Crimson Paradise

CRIMSON PARADISE

EUGENE WEAVER

Eugene Weaver Publishing

ISBN
Paperback: 979-8-9910012-0-5
ePub: 979-8-9910012-1-2

Eugene Weaver
North Canton, Ohio 44720
Edited by Staci Frenes

Cover design and interior design by Rafael Andres

For my good friend, Steve. The one guy who gets my taste in cinema that's later splashed across the pages I write.

Contents

PREFACE

I remember it well. The day when, at the age of seventeen and working at The Video Connection, a local mom-and-pop video store, in small-town rural Ohio, I decided to borrow two of the "big box" VHS movies in the horror section. The big boxes were typically reserved for the more obscure and crazy-looking titles. Movies I had never heard of. But it was the jumping off point, so to speak, of my absolute love for all things Eurohorror.

Often times, the covers were grotesque and disturbing, another way to catch the eye of a young and budding horror fan such as myself. Films like *Faces of Death, Silent Night, Deadly Night, A Bay of Blood, The Prowler* and *Dr. Butcher M.D.* stared at the customer, daring them to bypass the next *Halloween* sequel and dip their toes into something a bit more risqué. Because I worked at the video store on weekends and after school, I had the luxury of borrowing anything I wanted. A perk of being employed there, one that I took advantage of every chance I got. Stacks of movies would go home with me. I always had something from the video store sitting in my room waiting to get watched.

But this night was different. I had watched *Evil Dead 2* countless times already and had gone through all of the *Friday the 13th* films, along with the numerous other studio fare lining the walls of that room in the back of the video store (of course, the horror section was in a far corner of the building, so us deviants could peer at the grisly covers without the moral majority giving us sideways looks of disproval). And I decided to take a chance on a few of the "big box" movies.

Later that evening, I sat down in front of my 32-inch tube TV and popped the VHS tape into my player and watched two Italian horror movies, back-to-back. The first was a movie called *Make Them Die Slowly*, directed by Umberto Lenzi and staring the late, great Giovanni Lombardo Radice. Its original title, *Cannibal Ferox,* wasn't quite as fetching as the American title. I loved it. I loved the over-the-top acting and equally over-the-top gory violence. Everything about it seemed dangerous. After my first foray into the world of Italian splatter movies, I popped in my second big box VHS cassette: 1979's Lucio Fulci directed masterpiece simply titled, *Zombie*. This was the movie I had stared at for years at numerous VHS rental stores. The rotting face of the zombie with worms pouring out its eyes coupled with crooked teeth stared hungrily at the poor soul inspecting the box, as if daring them to watch it.

And so, watch it I did. And it was this movie in particular that broadened my horizons of cinema. No longer was it the safe and easy stuff. Now, it was whatever looked the weirdest and most bizarre, I wanted to check those out! Everything from Lucio Fulci, Rugero Deodato, Umberto Lenzi, Mario Bava and his son, Lamberto Bava, Sergio Martio, and of course, Dario Argento, were all digested in short order. Many of the films were heavily edited but it didn't matter. I was seeing things totally alien to my eyes.

The soundtracks by Goblin, Fabio Frizzi, and Riz Ortolani, to name just a few, were incredible and other worldly. The clothing styles oozed *cool*. Everyone smoked cigarettes and drank J&B Scotch Whiskey. The women were stunning: Edwige Fenech, Barbara Bouchet, and of course, Barbara Steele to name but a few. And the gory violence, oh, the violence! Everything about the special effects were just that, special. Crimson red was flung across and at the screen with reckless abandon, entirely different from what I had been used to. Especially Fulci's *Zombie* with effects by Giannetto De Rossi.

Which brings me to this novel you hold in your hands. I had recently rewatched *Zombie* for what felt like the hundredth time (I've watched it pretty much every year since I saw it for the first time with mouth agape back in the early 1990s). This most recent viewing got me thinking, I need to write my own zombie novel. I knew it needed to have an island setting, really rotten zombies, brutal set-pieces, and it had to take place in the late 1970s and early 1980s.

I hope I have succeeded in writing a compelling page-turner for you, reader, and that my love for classic European horror from my personal favorite era shines through here in all its blood-drenched glory. *Goditi il libro!*

*"Then you can tell me what it's like to pass from life
to death, and death to life."*

-Dr. Obrero, from the film "Dr. Butcher M.D."

PROLOGUE: FAILED EXPERIMENTS

The meteor flew forward from deep space for thousands of years, crumbling away the farther it traveled, until, at last, it breached earth's atmosphere, at which point it was no larger than a small boulder. Plummeting downward, it smashed into a small island, instantly creating a new crater as it shot forward, tunnelling downward until breaking apart entirely.

Hundreds of thousands of years passed and what had once been a crater devoid of life had now grown into a lush jungle spreading outward, covering what had been sparsely populated with just several palm trees and minimal vegetation in the middle of the ocean into a tropical paradise.

Plants thrived with various new species of plant life introduced to the island's natural habitat. Small animals fed off of it and lived much longer than their natural DNA could have allowed them.

Purple-colored flowers bloomed throughout the island, primarily inside the crater, and thick storms swirled around the island frequently, keeping most, but not all, human beings away.

In the middle of the Solomon Sea off the coast of Papua New Guinea sat la Isla de Sebria, the small island so named by the Spanish Conquistadors that had settled there in the early 1500s after their ship wrecked off its coast. After those first pioneers had long since died off, all that remained of the original occupants was a deserted town whose ancient structures had begun to crumble into ruin along with a small church in the island's center.

The original settlers weren't the only ones that resided on de Sebria in the years that followed its discovery. Natives from the nearby Solomon Islands, banished from their village when a rare, incurable strain of leprosy spread throughout their town, set sail for a new place to call home for the rest of their short lives and discovered the island in 1970 by mere chance as they pushed forward through tumultuous, swirling storms and soon inhabited it, claiming it as their own. Their leprosy remained but slowed at a significant rate, and they continued to exist in a sort of *leprosy limbo*. The rest of the world, including those that had banished them to the seas, moved on, and no one knew the fate of the lepers of la Isla de Sebria. Planes flew overhead on rare occasions, but the constant swirling storms seemed to obscure the island, as if wanting to conceal the poor souls from the rest of humanity.

June 14, 1979

Dr. Márcio Prestes Pedroso stood outside the small, dilapidated church in the middle of the jungle smoking a Marlboro Red cigarette. He looked up through the thick forest at the crater on the far side of the small island as Nurse Sara Luz and Luiz Melo Velho approached him.

"Velho and I buried the body as you requested." The nurse fell silent, waiting for his reply.

In a thick, Spanish accent, the large man in the blood-streaked grey surgical apron replied, "What about the body inside the church?"

"Nurse Luz, go inside with Velho, I'll be in in a minute." Pedroso needed to finish his scotch whisky first, his drink of choice when getting liquored up.

He watched his assistants leave in silence then brought the glass to his lips and let the stinging heat burn all the way down his throat. They had all led hard lives on the island since coming here with him, nearly a year ago and counting after he and his partner, Dr. William Joyner, had picked Sara Luz to help with their research when they had visited Spain. Velho, also from Spain, had simply been living off the streets and was easy to recruit with the promise of living arrangements, food, and a better life than the homeless squalor he had been found in.

Sara was a bit tougher to persuade, being educated.

The allure of breakthroughs in medical science through Dr. Pedroso and Dr. Joyner's research would bring her much fulfilment and, not to mention, possible financial independence. However, that was over a year ago, and they were now slaves to this island. Pedroso had turned to drinking heavily after numerous failed attempts at his cure for brain cancer, along with finding a cure to the cursed virus that only seemed to plague the people of this small island.

The makeshift church building was the centerpiece that sat almost squarely in the middle of the six-square-mile island. Roughly one mile behind it lay rows of thin-walled white structures with roofs, what constituted the housing on la Isla de Sebria.

As Dr. Pedroso finished off his scotch outside, inside the church Velho stood looking over a table covered with a body under a white sheet drenched in crimson red. He wiped his blood-covered hands on his apron, then pulled his face mask over his mouth and nose, as did Nurse Luz.

Luiz Velho sighed. "Another likely soon-to-be failed experiment. We are running out of bodies and running out of time. He looked over at Nurse Luz wearing an old, white nurse's uniform, her dark, curly hair pulled back tightly into a bun. She hung her head as he gazed at her.

Nurse Luz looked morosely over at her partner. "The doctor says he is on the cusp of a breakthrough, he claims he just needs more time. He is convinced the cure for advanced brain cancer is found within the blood of the people on this island who are dying of this strange mutation of leprosy. Sulfone therapy simply does not work on these people, they are doomed regardless! We all know that now!"

Velho glared angrily at the corpse under the sheet. "If we don't find a solution soon—"

"If we don't find a solution soon, what?" Dr. Pedroso quickly said as he made his way into the operating room that had once been a house of God. He stood beside Velho who had fallen silent. "Look, I know what we're up against, but we *must* keep trying! We've seen results in test animals, completely cured of the cancerous cells with Dr. Joyner and my serum that we created using the blood from the people of this island. Their disease is specific only to these poor souls, yet the natives here appear, by some miracle in their genetic structure, to continue existing even with the leprosy. They have no other diseases; they don't get sick. They just slowly rot away. They should all be long dead by now! We must draw more of their blood and we will eventually find a cure for what is eating away at them while they..." the doctor paused, choosing his words, "continue to live far past their expiration date, I suppose you could say. And of course, let us not forget the real reason we are here, to find the cure for brain cancer!"

"We've been here for nearly a year, though, how much longer until they turn on us? We continue to use them then bury them! Why not listen to what Dr. Joyner has to say about the purple plants near the village? He told me the natives call it the Violet Laceflower!" Velho exclaimed.

Sighing, Dr. Pedroso shook his head, "No! We have tried that and it has brought us less results than my methods! It's wishful thinking from a dying man. The answer lies in these people and the virus they carry while still living long past their expiration dates—that, along with my serum! I must believe we are nearing a breakthrough, then we will be off this island."

"You mean, *if* we get off this island!" Velho exclaimed angrily. "You remember the boat ride in? I'm still surprised it survived the storm! Meanwhile, they will be left to continue dying off since being exiled here! We are using them as guinea pigs for your experiments and you lead them on with a possible cure! They are too weak to resist and come willingly, like lambs to the…" he trailed off in disgust, shaking his head.

"You don't think I am trying to find a cure for these people while I do my research? I'm working on this! But brain tumor research is more important! Dr. Joyner is foolish not to follow what we had begun, off on a wild-goose chase with plants. He is wasting what little remains of his life on this research! Spending more and more time off on the other side of the island doing God knows what!"

"But what if Dr. Joyner is right? I mean, these people, they continue to live long after they should have all died off from their incurable leprosy!" Velho said urgently. "Don't you think it could have something to do with the island itself? Why not at least try looking into his research more? Or is it all about becoming rich and famous once you've found your success that continually eludes you at every turn?"

"Because it's a waste of *fucking* time! Time we do not have! And I would watch my tone if I were you!" the doctor shouted.

They all fell silent.

"Are you sure there is no hope for this one, Dr. Pedroso? We don't know for sure until," Nurse Luz asked, putting her hands on her hips, looking at the body on the table.

Glaring from Velho to Nurse Luz coldly, Dr. Pedroso said through gritting teeth, "Nurse Luz, prepare the body for the injection."

The small church had been cleared of the pews and a generator could be heard humming outside the building, bringing power to the doctor's equipment and much-needed lighting when conducting his critical experiments.

The building was in a state of disrepair: the flooring needed replacing, the wood was slowly rotting, the bricks originally used for its construction coming loose. It hadn't been properly retrofitted for the work that was now being done inside. Still, it was better than the alternative, the village. The church had to hold out just long enough to see the breakthrough Dr. Pedroso knew was near.

Dr. Pedroso spoke once more. "I need more time, and I need more bodies."

"How much longer must we do this? How much longer can this go on?" Nurse Luz said sadly, almost afraid to raise her voice.

"As long as it takes! *As long as it takes, damnit!* My serum can cure these people *and* brain cancer, I am convinced of this, it's why we came here! We've seen the results back on the mainland when we worked first on mice then on monkeys! I am convinced this will also work on humans! Now, enough of this chatter, let's get to work."

It worked twenty-five percent of the time, Nurse Luz

thought as she looked away from the doctor, filled with rage at the injustice that was continually being perpetrated on the poor people of la Isla de Sebria. *If he would just listen to Doctor Joyner...*

The bloodied sheet on the table moved slowly. Dr. Pedroso sighed as he put on a pair of operating gloves and looked to Velho and Nurse Luz for their assistance.

Nurse Luz moved toward the table; she had seen this before. Many times, in fact, but it never got any less grizzly. As she watched what lie under the sheet continue to come to after being heavily sedated, her mind went to her previous life. Her happy life, until the doctor had recruited her fresh out of nursing school. Happily taking the position of doctor's assistant in much-needed medical research for the betterment of humankind. And now here she was, a witness to mounting atrocities.

Dr. Pedroso pulled out a large hypodermic needle completely filled with a clear fluid and pulled the sheet back to expose the grotesque figure beneath. What had once been a boy, no older than thirteen, was now a mutated monstrosity. His nose was gone, in its place an oddly-shaped hole. Dark lesions had spread throughout his torso and his lips seemed to have receded upward, causing his teeth to be perpetually exposed. The boy gazed groggily at the doctor and his assistants through milky, white eyes. Patches of the boy's hair were all that remained of the dark-skinned child.

Nurse Luz flinched at the grotesque, pathetic spectacle in front of them. The boys' parents had both perished earlier in the year. At the rate they were going, there would be no more natives to conduct these experiments on within a year. Only slightly over fifty natives were left on the island, all of whom were worsening in their conditions.

Even with his face mask on, Velho grimaced at the smell of rotting flesh that seeped through, hitting his nose. No matter how many times he smelled it, it revolted him.

The doctor blinked hard, trying to clear his mind of the alcohol that had numbed it, and jabbed the needle deep into the boy's neck. Not feeling the sting of the syringe, the boy simply continued rocking his head back and forth as the liquid mixed with his blood shot through his bloodstream.

Dr. Pedroso pulled the needle out and handed it to Nurse Luz who had turned her head away from the ghastly sight. "Here, take it and dispose of it," Dr. Pedroso said hastily, shaking his head. He had consumed several glasses of scotch at this point in the day and the alcohol had indeed taken hold. He blinked hard, trying to keep his wits about him, but he felt the effects hitting hard.

Luz took it to the small wash basin near the table and was about to drop it in when she saw that it was empty. She came back and stood beside Velho who looked gravely down at the skeletal figure.

The boy involuntarily vomited. Thick yellow liquid spilled out across the table and onto the floor.

"Doctor, how much did you administer to the child?" Nurse Luz asked.

"Velho, turn his head so he doesn't choke on his own vomit!" the doctor shouted out, ignoring her question.

Grimacing, Velho did as he was ordered, turning the

boy's head while the sickly substance poured out. He knew the clean-up would certainly fall on him. He shuddered at the thought while keeping the boy's head turned.

"Doctor, how much of the serum did you administer? It's empty! You didn't inject him with the full dose that was in the tube, right?" Nurse Luz asked once more.

Dr. Pedroso shook his head and waved her away with his hand then took another needle out, jabbing it into the boy's neck and drawing blood. Pulling it back out, he quickly walked over to his microscope and put a small drop onto the glass to inspect the results of his latest test. He looked through the microscope at the thick liquid attacking the blood cells, ingesting them and mutating them at an exponential rate. He quickly shot up from the eyepiece, suddenly very sober, and looked in horror over at Luz and Velho. *How much did I dose that boy?*

"Doctor! Something is wrong with him, come quickly!" Velho shouted as he continued holding the boy's head to the side. The boy was now shaking on the table while still expelling fluids from his stomach.

Nurse Luz grabbed the boy's shoulders to keep him stabilized on the table, but it did little good. The table was becoming a disgusting mix of rotting human flesh and vomit. They had never needed to strap down their patients as all had been the worst off of the tribe and nearly immobile. This boy, who was one such patient, had suddenly gained strength.

"What the hell did you administer to him, doctor!?" Velho exclaimed.

"I, I gave him the normal dosage!" Dr. Pedroso replied

but his shaken voice said otherwise. He felt the inside pocket of his lab coat where a second syringe lay, reached in and pulled it out. It was the correct dose of test drug Neural Regenerator 485, or NR485 for short. He looked in horror at the scene unfolding in front of him.

"Doctor, I gave you a fresh batch of undiluted NR485 earlier today for you to ration out with saline into another ten doses. You didn't just…" Nurse Luz called out, continuing to hold the boy down on the table.

The boy on the table quit vomiting but was now biting his top and bottom row of teeth together, making a clicking sound, several of his already weakened and brittle teeth shattering at the force of it, leaving broken, jagged pieces sticking out of his gums.

Velho stared on in horror as the boy's veins began popping out of his skin and pumping with mutating blood cells.

"Something's wrong, this is wrong!" Velho shouted, trying to help Nurse Luz hold the increasingly struggling and agitated boy on the table.

Doctor Pedroso ran forward to the unfolding chaos. "This boy, we need to…" He fumbled with his words, trying to think of a solution but only coming up with one.

"I wish Doctor Joyner were here! Hurry up, do something!" Nurse Luz shouted.

The vomit and bile smeared across the table had made the boy's body slippery and twisting, and he escaped Nurse Luz's grasp on his shoulders. He instantly bit down onto her hand with snapping jaws.

Screaming in terror and pain, Nurse Luz tried to pull away from the boy whose jaws had a death grip on her thumb and index finger, blood pumping from the deep wound, flowing into the boy's mouth and down the front of his shirtless chest.

For a brief second, neither Velho nor Dr. Pedroso moved, then Velho pulled back and punched the boy as hard as his large fist could swing, connecting with the side of his face. This seemed to work as the boy released Luz's hand, turning his attention to the man that had struck him.

Nurse Luz, crying out in pain, grabbed hold of her hand, now missing a thumb and index finger, blood spilling out from the open wounds onto the floor. Slipping on her own blood, she fell backward, smashing her head and falling unconscious.

Dr. Pedroso ran to his desk and pulled open the top drawer. Inside amongst the papers and various haphazard files was an old revolver; he grabbed it, pulled the hammer back and ran back to the table, aiming it at the boy but unable to get a clear shot at the fast-moving subject. He fired at the boy but missed completely, hitting Velho in the arm instead.

The boy, meanwhile, had swallowed the nurse's thumb and index finger then leapt off the table on top of a stunned Velho who had just been shot in the arm, quickly sinking his broken teeth into the man's exposed neck, biting down as hard as he could against the jugular vein and pulling back.

Velho, caught completely off-guard by the aggressive nature the boy was exhibiting, stumbled backward in surprise, then, like Nurse Luz, tripped over himself and fell to the ground with the boy on top of him, continuing to bite and tear. Velho simply could not get a solid hold on the blood and vomit covered assailant slipping through his fingers as he felt his life quickly draining out of him onto the floor and down the boy's throat.

Dr. Pedroso came up behind the boy, aimed the gun against his head and pulled the trigger. The top of his head exploded, covering Velho in blood and brains. The boy fell with a thud on top of his prey, both unmoving.

Stepping back, Dr. Pedroso surveyed the carnage caused by his incompetence mere minutes earlier. Velho's jugular was nearly ripped out of his throat, blood spilling from the wound onto the floor. He was already dead, eyes unmoving.

"Oh, Lord, what have I done?" Dr. Pedroso muttered shaking his head in disbelief. His mind raced, thinking of his options. He didn't think for long. Behind him, Nurse Luz climbed to her feet and walked toward him. Unaware of her revived state, the doctor stepped back, away from Velho and the leprosy infected boy full of NR485.

Nurse Luz's eyes had turned milky white. Blood spilled out of the holes where an index finger and a thumb used to be onto the floor and across her nurse's dress.

Hearing the creaking of the old wooden floorboards, Dr. Pedroso spun around, seeing his nurse of the past year moving toward him slowly, opening and closing her mouth, biting into the air. *She's been infected with the mutating leprosy from the NR485 serum, I must destroy her!*

He aimed his revolver at her as she moved toward him, eyes blank and white, cocking the hammer back as he aimed.

Before he pulled the trigger, he heard movement behind him. Glancing back, he saw Velho stand to his feet, eyes blank and unmoving, as though nothing was wrong with his ravaged throat that still pumped blood from the large hole the boy had made minutes earlier.

Velho extended his hands toward his intended victim, the doctor that had caused his and the nurse's demise. He opened his mouth, exposing his teeth and, much like Nurse Luz, began biting the air, snapping at Dr. Pedroso.

Nurse Luz lunged forward toward Pedroso, but he stumbled out of the way just in time before she made contact. He fell to the floor and instantly began scooting away from the approaching staff of la Isla de Sebria. Once more aiming his revolver, he pulled the trigger, connecting with the nurse's chest and sending her back to the floor. His aim was poor. He had sobered up, but the alcohol still flowed through his veins, making him shaky, along with this sudden, horrible turn of events.

Glancing over, he saw Velho had turned and was climbing out a window of the church. *He still has some processing power in his brain, he's fleeing!* He aimed his revolver at the large man and pulled the trigger, hitting him in the back, but this had little effect on Velho who slid forward, dropping outside.

Nurse Luz was back on her feet once more, blank eyes looking toward the doctor. The gunshot wound that should have ended her life covered the front of her nurse's dress with her own blood mixed with the fluids from the dead boy on the floor. She took off in a sprint, the infected blood of the boy now fully pumping through her veins. Dr. Pedroso aimed his revolver once more and fired, this time hitting its intended mark, the woman's forehead.

Skull and brain matter exploded out the back of her head and she instantly fell to the ground in front of him, unmoving.

Standing to his feet, Dr. Pedroso ran to the opened window and gazed out, but Velho was nowhere to be seen. "He's making his way to the village!" he exclaimed in a panic, realizing the magnitude of what was happening. A group of over fifty natives, all of which were infected with a foreign offshoot of leprosy and helpless in their current state, now faced an all-new threat.

"No one must leave this island, ever! I'm sorry I could not fulfill our work, Dr. Joyner," he uttered gravely as his mind went to what he believed to be the final resting place of the far more accomplished doctor, buried nearby with the rest of the fallen inhabitants of the doomed island. Standing to his feet, he walked to his desk once more and dug through it, pulling out the box of remaining shells for his small revolver, opening it and counting its contents.

He sat on the chair by his desk, surveying the carnage around him, and pulled out another bottle of scotch from a half-opened drawer, poured a shot into a dirty glass sitting atop the desk, then downed it. Setting his loaded revolver beside him, he pulled his reel-to-reel audio recorder toward him and hit record.

"This is Dr. Márcio Prestes Pedroso, age forty-five, here to explain the grave misfortune that has befallen la Isla de Sebria at my own hands. All I wanted to do was help…" He trailed off, trying to collect his thoughts from the disastrous past year. He looked at the revolver in his hand and sighed heavily.

In the distance, shouts of terror began echoing through the dense island jungle.

1
THE DRAGON'S BREATH

Twenty-four-year-old Sam Berry sat alone at the small round table in the dimly lit, cigarette-smoke-filled bar in the town of Kokoda in Papua New Guinea. The Dragon's Breath Bar, situated on the outskirts of town, was certainly not appealing to nearly any of the locals other than those with nowhere else to go. The locals inside consisted of a handful of characters that looked to be of quite ill-repute: heavyset men with cowboy hats pulled far down on their foreheads to hide their faces, and women who appeared to have been used up many years prior from either prostituting their bodies or worse, heavy drug and alcohol use. The ceiling fan was set on high, but this had little effect on the stifling heat inside what was essentially just a hole in the side of a dilapidated building haphazardly turned into one of several local watering holes.

Taking a sip of his SP Lager from the bottle, Sam grimaced at the near room temperature beer that slid down his parched throat. It was either this or drinking it on draft and he didn't trust this establishment's staff, much less the keg the beer was housed in. This part of town was dangerous. He knew it and so did his twenty-five-year-old traveling partner, Edward Brant. One look at the street the bar was located on was enough to send any and all tourists running in the other direction, but not if their name was Edward Brant.

The street leading up to the Dragon's Breath was littered with empty beer bottles and trash and the air smelled of rotten food and stale piss. Several people, likely homeless, lay on the side of the small road surrounded by dilapidated buildings that had long since seen better days. Many of them were uninhabited or turned into makeshift bars, and some most likely had been turned into brothels.

Sam glanced at the watch his father had given his as a graduation present. It read 6:38 PM. He felt eyes on him and knew when they had entered the establishment that this was not a place that welcomed tourists. Especially those of the American variety. He and his traveling partner from Burbank, California stuck out like sore thumbs since arriving in Papua New Guinea earlier in the week.

Continuing to wait for his long-time college friend, his mind wandered back to what had caused them to take this trip in the first place. *Research into the religious practices of the island natives off the coast of Papua New Guinea* had been the official reason to his wary parents for the sudden purchase of plane tickets. He knew they wouldn't like the idea of he and his best friend traveling this far *just because we're young, horny and want to go on a crazy adventure.*

It was time for him to spread his wings. He was living on his own, but his parents still loomed large over him. This was another means of breaking free of the family bonds that had their talons in him ever since he was a boy. Being the only child had its advantages, for sure, especially when Christmas rolled around, but also numerous disadvantages. Primarily, that of being hovered over by overprotective and rather strict parents.

He had decided early in his teen years that he wanted to go to college straight out of high school, something his mom and dad, Cindy and Blake Berry, surprisingly were okay with. As long as it was local. And so, he enrolled in Woodbury University in 1975 and soon after, while working out at the gym on campus, made friends with Edward Brant who was a sophomore while he was a freshman. Both men were athletic and blessed with not only well-built bodies due to their rigorous exercise regimen but God-given good looks as well. They had both played on the football team and quickly found that they had many similarities, including drinking, smoking pot, and most importantly, women.

Once Edward graduated from Woodbury, they stayed in touch and decided that upon Sam graduating, they would go on an adventure. Nothing specific at the time, other than getting the hell out of Burbank and off to see the world. Sam liked the idea of an adventure in a foreign land, as he had been in Boy Scouts and earned his Eagle Scout badge many years earlier, something his mom and dad were proud of. Ed had teased him about the pictures adorning his mom and dad's walls, those of him in various uniforms, winning awards and badges.

After he graduated, instead of jumping right into the workforce with his undergraduate degree, he chose instead to sling burgers at the local hamburger spot, *Hero Howie's* near his home. This was a forgettable job, for sure, but he didn't want to get tied down to the well-paying job that awaited him after college just yet, likely in the realm of small business. And this job was as forgettable as they came. And so, he saved up for the adventure he and Edward were concocting.

Once the funds had been saved and the excuses dropped on his parents, Sam bought his one-way airline ticket and he and his best friend set off on what they hoped would be the adventure of their lives.

Finishing off his room temperature SP Lager, Sam glanced warily back at the rest room, if it could be called that. It looked more like a closet than a spot to relieve oneself of the contents of the lousy skunked beer the establishment served. "Come on, man, what the hell is taking you so long?" he muttered under his breath. He felt the locals' eyes glancing over at him, this blond-haired, blue-eyed American intruding on their turf.

Sandals sticking to the floor, Sam shook his head in disgust as he shuffled his feet and contemplated going to the bar to get another beer. As he pushed his old, wooden chair back, about to stand up in the low-ceilinged room, he heard his friend call out to him.

"Want me to grab you another one there, buddy?" Edward called out, leaving the piss closet while wiping his hands on his pants. Without waiting for an answer, he pivoted from his journey to their table and headed to the small bar where several patrons glanced over at him wearily.

"How's it going, friend?" Edward said casually to the old gentleman sitting inches from where he stood. He looked the dark-skinned man over. A cowboy hat covered most of his scar-riddled face, a thin mustache lining his upper lip.

The man looked at him blankly, giving him a once-over, then he shook his head, raised his mug of beer and continued drinking.

"What can I get you?" an old heavyset woman behind the bar asked Edward with more than a hint of disdain.

Taking his eyes off the large man beside him, Edward raised his index and middle finger. "Two more of your Dragon's Breath specials, ma'am."

She stared back at him, her eyes heavy and world weary. She was none too impressed with his attempt at lighthearted banter. Nodding slightly, she pulled out two more SP Lagers from under the counter, twisted the tops off, and set them down roughly on the bar top, causing both to foam up and spill some of their contents.

"That'll be ten kina," the woman said in a voice that sounded as if she had chain smoked since birth. She looked at him blankly, waiting for payment.

Digging into his front pocket, he pulled out a ten-kina bill, the currency of Papua New Guinea, and tossed it onto the wet bar, instantly soaking it. "Keep the change," he muttered with a smirk as he grabbed the beers, turned and headed back to the small table in the middle of the dimly lit bar where Sam sat.

Sam shook his head at Edward who carelessly set the beers down slightly too hard, causing more foam to bubble and spill over.

The fun but reckless Edward had lost his father Wilbur at the young age of five in an automobile accident and his mother, Aurora Brant, was an ex-hippie, so he had grown up relatively free of parental guidelines. He coasted through school on his charm and good looks. Always able to slink through each grade with average scores. Sam surmised this was likely due to his quick wit and ability to cozy up to the right people with the right answers that were happy to lend him a hand on his tests and homework. Especially those of the opposite sex. Even his teachers, who generally liked the free-spirited young man, were happy to pass him through to the next grade to be rid of his wandering eyes and snarky comments.

"Nice, Ed, real nice. We seem to be endearing ourselves to the natives here quite well," Sam said with more than a hint of sarcasm, glancing up at the angry bartender wiping off the wet bill she had just been handed.

Smirking back at his friend and sidekick, Ed replied, "Hey, she was the one that set these bottles of skunked garbage down hard enough to not only cost her a tip but also work a bit harder for that ten-kina bill. Don't worry, honey, it'll dry soon enough in this humid stale pit!" he said just loud enough for the old woman to hear along with the rest of the unhappy patrons of the Dragon's Breath.

Glancing back at the bar, Sam saw that the woman was glaring at them, as were several men sitting on their barstools. Shaking his head, he turned to look at his traveling companion once more. "What's the plan? We've been traveling through Papua New Guinea now for nearly a week. We've made it to the coast, so now what?"

Taking a swig of his SP Lager and grimacing at the stale taste, Ed wiped his mouth and cleared his throat of the foul beer. "Well, good friend, I know we talked about doing the hike back to Port Moresby and from there making our way to Australia, but I have another idea—now, just hear me out before you start bitching about changed plans, okay?"

Sam immediately wanted to protest but held his tongue as Ed pulled out the large, folded map he carried with him in his backpack that sat at his feet. A backpack that one particularly large man sitting near them had been eyeing ever since they sat down at the table thirty minutes earlier.

Noticing the brutish man staring at him, Ed immediately piped up, "Something wrong with your eyes, there? Mind your fucking business, Papuan." Ed glared at the man, not breaking the stare they were locked into.

"Damnit, Ed, let's finish our beers and you can tell me about this plan of yours somewhere else. We need to get the hell out of here before we get our asses kicked and robbed, or worse," Sam said under his breath.

Taking his eyes off the large, sweaty man, Ed moved his beer bottle and unfolded the map, laying it out on the table.

Sam shook his head at the vulnerable position they were now in. A large map sprawled out on the table of quite possibly the dingiest, most unsafe bar in all of Papua New Guinea. Ed's backpack haphazardly lay on the floor beneath him just asking to be swiped. Sam was glad his backpack remained back at the hostel they were shacked up at. They had a room to themselves, and the door was securely locked behind them, even though Ed thought it unwise to leave a backpack behind in this part of the country.

Ed pointed on the map. "Okay, we're here and to get to Australia, we have to travel this route to get to any airport that'll take us there." His finger moved across the map a significant distance before reaching the city of Port Moresby, which was the route they had originally intended to take to get to their next destination of Queensland, Australia.

"Yes, I get it. It's far, but we knew this when we landed at Jacksons International Airport and traveled across this hot-as-hell country on the Kokoda Trail before hitching rides over to town. We both agreed we would do the trail walk then turn around and head back to Port Moresby. Right?" Sam said as he angrily took a swig of his stale beer, glaring at his friend who was now likely changing plans on the fly.

"I know, good friend, but right here, there's the Kokoda Airport. It's small but hot damn, we could fly east and go to the Solomon Islands! You want to talk about adventure? That right there is adventure!" Ed exclaimed, keeping his finger on the small airport nearby.

"There's beaches in Australia, Ed, I see no reason to—" Sam began but was cut off.

"Listen to me," Ed said, changing his voice to a significantly more serious tone. Something Sam had gotten used to over the course of their knowing each other and being friends. This was Ed's *I've made up my mind* tone. "This is our chance to do something truly bat-shit crazy and unexpected. I've been looking at this map for a while and between you and me, Solomon Islands is unexpected. We spend some time over there, then make our way back to Australia. From there, we head back to the real world. Back to waiting jobs and eventually wives, houses, and kids with shitty diapers. But this here, this is adventure, and it's staring us in the face. We can do this!"

Considering this, Sam replied, "But why, Ed? We're already here! We had Australia all planned out. We can't be gone for an unlimited amount of time. We don't have unlimited resources, as you well know. Hell, I'm already getting low on funds!"

"You think Australia is gonna be cheap? If we can fly into the Solomon Islands, it's not going to be much less expensive than that. The place is impoverished. And we can likely find someone to fly us in from the Kokoda airport. Lord knows they need the money," Ed answered abruptly, not wanting to give up on this change of plans.

Sam sighed heavily, looking down at the map then back up to Ed. "Heads up, we've got company," he whispered.

"How many?"

"Two, they're not small so we should get going," Sam said under his breath.

"American, huh?" A large man in a dirty baseball cap

and mechanics clothes that looked as though they had never been washed had stopped right behind Ed's chair.

Ed didn't look back at the man but saw the other individual, a tall, skinny man in a cowboy hat, tank top, and ripped jeans coming up beside Sam. Everyone in the bar seemed to grow silent at what now appeared to be a stand-off, the local drunks versus the affluent, cocky Americans.

Glancing behind him, Ed saw the large man that had been watching them earlier still sitting in his seat, sipping his mug of beer. This man pulled his own cowboy hat further down over his face to cover his features as he looked on at the unfolding confrontation.

"I asked you a question. What do they call your kind in Mexico? Gringo, is it? That means, green...go," the large, heavyset man in the baseball hat said in a calm but menacing voice.

The skinny man chuckled at this and took a sip of his bottled bear, standing close to both Sam and Ed.

"Anyway, as I was saying, I vote we pack up and head for the airport, find us a ride to the Solomon..." Ed began, ignoring the men.

"Hey, you motherfucker! I'm talking to you!" the large man shouted, now putting his hand on Ed's shoulder.

Without batting an eye, Ed grabbed his beer bottle, turned it upside down, spilling the remaining contents onto the table, jumped to his feet and smashed it against the large man's face, shattering glass everywhere.

The man staggered backward, dropping his own beer to the floor and bringing his hands up to his bloodied face, letting out a shout of pain.

Sam immediately scooped up the map on the table and crumpled it up while the skinny man standing beside him was caught off-guard by the abrupt assault on his friend. "Time to go, now!" Sam shouted.

The rest of the patrons were now either getting to their feet or had turned to see what the commotion was all about.

"You two! Out, now!" the woman behind the bar shouted at Sam and Ed, pointing to the door angrily.

"Gladly," Sam began, turning to look at the bartender but was cut off by a fist slamming into his left cheek. He stumbled backward, falling onto the sticky, beer-stained floor.

Ed, meanwhile, had grabbed his backpack, slinging it over his shoulder, and as hard as he could, he kicked the skinny man directly in the crotch. The man instantly dropped to the floor beside a dazed Sam.

"You broke my fucking nose, gringo!" the large man shouted, pulling his bloody hand from his even bloodier face. Blood poured from his nose onto his filth-covered shirt.

Now several other patrons, all intimidating, were standing to their feet, beginning to make their way to the commotion in the center of the Dragon's Breath.

Sam shook his dazed head and saw Ed's hand reach down to help him to his feet. He grabbed it and was quickly lifted up.

"Ready to go?" Ed said mischievously.

"You're not going anywhere, filthy fucking American scum!" the bloodied large man shouted, making his way toward Ed along with the rest of the angry patrons.

A gunshot rang out inside the bar, causing everyone inside to freeze in place. The large woman behind the bar held a six-shooter in her hand, raised to the ceiling as bits of dust and soot wafted down from the new bullet hole it had produced above.

"Alright! Show's over! Back to your beer and ruined livers, the lot of you!" she shouted from behind her station.

Slowly, everyone dispersed, heading back to their places of origin, and uneasily took their seats, all eyes shifting from Sam and Ed back to the drinks left unattended in front of them.

The bartender looked over at the bloodied large man standing near Sam and Ed, stunned by the bottle blast across his face as he stared at his blood-covered hands. "Get yourself cleaned up. You're pathetic, go!" the bartender shouted, pointing to the bathroom.

Quickly, the bloody-faced man hung his head and made a beeline to the washroom in silence.

At Sam and Ed's feet, the man that had been kicked in his manhood scrambled back up and quickly headed back to his table, head hung low and both hands cupping his aching balls.

"Both of you, get the hell out of this place, now!" the unnamed and still armed bartender shouted at the shaken American men.

Ed made sure to keep a tight grip on his backpack and both men nodded in the bartender's direction as they made their way outside.

Once outside Sam looked at Ed angrily. "Well, that could

have gone...better."

"Sorry about your face. You took that punch pretty damn good, if I must say so myself," Ed replied, trying to diffuse the situation.

"I'll be fine. Guy hit like a fairy anyway," Sam answered with a grin.

They both walked in silence for a bit longer, putting distance between them and the Dragon's Breath before Sam spoke again. "So, why in all of Papua New Guinea did you have to pick the absolute world's worst bar to drop that shit on me about a detour to the Solomon Islands instead of sticking with the game plan?"

Contemplating this, Ed replied, "I don't know, just seemed like a place we wouldn't belong and that, to me, is fun."

"You are truly one crazy sonofabitch, you know that, Ed?" Sam said shaking his head as they both turned the corner on the edge of the street.

"Excuse me! Gentlemen, excuse me!" a voice from behind them called out.

The tall and slightly heavyset man in the cowboy hat pulled low across his brow who had been sitting near them back at the Dragon's Breath approached from behind.

Ed glanced at Sam then back to the cowboy hat-clad man.

He took off his cowboy hat, revealing dark skin, a black mustache, black hair slicked back, and a long, thick scar running from his forehead down across his face. He was dressed in a button-down white shirt stained with sweat, and blue jeans with a relatively nice pair of cowboy boots.

"Allow me to introduce myself; my name is Benício Pinto Guedes. I'm known in this town as Pinto. You seem to have dropped this back at the Dragon's Breath." The imposing man held out a crumpled-up map that had fallen out of Sam's back pocket when they abruptly left earlier.

Sam's hand went to his back pocket instinctively.

Pinto looked at both Sam and Ed as he continued holding out the map. "I couldn't help but overhear you discussing a possible trip to the Solomon Islands. Is this true?"

Uneasily, Sam took the map out of Pinto's outstretched hand and quickly pulled it back, not breaking eye contact.

Ed, sizing up the large man, spoke first. "Look, we were just passing through. I don't take kindly to strangers pushing me around, much less, my buddy Sam here. And with regards to what you heard back there, that's between Sam and me, alright?"

"I can take care of myself, Ed," Sam retorted, not liking when Ed took on the alpha-male role.

Pinto waved them both off. "Think nothing of it. You realize where you were? That place is a dive, and quiet honestly, that was mild compared to what goes on there after hours. I could tell the minute you both walked in it wasn't going to end well. That lot aren't fans of Americans, or any outsiders for that matter." Pinto fell silent, looking back and forth at the Americans standing in front of him, then up at the setting sun casting an orange hue over the beautiful and lush landscape. While the small town was made up of old buildings, the countryside surrounding them was stunning.

"So, what exactly do you want with us? Why chase us down to give us the map back? Out of the kindness of your heart? I doubt that, Mr. Pinto," Ed asked cautiously.

"Yeah, we need to be getting back to our hostel. It was nice meeting you and all but," Sam began.

Pinto wiped his sweaty brow with a red handkerchief pulled from his front pants pocket. "I can get you to the Solomon Islands. If that is indeed where you are heading. I've got a plane over in hangar B at the Kokoda airport. It's not much but it'll get you there. I'm a pilot and it's how I make my living, flying all over this island and the surrounding islands. Solomon Islands are a bit far for me, but I can make the trip." He fell silent, waiting to see how the two young men would react to his proposal, noticing that Ed had come to attention.

"You're a pilot, huh?" Ed responded.

"I am, and a damn good one, I must say. I am making a delivery to the islands and I could use the extra money for much-needed and quite expensive fuel. And since you need transportation, win-win, no?"

"Ed, we need to talk about this more, in private. Australia…" Sam said quietly.

Pinto's eyes shifted from Sam to Ed than back to Sam. "I have room for six on my plane. Myself and my copilot, Fernando Conceição Barroso, along with two other seats have been filled, going to the same location. With you two I would have a full plane. Come on, what do you say?"

"Two others traveling? Who are they?" Ed asked, interested in this new information.

"Two girls, young, one of them is searching for someone. I believe her father is there. They need to get to the Solomon Islands, so they hired me, and I go. Tomorrow. Choice is yours, my friends." Pinto answered.

"We really need to talk about this, Ed, right?" Sam answered, motioning with his eyes to end the conversation.

"The plane, it's yours?" Ed quickly asked, attempting to gauge the man's honesty.

"No, no, I cannot afford such a thing. The man I transport goods for," Pinto paused as though considering how much to tell his passengers, "it is his plane. I fly for him. A shipment of medical supplies needs dropping off for a poor village at the far corner of the island. I make the delivery for him."

Sam immediately asked, "So, why can't your boss cover the fuel? Why do you need us?"

"Oh, I don't need you, good sirs, I merely overheard you talking. I'm going to the destination with or without you. Just trying to help out. The choice is yours. It is no sweat off me," Pinto said, pulling out another cigarette from the breast pocket of his white, sweaty shirt.

Ed glanced from Sam back to Pinto and was about to speak but Pinto cut him off.

"Tomorrow, plane leaves at eight AM sharp out of hangar B. Look for a blue and white Piper Turbo Seneca II airplane with the serial number 8088N on the side, can't miss it. If you're there and want a ride, it's one-hundred dollars per person. It was a pleasure meeting you both." Pinto turned and walked back in the direction of the Dragon's Breath.

Ed looked and Sam who was staring at the large man making his way back to the Dragon's Breath, adjusting his cowboy hat before lighting his cigarette.

"Sam, come on! Can you believe our luck! That shithole bar literally dopped a pilot in our laps! One that's going to Solomon Islands! That's more than luck, that's divine intervention, my friend!" Ed exclaimed happily.

Reaching up and placing his hand on his still red cheek from the punch earlier, Sam replied, "Damnit, Ed. Damnit all to hell."

48

2
A FEW MORE PASSENGERS

Ed and Sam quickly headed back to the hostel where they were staying, thankfully, in a significantly better part of town. Most of the walk back was in silence, both men contemplating their next move on this post-college adventure, each wanting something slightly different out of the experience.

Sam wanted to take in the sights and make memories that he would take with him the rest of his life. Ed, on the other hand, wanted something more. Danger is what came to Sam's mind, thinking of the bar Ed had chosen to stop by for a few beers. There were other bars, all of which were closer to their hostel in the town of Kokoda, but instead of those easier and far less threatening locations, Ed had decided to put them in harm's way.

Ed had always been like this, to a certain extent, as they became good friends in college. Always one to take college hijinks a little too far. Always the ladies' man, Ed had taken many to bed through the years and had gotten a sort of reputation as not just a ladies' man but a "love 'em and leave 'em" type of guy. Something that came to haunt him toward the end of his time at Woodbury University when he found it more and more difficult to snag a date other than new Freshmen pledges.

After college, Ed swore he would calm down with his shenanigans, and he did, even going so far as to land a girl-friend, Barbara Jenkins, for almost six months. His free-spir-ited personality eventually led to their ultimate breakup, though, when Ed informed her of his planned trip to Papua New Guinea, Australia, and beyond. It was for the best; they were never meant for anything as long term as even the six months they had lasted. The breakup was amicable, and they remained friends, but it was a good lesson for Ed. Not everyone was going to wait on him hand-and-foot and be around through his many wild ideas.

Sam thought back to his own love life, such as it was. While Ed had been sleeping with anything that moved in college, Sam, meanwhile, focused on his studies and gradu-ated with honors in small business management. Something he was quite proud of, along with becoming an Eagle Scout when he was younger, which his father had insisted on as a way for them to bond. At the time, Sam hadn't wanted to do it, but looking back, those had indeed been good times with the old man, and he had learned a great deal more than he had expected to. Even if he hadn't had any opportunities to use many of the skills acquired during those young, formative years.

Another major reason he decided to take on a menial job after college was to save up for and go on this adventure. Once this was out of his system, it was full-on work force. He already had some solid leads that if he played his cards right, would pay handsomely for someone with his credentials.

Because of all of this, time with girls had been kept to a minimum. A few dates here and there as well as a couple one-night stands. Nothing substantial, but nothing that got him into trouble, either, and it had more or less taught him the ropes. As excited as he had been for this trip once the funding was secured and airline tickets had been purchased, Sam was already looking forward to it being over so they could get back to the real world, not out risking their lives in hole-in-the-wall bars at the ass-end of civilization in the stifling heat. The same could be said for Sam's worried parents but he had assured them, upon returning, he would line up interviews for his career of choice.

Ed watched the sun set across the beautiful jungle that surrounded them. Lush vegetation flanked them on either side of the road as they arrived at their hostel. This was all he imagined it would be and then some. And he felt deep in his soul that even more awaited them. "Look, Sam, I know I sprang this on you sort of last minute."

"*Sort of* last minute? That dude we just met is leaving tomorrow morning at eight! That's in roughly twelve hours if we hitch a hundred-dollar ride with him, and I don't know about you, but I sure as hell don't trust him," Sam retorted.

They walked through the front doors of the unremarkable looking hostel they had called home since finishing their hike through the Kokoda trail, glad to be back to their home base and looking forward to a long night's sleep. One Sam hoped didn't involve getting up early and heading to the Kokoda airport, hangar B.

Both nodded to the front desk as they made their way to the small room. Once inside, Ed looked at Sam with his serious look that Sam knew well. It signaled Ed attempting to get his way, when all joking ceased and a life lesson would be dropped into Sam's lap.

"We can go to Australia like we had planned, I'm cool with it. It would have been fun to head out to the islands off Papua New Guinea, for sure, but we're a team and this is what we originally agreed on. Australia it is, just glad to be with you, buddy! Especially since you took one on the chin for me back there at that shithole bar I dragged you to," Ed said with a grin, giving Sam a light punch on the arm as he headed to his bunk to drop his backpack and get ready for a quick shower.

This line of talk threw Sam off. This wasn't like Ed. Usually, if he wanted something bad enough, he pressed until he wore his opponent down. What likely had drawn Ed to Sam in the first place was Sam's low-key, chill personality. As long as Sam was in relative safety, he was fine with Ed's antics. But he still knew how Ed could be, and this was a side of his friend he rarely saw. Backing down and giving in.

Sighing heavily, Sam pulled a coin out of his pocket. "Heads we go to Solomon Islands, tails we stick to the plan. How's that sound, buddy?"

Smirking, Ed replied, "You're on."

The coin resting on Sam's thumb was flicked into the air. A second later, he caught it, cupped it in his hand then slapped it on top of his other hand and looked down at the next destination in this adventure.

"Well? Come on, now, where are we heading?" Ed asked, craning his neck to get a look at the coin's answer.

Blowing out a deep breath, Sam shook his head, "Looks like we're going on an airplane ride with Mr. Pinto tomorrow morning."

"Time to get up, sleepy head!" a voice called out.

Twenty-three-year-old Laura Joyner slowly opened her eyes, blinking. She looked around the room until her still waking eyes fell on her twenty-one-year-old traveling companion, Eva Barnes. Laura sat up in bed and stretched. The white t-shirt she had worn the previous night to sleep was slightly sweaty from the distinct lack of air conditioning in their small ten-room motel.

"Yuck, I stink," Laura said, getting a whiff of herself before recalling their previous night out at the local watering hole, the Golden Spirits, just up the street in the small town of Kokoda. She scratched her tangled brown hair, running her fingers through it while yawning deeply.

"You are indeed a lightweight, Laura, you know that,

right?" Eva replied, more chipper than she typically was in the morning.

Still blinking, Laura looked at Eva who was already showered and getting dressed in a pink bikini top and cut-off jean shorts that came just under her firm butt.

"I'm thinking of pigtails today for the trip over to the islands, thoughts?" Eva said, mock pulling both sides of her still wet blond hair.

Sliding out of bed, Laura looked at her friend of over ten years and smiled. "Eva, you look great, as always. But I'm not sure if that's proper attire for the flight we arranged with the local pilot. I mean, it's going to be a three-hour flight from what he says, you really want to just be wearing that?"

Putting her hands on her hips and shaking her butt, Eva replied, "Well, for your information, I plan on hitting the ground running once we land on your Solomon Islands, honey! And before you start, I know why we're going, but you promised me there would be fun to be had along the way!"

"You're right, Eva, I did say that. And as you mentioned, we are here for the primary reason of finding out what happened to my father. All signs point to Solomon Islands from the little information I've gathered over these past two years and now we're this close! So, last night, while fun, won't be happening tonight. I don't want to touch rum for the rest of my life."

"You literally had—what—four drinks, maybe?" Eva said laughing.

"Yeah, I did, that's about three too many, and you know

that!" Laura said jokingly.

Eva chuckled. "Such a lightweight. Just promise me, you'll still have some fun, okay? I mean, it's not every day I up and turn twenty-one. We're from Texas, honey, and we party hard!"

"Well, I hope you had a good birthday, and yes, we had a good day yesterday. But today, it's back to business, okay?" Laura responded.

Sighing, Eva nodded. "Okay, so I'm going to go grab some breakfast. I'll bring you back something for when you're done showering up. You think that Pinto guy will actually follow through on taking us over there? I mean, he's kind of gross."

"Let's hope so, it's not been easy getting here and that small airport is the most direct route. And at only a hundred dollars each, that's a good deal," Laura answered, thinking back to how they had gone to the airport the previous morning inquiring about a flight to the Solomon Islands and met him there, working on a small plane with a man named Barroso.

"You're still sure your dad was last seen in the Solomon Islands? I mean, that was a long time ago, right?"

"Well, that's my best guess, after all the phone calls I made and pictures of him I sent over there to the local law enforcement after he quit communicating with my mom and me. It lined up with what the doctor he spoke to before leaving us told me, that they were indeed on the Solomon Islands," Laura replied, instantly cooling upon thinking of how desperate and alone she had felt when her father up and left them.

She shrugged off her feelings of resentment, determined not to lose her focus. "At the very least, I'm hoping to find out more information about a specific island called la Isla de Sebria. From what I've gathered, it appears to be an uncharted island, so it would make sense to lose communication with my dad if he ended up there, somehow. But it's likely a dead-end. The local police in Kokoda said something about constant storms out there and no one could make it there even if they wanted to. But, I'm not ruling anything or any place out just yet."

"I just—how do I say this, Laura? I thought at one point your dad told you there might be a cure, but he needed more time?" Eva asked thoughtfully.

"Yes, and then remember I told you that correspondence ceased after several phone calls over several months of vague answers? He got harder and harder to track down, until, finally, poof. He vanished. But I have to believe he's out there somewhere. I have to find him, even if he abandoned Mama and me, something I cannot forgive him for. Two years we could have had with him…"

Seeing how the conversation was bringing Laura down, Eva changed the subject back to food. "Breakfast burrito okay for you?" she asked sweetly as she turned to leave the room.

"Fruit and vegetables please," Laura replied with a smirk.

"You're *so* damn boring!" Eva teased, closing the door behind her.

Laura glanced around the room and saw Eva had started packing, which surprised her. Eva was the partier, the one that slept in. But this was an adventure for the now twenty-one-year-old and getting out of this rather drab town and going to a tropical island paradise was exactly why she had convinced Laura to let her tag along.

As Laura hopped into the shower, washing the booze away, she reminded herself of why she had ultimately agreed to allow Eva to come along in the first place. Her mother was the primary reason. Alicia Joyner had at first forbid her daughter from traveling from Port Aransas, Texas all the way to Papua New Guinea to try and locate her missing husband, but when Laura insisted with the information she had gathered on his possible whereabouts, her mother agreed only if "Eva could travel along and keep an eye on you, dear." Her mom should have known better, it was she that would have to watch over Eva and her partying ways and keep them both on track.

Laura's mother later admitted that Eva's parents had called her and plead their own case for Eva to travel along with Laura, claiming it would keep her from running around with any number of unsavory characters in Laura's absence. Even going so far as to pay for their daughter's airfare and supply her and Laura with a bit of extra spending money for the trip.

She loved Eva, even if they were quite opposite in most ways. Eva could bring out the fun side of Laura while on occasion, Laura could instill some wisdom into her younger friend. Plus, Eva's mom and dad had on numerous occasions reached out to the Joyners, telling them how appreciative they were of Eva's grounded friend Laura and how she brought some much-needed stability to their "free-spirited" daughter's life. Their town was small, and because Eva was incredibly attractive, men took advantage of her regularly, something her parents were continually dismayed by. They had put her on the pill at an early age and, along with that, counted on Laura to be Eva's voice of reason on many occasions.

Their friendship had a checkered history, for sure, dating all the way back to junior high, but in the small town they had come from, friends were hard to come by, so they had stuck together.

Laura had decided to follow in her father's footsteps in the world of medicine upon graduating, although this was put on hold when her father's grim diagnosis was later made public. Eva, on the other hand, was content to just "wing it" and see what happened. Focusing more on boys and partying and what she saw as menial jobs, waitressing being one she had tackled and quickly failed at.

After her much-needed shower, Laura quickly got dressed, putting on a cropped brown t-shirt and hip-hugging jeans. She looked at the clock. 7:15 AM.

The door opened and Eva returned with the requested fruit and vegetables for Laura.

"Yes! Oh, thank you, I'm starving!" Laura said happily, taking her breakfast from her friend's hands.

"The burrito was delicious, your loss, honey," Eva said as she went to brush her teeth and finish packing.

"I'll take your word for it," Laura replied, peeling a

banana. She loved the fruit and vegetables the country of Papua New Guinea had to offer. Much better than anything she had in her small hometown.

While Eva brushed her teeth, Laura quickly packed her belongings up into her small backpack, keeping an eye on the clock. "Come on, Eva, we need to get moving!"

"Yeah, yeah, I'm just about done. Hey, so, do you think that Pinto guy got a few more travelers to ride along? He said he was hoping to fill the plane, seats six. If so, please let them be hot guys," Eva said, tossing her belongings into her own backpack.

"*Hot guys* are the furthest thing from my mind, Eva," Laura replied, knowing where this conversation would lead.

Eva stopped packing and glanced up. "Laura, you need to find a man! I know you're looking for your dad, I know how important this is, but...how shall I say this?"

"Let me guess, I need to get laid?" Laura responded with sarcasm.

"Exactly! You said it!" Eva said, pointing at her friend.

"Yeah, well, you put the thought there. Once this is behind me and I can put the whereabouts of my missing dad to rest, then we'll see," Laura answered.

"We'll see. You always say that. Always an excuse with you!" Eva said, this time a bit more serious.

Laura stopped packing now and looked at her friend. "Eva, it's easy for you. But for me, well," she paused.

"If you would just let me set you up," Eva started as she attempted to put her hair into the pig-tails she had planned on earlier.

"You have. Numerous times."

"You didn't like Mike Shaw? That guy was so damn sexy! And he was into you!" Eva pleaded.

"He was into me all right. That's all he was interested in. Being *in* me," Laura said coolly.

"And sometimes, Laura, that's all there is to it. Just wait, honey. Solomon Islands are going to be great! And after we find out what really happened to your father, you're going to live in the moment. But until then, I promise I'll do my best to keep on the straight and narrow, deal?" Eva said, walking over to her friend and looking her in the eye.

"Straight and narrow until we find out what happened to my father—and if he's still alive, then I'll relax, a bit," Laura said, giving her friend a little shove on the arm.

"Laura, are you prepared for the possibility that your dad is dead? I mean, two years is a long time and with his condition..." Eva trailed off.

"I have to believe he's still out there. My poor mom, all she's been through," Laura said softly.

"I know, Laura, it's why I'm here," Eva said, leaning over and giving her a hug.

Laura returned the hug. They were certainly opposites, but on occasion, Eva had her good moments.

Laura looked at the time. "Whoa, we've got to get going! Plane leaves in forty minutes!"

"Lead the way, sister," Eva said as she grabbed her last piece of gum from the dresser and popped it into her mouth.

As they left, Laura, not a religious type, felt a chill go through her. She patted her front pants pocket that contained the letter her father left before abandoning their family two years prior. *Dear Lord, please let this go well. Please let me find my dad and please help me keep Eva under control. Amen.*

3
HANGAR B

Morning came quickly for Sam and Ed. By the time both men had talked through the sidetrack in their plans, packed up, and washed off, it was nearing midnight. The nights were a bit cooler, which was a nice reprieve from the stifling humidity of the daylight hours. The hostel didn't have air conditioning so the ceiling fan in their room was always on high, but it did little to lower the heat during the day, simply recirculating the already hot air around the room. They both agreed it would be good to get out of the cheap hostel, even if it had provided them the basics of creature comforts in a town as small as Kokoda.

Both Sam and Ed slept restlessly through the night, knowing that a sudden change of plans awaited them in the early morning hours. Ed was excited while Sam was apprehensive, but both agreed, the plan was set, Solomon

Islands was the pair's next destination, for better or worse.

Sam's eyelids fluttered then opened as sunlight shone into the small room they had called home for less than a week. Their admittedly fantastic hike through the Kokoda Trail before arriving, even if it was hot, had provided them beautiful scenery and they hadn't regretted doing it.

Sitting up in bed, Sam blinked hard and looked down at his wristwatch that read May 18, 1980: 7:05AM. The compass on his watch bobbled in a southwest direction. Fifty-five minutes before Pinto was likely to be wheels up on the Kokoda airport runway, if he was indeed sticking to that flight plan.

"You're up! Man, you were tossing and turning last night, buddy," Ed said from the ground as he continued with his push-ups, his normal routine since the days of significantly more rigorous exercise and training back in college. He started the day banging out one-hundred push-ups, no matter what the previous night had entailed or how much or little sleep he had gotten. On good days, he would do significantly more weight training as well as jogging. Sam, on the other hand, while still quite physically fit, stuck more to jogging from time to time.

Ed hopped to his feet, stretching his arms across his chest and letting out a large breath of air. "I've been up since six, went for a jog then a bit more training. I'm gonna hit the showers once more then grab some food. We need to be heading to the airport by seven-thirty, so be ready."

And with that, he turned and headed toward the door leading out into the hallway to the small shower provided for the hostel guests. On his way out, Sam hollered out, "You snored like a sonofabitch last night, so that accounts for my tossing and turning, you asshole!"

Ed laughed and without turning around, closed the door behind him. Sam sat on his small cot alone in their room, yawned, stretched his arms and crawled out of bed. He had showered the night before, so breakfast was the only thing that interested him at this point. That and what lay ahead for them.

His mind drifted to Australia and all they had planned once they arrived. They were still going to Australia, and this new plan would be fun. Tropical paradise and snorkeling and *Lord only knows* what else with two girls on the flight. *Enjoy this!* he tried to convince himself.

He quickly changed into a white tank top and brown cargo pants made for this type of travel. After lacing up his hiking shoes, he put on his Aussie Slouch hat specifically purchased for this trip. "You're gonna see Australia, my friend, it's why I bought you in the first place," he joked about the hat he had grown quite fond of after their relatively strenuous hike on the Kokoda trail earlier.

Sam looked at himself in the small mirror in their room, thankful the smack he took the previous evening hadn't left his cheek black and blue. He wished it had been him that had delivered the hard kick to the balls on the nameless barfly. Raising his hand to his mouth, he blew out and breathed in, then grimaced at the sour morning breath of stale, yeasty beer and the constant flow of ethnic food his body wasn't used to. He quickly brushed his teeth in the small sink in their room.

Ed came back from showering and dropped his towel, quickly dressing in a Black Sabbath t-shirt and bell bottoms that were no longer in style, but Ed liked the way they felt on him. Sam secretly figured this was Ed's way of constantly going against the grain. His mom was a hippie, after all, and his attire typically exemplified that, even if he was more a jock than metalhead. That was Ed being Ed.

Slinging his backpack over his shoulder, Ed exclaimed, "Come on, buddy! Time's ticking!"

Nodding, Sam slung his own backpack over his shoulder as they made their way out of the hostel onto the sunbathed streets of Kokoda. After a quick breakfast of pineapples and bananas blended with local coconut milk and a bag of karuka nuts native to their particular area, they headed to the Kokoda airport. Along the way, they chatted lightly about the next leg of their adventure but were mostly left to their own thoughts, taking in the natural beauty that continually surrounded them. The morning sky was perfect, clouds slowly rolling across the atmosphere with a light breeze on their faces.

"This is a good sign, my friend, it's a beautiful day and perfect for air travel. In a few short hours we'll be exploring the Solomon Islands," Ed exclaimed as the airport came into view, a short walk from the center of town.

"I guess so. I'd rather see kangaroos, to be honest," Sam replied sarcastically.

"Hey, you not only suggested the coin flip but you called it! This is on you, my friend!" Ed retorted jokingly.

"Oh, that's bullshit Ed! We wouldn't be heading to this

tiny airstrip if you hadn't suggested it after going to that bar! So, it's on you actually," Sam shot back, giving Ed a friendly shove.

In a more serious tone, Ed said, "Hold on, I wanted to give you this."

Sam stopped and looked over at what Ed was fishing out of his backpack. He pulled out a brown sheath and extracted from it a sixteen-inch survival knife complete with a saw on one end of its shiny, silver blade. He pushed it toward Sam whose eyes widened at the weapon in front of him.

"Ed, what the hell?" Sam said.

"Go on, it's yours. I bought it from a street vendor on my jog this morning. Trust me, I looked quite the fool finishing my run carrying that damn thing with me. I couldn't resist. It's my way of saying *thanks* for going on this unexpected detour," Ed answered warmly.

"I just, well..." Sam took the knife by its gray handle and observed it. He ran his finger along the tip of the blade that was indeed sharp, as he quickly surmised.

"Come on, Mr. Eagle Scout, just say thank you for the knife and let's get to hangar B, alright?" Ed said chuckling.

"Thank you, Ed, for this. I'm not planning on murdering any natives, though. But I accept the gift. Hopefully, Mr. Pinto will allow it on the plane," Sam replied.

"*Allow* it on the plane? Stick that thing in your backpack, we aren't flying commercial, dude," Ed answered jokingly.

Sam smirked, opened his backpack and slid the sheathed blade into it, zipping it back up then continuing on their way.

"You sure you trust this Pinto guy? We literally met him

for only a few minutes yesterday. And now he's taking our lives in his hands, flying us across the ocean on a small plane to get to an island we haven't done any research on," Sam asked his traveling partner.

"I trust that guy as much as I can hold my liquor. Not that well. But I do know enough about airplanes to know the one he's flying and it's a beauty. If he can afford that, or has been granted access to fly it like he says, that's good enough for me," Ed answered.

They arrived at the airport shortly after the knife changed hands and saw quickly that there were exactly two hangars—A and, unsurprisingly, B. The door was opened and the blue and white Piper Turbo Seneca II airplane with the serial number 8088N on its side was parked with its door open. Several people stood near it talking. One appeared to be loading two pieces of luggage into the rear of the plane.

The airport was barely an airport at all. Just a small control tower beside the lone, relatively short runway.

"Come on, that's it up ahead," Ed exclaimed excitedly as he pushed forward toward the hangar, waving to the two men stationed inside the control tower as they passed by.

"Wait up!" Sam shouted after him, also picking up his speed.

Seeing the two approaching figures, Benício Pinto Guedes quickly raised his hand waving at the newcomers. "Gentleman! You made it! I wasn't sure you would take me up on my offer!"

Ed and Sam came to a stop in front of the man wearing the same cowboy hat as the previous day but now sporting fresh clothes. Another button-down shirt, this one a dull orange color and loose fitting, making him appear even bigger than he already was. His jeans were acid washed and had several holes in the knees. Dropping his cigarette and squashing it on the tarmac, he extended his hand. Ed was the first to stretch out his own and Pinto took it, shaking it firmly. After shaking Sam's hand as well, he turned to the other three people standing around them.

"Introductions! Sam and Edward, this is my copilot, Fernando Conceição Barroso. I trust him with my life so you can too, okay?" The man they were introduced to was significantly smaller than Pinto and wore a New York Yankee's baseball hat with large aviator sunglasses covering a good portion of his dark-complected face.

Finished with loading several medium-sized boxes labeled with a red cross into the rear of the plane and securing them with trailer ties, the skinny man walked over to introduce himself. "I go by Barroso, nice to meet you both," he said, shaking their hands quickly before adding, "Pinto, we need to get airborne if we're going to beat that storm that's forecast out over the Solomon Sea. It's due to cross our flight path in about an hour if we take off soon. We may beat it, but we must leave."

"Okay, okay, we go. Gentlemen, we must leave, it is now eight-oh-five. These are the two I spoke of yesterday that will be traveling with us," Pinto said, turning to look at the two ladies standing directly behind him near the airplane's entrance.

The women stared at the new arrivals. After a brief

awkward silence, the first woman, tall with brown hair pulled back in a ponytail, nodded and said, "Hello, my name is Laura Joyner." She extended her hand to Sam first who took it as he introduced himself as well.

"Sam Berry, pleased to make your acquaintance," he replied, quickly noticing the woman wore a short, cropped brown top and hip hugging jeans and was quite attractive. She also had a small backpack slung over her back.

"Well, hello, Miss Laura, name's Edward Brant, but my friends just call me Ed. So please, call me Ed," Ed was quick to say, shaking her hand as well.

"Laura, it's just Laura, not *Miss Laura*," she replied with the slightest hint of cool. Something Ed picked up on as he pulled his hand back.

"This is my friend and traveling partner, Eva Barnes," Laura said, looking over at the blond, pig-tailed woman standing beside her in the pink bikini top and cut-off jean shorts riding high on her upper thighs. The wad of gum in her mouth popped as she first took Ed's hand, shaking it.

"Ed. Call me Ed," he said to the stunningly attractive blond woman with large, nearly exposed breasts.

"Nice to meet you, there, Mr. Ed. Get it? Like the horse show?" Eva joked.

"Yeah, like the horse," Ed replied with a grin, already imagining her naked in bed with him after a night of hard drinking and an even harder night of sex.

"Hi, Sammy, nice to meet you," Eva said, now shaking Sam's hand. He took it and nodded back to her.

"Nice to meet you, Eva Barnes."

"Let's go," Laura said, ending the introductions and looking toward Pinto who was making final preparations for takeoff.

"Yes, yes…time to go! Ladies first, also, I need payment from you two. Are you carrying anything other than the backpacks?" Pinto asked as Barossa settled into the copilot's seat inside the plane.

"I got this," Ed said, pulling out two hundred-dollar bills.

"Wait, what? Ed, I can pay for my own ticket!" Sam retorted.

"Don't worry about it. Hey, you get our tickets to Australia once we're done on the islands, deal?" Ed came back.

"Sure, okay," Sam answered. He knew this, along with the knife, was Ed's way of thanking him for putting up with the abrupt change of plans and he appreciated it.

Pinto took the cash and then motioned for the men to climb aboard. Once Sam and Ed boarded, Pinto looked up to the beautiful sky above. It was perfect, but Pinto, an experienced pilot, knew that perfect didn't always mean *safe*.

He put on his sunglasses and climbed aboard the six-seater Piper Turbo Seneca, closing the door behind him.

Sitting in his pilot's seat, he began hitting switches and the plane's engine fired up. Once the engine was running on high, he glanced back to his seated passengers. Four seats total, two per side and each with its own window. Sam and Ed were sitting in the two seats nearest the rear of the plane and Laura and Eva sat in front of them.

"Everyone ready to go to Solomon Islands?" Pinto said happily, wanting to keep the mood light.

"Hell, yes!" Ed replied from the rear, causing Eva to glance back with a grin as she took her gum out of her mouth and stuck it under her seat.

"Good, good, then buckle up, we have a three-hour flight in front of us!" Pinto exclaimed as he pushed forward on the steering yoke of the small plane. Once it cleared hangar B, they made their way out onto the runway and waited for clearance from the tower.

"This is Kokoda tower, Piper Turbo Seneca II number 8088N, you are cleared for takeoff. Keep an eye out for that storm rolling in over the Solomon Sea. You should beat it but be aware of your surrounds. Your destination is Buka Airport on Bougainville Island, correct?" the nameless control tower employee uttered through the pilots' headsets.

"Yes, it is, control tower, Seneca II out," Pinto replied, glancing over at Barossa who slid his large sunglasses down slightly to reveal a worried look.

"Safe travels," the man replied.

Not bothering to reply, Pinto turned his attention to the runway and pushed forward on the yoke, picking up speed until, near the end of the runway, the plane lifted up off the ground and was airborne.

The plane continued to climb, gliding through puffy, slow-moving clouds before reaching cruising altitude.

Pinto looked back at their four passengers, all gazing out their respective windows lost in their own thoughts. Glancing over at his copilot, speaking just loud enough for Barossa to hear, Pinto uttered, "Regardless of the storm, we must make it to the Solomon Islands with the drugs. Our contact should be there waiting for us when we arrive. The Americans' money will get us refueled and pay off the security as well as buy us their silence. We'll get the hell out of there before the boss figures out what we're doing with his dope. If we mess this up in any way, he'll kill us both, you understand?"

Barossa nodded grimly. "I sure hope this works. The right engine was giving me some problems earlier when I was looking her over. This plane needs a serious once-over top to bottom. If either of these two engines acts up, the other can't withstand the added strain, especially those damn storms that hang over the middle of the Solomon Sea."

Shaking his head, Pinto replied, "Barroso, my friend, once we make it to the Solomon Islands, we're ghosts. All this plane has to do is get us there as it has countless times before. We'll beat the storm and if not we climb above it. We're good, relax. And hey, I got us some quick and dirty extra cash to help us vanish faster. You have to admit, that's going to help us out."

"Man, if there are any issues and Paim finds us—"

Pinto interrupted, hissing, "There will be no mistakes! We play our cards right and we will be two rich men free of this place and free of that sonofabitch! I'm just glad those two gringos showed up at the last minute or this would have been cutting it too close. Two hundred dollars will only refuel the plane, not pay off the security once we land."

Barossa looked over at Pinto and nodded gravely in agreement.

"Anything goes sideways," Pinto added, then pointed to his chest where an old Colt Python double action revolver lay holstered.

4
BUMPY RIDE

The first part of the flight was filled with mostly minor chitchat among the passengers. Sam talked to Ed about what exactly he intended to do in the Solomon Islands upon arrival. The answer was as expected, "I don't know, let's play it by ear when we get there." Typical Edward.

The women, on the other hand were mostly silent, both lost in their own thoughts as they stared out their windows and the miles and miles of sprawling ocean beneath them. Periodically, chatter could be heard up in the cockpit with Pinto appearing to glance back at his passengers then over at his copilot Barossa, muttering under their breath before going back to staring straight ahead out the window in front of them.

After the fourth time this happened, Laura, who had been noticing this, inadvertently glanced back at Sam who was sitting behind and to the right of her. She saw that unlike Eva, he too seemed to be watching their pilot with the utmost interest.

Sam glanced at Laura and their eyes locked for a brief second. But that was all that was needed for Sam to figure out she was thinking the same thing he was: something seemed off. The ease of which this entire trip was arranged, for one. Sure, the Solomon Islands were a popular destination and many tourists visited it, but this seemed too last minute and well-timed with regards to this Pinto guy getting things set up. And now he knew he wasn't the only one who had suspicions about this man's intentions. His mind shifted to the boxes with the cross on them. *What's in those boxes?*

Ed leaned forward and struck up conversation with Eva who was sitting to his right. "So, tell me about yourself, Eva, where you from? How old are you?"

Glad the good-looking man in the Black Sabbath shirt was striking up conversation with her, she turned to him and answered, "Well, we're from Port Aransas, near San Antonio, Texas. I'm twenty-one, just had a birthday, yesterday actually. And Laura here is twenty-three."

"Well, happy birthday, Eva! Twenty-one, great age," Ed exclaimed, immediately thinking of what he would enjoy doing with her after a hot night of dancing and drinking. She was incredibly sexy, especially in the bathing suit top exposing her golden tanned midriff and chest. He started to imagine her pressed up against him when he noticed Laura, who was sitting directly in front of him, had turned around and caught him glancing at her friend's chest.

Looking up at Laura, he read her face instantly. *Stay the hell away from my friend.* Ed averted his eyes quickly while Laura looked over disapprovingly at her friend who also averted her eyes but kept her sly smile.

"So, what's your story?" Ed asked Laura whose eyes fell back on him.

"My story, hotshot, is none of your business, alright? I'm not here to get to know people I'll never see again," Laura shot back, glancing once more over to Sam who was watching the back and forth. Her eyes softened when they locked with Sam's. His eyes seemed trustworthy.

Figuring he should smooth things over, Sam leaned forward. "We were heading to Australia. In fact, after this slight detour, we'll likely make our way over there next. This is our last big hurrah before entering the business world and settling down, so to speak."

Taking a second, Laura contemplated this then said, "This isn't a pleasure trip for us. Though Eva's attire would have you believe otherwise."

"Hey, it's hot and I'm working on my tan while we're down here! I need to find some way to entertain myself while you search for your..." Eva began but stopped short when she saw Laura's glaring eyes on her. She quit speaking.

Glancing back at Ed, she sighed. "My apologies for being curt, but I have business here, nothing more."

All four of them fell silent, Ed glancing over at Sam while rolling his eyes and mouthing *What a bitch*.

Ignoring his friend, Sam continued watching Laura, who was now facing forward once more. She was beautiful, tall and slender, with long straight brown hair neatly pulled back in a ponytail. Unlike her friend Eva, she wore no makeup at all, she didn't need to. Her face was smooth and tan. But her eyes spoke a message of concern and worry. She and her friend were indeed not here for pleasure but something else. He wondered if she would expound more or if this short flight would be it, all parties going their own ways once they landed.

Laura was deep in thought, staring out the window at the water below. She reached into the front pocket of her jeans and discreetly pulled out a piece of paper. Opening it, she read over it for what must have been the thousandth time.

My Dearest Laura,

How do I put into words how I feel? My love for you is so tremendous that I must leave you and your mother. For a time. I cannot have you watch me whittle away to nothing in front of your eyes. That's not how I want you to remember me. I want you to remember me as the man who tried to find a cure for this. Not just for myself, but for the whole world. For the countless people that pass through this life onto the next at far too young an age. It is my calling. Know that I will forever and always love you, my dear, sweet Laura. Watching you grow up to be the strong independent and kind-hearted woman you've become has been the greatest joy of my life. Following in your father's footsteps in the field of medicine has made me so proud. I couldn't have asked for a better daughter! If I have let you down, I am truly sorry. But out there, somewhere, is a cure for this. And your old man intends to find it, one way or another.

I love you always,

Papa.

Laura felt the tears welling up and quickly stuffed the letter back in her pocket, hastily wiping her eyes. Without thinking, she shot a glance back to Sam who had just turned his head to see her somber expression staring back at him. She quickly turned forward once more. *Get a grip, Laura. You don't know these people and you never will. Stay focused!*

"So, Sam, when we land, I think we should first—" Ed started to say as Sam glanced over at him, away from the mysteriously beautiful and troubled woman sitting in the front row of the small plane.

The plane suddenly began to shake and then dropped straight down a short distance before regaining its flight path.

"Everyone, we seem to be hitting a storm. I thought we could make it through before it crossed our path, but it looks as though we are in for a bit of a bumpy ride for a short time. Nothing to worry about, I've flown through much worse," Pinto called back to his passengers, glancing over at Barroso.

In front of them, the sky had turned black as rain began to spritz against the Piper Turbo Seneca II before quickly turning to a hard, drumming onslaught.

Instantly, the plane began rocking back and forth in the strong winds before taking quick dips downward then back up as Pinto and Barroso fought with the controls, trying to keep it steady.

Sam instantly grabbed the sides of his seat, looking in terror at Ed then up to the two women in front of them doing the same thing he was, hanging on for dear life.

"Holy shit," was all Ed was able to get out before the plane took another dip down, this time further than the last. His backpack, which had been laying at his feet, shot up onto the ceiling of the plane before dropping back down on his head with a thud. He quickly put his hands up to his head while grabbing at his loose backpack. "Ouch, damnit! Get us the hell out of here Pinto!" he called out.

All around the plane, blackness now filled the sky as not only pelting rain but cracks of lightning surrounded them on all sides, streaking through the sky in brilliant displays of shiny yellow. As if cracks in the atmosphere were being created and just as quickly, sealed back up. The plane continued to sway back and forth, then quickly descending before Pinto gained control. This went on for several minutes. All aboard clung on for dear life as the plane shook violently even when not rocking back and forth. A loud crack reverberated through the cockpit and hull of the plane as the lights inside flickered.

"This is not good, Pinto!" Barroso exclaimed into his headset. "We were just struck by several bolts of lightning! The engines, they can't take this! The storms in this region… we should have never attempted this in the condition of this plane's engines! She's old and needs work!"

"I'm going to attempt to climb out of this storm and get on top of it, hang on everyone!" Pinto shouted back to his passengers.

Barroso fell silent, gritting his teeth, doing everything he could to help maintain control of the plane that was far too small to be traveling through this massive of a storm. He knew it and so did Pinto. Both men gripped the steering yokes tightly and pulled back hard. The plane pitched up and began to climb while still rocking back and forth violently.

"That crack we heard; I think the plane was hit by lightning!" Ed shouted, looking at Sam with eyes wide.

Neither of them expected this, in the middle of the Solomon Sea battling a torrential storm in a small, six-person plane. This would be rough going for a commercial airliner, much less the puddle-jumper they found themselves trapped in. Unlike Ed, Sam clutched his backpack tightly so it wouldn't injure himself or anyone else. In the chaos that was unfolding, he noted that neither Laura nor Eva had backpacks. Laura had a leather satchel draped over her shoulder but nothing else. The suitcases he had seen their copilot loading when they arrived must have belonged to them.

"This is bad, this is *really* bad, Laura! I want off this damned plane!" Eva shrieked as the plane took another sharp drop before stabilizing and once more climbing.

"Hang on, girl! We're climbing; in a little bit we'll see sunshine!" Laura called out, hopeful but not believing what she was saying.

"Shit, shit, shit!" Eva continued gripping the sides of her arm rests as tight as her fingers could squeeze.

Sam looked over to Ed and noticed a thin line of blood running from his full head of hair down the side of his cheek. He wanted to ask if he was okay but could only grit his teeth and, like the rest of them, hang on for dear life.

Farther and farther up the plane climbed. Everyone on board, the pilots included, couldn't believe they were still in one piece and not already sinking to the ocean depths below.

Pinto wanted to wipe his sweat-covered brow but refused to take either hand off the violently shaking steering yoke. Neither man looked at each other.

Pinto called out into his headset, "Mayday, mayday! This is Piper Turbo Seneca, number 8088N. We are in the storm over the Solomon Sea. Our bearings are latitude -9.28766, longitude 153.69020. Attempting to climb over the storm, unable to go around! Repeat, mayday, mayday, this is Piper Turbo Seneca, number 8008N..."

For a brief second, a voice attempted to crackle through "Piper Turbo Seneca, Fabian Amill speaking from Honiara control tower, repeat your bearings..."

Then, only static.

"We've got to get on top of this thing!" Barroso shouted to Pinto, hoping to reestablish communications with whoever was on the other end of the radio.

As he spoke the words, the plane breached the storm. Sunlight instantly shone through the windows of the Seneca. For a brief period, no one spoke, all staring in awe below at what they had just escaped. A blanket of black hovered below them, occasionally lighting up with streaks of lightning and rumbling thunder.

Quickly, Pinto tried the com once more, to no avail. "I think communications are down, I can't reach anyone." Turning behind him, he looked at the four Americans, all frazzled, still gripping their arm rests. "Sorry, my friends, I wasn't expecting that. We're going to stay up here and stay on course. The storm is pretty widespread, but we went through the worst of it. I see its end up ahead a ways. Everyone okay?"

"Shit, am I still alive?" Eva called out, suddenly freezing cold in her bikini top and short shorts.

Laura reached her hand out to her friend across the aisle who quickly took it into her own and squeezed hard. Laura glanced back to Sam, "You hanging in there, hotshots?"

Forcing a thin smile, Sam replied, "I echo Eva's sentiments, are we still alive?" He remembered the thin line of blood on the side of Ed's face and looked over at him.

"Ed! Ed, buddy, open your eyes!" Sam shouted, reaching over and shaking his friend whose head was hung and eyes were closed.

At this, both women turned to look at Ed who appeared to be unconscious.

"Oh fuck! Is he dead!?" Eva called out, horrified at seeing the unconscious man behind her.

Ed's eyes fluttered then opened, he slowly raised his head. "Did someone say dead? I'm not dead but I think I may have a concussion, or just a nasty-ass bump on the old noggin."

"Stay with me, buddy, keep your eyes open, we need to stay sharp. I think Pinto's gotten us out of the worst of this storm, he said the end is up ahead," Sam said, thankful Ed was keeping his eyes open and remaining coherent.

"The *fuck* was I thinking going along with this! Damnit Sam, you're smarter than this!" Sam muttered under his breath then looked back out his window, thinking of the lightning cracking violently against the plane earlier and fearing the worst was yet to come. Below him the sea of black cloud cover remained.

"Laura, still with us up there?" Sam said, glancing up

at the visibly terrified woman trying to calm the even more terrified friend beside her.

"I think so. Ask me when we land, okay?" She glanced back and gave him a small smile which he returned. He didn't know this woman but was glad she was along. She seemed to have a calming effect on him and likewise, he on her.

From the cockpit, Pinto kept a steady hand on the steering yoke of Sérgio Melo Paim's private plane. One that he had used many times. Now that things were under control, his mind wandered. He was thankful he had a good rapport with the control tower back at the Kokoda airport; otherwise, he knew he wouldn't have been able to leave that easily. This was just another run he was making, one he wasn't planning on returning from, nor was his partner Barroso.

Stealing from a drug lord in Papua New Guinea, especially from the dreaded Sérgio Paim, was an instant death sentence, and not a quick one. They both knew the risks, but the rewards would be plentiful. They would make their way to the Solomon Islands, offload the drugs according to the plan, then sell the stolen plane. With the money, both men planned to get new identities and passports and from there, make their way to Columbia and blend in, vanishing forever from the tight grasp of Sérgio Paim.

Pinto and Barroso were considered *higher ups* in Paim's drug operation. Running large quantities of marijuana and cocaine from their home base to the numerous islands surrounding Papua New Guinea was their main job and they did it well, either avoiding police or paying them off. The racket had been quite lucrative, mainly for Sérgio Paim himself, and as the years ticked by, he got wealthier and greedier. Thus, Pinto and Barroso decided a change was in order. The fifteen pounds of cocaine stored in the back of the plane was enough to set them for life, especially in Bogota, Columbia.

Thinking of Sérgio Paim, Pinto wondered how long it would take for him to know something was amiss. Likely, later in the day when neither of them reported for work, he would do some searching, leading him to get in touch with the Kokoda airport and find that his plane was taken. That would lead him to quickly search his large stash of pure, uncut cocaine to find fifteen pounds of it missing. A quick call to the airport would lead Paim to believe they traveled to Buka Airport on Bougainville Island. A stop they had taken before but one that would throw him off their trail long enough for them to vanish with his cocaine. And that was that, they would be wanted men from this day forward in all of Papua New Guinea. But they planned to never return, as long as they could make it out of this plane ride alive.

Barossa shook his head, wiping the sweat from his brow. "I didn't think we were going to make it out of that storm alive. We've been through some storms in our time, but never one like that."

"Well, we certainly wouldn't have continued on with the flight knowing the storm was out there under different circumstances, but the drugs were taken early this morning, it was now or never, am I right?" Pinto replied, hoping his partner in crime would agree.

He needed Barossa to stick with him to the end on this.

His traveling partner had been to Columbia before and knew the lay of the land, along with several unsavory characters that could help them blend in and possibly hook them up with more work if they played their cards right.

But first...*survive this damn storm.*

Pinto turned to his passengers. "How is everyone holding up?"

Sam called out to the front. "Ed here has a pretty bad bump on his head, maybe a concussion! We're just glad to be alive. How soon until we arrive?"

"Ah yes, I am so sorry about your friend. We will make sure he gets to a doctor once we land," Pinto said as convincingly as he could manage, then continued. "To answer your question, Mr. Sam, we are roughly one hour away from Solomon Islands, possibly a bit longer as the storm has blown us off our flight plan slightly and I need to conserve fuel given what we just went through. So, it may be closer to ninety minutes. But, rest assured, the worst is over. Just sit back and rel—"

Pinto stopped speaking, looking at Barossa's finger pointing to engine one's gauge in front of them. It was blinking red. His eyes traveled up to meet his copilots as both looked out Barossa's window. *The lightning strike! Oh no, please God no!*

"Why are there sparks coming out of the engine?" Eva called out, her eyes glued to her window, looking out at the engine where sparks were sizzling and smoke was leaving a trail behind them.

Sam instantly looked out his window and saw she was

right. Sparks and smoke, heavy smoke. Laura and a drowsy Ed both strained to see what the commotion was about right outside Eva's window.

"Shit, not good, Pinto, this is not good!" Barossa exclaimed "We can't afford to travel back through that storm, not if we want to make it to the Solomon Islands in one piece. Like I said, if engine one goes, the second likely won't be able to handle the added stress!"

This time Eva and Laura, in the front seats directly behind them, heard his words.

Eva quickly reached over and grabbed hold of Laura's hand which she instantly took into hers, both squeezing tightly.

Ed looked over at Sam and said slowly, as though he was drunk, "Sorry about this, buddy. Wasn't my intention to get us killed and all, just some fun and adventure, know what I mean?"

Sam knew Ed wasn't in his right mind right now and was taking this far too lightly. He continued looking out at the engine that spewed out sparks and smoke.

The sparks had now turned into full-fledged flames. The engine coughed and sputtered then the propeller slowed to a stop in a matter of seconds, the flames becoming larger as they shot out the rear of the engine.

Pinto called out, "Do not worry, my friends, we can fly on one engine! These planes were built to fly on only one engine if necessary! Trust me!"

Barroso looked at Pinto gravely, thinking back to their conversation on the tarmac.

"Yeah? What about the fire?" Laura shouted back at him, glancing back at Sam as she did. Their eyes locked once more, each one's expression telling the other, *This is going from bad to worse.*

They waited for a response from Pinto but got none. All fell silent inside the plane as the right engine continued to shoot flames and cough smoke.

Ed spoke groggily while pointing out the window on his side of the plane. "Hey everyone, I know things are fucked with the right-side engine, but what's up with this engine out my window?"

The engine two gauge began to blink red in the cockpit.

5
SURVIVORS

Sérgio Paim ran his hands through his black hair, slicking it back against his scalp. This is how the muscle-bound man wore it most of the time, making him look exactly like what he was portraying, a gangster. He picked up the phone in his villa and called the Kokoda airport. "Control tower, now," the tall, well-built man said as he paced the room in nothing but small bikini briefs and an empty gun holster strapped around his bare chest.

Two dark-complected men in suits stood near him, both keeping their sunglasses on, staring straight ahead, avoiding any glances at the beautiful naked woman lying on the large, king-size bed.

The villa was near the airport but situated just out of town. Behind it, up in the hills, was Paim's highly lucrative cocaine operation. He had worked hard for this life, paying his dues as well as paying the right people off to turn a blind eye to what went on in and around his villa.

"Control tower speaking, Mr. Paim, how may I be of—" the man on the phone began.

"Listen to me and answer my question. My Seneca, is it still in hangar B?" Paim said in a calm but utterly threatening tone.

There was a moment of silence as the man on the other end quickly connected the dots and was likely afraid to give this man bad news. "No, sir. The plane 8088N departed shortly after eight AM. I cleared Mr. Benício Pinto Guedes for takeoff. He and Mr. Barroso informed me upon their arrival you had cleared them and their passengers."

The two men in Paim's room stood by, stone-faced as the black naked woman stood up in front of them. Her large afro puffed out all around her perfectly shaped head, complimenting her perfectly shaped body. She grabbed a tiny robe and instead of putting it on, slung it over her shoulder as she made her way to the shower in the bathroom connected to Paim's bedroom, closing the door behind her.

"How many passengers?" Paim asked the shaken control tower employee.

"They were traveling with four others. All appeared to be American from what we observed. Two young men and two women, one actually waved at me as he ran to the plane," the man replied.

"The next question I ask you is important, and you had better answer truthfully, or I will kill every member of your family, slowly. Then I will kill you. Do you believe the words

I say?" Paim said in an even lower, more calculated voice.

Stuttering, the man replied, "Y-yes, I believe you, Mr. Paim." He fell silent.

"Were there any briefcases loaded onto my plane? Black briefcases with red cross labels on their sides?" Paim asked.

"Yes. Two, I counted two, sir."

Paim looked from his phone over to the two men standing in his room as the shower ran in the bathroom nearby. Staring at them, he asked the man, "Why did you not notify me that there were four Americans traveling on my plane?"

The man attempted to choose his words carefully. "Mr. Paim, I spoke with Mr. Pinto himself and he assured me you had given your blessing on traveling with several other passengers. It was…a way to cover the fuel when they arrived at Buka Airport on Bougainville Island. He assured me they would be returning later to—"

The control tower employee was cut off by a visibly furious Sérgio Paim. "You will do as I say! Whatever plane is in hangar A, prepare it for my immediate departure. Have it fueled up and ready. I will be there in thirty minutes. If it is not ready and waiting, I will kill your mother and your father, your wife and your children. Do you doubt me?"

"No, sir, I do not doubt you. The Cessna Citation will be ready. Would you like me to—"

Paim slammed the phone down onto the receiver and glared at the two men, both of whom were dressed entirely in black. A requirement for Paim's muscle, you must *look* intimidating as well as *be* intimidating.

"Call Buka Airport, tell them to be expecting a Piper

Turbo Seneca II airplane serial number 8088N within the next hour. Also, get me in touch with all other surrounding airports on nearby islands that my plane could potentially make it to on one tank of fuel. Then, we are going to take a trip," Paim hissed, pulling a cigarette out of a Marlboro pack laying on his dresser. Next to the pack was a shiny, silver Browning 9MM pistol. He picked the loaded handgun up and put it into its holster strapped around his chest.

Pinto stared wide-eyed at the blinking engine one gauge. The red flashing light seemed to call out to him mockingly, *Are you prepared to go through the storm once more, you thief?*

"What's the plan?" Barossa asked in an even tone, masking the panic he felt.

"What the hell are you going to do, pilot?" Laura shouted out from behind the pilots.

Eva sat silently in her seat, eyes closed, mouthing prayers she had learned as a young Catholic schoolgirl. "Hail Mary, full of grace, the Lord is with thee…"

Staring lazily out at the sparking and smoking engine, Ed turned to Sam and shrugged, "Well, I promised you an adventure and this is certainly an adventure, am I right?"

"Shut the hell up Ed, just *shut up!*" Sam retorted angrily, knowing he wasn't entirely coherent. Otherwise, he would be freaking out along with the rest of the terrified crew of the seemingly doomed flight number 8088N.

Ed appeared to be ready to retort but fell silent, closing his eyes. Sam peered past him, trying to glimpse engine one's problems. All he could see from his vantage point was a line of smoke obviously shooting out the rear of the engine.

"The engine is going! Damnit, I knew we should have…" Barossa began shouting, leaning toward Pinto who sat looking at the engine now beginning to catch fire.

"Tell me something I don't know! The lightning must've done irreparable damage to our already weakened engine! The second engine couldn't take the stress of the storm on its own!" Pinto replied then shouted into his headset, "Mayday, mayday! Can anyone read me! This is Piper Turbo Seneca number 8088N, anyone!"

All that came back was static. He shook his head, took off his headset and threw it against the control panel, glancing back at the four passengers behind them, all clutching their respective seats.

Laura looked out her window, seeing the growing flames on engine one. As with engine two, the propeller shuddered then abruptly stopped. "Oh shit," she muttered under her breath.

Flight 8088N quickly descended and, in less than a minute, tumbled back into the storm. Rain began pelting the Seneca II as it continued its downward descent through the storm. Everyone on board shimmied in their seats as the plane rocked back and forth violently. Lightning crashed around them, one bolt making contact with the roof of the plane, sounding like a stick of dynamite being set off. The vibration and force of the lightning strike against the small airplane acted as a weight, thrusting it straight down.

"We're going down! Brace for impact!" Pinto shouted

to everyone.

Even Barossa, the furthest thing from a religious man, made a sign of the cross and closed his eyes while more wind and rain crashed against the plane. Farther down it fell through the storm, the instruments in front of Pinto and Barossa all blinking the numerous catastrophic malfunctions happening inside and outside of the plane.

Eva screamed out, "I don't want to die! Momma, Dad!"

Behind her, Sam kept his eyes shut tight, his hands gripping the sides of his seat as tightly as he could. Only once did he glance at his watch to see the compass spinning in circles.

Beside him, Ed's head bobbed back and forth as he tried to stay conscious.

In front of Ed, Laura gritted her teeth. "I will survive this, I will survive this, I will…"

The plane breached the storm clouds and sailed forward, both engines dead now, coasting quickly to the watery grave below.

Pinto squinted out the front, looking for any sign of land, rain continuing to pummel them.

Laura peered forward, trying to glimpse what was in front of them, only seeing rain smashing against the windshield, but it appeared to be slowing down as the plane continued gliding forward.

Pinto and Barossa stared wide-eyed at the ocean rushing toward them, both trying in vain to pull back on their steering yokes, trying to slow it down any way they could. The plane was dead, and soon they would be also. All the planning, all the dope, would soon be resting at the bottom of the Solomon

Sea with their corpses.

Suddenly, the rain ceased, and sunlight shone in throughout the plane. They had passed the storm just as the plane, mere seconds later, smashed into the ocean. The right wing instantly ripped off at the base of the Seneca, causing it to veer to the right, tilting everyone to the side as they all lurched forward from the catastrophic impact.

Eva screamed while the rest of the passengers continued gritting their teeth.

The left wing broke off as the vessel shot forward like a torpedo through the water, bouncing off waves then crashing back down. The front windshield smashed in and, along with it, torrents of water.

Pinto and Barossa screamed out as water smashed against them before flowing quickly to the four passengers behind them.

The plane came to a sudden, abrupt halt.

"Are we still alive!?" Eva yelled.

Sam shook his head and quickly looked over at Ed. "Ed, can you hear me? Ed, look at me!" he shouted.

Slowly, Ed turned his head. Blood was trickling out his mouth. "I think something is stuck in me." He looked down at his stomach where a red circle was pooling around him in the water that was now up to everyone's waists.

Hastily, Sam fumbled with his seatbelt, unlatched it, and pushing through water, came beside him. Laura got out of her seat as did Eva who was softly crying, both turning to see the pool of blood forming around the two American men behind them.

Pinto shook his head, dazed, but alive. His copilot wasn't so lucky. A large shard of the windshield that had just exploded inward had sliced through Barossa's neck, nearly severing his head completely. The thick glass had embedded itself into his copilot's seat but not before taking Barossa's life from him. Blood pumped out into the quickly filling husk of the sinking Seneca.

Having seen numerous dead bodies before, some by his own hand, the sight of Barossa still came as a shock to Pinto. He had known the man for many years and had gone on many drug drop-offs and pickups with the man. They had even shared women from time to time after killing a bottle of whisky at the Dragon's Breath. And now he was gone. *But I'm alive.*

He looked back to the passengers who appeared to be huddled around the man named Ed. "We must get out of this plane! It is sinking!" Pinto's mind went to the fifteen pounds of Papua New Guinea's finest pure, uncut cocaine, stored in the back. Seven-point-five pounds per briefcase. There was no way to get it from inside the plane in the shape it was in, quickly sinking. He leaned forward, peering out the shattered windshield.

In the rear of the plane, Sam had managed to unbuckle Ed who looked at him wearily. "How bad is it, good buddy?" he asked groggily. A steady stream of blood trickled out his mouth and from the earlier wound on his head.

"Is he gonna die?" Eva shrieked.

Laura and Sam ignored her. Laura, beside Sam now, said, "We have to get him out of this plane."

"And go where?" Sam retorted, before he answered his best friend. "Look, Ed, a piece of Laura's chair broke off when we crashed into the ocean, it's impaled in your stomach."

"What's the bad news?" Ed replied with a chuckle.

From up front, Pinto shouted, "Land, I see land!"

Eva was the first to move forward, screaming when she saw the deceased Barossa continuing to spill blood into the water. "He's dead, the copilot is dead!"

Sam glanced up to Eva but didn't reply, focusing on his friend.

Ignoring her friend as well, Laura looked up from the gravely injured Ed, and said quietly to Sam, "He's losing too much blood."

Pinto pushed his way out the busted windshield, not waiting on the four American passengers. Once on the nose of the plane, he surveyed the crash site. "We hit an islet near an island!"

Eva, trying to avoid the dead man and pool of blood, repeated what Pinto had said back to Laura and Sam.

"Ed, you hear that? Land is nearby, we've got to get you up. Laura, do you have any supplies in your luggage?" Sam asked urgently.

"Clothes, toiletries. The basics. Eva has the same, but they're stored in the back, I don't think we can even get to them."

Nodding, Sam grabbed his backpack and handed it to Laura then grabbed Ed's backpack, slung it over his shoulder and lifted Ed's arm, pulling him up.

Ed groaned loudly in pain.

Laura quicky lifted his other arm and slug it over her neck and with Sam, began making their way to the busted front windshield.

Ed looked over with eyes half shut to Laura. "Hey, you take care of Sam, here. He's a good guy. He shouldn't have been on this plane. It was my fault. Good guy, I tell ya."

Laura looked at Sam and contemplated shaking her head that this was no use but held off. "Come on, hotshot," she replied instead.

They reached the opening where Eva now forced herself to push past the blood-covered, unmoving Barossa, climbing out onto the nose of the plane and standing beside Pinto who continued surveying their surroundings.

"Give us a hand down here!" Sam shouted up to Pinto.

Glancing at them, Pinot replied coldly, "He's not going to make it, why bring the unneeded pain? You see what's sticking into his guts, right?"

Laura instantly became flush with anger. "You are the pilot on this doomed plane and as the pilot, you will help us! We paid you, remember? Speaking of this plane, did you know about the faulty engines before taking off?"

"Bad storm, nothing we could do. We're alive, that's all that matters right now," Pinto mumbled before he begrudgingly reached his arm down into the open cockpit, took Ed's hand and helped pull him up and out with Laura and Sam pushing him up from behind.

Once out, Ed nearly fell over, but Pinto continued holding onto him. He looked down at the chunk of steel sticking into his lower intestines. *This man is not going to make it,* he thought, but kept silent for now.

Laura began climbing out of the wreckage with Sam's backpack slung over her shoulder, Sam attempted to help her but saw no way of helping that didn't involve pushing her up by her butt. Glancing back and seeing his awkwardness, she grinned slightly. "I've got this, Sam, but thanks."

Nodding, he waited until she was fully out of the plane then he was about to climb out, still clinging to Ed's backpack when Pinto shouted down at him, "Flare gun! There's a flare gun under my seat! Grab it."

Sam fished through the waist-deep water, having to submerge himself to fully reach under Pinto's seat. His hand felt around until it bumped into a container with a handle. Grabbing hold of the handle, he gave it a yank and it released from its location. He pulled it up as he blew out the breath he was holding while submerged. He yelled up as he spat water out of his mouth, "Not a pleasant thing being submerged in bloody water—this it?"

"Yep, hand it up here," Pinto replied.

Sam held the gun up to Pinto, then made his way out of the bloody waterlogged cockpit, glad to get away from the dead body. His white tank top was soaked with a hint of red.

Ed, held upright by Laura, looked over at Sam. "Your hat, where's your Aussie hat?" he asked with a chuckle that produced blood that he spat out.

"Flew off when we crashed, I suppose. More pressing matters, like getting you to that island," Sam replied as his eyes went to the land mass near the downed plane.

"I don't know if I can swim that far," Eva exclaimed,

looking at the island in front of them.

Laura looked at the sky, the storm had indeed passed, then down to the small islet that had stopped their crash. If it had not, the plane would have sunk and likely wouldn't have given them enough time to escape before drowning.

Pinto stood on the roof of the plane to give the four passengers enough room to stand. Behind them was nothing but ocean; there were no other islands nearby other than the one in sight, roughly two-hundred yards away. "We must swim. We may be in luck!" he exclaimed.

"Why do you say that?" Laura asked.

Pointing to the island, he replied, "Look at the large crater toward the back of the island, then look straight down and slightly to the left. There appears to be a church past the palm trees. I can see the top of a cross."

They all stared in the direction of Pinto's finger. "He's right," Sam added, also seeing what looked like the very top of a church. Or so he hoped.

"Thank God in heaven, my Hail Mary's worked!" Eva exclaimed, thankful for the memories of her childhood church-going days.

"Ed, we need to go for a swim, okay? If there's a church here, there could be help," Sam said grimly, holding on to his friend.

Nodding in reply, Ed hung his head.

"Laura, Eva, Pinto, let's form a chain, hang onto each other as we swim for shore. All of us, okay?" Sam called out.

Pinto was about to protest but saw the looks they all gave him, except for the dying Ed. He nodded in agreement, pulled out the flare gun and two shells. "Sam, here, put this in one of the backpacks."

Sam took the flare gun and shells and stuffed them into Ed's backpack and nodded his thanks.

"Is there any way of getting back to the rear of the plane to get our luggage?" Eva asked.

Sam added, "Yeah, you said you were transporting medical supplies? Well, we are in need of them. Let's hope they're still back there."

"Good question, I will go look," Pinto replied, shifting his eyes to avoid looking at Sam, remembering he had told them the plane was indeed transporting medical supplies to poor villagers. He jumped into the water and quickly realized he was able to walk to the rear of the plane in the chest-deep water. Once there, he was no longer able to stand and had to swim to the very rear that was completely submerged. He wasn't interested in the women's luggage. What he was interested in were the briefcases with fifteen pounds of cocaine.

"See how he didn't want to make eye contact with you when you asked about the medical supplies?" Laura asked Sam.

Before Sam could reply, Ed said quietly, "He's full of shit. I can tell a bullshitter because I'm one myself. That man doesn't have medical supplies. Also, when he pulled me up, I saw he's packing heat, there's a revolver under that baggy-ass shirt."

They all looked at one other with concern, mistrust and outright fear now adding to the plethora of misfortune that had plagued flight 8088N.

Please be okay back there, Pinto thought. He saw the tail of the plane had been ripped off, likely when it first connected with the ocean. He was glad the impact hadn't ripped the plane completely in half which would have likely killed all onboard instantly.

He took a deep breath and sunk down to see the damage below. The storage compartment was busted open, the steel hull torn apart by the devastating contact with the ocean. Sharp, pointed rocks pierced the bottom hull of the plane, securing it fast to the islet they had smashed against.

He peered inside the busted cargo area but there were no suitcases to be found. He was in luck, though, as his two briefcases marked with Red Cross symbols hadn't flown out. Barossa had secured them to the hull with several trailer ties so they wouldn't shift around. *Good man, Barossa! And with you gone, all of this now belongs to only me!*

He came up for air and saw Eva leaning over the side of the plane yelling to him, "Our luggage, is it there?"

"No, your luggage is lost, the rear hatch is destroyed!" he shouted back. *Do I tell them about the other briefcases? I told them they were medical supplies.*

"Shit, oh fuck! What are we gonna do!?" Eva exclaimed, looking to Laura.

"Swim to the island and go from there, that's what. Pinto, are the medical supply cases back there?" Laura called out.

His mind raced; he knew he couldn't tell them the truth. But it looked as though they were about to find out what was in the briefcases; he couldn't afford to have his dope float out to sea along with the rest of the wreckage once the tide rose.

He put his hand against his chest, feeling his loaded Colt Python revolver safe and secure in its holster, then he moved into the opened hatch, unlatched the trailer ties and pulled out the two briefcases left inside.

Dragging the cases behind him in the water, he moved up to the front of the plane, his mind now focused on how soon he would need to dispatch the four Americans.

6
BACK TO WORK

Augusto Bezerra Vaz lay in bed when his phone rang. After three rings, his wife of twelve years, Amanda Vaz, answered in the other room of their small house outside of Kokoda. Vaz wiped his tired face with his hands and blinked at the light shining into their bedroom.

"Daddy!" a tiny voice called out.

"Is that my angel calling me from the heavens? Is that angel named Angelina Sophia? Does she have curly black hair like her mama?" Vaz called out, hearing his daughter's voice.

Ten-year-old Angelina ran into the room, still in her pajamas, and jumped onto the bed, giving her father a hug. Vaz returned the hug, then, as was the tradition, she tried to tickle him and he in turn tickled her back until both said, "I give up!" at the same time.

While Vaz and his daughter were tussling, he tried to

hear what his wife was saying on the phone in the kitchen. He could smell bacon frying and he was instantly hungry.

After the tickle fight ended, Vaz sat up, running his hand through his daughter's thick, curly hair. "What are you doing today, Angelina honey?"

Smiling her beautiful, big smile, the dark-complected girl put her finger to her lips thinking. She had already taken on many of her mother's attributes. She was kind, caring, and looked like her mom, who was much darker than Vaz, who could nearly pass as Caucasian if not for his tight black hair and well-groomed thin black goatee. Many people, when asked where he was from, were surprised to hear he was a native of Papua New Guinea and not Rome, Italy.

Finally coming up with her answer, Angelina said, "Today, I think I will make you take me to the market. I need a new dress and you know that store that—"

Angelina was cut off by thirty-one-year-old Amanda peeking her head inside the bedroom door. "Phone call for you, it's Rodolfo from the airport. Said it's urgent." The look on his beautiful wife's face told him everything he needed to know. He was off duty for the next three days and had promised his wife and child they would be doing a great number of things together, as he was often times much too busy to play with his daughter like he would like to.

Amanda looked both concerned and annoyed, an expression she had perfected to a tee. Her eyes were unblinking while her chin shifted back and forth. He had brought up this quirk of hers on numerous occasions, but she always denied doing it. So much so, it had become a joke. But not on this sunny morning. This morning, as her jaw moved back and forth and her eyes bore holes into his, he knew she was concerned. What the hell did Rodolfo say to her to get her this worried?

He patted Angelina on the back, motioning for her to hop off and let Papa up. She quickly obliged, sensing the sudden tension in the room. Vaz pulled the covers back; he was still in his black boxer briefs. He was physically fit and even in his early thirties, still had the six-pack abs he had worked hard to get in his twenties. A strict regimen of healthy eating and one hour of either jogging or weight-based cardio lifting on the days he was able to kept him tip-top for his job as a pilot.

Amanda quite enjoyed being married to such a handsome man and father. He was a good and faithful man and she loved him dearly. That was hard to find in this area of the country that had been so corrupted by drugs and crime.

Squeezing past his wife still standing in the doorway, he made his way to the kitchen, trying to ignore the smell of sizzling bacon, and picked up the old rotary phone sitting on the counter. "Vaz here."

"Vaz, Santana here in the control tower. We have an issue."

"I'm off duty. Check with—" Vaz began.

"It's urgent, Vaz. I wouldn't be calling you if it wasn't. Listen, I need a pilot in twenty-five minutes here, ready to go," Santana blurted out.

"What?! You must be out of your mind! Next flight I'm scheduled for isn't until—" Vaz was once again cut off.

"It's Sérgio Paim. He needs a pilot in less than thirty minutes. Please, Vaz. If you don't help me out, I am afraid…" Santana was now the one cut off.

"That man has his own pilots! He doesn't need me, damnit! What are you getting at, Santana?" Vaz said, getting visibly angry. He glanced over at Amanda who was flipping the bacon while trying to listen in on the heated discussion.

Angelina had gone to her tiny bedroom. She could tell Daddy was doing his "work stuff."

"I would not be calling you if it wasn't an emergency. You live near the airport, and it would be the red and white Cessna. She's all fueled up, ready to go," Santana said desperately.

"How many passengers?" Vaz asked, sighing. He heard his wife putting the bacon down on the table slightly harder than normal. *She's pissed off, and so am I, damnit.*

"Only you, Paim, and two of his—"

"Two of his goons, yeah, I know that man never travels alone. Destination?" Vaz spat out.

"Buka Airport on Bougainville Island. Three hours there, fuel up, and three hours back. Pay is double your standard rate. If all goes as planned, you'll be back before supper with your wife and little girl," Santana pleaded.

"And if there are complications? If I'm stuck over on Bougainville Island overnight? Then what? And I might add, I'm not one-hundred-percent certain Buka Airport is the actual destination. Not with the passengers you're telling me I'm to transport," Vaz said angrily.

"Please, Vaz. Every second the clock gets closer to his

arrival at Kokoda airport and if the plane is not ready for takeoff…" Santana said shakily.

Vaz knew what he meant. The man on the phone pleading with him had likely had his life threatened. Or worse, the lives of his family. He had heard the rumors of what happens to the poor souls that cross Sérgio Paim. They either vanished or were discovered later in various forms of pain filled, brutal deaths.

After the silence, Santana spoke again. "You are literally my only hope. The choice is yours."

Shaking his head, he glanced at Amanda who sat silently at the breakfast table. She looked lovely in an orange summer dress, her long, black hair flowing down her back. But her fear and anger were written all over her face. "Fine, double for every hour I am not back in my home, on my much-needed break from flying all over Papua New Guinea."

"You, my friend, are a life saver. Literally. Please be there in twenty min…"

Vaz hung the phone up. His head hung low.

"Santana needs me to take Sérgio Paim to a nearby island," Vaz said with a sigh, not mincing words and not wanting to hide the very dangerous task that lay ahead of him from his wife. He watched as Amanda's face turned to utter dread at hearing the name Sérgio Paim.

"No! Please! You don't have to do this, Augusto. You don't owe that airport anything! You work your ass off and you deserve this break! Now you're going to fly a piece of shit like Sérgio Paim around? Do you realize how dangerous this is?" Amanda nearly shouted, shaking her head in anger.

"Daddy, are you leaving?" Angelina had reappeared after hearing the shouting. She wasn't used to that in the Vaz household, so this frightened her and it showed in her concerned expression.

"Yes, Augusto, answer her, are you leaving?" Amanda demanded.

His wife always called him Vaz. Everyone called him Vaz. When she used his first name, he knew things were serious. He looked down at his dear daughter, feeling a lump in his throat forming. Kneeling down, he put his hand on her shoulder. "Yes, honey, but I will likely be back by supper. Then we can go shopping this evening if Papa isn't too tired. I will do everything I can to make it back today, okay?"

Angelina nodded her acceptance of the new plan then wrapped her small arms around her father. He returned the hug tightly. "You be good for Mama, okay? I fly a lot, and this is no different. Now, you go get dressed then come back out here for some of your mom's delicious bacon, alright?"

She smiled wide then ran back to her room, obeying his command.

"Honey, I must get ready," Vaz said but was greeted with silence.

Quickly, he got dressed into his secondary pilot's uniform as his primary one was in the laundry. He wore a white shirt and tan pants, opting for more comfortable shoes as he figured, *This is my off day so screw this Paim character.* He grabbed a few items including his billfold where he kept a picture of his lovely girls. After grabbing his sunglasses and pilot's hat, he was met in the kitchen by Amanda, tissue in hand as she fought back tears.

"Honey, I," he began.

"I love you, my Augusto. I know you must do this because you are a good man, and you are doing the right thing. You always do the right thing. That is *why* you are a good man. You be careful and come home to us, promise!"

"I promise you, Amanda, quick and easy, and a big payday. We will go somewhere nice with the extra pay, okay?" Vaz said softly.

Tears spilled out of her eyes. This would be just a minor annoyance for the Vaz family in any other circumstance, but this was different. Her husband, a damn good pilot, always doing things by the book and keeping an impeccable record of trouble-free hours logged in the air, had suddenly in the timespan of several minutes become a taxi service for the most feared man in the region. And even if this went smooth as butter, whatever the reason, Vaz would be in Sérgio Paim's back pocket. That's how he operated. They had managed to avoid the man and his drug empire for years, being harassed only once outside a local bar by several of his thugs.

Vaz wiped the tears from his beautiful wife's eyes and kissed her passionately. He pulled back, looked at his watch, and mouthed, "I love you," then turned and closed the door behind him, making his way to his Cutlass Supreme parked beside his wife's light-blue VW Bug.

Climbing into the car, he sighed, "Back to work," then left for the Kokoda airport with ten minutes to spare.

Inside the house, Amanda looked over to see Angelina come out in her favorite outfit, a white sundress and a yellow bowtie holding back her curly hair.

Seeing her mom in tears, the young girl hastily ran over and threw her arms around her. "It's okay, dad's my superhero! He'll be back before we know it, just like always!"

Amanda nodded in agreement. But her mind told her otherwise.

7

AN UNPLEASANT SWIM

Sérgio Paim and his two goons, Ruiz and Vidal, made their way to the Kokoda airport in a black Dodge Ramcharger with dark tinted windows. The vehicle had been retrofitted with bulletproofing due to the nature of Paim's business dealings and the many unsavory characters he had crossed paths with on his rise to the top of the drug trade in Eastern Papua New Guinea. He enjoyed his infamy and the power that came with it. He was feared by many and considered himself near the top of the food chain within the world of narcotics and prostitution.

"I made some calls, got a list of islands that they could have chosen if the goal was to throw us off the path," Ruiz said bluntly in a deep, thick tone.

"Good. We will take the Cessna to Buka Airport on Bougainville Island. Along the way we shall reach out to the airports on this list informing them of a possible Piper Seneca number 8088N requesting clearance to land," Paim replied.

Vidal, the driver of the Ramcharger added, "Do we take them dead or alive?"

"Once I have my thirty pounds of dope back, Pinto and Barossa shall receive no mercy, but it will be slow."

Vidal and Ruiz nodded their understanding.

Once they made it to the airport, they were greeted by the man Paim had spoken with earlier. They parked the Ramcharger and stepped out onto the tarmac.

"Hello, gentlemen, my name is—" the short and quite nervous man began.

"Do I have a pilot?" Paim replied, taking his sunglasses off, staring daggers at the man then looking over to the Cessna Citation ready and waiting. It was a sleek looking white and red airplane that was quite fast, much faster than his own. He could make up for lost time, for sure.

"Your pilot will be arriving momentarily. I informed him of the urgency in this matter."

"What is your name?" Paim asked, taking a step closer.

"M, my name is…is Rodolfo Pimentel Santana," the man stuttered out meekly.

"Very good. Santana, you have done well under this stress. If all goes well, I shall repay you handsomely," Paim uttered, liking the fear that gripped this man.

Santana nodded his thanks quickly, not wanting to speak out of turn and wanting Paim and his two goons to leave as soon as possible. He knew well this man's reputation and had silently sat by as numerous drug runs happened under his nose at the airstrip where he was stationed. He had a wife and kids to think about so staying out of this business was of utmost importance.

Santana turned to see a dark green Oldsmobile Cutlass Supreme pull up and a man with an intensely serious expression stepped out of the car. He sported black, well-groomed hair and a thin goatee and was dressed to fly a plane. "Gentlemen, I am told you are in need of a pilot?"

"This is Augusto Bezerra Vaz; he will take you where you need to go," Santana said quickly.

Vaz shot Santana a quick, nervous glare who quickly averted his eyes, saddened at what he was making his best pilot do.

Paim took Vaz's outstretched hand and shook it. *Good, a man of few words.*

Santana nodded to Paim and his henchmen who glared back at him as they quickly made their way to the Cessna Citation.

Once they had climbed aboard and taken their seats, Vaz turned in his pilot's seat and finally spoke. "I am told you need to go to Buka Airport on Bougainville Island. I will take you there now."

"Good, good man. You will be paid well for your troubles. You must know, we may need to travel elsewhere depending on information I will be requiring you to obtain for me. You will need to reach out to the airports on this list while we are in flight. Make haste," Paim replied with an stern expression covering his face.

Vaz didn't bother asking if the three men were carrying weapons. It would be dangerous to ask such questions of a man like Paim. Vaz knew what was at stake. Fulfill his obligation and get a nice payday. Fail to fulfil his requirements and he would vanish, as many had over the years in the town of Kokoda.

He put on a pair of aviator sunglasses, his pilot's hat, and began moving the plane forward to the small runway, plotting a course for Bougainville Island. Glancing down at a list of small airports in the general vicinity, he thought, *They're hunting people and there is no way in hell I'm getting back home today.*

Pinto made his way to the front of the plane whose nose was half covered in beautiful, blue water. If not for the devastating plane crash, this appeared to be a tropical island paradise. Standing in the waist-deep water and looking up at the passengers still on the nose of the plane, he motioned for them to jump in.

"Let's hope those medical supplies can save my friend's life," Sam said when he saw the black briefcases marked with a red cross on them.

"Come on, let's go to the island, try to figure out our next move!" Pinto exclaimed, ignoring Sam's comment.

Looking at Ed, Sam said quietly, "Okay, buddy, this is gonna hurt, you ready?"

"Pain? I don't know the meaning." Ed attempted a joke

but was dreading the saltwater hitting his stomach wound once more. He gritted his teeth and with Laura and Sam's help, slid off the plane's nose and into the water below, shouting out in pain as soon as it hit his stomach.

"I know, Ed, I know. Come on, we have to start swimming. We might find help on the island, we've gotta go," Sam said gently.

Laura, who still had Sam's backpack, took Ed's other arm and with Eva at her side, began moving forward to the shore that seemed so far away. She was glad the waves weren't rough, at least for now.

Pinto was offering no help. He had swum forward, looking back to ensure they were still coming, pulling ahead of them with his two briefcases.

"I'm liking our fearless pilot less and less. Especially knowing he has a gun on him. We aren't safe," Laura said just loud enough for Eva, Ed, and Sam to hear.

Sam nodded his agreement as his mind went to the large knife Ed had bought him back on Kokoda. He was thankful he had not only the knife but the flare gun as well. "I still have the flare gun and I'm going to do everything I can to keep it."

Laura and Eva nodded as they all continued moving forward toward the beach in the distance.

"Do you believe there's medical supplies in those briefcases?" Eva asked before spitting out a bit of salt water that was now up to their necks.

"I'm starting to have serious doubts. Sorry, Ed," Laura answered.

"Agreed. Everyone, watch yourselves and each other,"

Sam added.

"Don't have to tell me twice," Eva said.

Below them, the bottom dropped out, and Eva, Laura and Sam, holding onto Ed, began paddling forward, made infinitely more difficult with the gravely wounded Ed and the backpacks.

Eva reached out and took Sam's backpack from Laura who nodded her thanks.

"Come on, Ed, keep your head out of the water!" Sam exclaimed.

Raising his head slightly, Ed spat out a mouthful of salt water, then looked at Sam and smiled.

Shit, he's dying, Sam thought, noticing the color in Ed was draining and he was becoming less coherent by the minute. He loved this man, warts and all. No matter how rough around the edges Ed was, they were best friends. He pushed forward with newfound determination to get to the beach.

All of them remained silent, focused on their own doggie paddling. Periodically, Pinto turned to look back, significantly farther ahead at this point, which upset Sam more and more. *Sonofabitch is making these two women help me with my dying friend.*

Ed began groaning and coughing up blood. He looked at a worried Sam and muttered, "Dude, you should leave me. I'm having my doubts on making it. I think it might be my time to punch out."

"Damnit, you shut up, Ed! Just shut the hell up! Don't talk like that, we're getting close then we're going to take a look at your stomach, so you hang in there, buddy!" Sam said as he coughed up a bit of water himself. They were all struggling at this point.

"What's Pinto doing up there?" Eva asked as she continued doggie paddling with Sam's backpack in front her, thankful that it was staying afloat.

Sam and Laura looked up at Pinto who was now able to stand again, and was staring at something past them. All three turned to look behind them at the crashed airplane resting on the islet as light waves sloshed against it, moving forward toward the shoreline. Something else appeared, as well. The tip of a gray fin pierced the water, zigzagging in what seemed like a frenzy.

"Oh Lord, a shark! The blood from Barossa and Ed!" Laura shouted.

Instantly, Eva screamed out and began paddling faster. Taking their cues from her, Laura and Sam both began swimming as fast as they could while still holding onto Ed.

"Help us, you bastard!" Sam shouted toward the shore. He watched as Pinto turned his back, continuing to head inland.

"Come on, Ed, head up!" Laura shouted, spitting out water as she struggled with the nearly unconscious man.

The fin had come closer and was now moving around them in a wide circle. *It's stalking us,* Sam thought.

"This just isn't our day, is it?" Ed mumbled, coughing up more blood into the water.

Sam watched in horror as the fin that circled them got closer.

"We have to do something, it's going to attack us any minute," Laura said, scared out of her wits. She looked at Eva who was flailing in the water and yelled, "Eva, stop splashing! You're just drawing its attention!"

Thinking quickly, Sam pulled Ed's backpack to him. "Laura, can you hold onto Ed?"

She nodded and he released Ed's arm. Ed was able to stay afloat and ease some of Laura's burden.

"You've got to leave me," Ed mumbled.

Ignoring him, Laura looked at Sam. "What are you doing?"

"This," Sam replied, pulling out the flare gun and two shells. The rest of the backpack's contents sank to the sandy bottom, now out of Sam's grasp. Bobbing in the water, he slammed the first flare into the gun, closed it and aimed, waiting for the shark to get closer. He glanced back at Pinto, who still had his gun drawn but likely couldn't get a clean shot. This was on him.

Eva had thankfully quit splashing around and was now treading water softly, her eyes filled with terror. She made eye contact with Laura and exclaimed, "How much more of this shit do we have to take? We crash into the water and now a shark is gonna eat us!"

Laura didn't respond and continued holding up Ed. She looked at Sam. *Come on, guy…you can do this.*

The shark rounded in front of them, Sam turning with it. In the clear water, he got a good look at it just below the surface. "Sonofabitch, that thing is big!" he exclaimed as the tiger shark drifted closer and closer.

"Take the shot, Sam!" Eva shouted.

The gun erupted, sending a white-hot flare out toward the approaching shark, breaching the water and connecting with it. Instantly, the fifteen-foot creature took off, away from its prey as its thick outer sandpaper-like skin caught fire. Sam opened the flare gun, pulled out the empty cartridge and slammed the second and last flare into its chamber, closing it up and pointing in the direction the shark had fled.

"Good shot!" Eva called out.

"Yes, indeed, good shot Sam!" Laura echoed.

"Is it gone, for good?" Eva screeched.

"I assume no. There's blood in this water and we may have scared him off, but where there's one shark, there's likely going to be more. We have to hurry, come on!" Sam replied urgently.

"Don't need to tell me twice!" Eva began once more, swimming as hard as she could, still clasping Sam's backpack.

Sam and Laura continued on, gripping both of Ed's arms. "You did good, Sam," Ed mumbled.

"Shh. We're almost to the island," Sam replied, pushing forward determinedly.

In a few short minutes, they were able to find their footing in soft sand, making it significantly easier to haul Ed along. The water level soon fell to their chests, then waists, then knees. Up ahead, Pinto stood on the beach, his gun had been holstered under his shirt. When the four were almost to the beach, he went to help Ed.

The noonday sun beat down as Eva, Laura, and Sam gently laid Ed down onto the sand.

"We could have used your help out there, Pinto," Sam said, glaring at the large man.

"And when were you going to tell us you had a gun on you?" Laura added, seeing that Pinto had now pulled out his revolver.

"There aren't any medical supplies in those briefcases, are there?" Sam added.

"Very perceptive, you Americans are," Pinto said with a smirk, then raised his revolver at Sam.

Instantly, Laura raised her hands as did Eva.

"So, what are you planning on doing with us?" Sam said, still clenching the flare gun.

"Hand it over, now," Pinto replied coldly.

Glancing down at his friend, Sam saw blood oozing out of the metal sliver that appeared to be about an inch thick and several inches long.

Slowly, Sam did as he was instructed and gave the flare gun to Pinto who had set the briefcases down in the soft, white sand at his feet.

Pinto motioned for the women to go sit on the beach with a wave of his gun. They both quietly walked fifteen feet away and sat down.

Eva sat on the beach, Sam's backpack sitting beside her. Her face was quickly buried in her hands as she softly cried, thinking of her mom and dad who she now missed more than ever before. The only thing on her mind was home. All the way back in Port Aransas, Texas.

Laura dropped down to sit beside her friend. She put her arm around Eva who quickly leaned in, resting her head against her stronger and more resilient friend. She wept softly while Laura glanced at Sam still standing in front of Pinto. Both men looked deadly serious, but it was clear Pinto was now in charge.

Wanting to get Eva's mind off of their ever-increasing bad luck, Laura asked, "Eva, remember when we met for the first time?"

Wiping her eyes, Eva, whose hair was no longer in pigtails but a tangled mess of blond, nodded her head and catching her breath, answered, "Yeah, junior high. I was getting made fun of by the freshmen cheerleaders because of my big boobs and you were a sophomore. You told them you'd beat the ever-loving shit out of each and every one of them if they messed with me again."

"That's right," Laura said smiling. "I've had your back and you've had mine ever since. And I intend to keep having your back. We both need to remain strong, we both survived more than any human could survive. What stories we'll have to tell after this, right?"

"You're right about that, if there is an *after this*." Eva glanced over at Sam and Pinto.

Pinto's demeanor had changed, even his expression was different since the plane came to a rest on the islet. He was becoming more and more himself, the *real* Benício Pinto Guedes. The one who had murdered, raped and stolen. Who wasn't to be trusted for any reason, ever.

He spoke to Sam now, with a smirk on his face. "You see, Sam, in Kokoda one must be protected. You saw what happened at the Dragon's Breath yesterday. Actually, I should say, you felt what happened when the man's fist connected with your face. So, this is essential." He waved his Colt Python in front of Sam's face then continued. "So, now you will all walk to whatever that structure is deep in the jungle past this beach. I need to find a way off this island, with my briefcases."

"What's in them?" Sam asked, figuring he wouldn't say.

"Fifteen pounds of Papua New Guinea's premium cocaine, pure as the finest snow."

Sam raised his eyes, surprised he had divulged this information.

"Okay, so we go to the structure, what about Ed here?"

"Ed is your responsibility, not mine. He is as good as dead. We need to think about ourselves and how to get off this island," Pinto shot back coldly.

Sam's mind raced as he and Pinto stared at each other. *If I could get to my knife, then what? What good would that do? The guy has a revolver and a flare gun!*

The women watched this tense back-and-forth. "If I get the slightest chance…" Laura said softly.

"You'll what? You can't take that beastly man on! He's armed and obviously dangerous. Please don't get yourself killed!" Eva said in a loud whisper.

"Timing is everything. I just hope the opportunity arises. Otherwise, Eva, I'm not sure any of us are making it off this island alive."

8
NEW ARRIVALS

Vaz piloted the Cessna Citation through the clear blue skies over Papua New Guinea with his three passengers. Paim, Ruiz, and Vidal sat silently behind him. Paim puffed a cigar—Vaz hated the smell, especially in tight, closed quarters such as this, but he knew better than speaking out. *Just do the job, get paid well, and go home then get your daughter that dress she's been wanting.*

Once they reached cruising altitude, Vaz began his task of contacting Buka Airport on Bougainville Island. "This is Cessna Citation 649, pilot Augusto Bezerra Vaz, checking to see if you have any information on a Piper Turbo Seneca II, blue and white, serial number 8088N, passenger count is six, landing at your airport."

"Hi there, Cessna 649, hold on a second let me check," came the reply through his headset.

After a brief pause, the voice came back. "Sorry, but there are no records on our end of a Piper Turbo Seneca II landing. However, contact was made earlier today that your plane in question was about to depart from Kokoda airport shortly after eight AM for our airport. Haven't heard from them since. Hold on…"

Vaz glanced back at his passengers, all staring at him, then continued waiting for some more news. "Ah, I see. Okay, thanks for the information. Yes, I would appreciate any updates if you receive them, thank you. Pilot Augusto Vaz, out."

"Well?" Paim immediately asked, leaning forward in his seat awaiting news of his stolen plane and more importantly, stolen drugs.

"Well, the transponder was disabled. So, they have no information on the plane other than Pinto contacting them earlier this morning. However, I will contact other airports within the area where they may be heading."

"Do it, and keep me posted," the imposing man called out, taking another puff on his cigar.

"One other thing," Vaz said. "The gentleman I spoke with mentioned a severe storm that plowed through the Solomon Sea, dissipating before hitting Queensland. He said he hoped the plane didn't run into trouble out there. Said those storms are common in that area."

Nodding, Paim called out once more, "Keep making contact."

"Roger that," Vaz mumbled under his breath. He had a bad feeling about how the rest of his day might go.

The survivors of Piper Seneca 8088N peered into the jungle past the soft, white beach. It was quiet, other than several seagulls sailing by overhead and the ocean crashing against the shore behind them.

"To the church, now!" Pinto exclaimed, motioning with his gun.

Pointing to Ed, who was lying on the sand with Laura and Eva on either side of him, Sam replied angrily, "Ed can't move! And how are you planning on getting your precious cargo through that jungle?"

"Luckily, I have you three to help carry my briefcases," Pinto replied coldly, keeping his eyes on the jungle now, planning where they would enter.

Sam kicked the sand in front of him, seeing a medium-sized rock embedded directly at his feet. He glanced over at Laura who returned his gaze. His eyes moved from hers down to his backpack at her feet beside an unconscious Ed then back up to meet her eyes once more, all while continuing to kick at the rock below, loosening it.

Laura got the message. *He's got something in this backpack that may be able to help us.* As Pinto tool several steps forward, toward the sprawling jungle, Laura quickly bent down, unzipped the waterproof backpack and peered inside at its contents.

Looking down, Eva immediately saw what Laura was looking at, a large, sheathed knife. Her eyes met Laura's who quickly raised her index finger to her lips to silence Eva.

Eva was about to protest as Laura reached inside the bag, pulled the knife out, and dropped it into the sand in front of Ed whose eyes remained closed, all while keeping her eyes on Pinto.

Sam watched the retrieval of the weapon unfold and was glad they hadn't been caught.

Pinto swiveled around toward the women, seeing Laura crouching down by the opened backpack. "You! Get up! What are you doing?" he shouted, immediately running over to where they stood.

Eva had stepped in front of Ed and quietly kicked sand on the knife and its sheath as soon as it dropped onto the ground. It was out of Pinto's sight for the time being, but any sort of inspection near the women would reveal its makeshift hiding spot.

"What are you looking for? Give me that backpack, woman!" Pinto shouted.

Laura pulled out a granola bar. "This, I was looking for something to eat, and drink. We're hungry and tired after everything we've been through. We need to think about how we're going to get food and water—that's more important that carrying around your precious briefcases full of dope!"

"Give me that!" Pinto exclaimed, ripping the backpack from her hands while still clutching his Colt Python revolver, aiming it back and forth from Eva to Laura. He dumped the contents out onto the sand. Toiletries, clothes, and several more granola bars spilled out.

"Worthless. Nothing substantial in here," Pinto said, kicking around the loose items in the sand, his right foot dangerously close to the buried knife.

Laura knew she had to get him away from the immediate area so she took several aggressive steps toward Pinto.

Surprised at the sudden boldness of this skinny American woman from Texas, he took several steps back while extending his right hand, aiming the revolver at her.

"How do you plan on getting us out of here when all you care about is hauling drugs into the jungle? How will that help our situation?" Laura shouted.

"Silly American," Pinto said snidely. "You think I care about your situation? I care about one person, me! Now, enough of this arguing! Into the jungle to the church! The dying man stays here, on the beach. He's nothing more than food for seagulls and crabs at this point, got it?" He laughed at his own crude joke.

"Not just yet," came the raspy voice at Pinto's feet.

Pinto looked down to see a conscious Ed, rolled over onto his side, holding a large knife which he instantly slammed down into Pinto's foot. The sharp blade sliced through the man's cheap, fake leather cowboy boot and drove all the way through his foot, the force of it piercing the sole of the boot.

Surprised at the sudden turn of events, Pinto let out a loud scream of pain and tried to step away from the embedded knife. Eva and Laura, equally surprised, saw an approaching Sam from behind the brutish man, holding the rock that had been embedded in the sand by his feet.

Pinto lost his balance from the knife sticking through his foot and stumbled backward. Sam smashed the rock into the side of his head as hard as he could, instantly knocking him out. Pinto fell to his side, his large body rolling down a slight dip in the sandy beach and coming to rest roughly ten feet away.

Laura rushed forward, grabbing the knife and yanking it out of Pinto's foot while Sam bent down and scooped up the revolver and the flare gun. They backed away from the unconscious man and moved over to where Ed lay flat on his back once more.

"Ed, good job!" Laura exclaimed, kneeling down into the sand to inspect him.

Smiling, Ed spat a small bit of blood out. "I knew if I couldn't win you over with my charming wit, I could with my heroic deeds." He coughed.

Sam knelt down beside Ed as well. "Oh, Ed, you're really bleeding bad," he said in a near whisper.

Motioning for Sam to come closer, Ed looked his best friend in the eye. "Sam, I'm a sonofabitch, I know it. I got you into this mess. I should have listened to you but…"

"Shh! Quiet, Ed, we're going to figure something out. You've got to hang in there!" Sam pleaded.

"Find a way out of here, keep these ladies safe, tell my mom I love her and live a long life. For both of us," Ed sputtered out in a whisper.

Sam realized Ed had been holding his hand and squeezing it when it suddenly went limp in his. He looked into Ed's now unblinking eyes that appeared to be glazing over. "Ed? Ed! Come on, man!"

Eva stood beside Sam, softly crying. Laura put her hand on his shoulder while he stared in disbelief at his dead best friend. His mouth was partially open and a steady trickle of blood dripped from it onto the sand.

Sam shook his head and released Ed's lifeless hand from his own. Standing to his feet, he wiped his wet eyes then pushed his messy, blond hair back out of his face. His bloody tank top had dried in the hot sun of this tropical paradise they were trapped in. He looked at the blood, his friend's.

Laura was the first to speak. "I'm sorry, Sam. I don't know what..." She fell silent when Sam raised his hand.

"Come on, we've got to get this asshole bound and secured," Sam uttered, sticking the flare gun back into the side of his cargo pants and walking toward the still unconscious Pinto.

Eva suddenly felt exposed in her skimpy clothing and desperately wanted to cover herself. Seeing a white, button-down shirt laying in the sand, one of the spilled items from Sam's backpack, she quickly put it on, buttoning it up enough to cover her bikini top. She hastily threw the rest of Sam's clothes into his backpack, leaving the more cumbersome articles of clothing spilled out on the sand while he and Laura stood over Pinto.

"What do you think? Wait here and hope a plane flies overhead then shoot off the flare gun? Or make our way to the church?" Laura asked, standing close to Sam.

Looking down at the unconscious beast of a man, Sam replied, "I think we've got our answer from the sky." He pointed up to a large rain cloud moving in. Likely a remaining rain cloud from the massive storm that just passed by. This one, however, was heading right for the island.

"I think it's likely that no one will be looking for us, other than possibly the owner of those two briefcases." He pointed down to the red cross marked briefcases laying haphazardly around Pinto.

Laura scoffed. "I personally think chucking them back into the ocean would be a fitting gesture for this bastard, but I'd rather not set foot in that shark-infested water. Leaving them sitting out here doesn't seem right, though. I'll just bury them for now."

"Whatever, I can't think right now, Laura," Sam answered, still reeling from the death of his best friend.

Laura grabbed both briefcases and dragged them away from Pinto and threw sand over them until they were covered. Sam, meanwhile, put his hands on his hips, glaring down at the still unconscious man with a bleeding foot.

"And now, what to do with you," Sam said coldly, holding his revolver in his hand.

"Hey, look!" Eva called out.

Laura who had once more joined Sam, looked in Eva's direction. She was pointing to something in the far distance down the beach.

"What is that?" Sam said as he took several steps forward, squinting his eyes to get a better look.

Laura did the same. "Whatever it is, it's moving toward us. I think that's a person!"

Sam's eyes widened. "You're right, it is a person."

"Eva, come here!" Laura called out.

"I'm not quite done packing up Sam's stuff!" Eva replied.

"Why do I have a bad feeling about this in my bones?"

Laura said quietly.

Nodding, Sam kept his eyes fixed on the figure rapidly approaching.

"Whoever it is, they appear to be limping," Laura said, studying the approaching figure.

Sam got a sick feeling in his stomach the closer the individual got, realizing she was completely naked.

"Eva, get back here, now!" Sam shouted when he was able to get a good look at the facial features of what appeared to be a woman, now merely thirty feet from them.

Doing as he commanded, Eva ran back to Sam and Laura, leaving the unpacked backpack behind.

"Something's wrong with her," Laura exclaimed.

The woman was now merely steps away from Ed, coming to a stop beside his lifeless body. With milky-white eyes, she peered down at Ed then up at the three people standing in front of her. She appeared to be in a sort of late-stage rigor mortis, her body bloated with large black and blue swaths all over. Most of her hair was gone and one of her ears was completely missing.

"What the hell *is* that?" Eva said in disgust.

The woman opened her mouth and let out a raspy scream. From the nearby jungle came similar sounds.

Sam raised his revolver at the woman as she dropped to all fours and began sniffing Ed's body. "Hey, get away from him!" he shouted, instinctively rushing forward.

The woman looked up at him with white eyes and shrieked once more, then bit down into Ed's neck.

"No!" Sam shouted, pulling the trigger on the Colt

Python, hitting her in the shoulder. She didn't flinch at the bullet's impact. Sam ran over and, as hard as he could, kicked the woman away. She fell back and he got an even better look at the monstrosity lying on the sand. Not only were there lesions all over her naked body, but chunks of flesh had been eaten away, exposing muscle tissue beneath. She was literally rotting away.

"Oh my God," Sam uttered in disgust.

He saw the gunshot had done little to stop the woman, and the blood seeping from the bullet hole was a sickly brownish red.

The woman climbed back to her feet and began hobbling forward again, the blood from Ed's neck wound dripping off her teeth.

"Sam, we've got to get out of here! Look!" Laura shouted.

"What's going on? Give me my gun, you American bastard!" Pinto shouted from several feet away where he'd fallen and was now trying to pull himself up from the ground.

The woman lunged forward and pulled out the metal sliver jammed in Ed's stomach. Fresh blood pumping out of the now open wound caused her to let out a groan and a snarl. She buried her face over the wound, drinking and biting.

"You get the fuck off my friend!" Sam shouted, pulling the trigger on the revolver again, this time sending a bullet directly into the top of the disease-riddled woman's head, dropping her instantly. She lifelessly rolled off of Ed and onto the sand, her face covered in Ed's blood mixed with her own tainted blood from the two bullet holes.

Silence fell across the beach. In the distance, somewhere past the trees, more groans could be heard faintly.

Sam and Laura rushed over to the grisly scene, Eva following behind. All three ignored Pinto's taunts.

"Get back here! Give me something for my foot! Where the hell are my briefcases? What the hell did you do with them, you motherfuckers!" he shouted, alternating between rubbing his sore head and his pierced foot.

"She was trying to eat him!" Eva exclaimed in horror, looking at the deep bite marks on Ed's neck and around the wound from the doomed plane ride down to this infernal island.

Laura gazed at her in revulsion. "This woman appears to have been dead. I'm no doctor, not yet anyhow, but from the looks of this body, she was in late-stage rigor mortis."

Sam shook his head in rage at the violation perpetrated on his best friend. "You're right, she was alive but looked dead! Come on, there's more of those things out there from the sound of it. Let's at least cover Ed with sand, but we need to move quickly."

Nodding, Laura took her cue from Sam and helped him move Ed away from the dead woman. When Ed's body had been dragged a short distance away, she dropped to her knees and began digging. Seeing Eva standing still, she said, "You going to help?"

"I, I can't, I can't be around this anymore! I have to get out of here! Why, God? Why are we here! Get me the hell out of here!" Eva wailed.

Laura glanced over at Sam who was frantically digging in the sand, trying to create a makeshift grave for his friend as quickly as possible. Jumping up and grabbing hold of Eva's shoulders, Laura gave her a sudden shake to snap her out of her frantic state.

Eva stopped talking and stared at her, then a flood of tears came. "Oh, Laura, how are we going to get out of this, huh?" Eva cried and rested her head on Laura's shoulder for a brief time as Laura wrapped her arms around her.

Whispering, Laura said, "Eva, come on. We need to help Sam then we need to get off this beach. I need you to help, okay? You've been so brave so far. But we aren't out of this yet." She pulled away from Eva, looking her in the eye to see if she had regained her composure.

"Okay, I'm good," Eva said while sniffling.

"Little girls shouldn't be hiding what doesn't belong to them! You will pay for stealing from Pinto! I will kill you both, mark my words!" Pinto shouted from behind them.

Without missing a beat, Laura ran over and punched Pinto in the nose as hard as she could.

"Ahh!" he cried out, grabbing his face as he felt fresh blood begin seeping through his fingers. "You *bitch!* You broke my nose, damnit!"

"You, shut the fuck up, you sonofabitch!" Laura hissed through her teeth.

Pinto fell silent, looking up at her then down to his bloody hands. "Can I have something for my foot?" he uttered, calmer now. He didn't want to take a punch from this woman again.

Laura ignored him and joined Eva and Sam digging a grave for Ed.

Eva glanced back to see Pinto's demeanor had once more changed. He looked maniacal as he stared daggers into her. She quickly turned away from him.

"Hell of a punch you got there, Laura," Sam said without looking up.

She didn't reply, but quietly helped lay Ed down into the small hole dug out for him. All three of them covered the body then stood to their feet.

"I feel as though I should say something, but we don't have time. Those moans are getting louder," Sam said.

Eva pointed. "Over there, I see one of them!"

"See what? What do you see? What happened to this lady here!" Pinto called out behind them, staring at the bloody remains.

Sam and Laura looked where Eva was pointing and saw three figures slowly approaching out of the jungle onto the beach. Above the island, moving over the large crater, the rain cloud had arrived.

138

9

A RAINY STROLL THROUGH THE JUNGLE

"**T**his is Honiara air traffic control; how can I help you today, Cessna Citation 649?"

"Pilot Augusto Bezerra Vaz speaking, I am checking to see if you have any information on a Piper Turbo Seneca II, color is blue and white, serial number 8088N, six passengers including pilots possibly cleared to land at your airport today."

"Hold on," the voice came back. "Sorry, Mr. Vaz, I am not showing any information on a missing plane."

Paim leaned forward in his seat. "Who said anything about a missing plane?"

Vaz fell silent, glancing back at Paim and his goons. *He's right, I didn't mention anything about a missing plane.*

"Honiara air traffic control, request permission to land, we need to refuel our Cessna," Vaz said into his headset.

There was a long pause, too long. Finally, the man on the other end came back, "You are cleared to land on runway A. We'll have you refueled and back in the air soon."

"We're deboarding when we land. I would very much like to meet this man," Paim said coldly, sitting back in his seat.

"Roger that, and who am I speaking with?" Vaz asked.

More silence, too much silence. This is our lead right here.

"He only gave me his first name, it's Fabian," Vaz said to his passengers.

"That's our guy," Paim muttered. "Pilot, contact the Royal Islands Solomon Police Force headquarters. Ask for an officer Logan Pabon. Inform him that Sérgio Melo Paim is landing at the Honiara Solomon Islands airport and that I need to meet him on the tarmac with an employee of the airport. First name, Fabian. Will likely be fleeing the airport, so may have to apprehend."

"Yes, sir," Vaz came back, trying to mask his nervousness at the change of airports they would be landing at. As he made his way to the approaching island, he made contact with the Royal Islands Solomon Police Force and was quickly patched through to officer Logan Pabon. After giving the officer the message, he clicked off his headset, then turned to the men behind him and nodded.

Vaz lowered the landing gear and within minutes, they were taxying. Soon they would be fueled up, but before that, a man named Fabian was going to have a very bad rest of his day.

Sam, Laura, and Eva stared at the approaching figures of two men and what appeared to be a child. All had lesions covering their bodies and what little clothes they wore were in tatters. Brown and ripped to shreds, covered in what was likely blood and other bodily fluids expelled through the open wounds throughout their bodies. All were barefoot and from their states of decomposition and disfigurement, it was hard to tell what skin color they once had.

The first and tallest man stared out at the beach with unblinking white eyes. One of his arms was missing. All that remained was a partially protruding humerus bone, broken and jagged and surrounded by torn-off, rotting flesh.

The second man, smaller than the first but no less grotesque, had a face that looked as though the entire flesh had been torn off, and in its place remained an open, exposed skull. One white eye remained; the other was hollow. This man was slowly opening and closing what remained of his mouth, as if biting at the air. What remained of the second man's pants had been shredded, and where there should have been sexual organs were thick scratch marks revealing parts of his pelvis and nothing else.

The third creature was a young girl, evidenced by the long, tangled hair that remained atop her head and what once was a small dress that had fused to the putrid skin underneath. The girl's head was twisted to the side at an unnatural nearly ninety-degree angle. Her spinal cord was pushing its way out her skin.

"Oh my God!" Laura exclaimed, looking on in horror at the shambling figures that had once been human beings but now resembled something that had crawled out of hell to infect its surroundings.

Rain began dripping down onto the survivors of 8088N and the rest of the island.

"Come on, we've got to go. There are only four more shells in this thing, and I have a feeling we may need to save them!" Sam exclaimed.

"Hold on," Laura said, running over and grabbing the backpack then hurrying back to Sam.

"What about Pinto?" Eva asked as they passed him and slowed down, all of them thinking the same thing. He is a bastard but still a living human being.

"We ought to leave him here, but…" Laura started.

She spoke too soon. He lunged out from his sitting position on the sand, grabbing Eva's ankle and yanking her down, her hand slipping out of Laura's.

"You're not going anywhere without me!" Pinto cried out, squeezing her ankle as hard as his large hand could.

Eva screamed out in surprise, reaching for her foot. Sam ran forward and kicked Pinto squarely on his already broken nose with all his might.

Pinto screamed out as new shockwaves of pain erupted across his face. His foot had been impaled, the back of his skull smashed with a rock, and his nose smashed twice. Sam stood over him with his revolver drawn.

"Come on, let those things have him," Laura said coldly, pulling Eva to her feet.

Sam's hand was shaking, his finger on the trigger. He glanced back at the figures now on the beach then back to Pinto, put the gun away, and went to help Eva.

"Come on, Eva, we've got to go," Laura said, putting Eva's arm around her neck. Rain was now coming down at a steady stream. Sam put his arm around Eva's waist and they made their way slowly away from the figures into the tropical forest.

"Ouch, it hurts, damnit!" Eva cried out as she put pressure on her foot.

Hearing Pinto's screams, Laura glanced back to see the three walking corpses standing over him. He was flailing his arms wildly at the two men that wouldn't relent in their aggressive push forward toward their fresh meal while the little girl crawled up behind him, teeth snapping in the air.

The three remaining survivors breached the line of palm trees, leaving behind a buried Ed, buried briefcases of cocaine, a crashed plane, and one likely dead psychopathic drug runner.

The jungle terrain was rocky and slippery due to the rain which slowed them down. The dark cloud on top of the tree cover had cast a dark shadow making it difficult to see as they moved forward.

"What direction are we even heading in?" Laura exclaimed, wiping her wet face.

"I'm just moving forward, away from the beach. I imagine if we keep moving ahead, we're bound to find that church Pinto pointed out earlier," Sam answered, spitting water out of his mouth.

"When that bastard pulled me down, I landed pretty hard on my ankle!" Eva complained.

"We'll take a look at it once we find a place out of this rain," Laura replied.

They continued on, deeper and deeper into the ominous jungle. Strange noises from various insects could be heard through the rain, and in the distance they heard groans and wails.

This is a nightmare and I'm going to wake up on a plane heading for Australia. Or better yet, back to America, Sam thought. But he knew this was no dream, this was reality.

After trudging slowly for what felt like several hours through dense, unfamiliar tropical forest, Eva cried out once more before coming to a complete stop. "I can't go on! I need to rest, please."

"Okay, there," Sam said, pointing to a large palm tree that had fallen into several others, creating a makeshift area where they could find cover from most of the rain.

Setting Eva down gently, Laura quickly sat next to her to look at the wound Pinto had inflicted.

Sam bent down as well. Eva's ankle was swollen. Dropping his backpack in front of them, he opened it and pulled out a spare shirt, wrapping it around her ankle. "This will have to do for now," he said, looking through the rest of his things. Half of them had been packed back up, the rest remained on the beach.

Pulling out one of several granola bars he had packed,

he opened the wrapper, broke it in half and handed Laura and Eva equals shares. Both took it, nodding their thanks. They had all forgotten about hunger until now.

"God, I didn't think a granola bar could taste this good," Eva said and forced a smile.

Sam tilted his head up and let some falling rainwater drip into his mouth. They sat in silence a bit longer, listening to the soft drum of the rain, the insects and the distant moans. He looked down at his watch, the time read 4:53 PM and the compass pointed north.

"Come on, we've been on our feet for hours but we have to keep moving. Night will fall in the next few hours, and we can't be outside when it does. Once we find a more secure location, we can figure out our next steps. Let's keep heading north." Sam got to his feet and pointed.

Nodding, Laura pulled herself up and helped Eva up as well.

They continued further into the jungle, periodically seeing a monkey or two in the trees high above as well as small lizard scurrying away from their path.

"What do you think those things are?" Laura asked, breaking the silence.

"Well, I don't believe in zombies…" Sam answered. "I've seen enough of them in movies, but I do believe what my eyes see, and everything about those things back on the beach tells me they used to be living and now they're dead. Or infected with some sort of virus that causes those sores all over them."

"They were missing body parts! That one didn't even

have a face!" Eva said, grimacing at the sharp pain that periodically shot through her ankle.

"Yeah, they're dead. I don't believe in zombies either. But those things are displaying every characteristic I've seen in movies myself," Laura added.

They fell silent once more. Sam's thoughts falling to Ed. What would he tell his mother when they returned back to America? *If* they returned back to American. The situation was dire, and he knew it.

"What if all that's left on this island are more of those things? We can't get off this island. We don't even know what island it is!" Eva said with panic in her voice.

Laura piped up. "We're gonna get off this damn island! One way or another, we're alive and I plan to stay that way," she said defiantly, glancing over at Eva.

"There, up ahead," Sam said.

All three stopped and looked through the rain and dense tree cover to where a white building could be seen in the distance.

"Thank God. Come on," Laura said, pushing forward.

"We need to be careful; we don't know what we'll find inside that building. One of you should take my knife," Sam said.

"Not me, nope," Eva shot back, adding, "I don't like knives and I don't like guns."

"Thanks, Sam, I'll take it," Laura replied as she took it from him and stuck the sheathed knife into the side of her pants. Looking over to Eva, she added, "Eva, you're going to have to have some sort of defense. We don't know how many of those things are out there, and you're injured."

Sam began scanning the immediate area until his eyes fell on what he hoped was a sturdy branch. Picking it up and snapping the end off, he handed it to Eva. "Here you go, a walking stick and something to swat away anything unwanted, if it comes to that."

Taking it into her hand and examining it, she forced a smile. "Thanks, Sam."

"Time to move, the church is nearby," Laura said.

They continued on their route as moans seemed to echo through the entire jungle. Most sounded relatively far away, but some of it was far too close for comfort.

Eva was thankful for her new walking stick, which took some of the stress off of Sam and Laura. She was able to move on her own, albeit at a slower pace. She watched carefully where she stepped in the thick, wet, slippery growth under-foot when, suddenly, something moved in the weeds. A long, green and yellow snake slithered past her, causing her to cry out and lose her balance, tripping forward and landing on her face in the thick brush.

Laura reached out and grabbed hold of her. "Eva! Are you okay?"

Sam crouched down. "Let me give you a hand."

Slapping her hand down in the thick grass, Eva cried out, "Why the *fuck* is this happening!? I want to go home, damnit! Why did you bring me to Papua New Guinea to look for your dad, anyway, Laura?"

Laura knew Eva had not only willingly come along but had *insisted* she accompany her best friend on what would likely be a long, arduous trip. But things had been tough every step of the way since they had left Texas. Delays in air travel, the foreign food and customs, things the American born-and-bred Eva simply wasn't adapting well to. And now this.

Helping her to her feet, Sam tried to brush her off but she swatted him away. "I'm fine, let's just get to that church."

Sam glanced at Laura, both thinking the same thing. As annoying as she was, in this hostile place, Eva was in terrible danger with her injured ankle and finicky temperament. Real-world survival was clearly not her strong suit.

They continued on in silence, the rain continuing to drop from the sky while the thick tree cover did little to keep them dry. Always off in the forest, moans echoed. Every time a moan could be heard, the group seemed to pick up the pace until, finally, they exited the dense forest and stood in front of the small church with a steep enough chapel that had pointed the way for them.

The roughly 1,200-square-foot white church building was quite old and dilapidated, with peeling paint and dust covering the sides, along with heavy foliage covering most of its roof. A stone cross remained perched high atop the vaulted roofline. Regardless of its shabby condition, it was four walls and a roof, and Sam was thankful for it.

"Sam, look," Laura said, pointing off to the side of the structure. Markers had been placed in a clearing, signifying this was a graveyard. The markers, many of which had fallen over, appeared to be blank. These were simply placeholders for the dead and buried. There was no way of knowing how many markers had once stood there, but the ominous presence of them, along with the moans in the forest and the creatures that had attacked them on the beach, sent shivers through Laura.

Pulling his eyes from the morbid graveyard that looked like something straight out of an old Hammer Horror movie starring Peter Cushing and Christopher Lee, Sam made his way to the front door with Laura and Eva following close behind. He gripped the revolver tightly in his right hand as he grabbed hold of what appeared to be a large brass handle that had rusted through and gave it a push. It held fast.

After several more pushes on the door, Sam sighed, "It's either locked or stuck. This thing is old, so there is a chance it's just rusted closed. Stand back."

"I'm helping," Laura said, sensing what Sam was about to do.

Nodding at her, they both took several long steps back then ran forward, slamming into the closed door. It moved forward slightly but held fast again. In the crack big enough to peek through, Laura noticed a metal hook lock connecting the door to the wall inside.

She pulled out Sam's knife, slipping it through the crack, and lifted up but the latch stuck fast. Seeing what she was doing, Sam holstered the gun and took hold of her hands on the knife handle. For a brief second, their eyes met. Then, looking through the cracked door, with all four hands they pulled up.

The knife inched up slowly, releasing the latch from the metal loop it was connected to. Sam pulled his hands from hers as she glanced back to see Eva had now joined them.

Sam pulled the revolver back out and carefully pushed the door of the old church open.

10
LIVING DEATH

Pinto looked at his assailants standing over him snapping their teeth. *Holy shit, I crashed on an island with zombies. This is like that Italian movie I saw a few weeks ago.* His head ached and his foot throbbed from the deep cut inflicted on it. He was in grave danger, and he knew not acting fast would surely result in death.

A man with white eyes stood over him. The man had only one arm, the other appeared to have been chewed off, or ripped off. Pinto looked on in horror as the man wavered over him. Behind him, a girl whose head was at a complete ninety-degree angle to the side continually bit into the air. She was the nearest to him and looked as though she was about to lunge at her meal any second.

The third and final zombie lingered behind, completely missing a face with only one eyeball moving in its socket. This one appeared to be less coherent of what was happening. It was likely following the other two blindly and was certainly the most rotted and skeletal.

Move! Pinto thought. He rolled back, away from the ghastly sight looking for a quick meal. As he did so, the girl, the quickest of the lot, lunged at him, but even in his sorry state, Pinto still had his strength along with adrenaline.

From his prone position on the beach, with his large fist, he swung as hard as he could and connected with the girl's torso, sending her flying backwards onto the sand.

The man who was missing his arm slowly grabbed Pinto's shoulder, leaning forward about to bite his neck. Pinto felt through the sand and found a large stone. *The one that cracked me on the back of my head earlier?* Grabbing it in his hand, he swung hard, connecting with the zombie's chin, breaking it completely off.

In a grotesque display of blind animal instinct, the zombie reached up with his remaining arm to feel where a chin once was. What was left of a tongue hung loosely out, bobbing against his neck.

Pinto was too terrified to be revolted at the sight. The girl was getting up and the third zombie without a face stumbled forward, this one easy to avoid. Pinto pushed himself up to his knees, then stood to his feet. Pain surged through his sliced foot all the way up his leg. He screamed loudly but remained standing. Still clenching the rock tightly he had found earlier, he limped forward, slamming it against the skull-faced zombie.

The skull broke apart easily as did the rest of its head.

The blow sent what remained of its rotted-out brain falling to the beach, dropping it instantly.

With newfound vigor, Pinto swiveled on his remaining good foot to catch the armless and chinless zombie attempting another attack. Once more with the stone, he swung it hard, hitting the zombie on the side of its face, dropping it to the ground. However, this had sent searing pain once more shooting up through his leg and he fell forward, on top of the zombie.

In disgust, he rolled over, raised the stone and smashed it atop the zombie's face, crushing it completely. Pinto didn't stop, raising it and bringing it crashing down with such force that it only took three smacks and the head was completely flattened on the sand.

Two down, one to go. The girl had crawled over toward him while he finished off the zombie. "You want some of me, do ya?" Pinto uttered. Angry, he set the rock down, opting to finish this child off with his bare hands. Avoiding the biting mouth on her twisted head, Pinto easily grabbed her by the shoulders and rolled over on top of her. He grabbed hold of her neck and straddled her, pulling as hard as his large arms could. The sound of ripping tendons and pulling flesh emanated from the girl's body before the head was ripped clean off. A portion of her spinal cord yanked out of her body as well. What blood still remained in the leper zombie child trickled out of the newly-formed stump where her head had rested.

Satisfied at the carnage he had wrought against these ghouls, Pinto threw the girl's head into the ocean water behind him. He stood back up on his feet, surveying the damage. The sight was ghastly and worse than anything Pinto had ever seen in any horror movie, of which there were many.

"Fuck with me and that's what happens," Pinto muttered, now fully realizing what he was up against. "Where the hell am I?"

He surveyed the beach once more, seeing no other things like this approaching. He stared at the woman Sam had taken care of earlier, thankful he hadn't had to deal with this one as well. "My dope, where the hell is my dope, damnit!" He looked frantically around the beach.

Limping, he began moving toward the forest on the edge of the beach, scanning the sand as he did. "No way they dragged those briefcases into the jungle with them, no way! They're here," he muttered to himself, biting through the pain he felt in his head and entire leg. He had no revolver, no flare gun, and was gravely injured.

Shaking his head and pushing the desperate scenario he was in out of his head, he continued shuffling through the sand, looking for the briefcases. "I know they're here, I know it!" When he could no long stand the pain in his throbbing foot, he dropped to his hands and knees, crawling through the sand in the hopes he would inadvertently stumble across his briefcases.

His mind was foggy. *I'm dead. I'm dead and on my way to hell for the life I've lived. This is what awaits me. Total darkness.* He lay still, surrounded by blackness, waiting for the hellfire flames to overtake him if what he had heard about was accurate.

But the flames didn't come. He wasn't breathing or blinking or moving, for that matter. His mind was still coherent, to some extent, scrambled as it was. *So hungry! How do I get myself out of wherever I am?*

He felt cold and numb, as if he didn't have a body at all. Just a mind that could only think of one thing, food. *Who was I? Where did I come from? How did I get here? Must eat!*

A new sensation coursed through him. He could actually feel something, and it was painful. A burning feeling running through his veins. *Oh God, no! It's burning! Help me, someone!* This new feeling coupled with a sudden insatiable lust for meat was more than he could take, but he could do nothing for it. *Except I can. If I eat, this will go away!*

Along with what felt like acid replacing blood that once pumped through his system, this newfound insatiable drive forced him to move, or attempt it. His stiff fingers twitched, slowly moving themselves.

Along with this, he could now move his neck, slightly at first. Then his toes began wiggling and his feet moved, ever so slightly. He twisted in place and felt a substance on him. *What is this? I'm buried! Move your fingers.*

He found it easier and easier to movie both sets of fingers. They ran through something soft. Continuing to move them, he slowly was able to push the substance he was trapped under, away.

Now his whole arm began to function. Pushing upwards, his hand broke free of the substance he was under. Upon doing so, a bright light hit his eyes. *Move your other arm, push yourself up, then you will find something to take this pain away!*

He pushed himself up. Sand spilled off his head and, moving his feet, he was able to crawl the rest of the way out of the makeshift grave in which he had been buried. He stood to his feet as his eyes began taking in the sights around him. *Sand, trees, water, blue skies. Where am I? What happened? So hungry!*

What he could make out was blurry. He wasn't sure if this was due to the sand that had been on his eyes or the current state he was in. Poor as his eyesight was, it was better than where he had been minutes earlier.

He felt something on his neck. Raising his hand slowly, he felt something wet as his finger inadvertently pushed itself into a hole on his neck. He brought the finger back out and inspected it. Even with his blurry vision, he could make out blood mixed with sand.

His foggy brain transmitted distant memories into his subconscious. A woman that had taken care of him, possibly a mother. Glimpses of possible memories before…this. School, women, sex, parties, jobs, vacations, airplane ride. *Something happened on an airplane. A friend, I had a friend, a good friend. What was his name? Doesn't matter. That was from another time. Now all that matters is food.*

He opened his mouth to speak but no words came forth. A low groan slipped out as he continued trying to say something, but it was no use. His hunger was so severe he began biting out of sheer desperation to quench the insatiable appetite he now felt. *The food will stop this acid from burning me alive! Must find food!*

His blurry vision scanned the area while his hands felt over his new body, touching another open wound on his stomach. At this point, his mind could fully comprehend that he was indeed, dead. The reasons behind his ultimate demise were a mystery but that no longer mattered. Only one thing mattered.

He saw movement in the sand near what his eyes perceived as trees. Tiny nuggets of his previous life and things he had learned from it continued to blip through his brain. The movement meant something. Another being like himself? Food? Whatever it was, that was where he needed to go. He began to shuffle slowly in its direction, inadvertently biting at the air hoping to satiate the hunger pangs in his stomach and the acid coursing through his veins.

His feet touched the microscopic grains of sand beneath him but they didn't register in his mind, as if the sand wasn't there at all. As he bit the air, his mind knew that at one time, air had flowed through his body. This was how he had existed before. There had been a beating organ inside his chest, pumping life through him. *It no longer functions. I know that.*

Shuffling forward, the image in his peripheral vision became slightly clearer the closer he got. His mind deduced that this being, crawling on all fours in the sand, was like him. Two legs, two arms, torso, head, internal organs. Human.

His mind went from this thought to the much more important one. Sustenance, anything to sate this agony reverberating through his entire body. His hazy vision kept the moving image in front of him as focused as possible as he shambled on.

The closer he got, the hungrier he felt. His ears worked, to a certain extent. He heard a muffled voice exclaiming, "They must be here! I know they are, where did you hide them you motherfuckers!?"

The words meant nothing to him. What was important was what his nose was now smelling *fresh meat*. His damaged brain sent signals: *Do not moan, do not alert this being in front of you to your presence. You might scare off the only thing that will sate your appetite.* He moved closer, the moving image still unaware of his presence. The closer he got to his prey, the more he smelled food. *Nearly there now!*

"Sonofabitch! I found them!" Pinto cried out triumphantly. His hands frantically dug through the sand. He had followed footprints and, when they stopped, he dug in the hopes of finding his prized stolen treasure. His persistence had paid off. The cases were there, back in his possession.

Pulling them both out of the sand completely and brushing them off, he looked down at them, satisfied. "Okay, what are my options? I suppose I could attempt bandaging up my foot and huffing it through the jungle and try to find the Americans. These things used to be human so there is a chance there could be a boat here," Pinto surmised.

Putting his hands on his hips, he sighed. He would have to find a way to transport the drugs with him, and with his foot in the condition it was in…his mind trailed off. "Keep going, Pinto, you've survived this far, you'll figure it—"

A sharp pain pierced the side of his neck. Hands wrapped around his waist and pushed him forward. With his injured foot, he was caught off-guard and fell forward, his forehead smashing against the side of the nearest briefcase. Not knocked out completely, but he was instantly disoriented. Something had fallen along with him and was now on his back.

The impact of his forehead against the briefcase had caused him to lose much of his motor skills momentarily. All he could do was lie with his face in the sand as the pain in his neck increased. Something had latched onto it and was not only sucking but biting continually. Ripping chunks of flesh and muscle tissue away.

"Get off of me, you filthy sonofabitch!" Pinto gurgled out. He rolled over onto his back, causing whatever was attacking him to fall off. Pinto grabbed his open, gaping wound and felt far too much blood pouring out to survive without a miracle, and this island was devoid of any such thing.

He coughed up a mouthful of blood and stared up into the sky as rain drizzled down. Whatever had attacked him had climbed on top of him once more as he got his first clear look at the assailant. "You," Pinto gurgled, staring into Ed's blank, white eyes.

Ed peered down at his meal, blood covering his face and oozing out of his mouth. Now that he was this close, this human looked oddly familiar. *Plane ride, crash, my friend, what was his name?* The thoughts faded as hunger once more took over.

Pinto attempted to push Ed off of him, but he was growing weaker by the second. Out of the corner of his eye, he saw several more things appear. Unlike Ed, these beings were nearly unrecognizable in their advanced states of decay. What had at one time been clothing were now parts of their bodies, molded into their wet, rotting flesh. Blank, skeletal faces with hollowed-out holes from whatever disease this island had dished out to them stared hungrily.

His mind became foggy while he coughed up more thick blood that was now clogging his throat and choking him. The entities began feasting along with Ed, who continued with the opening he had created on Pinto's neck while the other two dropped to their knees and ripped open his blood-drenched shirt.

With their bony fingers, they pushed and pulled against Pinto's stomach. Unable to defend himself any longer, his skin finally gave way to their greedy hands and burst open. Instantly, rotting hands grabbed and groped at his exposed internal organs and ripped them out greedily.

As death washed over him, the last thing he saw was his insides being pulled from his stomach as creatures that barely resembled human beings hungrily began devouring them.

Once Ed had gotten his fill, he stood to his feet. It was raining now. He remembered rain from a previous life. One that no longer existed, all that existed now was *food*. He had gotten his first fill from this human but already craved more.

He shuffled to the bloody briefcases left on the beach as the other two zombies continued to slowly work their way through Pinto's insides. More living dead had arrived at the smell of fresh kill, hungrily pushing their way in and greedily eating to fill appetites that could never be sated.

Looking down at the briefcases, his foggy mind remembered their importance. The small part of him that remained human grabbed their handles and dragged them along with him into the jungle at the edge of the beach. One case popped open and began spilling its contents out onto the grassy surface.

Ed made his way through the jungle. His senses, while dulled, were still present as he had been dead for such a short period. He smelled the air as his milky-white eyes peered into the trees. *More, there is more of what I just tasted. Must, have, more.*

Behind him, the zombies continued to feast on Pinto, creating a grisly spectacle on the beach. Body parts were strewn about, and it looked as though the sand and small rocks had turned bright crimson. Their last act of desecration was the removal of Pinto's head from his torso and haphazardly dropping it into the blood-red sand.

11
THE CHURCH

Fabian Amill had plenty of time to make the wrong kind of friends with the various planes coming and going, transporting illegal narcotics, and it was now about to catch up with him. But he wasn't the only one with friends on the inside.

Sunglasses-clad Officer Logan Pabon sat in his police issued, light-blue Toyota Land Cruiser with the simple words *Police* in blocky white lettering on either side. He watched the front entrance of the small Honiara airport. He had his orders, pick up one Fabian Amill. He had a picture of the employee of ten years working out of the control towner.

The short, stocky, dark-skinned Logan was a bought-and-paid-for employee of Mr. Sergio Paim, and a law enforcement officer on the Solomon Islands. He was rarely called on by Paim, but when he was, it took priority over everything else. Such was the case today.

He knew it was important if the boss himself was flying in to the airport he worked near. Typically, a mere phone call was all it took to take care of any number of issues that arose when the transport of drugs or, at times, human trafficking was involved. There were several others on the police force who worked for Paim from time to time like Officer Logan, but none as prolific and hardened. He was called when things got tricky and bodies needed to vanish quickly and more importantly, quietly.

Logan watched as a man slipped out the front door of the single runway airport. Another benefit of such a small airport, one way in, one way out. Head hung low, trying not to draw any unnecessary attention, the man moved as fast as his large body would take him. Clad in sunglasses and pulling a baseball hat onto his head as soon as the door closed behind him, he made a beeline for the parking lot to the far left of the control tower.

Officer Logan held the black and white employee picture of the man in question and looked up at the individual leaving the building. "Got you, sneaky little bastard," he muttered, watching the heavyset man waddling as fast as his heavy legs could move.

He continued watching to see which car belonged to him. Fabian Amill stopped in front of an ugly orange AMC Pacer. Likely from the mid-70s. "Figures, a piece of shit driving a piece of shit," Logan said as he slammed his Land Cruiser into gear and slowly began driving up to the man who was fumbling for his car keys and glancing back and forth nervously.

If he had turned around completely, he would have seen the light blue Land Cruiser approaching and essentially block his Pacer from exiting its parking spot. When Fabian heard the rumble of the truck, he spun around, but it was too late. Officer Logan had already slammed the parking brake on and was hopping out of the police vehicle.

Glancing over, Fabian saw from the approaching man's demeanor that he was in serious trouble. His head sunk and his shoulders grew limp as he continued fidgeting with his car keys. Finally unlocking it, he opened the door, pretending Officer Logan wasn't approaching him on foot.

"Excuse me, you work here?" Logan asked the man whose back was turned, attempting to fit his incredibly large body into his tiny car.

"Y-yes, I do, I have to run though. I was informed my mother is not doing so well," Fabian replied, glancing back in his sunglasses.

"Well, I'm sorry to hear that. You most certainly need to tend to personal matters. I have a few questions for you before you leave though. It won't take long and would be a big help to me, if you could follow me to my cruiser," Logan said coolly, now standing right beside the man who no longer scrambled to get his fat body into his car.

"May I ask what this is about, officer? I really must be going, you see I—" Fabian began.

"Get in the fucking truck, you fat piece of shit," Logan muttered in a low, even tone.

Fabian froze in place, reaching up and slowly taking his

sunglasses off, shakily sticking them in the front pocket of his button-down shirt.

Officer Logan extended his outstretched hand and motioned for Fabian's car keys.

After a brief hesitation, he dropped them into the officer's hand.

Pocketing the keys, Logan took his sunglasses off, his eyes cold and calculating.

"Please sir, please I only," Fabian began.

Without taking his eyes from Fabian's, Officer Logan slammed his fist into the large man's ribcage.

Instant jolts of pain coursed through the large man who doubled over, nearly falling from the devastating blow. Officer Logan easily caught him and guided him to his waiting Land Cruiser. He opened the rear door and hastily pushed Fabian through it. Satisfied the man was far enough inside, he slammed the door behind him and climbed into the driver's seat.

Logan quickly drove around the airport to the tarmac where a red and white Cessna Citation I with the numbers 649 etched on its side sat at the far end.

Fabian's eyes widened in horror. "Please, officer, please, you must understand, I was only," he faltered.

"Your ass isn't talking its way out of this one," Logan replied.

Fabian began weeping softly in the rear seat, his rib cage throbbing in pain.

Logan drove in silence, devoid of any emotion, taking him to the waiting plane. He pulled his Land Cruiser up to the airplane that was unattended. It would be fueled up once its occupants had deboarded as per Paim's request.

The door on the side of the plane opened and Paim, Ruiz, and Vidal climbed out. Fabian watched in terror as the three men approached then looked at the pilot that remained in the cockpit, staring at him.

Climbing into the passenger seat of the Land Cruiser, Paim leaned over and embraced Logan. "Good to see you, my friend! I always know I can count on you to help when needed."

"Of course, Sérgio! You have been so good to me and my family," Logan replied, now showing a bit of emotion.

Ruiz and Vidal each climbed into the rear of the Land Cruiser, sitting on either side of the terrified Fabian. As soon as the doors closed the officer fell silent.

"Please, Mr. Paim, he, he threatened me. Yes, he threatened me. I had to keep his secret and allow him to land, or else…or else, my wife and kids," Fabian began.

"Shut up. You don't have a wife and kids. And that's probably a good thing for you, since you won't leave behind a widow. Slow and painful or quick and easy, up to you. Start talking," Paim said, emotionless.

The police truck took off and, as it did, several employees ran out to begin refueling the plane. Vaz watched it all from his pilot's seat.

Just get through this day, get paid, go home.

Sam, Laura, and Eva stood in the opened doorway leading

into the thirty-by-forty-foot church in the middle of the island forest. It was, as they expected, dark inside. Laura closed the door, locking it behind them as they entered and scanned the area.

Immediately, they could see this was no longer used as a church at all; in fact, no pews remained. The only thing that signified this had ever been a house of worship was the tall steeple outside. Otherwise, this appeared to be a makeshift laboratory. In the center of the room was a table with a sheet draped over it, covered in old, dried blood. Surgical instruments lay beside the table on a small cart. Around the table stood several light fixtures.

Cabinets around the room sat closed and in the far corner sat a desk with a mess of papers sprawled on it, the front drawer open. Everything seemed to be in a state of slow degradation. Spiderwebs draped everything and the whole building smelled of old, rotting wood, mildew and decomposed bodies.

Sam was the first to walk forward, floorboards creaking underfoot as if the humid tropical climate was rotting them away as well. With the door closed and the rain continuing outside, it was nearly too dark inside to clearly see.

"Oh gross! It stinks!" Eva exclaimed.

"Yes, but we've got to get a light on in here. Those lights, how are they powered?" Laura asked.

Sam quickly surveyed the lights. "I assume there's a generator outside. From the state of disrepair this church or operating room is in, the likelihood of a generator still working or having fuel to power it is slim. Let's try some of these drawers for candles."

Setting her walking stick down, Eva began looking through the drawers nearest her. Pulling out several candles, she held them up, "Found some! If we can find a way to light them."

"Good, Eva," Sam replied as he pushed aside the mess of papers and an old reel-to-reel audio recorder on the desk.

"Found a pack of cigarettes and a lighter," Laura called out from the drawer she was sifting through. Flicking it, a small flame shot out.

Eva made her way over with the candles and held them out for Laura. Once the wicks ignited, the room became much more visible.

They looked around at their surroundings, now able to take everything in much better. "Bodies, that's what we're smelling," Sam said, pointing to a corpse beside the desk and one on the floor near the center of the room.

"Gross! Gross! Gross!" Eva wailed, covering her eyes.

Sam and Laura looked at the first body which appeared to have been a young boy, the back of his skull blown inward from a close quarters blast to the head. The body barely resembled anything human anymore and it was heavily diseased judging from the hideously deformed skeletal structure that remained.

Moving past the first corpse, they went to the second, this one sitting upright, its head tilted abnormally upwards, a hole under its chin leading out the top of its head. The corpse was wearing a doctor's coat and in a heavy state of decay. In its right hand was a black revolver.

Eva glanced at the body then quickly turned away. "Oh God! Another one!" she shrieked, stumbling away.

Quickly turning from the corpse holding a gun, Sam and Laura saw what had caused her outburst. In a corner of the room, behind a trash can and piles of old tablets, lay yet another rotting corpse, this one dressed in a nurse's uniform.

Laura grimaced at the ghastly sight. "This is insane, what the hell is going on here?" she whispered in revulsion, involuntarily coughing and swallowing the bile that had formed in her mouth. A skeleton with a thin layer of human skin wrapping it was all that remained of the nurse. She appeared to have been shot in the head and the uniform she wore showed signs of further trauma to the body.

"I'm gonna puke," Eva uttered, seeing that a finger and thumb were also missing on the nurse's right hand. She quickly backed away from the dead body and wretched in the corner of the church building.

Sam looked from the vomiting Eva over to the corpses in the room. *Keep it together, Sam,* he thought as revulsion swept over him.

"What in God's name happened here?" Laura said, disgusted by the three corpses strewn about the room.

"I don't know but that reel-to-reel tape recorder on the desk might have some answers, if we can get it to work," Sam said, continuing to study the corpse in a doctor's coat.

Outside, the rain was slowing and daylight was quickly fading. Faint light shone through an exposed window.

"We've got to get that window closed," Laura said.

Prying the gun from the dead doctor's gnarled, skeletal

hand, Sam opened it and saw three shells remained inside. Closing the cylinder, he looked up from the body to Laura then stood to his feet and handed her the gun. "Here, you should have this."

She grimaced at the thought of now being in possession of a weapon that had likely killed both of the people in this makeshift laboratory but accepted it, looking it over in her hands.

Sam walked over to the open window. On the ground below and over toward the rear of the church sat an old generator, half covered in dirt and debris. A shutter above the window was latched in by an old metal lock and loop. Reaching up, Sam unhooked it and the wooden shutter fell forward, slamming against the window.

The noise startled him. As much as he tried to keep his cool, he was rattled by the dire situation they were now stuck in. His life and several other lives were threatened with the very real possibility of death. *Keep your cool, Sam, Mr. Eagle Scout.*

With the church closed off completely, other than two small windows on either wall, and cracks in the centuries-old wooden frame revealing small slivers of light, the candles were all that illuminated their surroundings. Not only was there a sheet covered in old, dried blood, but the floor appeared to be splattered in a brownish-colored blood.

Inspecting the sheets on the table, Sam pulled them off, draped them over the boy's body, then approached the body of the woman in the nurse's uniform. He noticed a small cannister sitting in the corner nearby. Picking it up, he shook it then popped the lid. *Gasoline.*

He then moved to the audio recorder and clicked the *play* knob. The girls joined him there, but all were met with silence. "Shit! We need to get power to this thing," he said.

"What are you going to do?" Laura asked.

Holding the revolver in one hand and the container of gasoline in the other, he stared at the door, "I'm going to go out and try to fire up that generator out there."

"Think that's a good idea?" Laura came back quickly.

"No. Not at all. But we could use better lighting and I have a hunch whatever is on that reel-to-reel is going to shed some light on this island and what's wrong with its inhabitants and possibly even explain what the hell happened in here."

"I'm coming along," Laura replied.

"No. Absolutely not, not with those things out there. You two stay put, I'll be back in—"

"I'm coming along," Laura said again, this time with a tone that said, *I'm not arguing about it.*

"I'm not taking one step outside," Eva said coldly, folding her arms in defiance.

Nodding, Sam replied, "Come on, Laura."

Laura was impressed with how well Sam, under such duress, was handling her whiny sidekick. She, on the other hand, was growing weary of her complaining.

Laura turned and followed Sam outside as Eva quickly closed the door behind them, bolting it shut once more.

They quickly made their way around the side of the church, past the makeshift graveyard, to the old generator sitting unattended for what appeared to be a significantly long period of time. Moans continued emanating from the thick forest.

Scanning their surroundings, Laura whispered, "How soon until those things out there come knocking on our door?"

"Too soon. I just hope that reel-to-reel has some answers."

The old generator looked as if it hadn't been fired up in ages. Wiping away much of the dirt and grime that had accumulated on top of and around the generator, Sam located the gas tank cap, popped it open and shook the generator lightly. No liquid could be heard inside sloshing around. Sam holstered his revolver.

Laura scanned their surroundings once more, feeling safer holding her own firearm before turning back to watch Sam pour most of the container's contents into the generator then sealing the cap back on tightly.

"What do you think happened in there?" Sam asked.

Giving this some thought, Laura replied, "From the looks of it, the man in the doctor's coat shot the nurse and the boy then blew his own brains out. The body of that boy is in a heavy state of decomposition, but I have a strong hunch he was like those things on the beach. Infected with some kind of virus that causes those lesions on the skin."

Laura thought of her father and the reason for her visit to Papua New Guinea, to locate him.

Sam turned the choke on then the starter switch, taking a deep breath. He gave a hard tug on the recoil cord. Silence.

"Damnit."

He tried it again and was met with the same result. Two more times, each time yanking on the starter cord harder, but nothing happened.

"Wait a minute," Laura said, crouching down to investigate the device. She found a value over to the side that was set to *off*. She quickly turned it to the *on* position and glanced up to Sam.

Grinning at her, he grabbed hold of the recoil cord once more and yanked. The engine turned over. He gave the cord two more pulls and on the third, the engine, coughed, wheezed and finally, fired up. Smoke instantly wafted out of its sides as Sam turned the choke off. After letting it run for a bit, the generator seemed to settle into a slow, steady purr.

"This is going to likely draw those things to us, you know that, right?" Laura said.

"Let's get inside," Sam answered, knowing she was right.

They quickly headed back to the front of the building and knocked on the door. "Eva, open up," Laura said.

After a brief pause, they heard the unlatching of the lock and the door opened. Both Sam and Laura quickly walked in, closing it behind them, noticing that one of the lights was functioning, but flickering sporadically.

"Took you guys long enough! I was getting worried, I don't like being stuck in here with dead bodies you know!" Eva said, nervously glancing over at the corpses in the room that were now covered with sheets she had found.

Noticing this, Laura exclaimed, "Good job covering the bodies, Eva."

Eva attempted a brief smile that quickly turned back to fear.

"Now let's see what's on that reel-to-reel over there," Sam muttered.

Outside the church, a skeletal being shuffled out through the heavy brush into the clearing directly in front of the church. Dragging its bare feet on the dirt in front of the church, it opened its jaws, biting at air. The large man's clothes were in tatters and his throat was completely torn out. Moaning, he stood at the edge of the forest, his white eyes remaining stationary, looking at the church.

Farther back and unnoticed, the corpse of Ed shuffled forward, clutching a briefcase in each hand. One had popped open from the movement, spilling its contents to the ground. Ed slowly looked down at the now empty briefcase then dropped it.

Unsure why, but somehow recalling them as a reason for his current state, he continued clinging to the second briefcase, Ed began to move forward. Awkward in his new undead skin, he inadvertently stepped down into a steep ravine and tumbled several feet forward, not even trying to break his fall. His head smashed into a waiting rock below and his dulled mind went foggy.

Almost as if the sudden crack had jarred deep, lost memories to the forefront, Ed lay in silence as his past washed over him in waves. Mistakes he had made, relationships severed, family disappointed, money wasted, a life wasted.

And then there was Sam. His only true friend. Always there for him, Sam.

He opened his dry, scab-encrusted mouth and mumbled, *"Sam."*

12
MORE QUESTIONS THAN ANSWERS

Vaz continued to peer out of the now fully refueled Cessna on the tarmac awaiting his passengers. He quietly ate a bag of peanuts, wishing this day would end and he could be back home with Amanda and Angela Sophia. But this was his job, and he was good at it. Especially the *no questions* part.

Flying around the Solomon Seas with the likes of this lot was dangerous and he knew it well, which is why he went out of his way to never, ever fly anyone that was questionable. However, this was a unique situation and one he knew he couldn't say no to. If Kokoda air traffic control employee Santana had been cornered, he might have given Vaz's name and address as the pilot that turned down the mighty, all-powerful Sérgio Paim. *Do your job, get paid, go home, kiss your wife and child. Thank God you are alive and well.*

The Land Cruiser with *Police* etched on the side came back into view. Soon it was beside the Cessna and Paim, Ruiz, and Vidal stepped out. Paim walked around to the driver's side, shook hands with the police officer and made his way back to the airplane.

Once inside, they took their seats.

"Destination?" Vaz asked without turning around.

"The unfortunate Fabian explained to us that there was a distress call that came in over the Solomon Sea. Coordinates are..." Paim looked down at notes scribbled on a sheet of paper. "Latitude -9.28766, longitude 153.690201 was their last known location. Fly us there and fly low. At the time of the distress call, they were flying through a very large storm. They are likely at the bottom of the ocean, but they may have crashed on one of the many uninhabited islands in that vicinity. At least that is what Mr. Fabian just told us."

"Entering those coordinates now. We're cleared for takeoff so we will be airborne shortly," Vaz responded. *What on earth happened to that pour soul?* he wondered.

"See his eyeballs? Never seen that before," Ruiz said quietly to Vidal.

"Yep," came the icy reply before both henchmen fell silent.

Vaz cleared his throat. "Excuse me, Mr. Paim, if we find your plane on one of the islands, we will either need to come back for a boat or..."

"Or you'll land this plane on the beach. Regardless, you

will do as you are instructed, is that clear?"

"Yes, sir. Perfectly," Vaz replied, pushing forward on the throttle. *Please let that plane be on the ocean's floor.* He was suddenly regretting becoming a pilot instead of taking over his father's small bakery years ago. He glanced at his watch; dusk would arrive soon.

Police officer Logan Pabon drove off as they taxied. Now, it was clean up duty. Starting with the AMC Pacer and the dead body stuffed into the passenger's seat with a cord wrapped tightly around his throat. His face purple, eyeballs hanging out of their sockets, and his tongue sitting in his lap along with two severed hands. Loose lips and greedy hands that help thieves are dealt with accordingly in Paim's criminal underworld.

Logan would make short work of him and his vehicle. After a few quick phone calls and a police report, Fabian Amill would be a mere afterthought. A man that barely existed at all, soon forgotten.

Inside the church, Eva fished through the backpack, looking for pants to put on per Sam's insistence after he had finally noticed she had "borrowed" one of his shirts to cover up back on the beach. It would likely get cool at night and her tiny shorts wouldn't suffice.

Sam said, "Eva, if you're looking for pants, what I had was dumped out back on the beach. I only have some shirts left." He thought back to Eva tossing only some of his shirts back in when they were dealing with Pinto earlier.

"Shit. Of course. Of...course. Of course they are, damnit," She replied bitterly. After tossing the backpack down to the ground, she held up another granola bar she had pulled from it and glanced at Sam for confirmation it was okay to eat.

Sam, who would rather have not used up the small amount of food they had on hand, begrudgingly agreed, knowing she likely needed it more than he did. Eva and Laura divvied it up along with a bottle of water found in the side of the backpack. Laura offered some to Sam who only took a gulp of water and waved away the portion of granola bar she offered him.

"Okay, fingers crossed this thing works," Sam said, clicking the *rewind* knob on the reel-to-reel the tape. It fired up, the tape spun backward until reaching the beginning, then clicked on. For a brief period only static crackled through its small speaker, then a voice came on.

"This is Doctor Márcio Prestes Pedroso. Date is October 19, 1978. I hope this thing is working and picking up my voice."

There was a pause in the audio and Eva gasped, "Laura, isn't that the doctor your dad was working with?"

"I believe so," Laura replied, stunned at what she had just heard, looking at the reel-to-reel in rapt attention as the voice continued.

"In the room with me is nurse Sara Alvarez Luz. We continue to run into dead ends trying to find a cure for brain cancer as well as for the cursed virus plaguing the people of this small island. The serum my partner Dr. William Joyner and I created, NR 485, seems to show progress but experimenting on the people of this island has put a strain on our relationship."

At the mention of her father's name, Laura's eyes welled with tears, her hand covering her mouth in disbelief.

The doctor continued. "Joyner is unwilling to perform the trials due to their unpredictability on the natives here, but if we continue to do nothing, he will die from the very disease we are trying to eradicate. This wasn't supposed to go like this. The plan was sure-fire and the cure, well... we both felt it would be rock-solid and, in the process, that we would be able to cure these poor people of their leprosy."

Sam and Laura exchanged glances, both fascinated and curious to hear more, while Eva picked at her fingernail polish.

The audio clicked off and then on again. "Dr. Pedroso, recording on January 10, 1979. Still no cure, more deaths as the people of this island are dying off. After being banished from the Solomon Islands, this place was essentially their final resting place. They're resilient and have lived far longer than any of us expected. My assistant, Luiz Velho, has buried another test subject. If we can just figure out what caused this mutated strain of leprosy in the first place, we are confident that NR 485 can not only cure them of this virus slowly eating them alive, but combined with their blood will lead to the cure for brain cancer.

"They are surviving long after they should have perished. What is allowing them to live on? The answer must lie in their blood, I just haven't found it, yet. It could be the leprosy itself in their bloodstream that causes the red and white blood cells to fight back at the invading disease. I need more time and more test subjects! Dr. Joyner has grown worse and wants to let these people die in peace. He is still convinced, falsely I might add, that the answer may actually lie in a plant of unknown origin he found near the village, Violet Laceflower. But this, I fear, is a dead end. However, I refuse to give up. Even at the cost of their lives. We have living specimens at our disposal to use. No, scratch that, to try to help!"

Another pause in the audio. By the now, all three of them stood mesmerized at what sounded like the rantings of a madman.

"Holy shit, they came here to experiment on these people. Use them as guinea pigs! What the hell have we been dropped into?" Sam said, disgusted at what he was hearing.

Laura sighed. "My dad. I've been searching for him ever since he left us after his diagnosis back in Texas. He told me on one of our final phone conversations after he left that he had been in contact with a doctor from Indonesia who was on the cusp of a breakthrough in brain tumor research and would be traveling to meet him somewhere in Papua New Guinea. I had tracked him to the Solomon Islands then lost his trail. He never returned. That was two years ago. It's why I'm here."

The audio clicked on again, and a tired voice spoke. "This is Dr. William Joyner, location: la Isla de Sebria. I am recording this on May first, 1979."

"Dad!" Laura cried, hearing his voice for the first time in nearly two years. "What have you done?"

Eva moved closer to her friend and put her arm around her.

"I don't have much time left. I'm dying and no amount of experimenting on these natives will save me at this point. It is not the natives we should be experimenting on, it is the mysterious plant life found on this island. Dr. Pedroso and I do not share the same views on this. This has been a failure; all we are doing at this point is giving false hope where there is none, at least not with what Dr. Pedroso has been attempting. We agree on one thing: the answer may lie in the serum my colleague has created, NR 485, but only in combination with the Violet Laceflower, found near the village and up into the crater a mile past it, has it shown the most promise. However, the conditions of this island are not suitable to continue experimenting. This needs to be done in a secure facility, with modern technology. Not using human beings as lab rats. I am considering leaving the island on our boat on the other side of this island."

The audio went silent at the end of Dr. Joyner's recording, then clicked back on after several seconds of crackling static.

"This is Dr. Pedroso, my final log entry. June 14, 1979. My staff are dead due to my negligence. And now, the people of this island will have their revenge. Revenge on the God that created them and inflicted them with the disease that forced them to flee their homes and relocate on this island. I'm convinced the cure for brain cancer and the leprosy that infects these people lies in the NR 485 formula, but I can do no more here…"

He paused, as if debating whether to go on.

"I have created something else, something much more deadly than leprosy. And if it escapes this island, it could quite literally be the end of life on this planet. Whatever it is, it turns those infected into rabid killers that eat flesh. Human flesh! It spreads through the saliva and is highly and nearly instantaneously infectious. I pray that my associate has left the island..."

A single gunshot rang out through the speaker of the reel-to-reel before the tape ran out.

Sam clicked the nob off and they all stood in silent horror.

Outside, the generator sputtered. "There wasn't much fuel in that cannister I found and that generator is on its last leg," Sam said, turning to Laura. "Now we know what those things were on the beach, and that your father was here." He grabbed up a handful of scattered papers on the desk and looked them over, seeing frequent mentions NR 485.

Laura wiped away her wet eyes and gently pushed Eva away.

"Sam's right! He was here...and you found out what happened to your dad, Laura," Eva added, not sure how best to comfort her friend in the middle of this rotting church with its rotting corpses.

"I found out that he was here. Not what happened to him. These bodies look thoroughly decayed, they've been dead a while. What if he's still out there somewhere?" Laura replied urgently.

Sam shook his head. "Laura, the odds..."

Laura shook her head defiantly. "Don't tell me the odds. I don't know you and you don't know me. But I was brought here for a reason. Look, I'm sorry about your friend. I'm sorry the plane crashed and all of this crazy insanity. But at first light, I want to get a look around this island and try to find out what happened to my father."

They all fell silent once more. Sam's mind raced through various scenarios of escaping this island of infected leapers, but short of a miracle, they would have to survive until help arrived. If it ever did.

"Your dad mentioned a boat, right? I mean, these doctors would need to get to the mainland at some point," Eva said, her voice hopeful for the first time since arriving on the island.

"Damn, she has a point," Sam said. "I mean, there must be a boat somewhere on this island. How safe it is to get to it is a whole other topic for discussion. I have a compass on my watch but that sure as hell doesn't make me an expert in navigating the island. However, it is imperative we do what we can to find a way out of here, and if there's a boat some-where in this god-forsaken place, that's our best option."

Laura, still coming to grips with this new information about her father, stared down at the dusty floor, at a loss for words.

The generator coughed, sputtered, and then fell silent. The lone light in the small church flickered then clicked off, shrouding them in darkness.

Sam hurriedly lit the two candles once more. "Night is falling, we need to hunker down here, then tomorrow morning we need to slip through this jungle and, as dangerous as it may seem, see if we can find that boat, even with those things out there."

Laura spoke up now, urgently. "I must find out what happened to my father. What if he's alive?"

"Laura, the most important thing is that *we* make it out of here alive! Our main goal is escape," Sam retorted.

"Look, I've traveled from Texas in search of a father who left my mother and me two years ago on some mission to find a cure for the brain tumor in his head. And we just so happen to crash land on *this* island?" Laura raised her voice, trying to get Sam to see her point.

Sam shook his head. "All this island has brought is death so far. My friend is buried back there in the sand! I feel for you, truly, I do. But we have got to figure a way off this island before those things out there get us! Because if they do, we're all screwed!"

Laura tried to stop the tears from coming but she couldn't. She was so close to finally getting some answers about her father. "But surely, we can do both! Look for a way off this rock while still looking for my father! I've come so far!"

"*We've* come so far," Eva said with a hint of bitterness in her tone.

Laura fell silent, thinking of Eva's parents pushing Eva onto her for this difficult journey. *Damnit! Why didn't I refuse them!*

Sam and Laura stared at each other in a silent battle of wills, Eva now quiet after her slight dig.

Finally, Sam sighed and said, "Okay, top priority: get to the other side of the island in the hopes of finding a boat to get us the hell out of here. On our way, if we stumble upon your father or anything else that could be of help to us, we investigate. But we must be careful! Those things out there don't appear to have any reasoning capabilities. Anything other than trying to get off the island puts us in greater danger and right now, keeping us safe is number one on my list."

Laura nodded, accepting these conditions, drying her tears and pulling herself together. "Thanks, Sam. I can handle myself just fine, though I appreciate you looking out for us." She was quietly thankful he was with them and even entertaining the possibility of helping her locate her father.

Eva looked away from the two of them, bitter over everything they had endured thus far and scared for her life.

The two women searched the remaining drawers for anything that could be useful. A few cans of tomato soup that even cold, proved to be good nourishment for their hungry and tired bodies. A large container of water was also discovered. Sam filled his water bottle with some of its contents and they drank their fill.

Sam wiped his mouth off and sealed his water bottle. "It's nine o'clock and we haven't heard any more moaning. Let's try and get a bit of rest before we make our way to the other side of the island in the morning."

He agreed to move the three corpses to a far corner of the room and cover them further with the sheet found on the examination table. Afterward, while Laura inspected Eva's swollen ankle and rewrapped it a bit tighter, Sam did a bit more reading of the doctor's notes about the mysterious disease that plagued the people of this unnamed island in the middle of the Solomon Sea. He learned that they had indeed been forced to relocate from their home by boat, pushed away and abandoned by the government officials back on the mainland and left to fend for themselves. A slow death for sure. Until Dr. Pedroso and his associates had found out about them and their mysterious disease. An island of guinea pigs. Lab rats whose lives were over anyway. He was sickened by what he read, throwing several notebooks back onto the desk after scanning through them.

With Sam's remaining clothes, the group attempted to create makeshift sleeping arrangements on the floor. Sam made sure the door was securely locked along with the sole window in the building. Nothing was getting in without significant force.

Eva fell asleep nearly instantaneously. They had found some pain killers which she greedily took. The pills not only helped with the ankle but also knocked her out quickly. While she slept, Laura and Sam lay in silence on the cold hard wooden floor of the church laboratory.

Sam spoke quietly. "I hope you understand my predicament, Laura. I truly am sorry for what you've had to go through with your father and that he might still be alive. And I am hopeful we'll discover something along the way..." His voice trailed off.

Laura remained silent. She understood the man's insistence that trying to find a way off the island was of utmost importance and the main objective. But she was determined not to give up all hope. Deep down, she felt her father could very well still be alive. She had to find him.

Noticing her silence on the matter, Sam changed course.

"Tell me about yourself, Laura, tell me where the both of you are from, Port Aransas was it?"

She remained silent for a short time, trying to decide if she should get to know this man better. She prided herself on not letting many people in, not after her father had abandoned them. "Decent town, decent life. That's how best to describe me. I've always been a bit of a homebody. My dad and I..." She trailed off.

"You were close?"

Laura put her hands under her chin, staring at the handsome young traveler. "Yeah. I was, I think that's the reason he left. He didn't want me and my mom to see him rot away and instead figured he would die trying to find an actual cure. Told us he had a good hunch about a serum a doctor friend had told him about."

She paused, contemplating her last interaction with her father.

"Then he left. Broke my mom's heart. I mean, I get it, I get the *why*. My dad is a brilliant man, and I truthfully think he was onto something big. Something that had him choose, well...choose this. But to just leave us behind? I don't know, it's been one hell of a two years, that's for sure."

"I must admit, the odds..." Sam said, then fell silent.

"Exactly, that's why I feel like destiny has just knocked on my door. Sam, I am sure my dad is still on this island and I have a strong hunch he might have a cure. Why he didn't leave though, that's another question entirely and one I plan on finding out. I know he's alive, Sam, I just know it." She glanced up at him with tired eyes.

"If he's out there, we'll find him...on the way to the boat," Sam added, giving her a brief smile. He couldn't help but feel empathy for her and want to help this beautiful and strong-willed woman lying across from him.

"Thank you, Sam. Thank you for staying strong. For Eva and for me. It's hard to fathom what we've been through already. I mean, plane crash, shark, murderous drug dealer, and mutated leper zombies? I'd pay money to see something like this at the local movie theater," she said with a grin.

Sam smiled too. They stared at each other in silence.

"What about you, Sam? What was your last name again? Sorry, I'm not the best with names, especially last names."

"Oh, I don't expect you to remember it. Last name is Berry. Not much to tell. The party animal is no longer with us. This was his plan; good old Ed. Damn, I miss him right now. The shit him and I would get into back in college. We couldn't be more opposite, but I guess opposites attract." Sam fell silent, missing his best friend.

"I'm sorry, Sam, really, I am," Laura said in a whisper, looking at him with sad eyes.

"I know we haven't really had time to mourn the dead. I gave your friend a hard time and for that, I'm sorry."

Sam let out a small chuckle. "Oh, Laura, trust me when I say, that stand-off attitude you threw his way, that's how I would say roughly fifty percent of the women he interacted with dealt with him. Some picked up on his flirtatious remarks and reciprocated, but the smart ones didn't take his bullshit."

Laura instantly looked over at Eva. "Eva is totally Ed's

type. She thrives on the attention. She's a good girl, but young and naïve even at twenty-one. This is the opposite of fun for her. For any of us, but for her, if you haven't figured out by now…she'd do much better sitting poolside at a swanky hotel with a cocktail in one hand, having her pick of the muscle-bound lunkheads swooning over her. That's my Eva."

"You two seem quite opposite," Sam said.

Nodding, Laura replied, "Oh, we most certainly are. Like you said, opposites seem to attract. Nine times out of ten, a friendship like this wouldn't work. I'm the tomboy-figure-shit-out-on-my-own type. And she, well, you get the picture."

"So? Why did she come along with you?" Sam pressed.

Sighing, she glanced at the sleeping Eva. "Her parents insisted she come along. To keep her out of trouble, which, truth be told, does seem to follow her wherever she goes. Plus, my mom thought it best, once I insisted on going to Papua New Guinea, that someone travel with me. And here we are…"

Sam soaked up this information. He had picked up, almost immediately, that the two of them were like him and Ed, opposites, but somehow it worked.

"You have a significant other waiting for you back in Texas?" he asked, hoping he didn't sound too obvious.

"Nah. I did for a bit, got cheated on. Swore I wouldn't let that happen to me ever again, so…single. Much to my mother's dismay. She already wants grandkids. And my dad did too. The dating scene isn't really my…scene. But anyway, how's about you?" She realized how awkward she sounded and felt her face go flush.

Sam hadn't noticed in the dark, the one candle between them the only light in the room.

"I've had a few relationships, none sticking though. Ed and I were just getting this out of our systems before we got fully taken over by jobs then family and all that middle-aged stuff, you know? My parents, if they ever see me again, are gonna say *we told you so!*"

Laura smiled. This was the first time she was enjoying a pleasant chat with someone of the opposite sex in as long as she could remember.

"So, it seems as though there are more questions than answers here on this island," Sam said, becoming serious.

Laura nodded. "Right. Was this Dr. Pedroso actually planning on helping these people? Sounded like he was basically using them like his own reserve of test subjects on relatively untested, experimental drugs, all in the service of finding a cure for brain cancer and maybe, if he was lucky, their leprosy. My dad seemed to abandon this doctor's mentality and bailed. I'm assuming the man and nurse on the reel-to-reel are the ones covered up in this room?"

"They have to be. And, how infectious is this? We know it's through the saliva. If that's the case, what if our illustrious pilot Pinto is up and wandering this island?" Sam replied. His mind went to Ed. Ed had been bitten but had passed away, thankfully. He couldn't imagine having to put a bullet in his friend.

"Well, I'm just glad we have a few guns, even with limited ammunition, I certainly feel safer, if such a thing can be said on this island," Laura answered, not wanting to think on Pinto's whereabouts any longer.

"Good talking with you, Laura. I know we're in a shit situation but I'm glad to know you, just the same," Sam said.

Laura smiled at him, nodded, then rolled over, sleep washing over her weary body nearly instantaneously.

After blowing out the candle, Sam lay in silence, the gun tightly in his hand. Somewhere outside moans could be heard. He remained awake for much longer than he hoped.

13
THE VILLAGE

Sam stood outside the church, gun in hand, scanning the immediate area. It was early morning and all was quiet. He was up before his companions and thought it best to check their surroundings before they all made their way outside. A true Eagle Scout move, he thought.

As he drained the contents of his bladder at the side of the church, out of view of the door should they come out, he peered around at his surroundings. He thought he saw brief movement deeper into the tropical jungle surrounding him so he quickly finished up his task, zipped up and, glancing up at the tip of the crater visible from his much lower vantage point, headed back inside the church quietly so not to disturb Laura and Eva.

Deep in the forest, Ed stood. His head was covered in blood from the smash it had taken, and while he still had an insatiable hunger, it seemed to have dulled. His stomach wasn't transmitting the messages to his damaged brain like it had been shortly after his resurrection. Instead, still clenching the briefcase of drugs that he knew meant something from his previous life, he watched Sam pee onto the ground then walk inside.

He tilted his head slightly, processing what he had seen. *Who* he had seen. His nose twitched. He smelled warm blood and fresh meat, but his mind continued telling him, *friend.*

Eva lay naked under the covers of her bed in a darkened room. She instantly knew this was a dream as dream logic had dictated that this was her own bed in her own bedroom back in Texas. But none of her surrounds were accurate. For one thing, she never slept in the nude. Even though she was twenty-one, she still liked her "jammies." Secondly, the bed she was lying in was much smaller than her own and the room she found herself in was cold—the actual temperature as well as the overall vibe.

Quickly realizing her vulnerability, she clutched the sheet draped over her and hugged it tightly. Several figures entered the room. *But where is the door they walked through? I must know for my eminent escape!* No door presented itself, however. The three figures were clad in doctor and nurse uniforms with masks on their mouths. The small portion of the exposed faces of her dream invaders was ghastly. Rotted flesh, peeling away from skull underneath. Eyeballs loosely bobbing in their sockets with only the whites showing.

Then there was the smell. Rotted, putrid meat hit her nose as the three stood around her. She realized she wasn't in a bed at all, but on an operating table. And she also discovered that she was no longer able to freely move her arms and legs. They were fastened with leather restraints, securing her to the table.

Eva struggled against the leather that bound her tight, but it was no use. She was at the mercy of her dream-stalking assailants. The faceless entities ripped the sheet off, exposing her nakedness underneath.

The presence closest to her pulled off his mask; it was the deceased doctor they had found in the room where she now slept. The next was the nurse, and finally, Ed. He had multiple bites and his eyes were milky white.

"I'm going to make you like me. Then we can be together forever, for all eternity, rotting on this island," Ed said without opening his mouth as he leaned forward, hands reaching for her throat, teeth biting the air.

Eva sat up in the small church screaming. Laura bent over her, shaking her, yelling, "Wake up, Eva!"

She shook her head and looked at her friend, sweat covering her face and down the back of Sam's shirt she still wore.

"Holy shit. What, where?" Eva began then fell silent as the realization of where she was flooded over her. She leaned forward and hugged Laura. "Oh, Laura, the nightmare I just had! That Ed guy was there, and he was…" She fell silent seeing Sam standing over her.

Laura stood to her feet and helped her friend up. "It's

okay, Eva, I'm here. Try not to think about it. How's your ankle?" she asked once Eva was standing in an attempt to get her friend's mind off the nightmare.

"It's okay. I've been off of it long enough and the pain meds really helped. I should be fine to walk for a while," Eva replied as she put pressure on the ankle, testing it out. "I need a shower, and a change of clothes, and real food and a real bed," she added glumly, still shaking off the terrible dream as she moved around on the ankle.

"We all do," Laura replied curtly.

Eva fell silent, knowing she was complaining once more. It was something she excelled at, even when things were going fine. Now, however, her life was literally in peril. *I'm allowed to hate this* she reasoned as she grabbed a few items in preparation for their departure.

"Have you two been up a while?" Eva asked, looking from Laura to Sam, slightly suspicious. She had heard a small portion of their conversation the previous night after being stirred from her restless sleep. She was adept at sensing attraction, and she was sensing it now. Only it wasn't her, it was her best friend. The one who wasn't interested in men, ever. A slight tinge of jealousy shot through her at this thought.

"I don't know, how long have we been up, Sam?" Laura asked casually, not picking up on the jealous vibe coming from Eva.

"Around thirty minutes now. Enough time to go through some more of the good doctor's notes," Sam replied.

Eva fell silent, feeling ashamed of her thoughts. *I want to be home, damnit! I want to be in my house, with my mama and papa. Fuck this place and fuck you for bringing me along, Laura!* She shook the thought out of her head.

"So, we still have my backpack, I'm going to take some of these notebooks with us. If we make it back to the mainland, someone, somewhere needs to know what happened here," Sam said, grabbing the incriminating evidence of Dr. Pedroso's crimes against humanity.

"I think we should keep our eyes peeled for those Violet Laceflowers my father spoke of. He mentioned they were around the village and that large crater in the distance. That could be a clue as to his whereabouts," Laura added making her way to the door.

Grabbing one of the candles, the flare gun, and some pain tablets, Sam placed them in the backpack, slung it over his shoulder and opened the front door cautiously. The morning sunlight hit his eyes. It was only 7:35 AM but already the sun was up on the horizon.

Peering outside, Sam could see they were alone, at least in the immediate vicinity. "Everyone ready?"

Laura nodded and Eva glumly followed suit.

With Sam's compass as their guide, they made their way into the forest. Sam, in the lead, had taken back the knife Ed had gifted him and, using it as a machete, sliced away at the thick growth all around them. It certainly wasn't made for this kind of activity, but he was quite thankful for Ed's gift.

The rain from the previous day had soaked the ground and the hike covered already dangerous terrain winding past large trees and thick brush. This, along with sudden steep inclines and sharp drops, caused all three of them to slip and fall frequently.

Sam and Laura took this in stride, but Eva, on a particularly bad slip and fall, shrieked out in anger and all-new pain coursing through her ankle, essentially reinjuring it. She smacked the ground with her open palm. When Laura attempted to pull her up, she pushed her hand away. "I can handle myself, damnit!" she spat out frustrated and angry.

"I'm just trying to help, Eva."

Eva waved her away bitterly. Sam and Laura looked on as she continued her temper tantrum. "I just, I cannot believe this is happening to me! Me! Laura, you're the tomboy, not me! I should be on a beach in Florida! That's where I should be! Instead, my ankle is fucked, I spent the night inside a room with three dead and stinky bodies and had the mother of all nightmares! I'm hungry, tired, dirty, and feel like I'm about to start my period! If you would have just…" She looked at Laura, falling just short of outright blaming her friend for her woes.

"Come on, Eva, let's go," Sam said calmly.

"Don't tell me what to do! I know what you're up to! I see you! I just want to go home!" Eva shouted.

"Look, I don't know what you're taking about but you've got to keep your voice down! We aren't alone here!" Sam replied, annoyed but still keeping his cool.

"We're stuck here, and you've got eyes for my friend. Fine! I'm the third wheel now. Is that what you want to hear, Laura? You've always been *my* third wheel and now the tables have turned. Look at poor Eva! Can't handle herself! All she's good for is fucking! That's what you're both thinking, isn't it?" Eva was now full-on shouting.

"What the hell!" Laura chimed in.

"I just want to go home! Fuck this place and fuck you for dragging me along on this stupid trek through third-world countries trying to find your dad who abandoned you!"

Sam wiped the sweat from his face, his frustration with Eva mounting. She had been obnoxious since the moment he met her on the tarmac back in Papua New Guinea. Now she was putting their lives in more danger than they already were with her increasingly loud, shrill voice.

Putting her hands on her hips, Laura let loose. "You, Eva, will now *shut up*. *You* were the one that pushed to come along with me and your parents begged, no, pleaded with me to bring you along! I knew the risks and shared them with you. I didn't plan on any of this happening, so we need to stop with this bickering. You're going to get us killed. Now, I've been sympathetic to you since the plane went down, but it's time to adjust your attitude! That means keeping your tongue and your tone in check! Because I'm not dying here, damnit!"

Eva fell silent, feeling both of their angry gazes on her. She pulled herself to her feet, grimacing at the pain.

They continued in silence a bit farther. The morning sun was already hot and getting hotter by the minute, soon they would be in full sun.

"We've got to find food. And this water will only last so long," Sam said, glancing from the sun down to his water bottle.

Laura pointed. "How's about that?"

They looked in the direction she was pointing. "Well, I'll be damned, papaya trees!" Sam said happily.

With this bit of good fortune, they made their way through more dense forest to the trees. The fruit wasn't high, so Sam made short work of cutting several down with the knife and handed them to Laura and Eva.

As they ate hungrily, Sam scanned their surroundings. Glancing at the compass on his watch, he knew they were heading in a relatively straight line toward the rear of the island but wasn't sure how long the hike would take. Or what they would find once they reached the other side, for that matter.

They each took several more gulps of water before Sam put the bottle back in his backpack and they continued on their trek through the jungle. Eva and Laura awkwardly avoided making eye contact, both still reeling from the obvious tension following Eva's outburst.

What they hadn't seen was a large man that had at one time gone by the name of Velho, now a rotting zombified corpse, shuffling toward them through the deep forest. Because his throat had been ripped out, he made no sound other than the slow drudge forward through the wet ground. His mouth slowly opened and closed, teeth clacking together hungrily. The whites of his eyes blankly stared forward as his nose followed the scent of living human meat.

The Cessna flew through the sky, searching for the longitude and latitude given to its pilot the previous day. After taking off from the Honiara airport the previous late afternoon, it had been decided, after more searching, to return and continue the search the following day. This had been met with significant pushback from Paim, but as the sun set, they all realized it was pointless to continue to search and would do nothing but waste fuel. A significantly smaller airport was found on an island closer to their search radius and, as Vaz suspected, they were quickly granted access to land.

Of course we're granted access. This guy transports drugs all over the Solomon Islands. They all know him. Vaz was liking this less and less. They had been put up in a nearby hotel where he made a quick phone call back home. After only one ring, Amanda picked up the receiver. He assured her he was okay and would be home the following day. She didn't give him much pushback as she was too scared. He could tell in her tone.

"Someone wants to say good night to you," Amanda said.

"Daddy, I thought we were going shopping tonight?" Angelina said softly.

Vaz grimaced at the disappointment in his daughter's voice.

"Honey, it's a minor setback. It happens to us pilots. Some things we simply cannot avoid. But listen to me, I will be home as soon as I can. And you'll get that dress you've been wanting for so long. I love you, baby girl. Now, put your mama back on the phone," he said, finding it too difficult to continue talking to his daughter when he sensed he was in even graver danger moving forward. He didn't make much as a pilot and the pay times two would be hugely beneficial to them, but none of it was worth the danger he had been thrust into.

"Please be careful and come home soon! I can't believe I let you go with Paim of all people. The hell was I thinking?" Amanda said angrily.

Vaz was silent for a bit, knowing she was right. "Honey, I know this is tough, trust me, I do. But I must do this and then I will return home."

"He's a drug kingpin! Not dealer! He's the *man*! Top dog. And you're shuttling him around! Oh Vaz, I am so scared right now! The man is known far and wide for what he does to people that step out of line!"

"I know you're scared honey, and so am I. Just hang tight, send a few prayers my way, and I will be back in no time and this will be behind us. Santana will literally be indebted to me the rest of his life. I expect fresh fruit and vegetables and the finest meats whenever I fly out of Kokoda airport from that man!" Vaz replied lightheartedly, trying to calm his rightly anxious wife.

"You watch your back, then come home to your little girl and her very worried mama," Amanda replied shakily.

"I will. I promise," Vaz said before hanging up.

After a short and restless night's sleep, they were immediately cleared for takeoff and once airborne, continued their search for the stolen Seneca.

Sailing through the clear morning skies, Vaz continued hoping this would all be a fool's errand, and nothing would be discovered. "We're back at the coordinates, -9.28766, longitude 153.690201 latitude. Like yesterday, I'm not seeing any uncharted islands in the vicinity."

"Fly lower, I want this entire area covered within thirty miles," Paim uttered from the back.

"Sir. Mr. Paim, I truly don't think," Vaz began.

"I'm not paying you to think. I'm paying you to fly this plane. If you are unwilling to do so, I will find a more willing pilot, do you understand?" Paim shot back, glaring at his pilot.

Shut your fucking mouth, Vaz. You're gonna get yourself killed! Grimacing, Vaz nodded and continued on with their plan. With the fuel they had remaining, he would be scouring the Solomon Sea for hours, certain to find nothing. He exhaled heavily, took the plane lower and pushed on with the search.

Shambling through the forest at a distance, still gripping the handle to a briefcase of cocaine, Ed looked on as his friend and two strangers made their way forward. His foggy mind desperately tried to recall why he was such good friends with the blond man. Fleeting images would zip through his mind then vanish. His hunger and curiosity kept pushing him forward. Slowly, he advanced.

Sam and Laura rounded a particularly thick area of growth and once out the other side, realized they were no longer alone. "That looks like the village the doctor was speaking of," Sam exclaimed, pointing in the direction of a long row of shacks in the distance.

"I wonder why the church is so far from the village," Laura pondered.

"Well, there's a good chance these people were not the island's first inhabitants. I think it was the Spanish conquistadors who sailed the Solomon Sea hundreds of years ago. Maybe they stumbled upon this island and settled? The church looks older than those huts so I'm guessing there was more than one settlement of people here," Sam replied.

Laura looked at him puzzled.

"College. History class. Amazing how things you find useless in the classroom can suddenly become incredibly relevant? I've always been fascinated by the Spaniards and well, it seems like we're walking on some ancient history right here," Sam answered.

Trailing behind, Eva had fallen silent after her meltdown earlier. She felt ashamed of her actions and, at the same time, completely justified. She tried not to pay attention to the quiet chats Sam and Laura had, walking beside each other. *They're probably talking about me.*

"I vote we stay away from there," Laura said, now in a whisper. From their vantage point, it appeared to be several rows of identical, small huts lining a clearing. All appearing as though one strong storm could blow them over.

Upon closer inspection, they saw that some of the huts had indeed been knocked down. What was once a small island village was now little more than a ghost town. Except it wasn't. Moans once more could be heard in the not-so-far distance.

"Hey, look, I wonder if this is some of the Violet Laceflower my father spoke about on the recording?" Laura pointed over to a thick area of brush. Inside were long-stemmed plants with violet petals on the ends arranged in a wide circle.

Sam moved forward and picked one, inspecting it. "Looks like a..."

"Oversized purple daisy," Laura finished.

"Exactly!" Sam replied. "I mean, I'm no expert on flowers, especially those of the tropical variety, but these must be the flowers."

He handed one to Laura, who raised it up and smelled it. "Smells quite nice. Sam, turn around, I want to put a few of these into the backpack."

As she unzipped the backpack and carefully put a few picked Violet Laceflowers inside, Eva stood glaring at them several feet behind. *They don't need me for shit. Now he's giving her flowers. Might as well just drop down and fuck right in front of me.*

Off to the right, a rustling sound emanated from the thick brush. They all froze and waited, guns in hand. Eva was the first to open her mouth. "What? What is it?"

Sam quickly glared over at Eva at the sudden noise she made.

Seeing this, Eva shook her head and mumbled to herself, "Of course, Eva fucks up again."

The brush rustled again, and this time, Sam and Laura quickly aimed at the area with their pistols. A small possum waddled out from within the greenery, smelling the air, taking one look at the intruders, and headed back in the direction it came from.

Sam and Laura slowly lowered their guns, breathing a sigh of relief.

"See, you guys didn't have to go wig out. It was a porcupine or racoon or something," Eva said glibly.

"Or a possum. An oddly colored one at that," Sam answered, biting his tongue at the asinine assumption that the small animal looked like a porcupine or a racoon. He was liking Eva less and less the longer he was around her. Especially when she was risking his life at seemingly every turn. Judging by the look on Laura's face, he wasn't the only one reaching the end of his rope with her.

"Let's keep moving," Sam whispered once the backpack was zipped up, shaking off Eva's latest infraction. He moved forward, hacking away at the tall overgrowth in front of him while keeping his eyes peeled on the village off to their left less than sixty yards away.

As they crept along quietly, they saw several people shuffling through the village and picked up the pace.

Eva, however, couldn't keep her thoughts to herself. "We're not going to get out of this alive. I know it, I can feel it. We're going to die here. Shit, we are going to die!" she said as she continued glancing over at the village and the few inhabitants.

"Shh! Keep it down, Eva!" Sam whispered hoarsely, abruptly turning around and glaring at her once more.

"Don't you tell me to keep it down! You aren't my—"

The living-dead man once known as Velho reached out from behind a palm tree Eva was standing beside, grabbing a large clump of her messy, tangled blond hair and yanking her back. He opened his mouth and bit down on Eva's ear, severing it completely.

Eva let out a deafening scream of pain and terror as the zombie continued with his assault.

Sam and Laura jumped back and extended their respective revolvers, attempting to get a clean shot, but at their current angle, they risked shooting Eva.

Laura cried out, "No! Eva!"

The large zombie man bit into the side of her neck and ripped flesh and muscle away. Blood gushed forth, spilling over the front of her shirt and onto Velho who eagerly feasted on his prey.

Eva tried to scream but all that came out was gurgled and muffled cries as her life spilled from her open wounds.

"Stand back, Laura!" Sam cried out as he took aim once more. Eva had grown limp, held up solely by the zombie's arms, giving Sam a clean shot at his head. He didn't hesitate, pulling the trigger.

The top of the zombie's head exploded, sending rotting brain matter and skull flying backward, hitting the tree he had popped out from behind a minute earlier. It instantly fell over, still grasping Eva in its clutches.

"Oh no! Eva, no!" Laura wailed, running over to her fallen friend.

Coughing up blood, Eva's eyes were glazing over. She looked at Laura and tried to speak, "Laura, why did you bring...me..." then she fell silent.

Laura stroked her dead friend's hair, sobbing.

Looking toward the village, Sam bent down and whispered urgently, "Laura, we need to go, now."

"But Eva!"

Gently but firmly, Sam pulled Laura to her feet. "She's gone, and we've been spotted."

Laura wiped her eyes and looked toward the village to see five leprosy-infected corpses shambling in their direction, their mouths opening and quickly snapping shut.

She took one more look at her friend sprawled out on the ground, a pool of blood surrounding her and lifeless eyes staring up into the sky. Then, taking Sam's hand, she quickly slid back into the jungle with him.

Once they had vanished, Ed shuffled over to the corpse of Eva, looking down at her. His mind tried to compute who she was and why she was here. He saw the damage done to her throat and lifted his hand, placing it on his neck wound. He groaned as his foggy mind realized that she would soon be what he had become.

He slowly looked toward the village and saw others, but he could not smell them. *Like me, they are like me.* His feet instinctively began walking in the town's direction. His curious, yet damaged brain wanted to know more.

14
WATERFALLS
AND BOOBY TRAPS

Eva's body lay still on the ground. It was dead, but her mind wasn't. Her mind was working and soon so were her motor skills. Blinking, she saw her surroundings through the shroud of a hazy, blurry fog. Slowly standing to her feet, her mind tried to comprehend what was happening.

She looked down to the ground. Large puddles of blood spread out from where she had lay. Nearby, a large man with the top of his head missing was slumped over on the ground, unmoving. Her mind processed this along with what had happened to her. She wasn't sure of anything, even who she was or had been before.

Pain began coursing through her veins. A pain she had never known possible. It was as if fire continually flowed through every inch of her body and the only thing that would sate it was *food*.

She sniffed the air as her mouth began slowly opening and closing, teeth slamming down on each other, desperate for the one thing that could take away the pain.

Once past the dilapidated village, Sam and Laura continued on quietly. Laura no longer spoke, still stunned at the sudden and violent death of her friend. What had started out as six people making a quiet airplane ride over to the Solomon Islands had suddenly been whittled down to two that would likely not survive another day on this island of death.

"I'm sorry about Eva," Sam began.

Laura shook her head, signifying she didn't want to talk about it.

Sam persisted. "Laura, my best friend was just killed yesterday. I get it. But we can't give up, okay?"

"Oh, I'm not giving up," she said bitterly.

"I know that. But we've got to keep our wits about us. We're still alive and I'm going to do everything I can to keep us that way," Sam replied.

She glanced over at him. Even in this time of turmoil and uncertainty, Sam had indeed kept his cool. She admired that in him. It was a trait she herself had displayed countless times when Eva was being…Eva. She realized, deep down, that their chances of survival had actually just increased without her in the picture. Her mind wandered, her eyes gazing off in the distance.

Sam tried another tack at drawing Laura out of the shocked state she seemed to be in. "Laura, I don't believe in zombies, or vampires, or werewolves. But I do believe what my eyes see. The people on this island are killing us off—first Ed, now Eva—by way of biting. And I believe it's from that NR 485 serum your dad and Pedroso concocted. Pedroso seemed to just be throwing caution to the wind and hoping something would work, eventually. That's what caused this mess. If I'm right, I'd guess we're dealing with, what? Leper zombies? Fuck me, what a nightmare."

"My dad didn't invent that stuff. I have to believe that. Anyway, I can't believe I'm even saying this, but our friends. Could they come back?" Laura said shuddering at the mere thought.

"I don't know, I just don't know. Logically, no. But we're no longer living in the world of normal reality. Quite the opposite. So, maybe, I guess?" Sam answered grimly.

She was about to reply when they both heard movement up ahead through more dense forest. They froze, listening.

"Do you hear that?" Sam said looking from her to the sound of the noise.

"Yeah, it sounds like…" Laura began.

They both moved quickly forward, pushing their way past the brush to reveal an open space with a large pool of water. Above it, from a jagged rock-covered slope leading to the crater they had seen earlier, flowed a stream of glistening clear water down into the small lake below.

Sam was about to step forward, but Laura quickly put her hand on his chest, stopping him.

"What, what is it?" he said.

Pointing down, Sam saw what had given Laura pause. Twine carefully wrapped around pieces of tree branches buried in the ground circled the perimeter. Their eyes followed it from one end to another. Numerous spots surrounding the small lake had similar contraptions set up.

Sam bent down for a closer look.

"What the hell is this?" Laura said shaking her head, puzzled at the strange anomaly.

"It's just twine. There's nothing connected to it other than these sticks," he said, puzzled. "Wait a minute. Wait one damn minute."

He picked up a medium-sized stone and tossed it past the twine. It instantly sailed forward through the grass, landing with a dull thud inside a concealed hole dug out of the soil, roughly twenty feet away from the lake they had just discovered.

Both Laura and Sam quickly peered over the edge where he had just tossed the rock. Below, in a hole that appeared to be roughly seven feet deep were large bamboo spikes carved from trees stuck into the ground. Stuck on several of the roughly thirty spikes were the skeletal remains of three humans.

"Just when I thought I had seen it all," Sam began.

"This wasn't created by those things out there. This was done to keep them out," Laura said.

"Do you think this could possibly be the work of—"

"My dad." Laura finished.

Sam put his hands on his hips, surveying the area and

the numerous areas where twine was tied to branches stuck in the ground. "This place is totally booby trapped. We've got to be damn careful. Boy Scout instinct is coming back to me," he tried to joke nervously.

"Yeah, tell me something I don't know," Laura replied.

"Come on, let's try the water, I'm thirsty," Sam said, giving her a quick nudge on the arm.

"Wow, I never thought I would say this here, but that's beautiful," Laura said, making her way cautiously forward with Sam following close beside her, both guns drawn. Watching where they stepped so as not to fall into another spike-filled dugout, they made their way to the lake of clear water and peered into it. Small fish zigzagged back and forth near the top of the water while small insects buzzed just slightly above it.

Sam set his backpack on the ground beside him, crouched down, and cupping his hand to the water, scooped up some of the crystal-clear liquid, pressing it into his mouth. Swallowing his first mouthful, he glanced up at Laura. "Well? You gonna join me?"

Dropping to her knees as well, she began to drink her fill. "Hot damn, that might be the best water I've ever drunk," she exclaimed.

"Agreed," Sam said, filling his water bottle up and looking around. "I would guess this lake is around fifteen thousand square feet."

Laura looked at him slightly puzzled by this information.

He smiled and said, "Boy Scouts of America. Always trying to figure shit out, I suppose. Old habits die hard."

Instinctively, Sam glanced at his watch, checking the time and his compass.

Laura smiled and nodded then cupped water into both hands and splashed it over her head. "Ahh, does that feel good after the hell we've been through. I need a shower more than I ever have."

"You and me, both," Sam replied, glancing at her. The water had drenched her long, brown hair and in that instant, he was taken aback by her natural beauty.

She looked at him, offering a weak smile. Their eyes locked for several seconds before each looked away quickly.

Laura broke the awkward silence. "There's nothing else here. Just waterfall and lake and these...traps."

As they approached the side of the lake where the waterfalls were crashing down, Sam, careful where he was stepping, heard a snap.

Instantly, a rope wrapped around his right ankle and a tree branch above pulled back, lifting him up into the air upside down. "Whoa!" Sam yelled as Laura quickly tried to stop him from swinging back and forth in the air. Sam dropped his gun and the backpack slipped off his back, falling to the ground.

Once he was steadied, she moved his body until he faced her as he hung upside down in the air. "Hang in there, I'm gonna cut you down!"

"Please, hurry! Wait, was that a joke?"

Grinning, Laura pulled out the knife and reaching up, began to saw at the rope tied tightly to Sam's ankle. "Grab onto my legs for stability," she said as he swayed back and forth in her attempt to get a good grip on his own leg.

He took hold of her legs and felt the knife sawing through the rope right by his foot.

After a bit of cutting, the rope broke, spilling Sam onto the sand and rocks near the lake. Brushing the dirt off of him, Sam grabbed his gun and was about to stand to his feet when Laura reached her hand down to him, "Come on, cowboy, off your ass."

Smirking, Sam slapped his hand into hers and she pulled him to his feet. Grabbing the backpack from the ground, he slung it once more over his shoulder. "This place is crawling with booby traps. And that means two things. One, there's someone else here that's human, or *still alive,* I should say. And two, that person wants to keep those things away from this particular area. But I don't see anything that could constitute a hideout. Do you?"

"My dad and I used to make booby traps when I was a kid," Laura said, thinking back to her childhood. "I loved it. The crazy things we came up with on the weekends when he wasn't at work. Just me and him, out in the backyard. We built stuff like this! Granted, we weren't putting spikes in holes, but this contraption here that you were just hanging upside down in? We did this!"

"Okay, so maybe your dad *is* alive on this island. But where?"

Laura nodded slowly, thinking. "Sure as hell isn't here. I mean, I suppose this is to keep those things away from what is likely the only water source here on the island. Don't want them infecting the water. It's what I would do if I were trapped here for an extended period of time."

They stood in silence, continuing to look around the area. "Hey, look, more of those Violet Laceflowers!" Laura said, pointing to several patches of thick brush with several of the long, beautiful flowers growing out of them.

"So, there's more than just one particular area where they grow. Interesting. I've never seen a flower quite like them," Sam said, admiring them.

Behind them, they heard movement. Spinning around, another grotesque monstrosity that had at one time been human shuffled through the brush and stopped, its white eyes blankly looking forward.

Sam and Laura raised their revolvers.

"Wait, hold your fire, Laura, look at it."

They continued watching the new arrival. A scrawny woman, completely naked but devoid of all feminine attributes. Sores covered nearly all of her exposed, rotting flesh. Small patches of long hair were all that remained. Her stomach was so thin her ribs were exposed. She was literally a walking skeleton draped with rotting flesh.

She moaned lightly and bit the air with what teeth were left in her mouth.

"Look, I think she smells us!" Sam said pointing at the zombie's facial twitches.

The pathetic display of bones and leathery, dried skin began shuffling forward, close to where Sam and Laura had initially discovered the concealed pit with bamboo spikes.

"Come on, just a little closer, come on," Sam said in a whisper, then shook the tall plant they were standing beside to draw its attention.

"What are you doing? We don't want that thing attacking us!" Laura whispered loudly.

"Wait, wait, I feel like this one can sense danger. Look, it's hesitating," Sam replied.

They both continued watching to see what the woman would do next.

The living-dead being stared aimlessly around at the noise while sniffing the air, then began moving forward toward their location. Snagging her foot in the twine, the zombified woman fell forward, crashing down into the pit with a thud.

Laura and Sam moved to the open pit to see the being inside that had ceased moaning.

"That thing was coming after its mealtime—us," Sam said with a shudder.

They fell silent as Laura looked back toward the waterfalls. "I have an idea. That backpack is waterproof, right?"

Puzzled by the question, Sam replied, "Yeah. It is. Why?"

"Because, unlike yesterday, trudging through the ocean and then the rain, I would like to keep my clothes and shoes dry this time." She began undressing, taking off her shoes and socks, then peeling off her shirt and tight pants, holding them out for Sam.

"Um, okay," Sam said, feeling his face grow flush, trying to not look at Laura in nothing more than her pink bra and underwear. He took the pants and shirt from her, carefully putting them into the backpack.

"You stay here and keep a lookout, got it?" she said,

handing him the knife along with the doctor's revolver.

"So, you're just going for a swim, huh?" he replied, stuffing gun into the backpack and sheathing the knife at his side.

"I'm going on a hunch. If I'm wrong, at least I got rinsed off. If I'm right…" Laura said, staring at the waterfalls.

"If you're right?" Sam asked.

"Then you'll need to take a swim yourself," Laura turned and leapt into the water.

"Laura, you are one interesting person," Sam muttered to himself, watching her swim toward the waterfalls.

The water felt wonderful against her bare skin as she swam. Taking a deep breath, she dipped under the water and opened her eyes. Even in a place as horror filled as this island, there was still beauty to be seen. Small tropical fish darted back and forth, away from her as she passed them. The bottom of the lake which she guessed was ten to fifteen feet deep, appeared to consist of smooth rocks and sand. *No zombies in here* she thought as she glided through the cool, refreshing water on her way to the falls.

When was the last time I undressed in front of a man? Her sparse love life consisted of only a few brief runs, all of which were forgettable—the relationships themselves as well as under the covers. Laura hadn't met any man, ever, that clearly *got* her. Her tomboy personality, her interests, or her quirks. Most of the men she met were of the Eva variety, out for one thing and one thing only. Something she despised.

With everything they'd been through together, undressing as casually as she had in front of Sam felt good.

The roughly hundred-foot swim didn't take long, and once at the splashing waterfalls, she glanced back and saw Sam standing by the edge of the lake. He gave her a brief wave to which she smiled and nodded in return. Taking a deep breath, she sank down into the water and began swimming through. She immediately was pushed down by the torrents of water but continued on. Soon it subsided and she was behind the waterfalls.

When she felt the pressure of the water subside, she shot up out of the water and wiped her wet face off, taking in her new surroundings. It was relatively dark but sunlight from beyond the falling water shone through and lit up the immediate area.

"I was right, a cave," Laura said, looking behind her. She swam over to the ledge of the rocks and pulled herself up and out of the water in what appeared to be a dome-shaped, hollowed-out rock formation behind the falls. Once out of the water, she shook herself off. Taking a few steps, she peered into the oblong hole directly behind her against the dome rock wall but couldn't make out much, other than seeing that it led somewhere. And she was going to find out where, with Sam.

She turned back toward the waterfalls and dove into the water once more, quickly swimming under the pounding pressure of the falls before coming out the other side. She popped her head up out of the water, looking in Sam's direction.

"What the hell," Laura uttered, looking around the lake.

Sam was nowhere to be seen.

15
TUNNEL TRAVEL

"We're going to need to refuel again soon if you want to keep searching this far from the mainland. We've got about half a tank remaining," Vaz said to his passengers.

"Keep going. I said thirty miles search radius and I meant it," Paim replied from the back.

"Yes, sir," Vaz replied rolling his eyes and biting his bottom lip while not once glancing back. He had grown beyond tired of this charade. The Turbo Seneca was almost certainly at the bottom of the Solomon Sea along with his precious drugs. And more importantly, innocent victims that had inadvertently hitched a ride on the doomed plane the previous day.

Pulling left on the yoke, the Cessna veered south for another pass over the sea Vaz was sure they had flown over previously. *This is your dime, I suppose, but why do I feel like it's on me to find this damn plane or it's my ass?* He missed his wife and daughter more with each passing minute, replaying the phone call from the previous night. Stuck on a fool's errand circling the Solomon Sea looking for something that likely wasn't there.

He decided to keep pulling the plane farther south. It was pointless covering ground previously flown over. *Screw it, they'll never know.* It was usually storm-riddled over this part of the ocean but today there were rare clear skies. *Give it a try, Vaz.*

The plane continued pulling to the left until Vaz was satisfied he was out of the immediate search area that, so far, had turned up nothing but miles of ocean. *Come on damnit, let there be something out here! Wreckage or floating debris, please God!* He took a deep breath, exhaling and stretching his arms.

"Is this boring you, Mr. Vaz?" came a sharp voice from the rear.

Glancing back at his passengers, he shook his head. "Nope, just doing my job. Hoping to find this missing plane for you then go home to my wife and kid. Been flying for a while now."

Paim leaned forward in his seat and ran his hands through his black hair. "Yes, you have. And I personally thank you. However, I cannot stress enough the amount of cocaine this former employee of mind stole from me. I do not take failure well and I do not intend to fail in finding my property, my very expensive property that has already been purchased and was ready for shipment. I need you to accomplish this. Do not *fail* me, understand?"

Vaz stared at him, then at the unblinking, unmoving men around him. He was more and more convinced that if he didn't locate this damn plane, he was going to be killed. Regardless of whether the plane was at the bottom of the ocean or all the way to Australian by now.

Vaz nodded slightly. Gritting his teeth, he pushed on, hoping against all hope this new section of sea might produce results even if it was a needle in a haystack's chance in hell of finding his drug lord's precious stash of dope.

Laura slowly tread water near the waterfalls. Absolute, unrelenting dread was creeping through her suddenly cold body. She felt vulnerable and utterly alone, as if she were the only *living* person left on planet earth. She contemplated shouting out but didn't think that wise.

She was about to swim forward to where she had last seen Sam when she saw something floating in the water near the shore. It was a backpack, Sam's backpack. "Oh Lord, no, please God, not him!" Laura felt herself begin to panic, her eyes darting back and forth, searching for life.

The backpack began moving toward her when it should have been moving away from the pressure of the waterfalls. From behind the floating backpack, she saw Sam's head peeking out. She put her hands to her mouth to avoid screaming out loud. Her emotions were all over the place as she felt a lump form in her throat.

He had nearly reached her. Her fear that had turned to

happiness was now devolving into anger. Glaring at him, she turned and dove under the water back toward the waterfall. Once more, she felt the rush of the pounding water crash down as she swam under them. Once she had pushed past, she came up for air in the hollowed-out cave inside the waterfalls and pulled herself up onto the ledge.

A minute later, Sam's backpack popped up out of the water along with him. He looked around, locking eyes with Laura and floating over to where she now stood. He tossed the backpack up beside her then began pulling himself up.

Reaching down, Laura grabbed his hand, yanking him up hard out of the water. As soon as he stood to his feet, he wiped his wet face off. He had stripped down as well, only wearing a pair of tight boxer briefs.

"Whew, I don't think I've ever been in a lake that felt that good!"

Laura briefly glanced at Sam's nearly chiseled body. He was trim yet his body was toned and muscular. She raised her hands and pushed him slightly backward. "What the *hell* were you thinking out there? Didn't I tell you to wait? I couldn't find you and all I saw was your backpack floating in the water! I thought one of those things got you and I was now completely alone! Damn you, Sam!"

Sam instantly saw how shaken she was, and his demeanor quickly changed. "I'm sorry. I heard movement in the brush and figured it was another one of those zombies. I didn't want to fire the revolver so I opted to jump in and join you before you came back to get me."

Laura stood with her hands on her hips, glaring at him.

Her face slowly relaxed. "I'm still trying to come to grips with everything that we've been through. Losing you next is not something I think I can deal with, okay?"

Bending down, Sam picked up the backpack, opened it and pulled out clothes. "Here, I still have a few clothes left. A spare tank top. I don't think my pants will fit you but at least it's a fresh shirt. Take it." He smiled warmly and handed them to her.

She took them, their hands touching for a second, and Laura instantly felt unmistakably attracted to the man standing in front of her. Quickly, she turned away from him and began dressing.

Sam pulled out his own clothes and did the same. He slipped on his shoes and turned at the same time Laura was turning. They nearly bumped into each other, but Laura stopped short of touching his chest, now in his own tight tank top.

"Looks like it fits," he said, glancing at his tank top she now wore.

"It does, and thanks," Laura she said shyly, and gave him a brief smile.

They peered into the cave behind them. "Where do you think it leads?" Sam asked curiously, trying to get a better look into the darkness.

"I don't know but there's only one way to find out. Hand me the backpack?" Laura said, reaching for the backpack.

Sam handed it over and watched as she unzipped it and dug through it. "The candle!" he exclaimed as she pulled out the lone candle they had taken from the church earlier.

She dug through the backpack a bit more until producing the lighter she had found as well. "We'd be screwed without your waterproof backpack, you know that, right?"

"Ed thought it was a waste of money back when I bought it. Said why would I ever get my backpack wet? And if so, a little rain never hurt anyone. Well, I beg to differ," Sam said, chuckling and thinking back to his friend.

"Come on, let's shed a bit of light on the situation," Laura said, making sure she was back far enough from the falls to avoid any water droplets hitting the candle. With a few clicks of the lighter, a flame popped out and she held it to the wick.

Slowly the candle's flame cast a dim light. Laura put the lighter back into the backpack and held the candle toward the open cave entrance.

Sam stood close beside her peering inside. "Looks like it heads up. Shall we?" He glanced at his compass as he drew his gun and handed Laura her own.

Laura moved forward as Sam slung his backpack over his shoulder and walked beside her.

Outside the waterfalls, past the lake and the beach, a lone figure made her way forward slowly. She sniffed the air while biting at it.

Something, there is something nearby and whatever it is, it will sate this gnawing, insatiable appetite. I must find it. That is all that matters.

Her mind had brief glimpses of things from her past

life. When she was still human. A tan, brown-haired person, slightly taller than she was, arguing with her. Something about not going along on a trip. *"You can't go along! It's too dangerous and it's simply not your thing! I need to do this!"*

Eva stared blankly up into the sky. More brief glimpses of an airplane. Maybe she was in it? She couldn't be sure. It was crashing into the water. Swimming. A shark. A dangerous man. Then her mind went foggy as her remaining blood, stagnant inside her body, once more burned. She groaned at the torture of it, coupled with utter despair. Whatever this new life was, it was that of hopelessness. No heaven, no hell. Just a pain that could only be stopped by feeding.

She looked toward the waterfalls and smelled the air. Her prey had stood here and now it was somewhere in the water. Eva surveyed the ground around her. Her still active mind peered into the open hole in front of her. She shuffled over to it and looked down. Inside she saw a figure squirming on the ground, several sharp objects rammed through its chest and neck.

Eva tilted her head causing blood to seep out of the wound inflicted earlier. *Traps, made to stop me. To stop us. Be careful where you step*, the foggy recesses of her mind warned her.

Eva looked around at the pond with water rushing into it from the crater above, then back down to the creature writhing in the small pit with bamboo spikes rammed through it.

I cannot smell this person. This person is like me, and it is in pain. The people that did this to her are what I smell, they will not only sate my appetite, but they must pay for what has happened here. Her still dying brain was able to process enough of her former life for her to come up with her own interpretation of what she saw around her. It was foggy and hazy inside her damaged mind, but it still functioned on a basic, primal level.

She shuffled away from the squirming body in the spike-laden pit. Back toward the waterfalls she stopped. Behind her came moans. Eva slowly turned, her eyes making out several new shapes, all in various states of decay. They moved forward toward her. One of them, a small child, blindly fell forward into another unmarked pit that had been covered by large palm tree leaves to disguise its whereabouts. The child's groaning instantly ceased. The walking corpses beside it paid it no attention, continuing on to the edge of the lake.

Eva, standing in the sand, turned her attention back to the waterfalls, her mouth in a constant state of biting while her nose sniffed the air.

Her dulled mind remembered water. *To drink, to bathe, to swim. Move forward.* She slowly moved her arms and legs haphazardly. Behind her, the small group of living-dead lepers blindly followed suit.

Sam and Laura made their way through the tunnel with the candle in front of them. Even with the dim light, they could see the place had likely been here long before any humans inhabited the island.

It was deathly quiet inside the cave. Dripping water

running down the walls was the only sound they heard along with their steps.

"How far do you think this goes?" Laura asked, moving the candle slowly back and forth making sure they were careful where they stepped.

"It's not getting any narrower, so that's good. But we're a long damn way from the beach and the crashed plane by now. Might be bigger than we think."

Side by side, their arms touching, both felt more and more in need of the other to get through the ordeal they found themselves in.

"Do you think your dad really found the cure for brain cancer in this place?" Sam asked.

Laura replied after thinking on this for a bit, "If there is even the slightest possibility, yes. He was, is, one determined man. So determined that he left Mama and me behind to either find the cure or die trying."

"How long did the doctors give him?" Sam pressed.

"Two years, at the most. At least, that's what we were told two years ago before he left us," Laura replied sadly. "I still cannot believe my father abandoned us. He was such a smart man, a kind man. We tried to have him stay but one morning, he was gone. He left a letter behind saying how he didn't want us to see him suffer and that there may be a cure for him but it would require traveling. He communicated for a time from Papua New Guinea and then later, the Solomon Islands until all communication with him was lost. He never lost hope though, that's my dad."

"Well, someone set those traps out there," Sam said,

adding, "I'm of the mindset that you are likely correct. Your father is here somewhere…alive."

"Do you believe in fate? That we crashed on an island in the middle of the damn ocean, and my father who took off two years ago is *here?*"

Sam glanced at her. "I honestly don't know. Regardless, here we are. I swear, we make it off this infernal island, first thing I'm doing is going to the nearest parish I can find and doing some much-needed penance."

They both chuckled lightly.

"I think I gave up believing in any higher being when my dad was given his death sentence. Being here hasn't changed my mindset either. What kind of God would give people a virus like this?"

Sam thought on this for a minute before responding. "Yeah, those random acts of God can really stick it in and twist, can't they? All I know is, I'm saying my Hail Mary's. Lots of 'em. If there is a God, I'm not about to piss him off any more than I already have."

Laura smiled as they continued making their way cautiously onward.

"So, you went to college for…?" Sam asked.

Nodding, Laura replied, "University of Texas, San Antonio. I wanted to follow in my father's footsteps. Dropped out though, after two years. After everything that's happened with my father, I no longer wanted to pursue that line of work. But that chapter of my life isn't over yet. I don't know, you could say I'm a lost soul looking for my purpose. Been like that since…"

"Since your father went missing?"

"Yes, after communications stopped completely, I began contacting the local law enforcement, hospitals, hotels, anyone I could think of to try to locate him. The only bread crumb I was able to latch onto was an island I was told was not on any map named la Isla de Sebria. Divine providence and here we are, for better or worse."

"We're going to find your dad, or at least what happened to him."

Laura glanced at him and nodded. "Thanks for being, hmm," she thought for a bit. "Thanks for being decent."

"Hey, you don't know me *that* well yet. I could end up being a complete basket case. Guess you'll have to wait and see."

Laura let out a small chuckle. She thought of Eva, how she had so desperately not wanted her to come along, but Eva's parents and her mother insisted. And now she was dead. How would she tell Eva's parents of the tragedy that befell their daughter if and when she made it back to Texas? *Sorry, Mr. and Mrs. Barnes, I took your daughter along on a search for my own father through Papua New Guinea, our plane crashed on an island inhabited by leper zombies and she got eaten.*

She shook the thought from her mind, focusing on the task at hand. "Hey, up ahead! I think I see sunlight!" Laura exclaimed.

"I see it too!" Sam replied, squinting.

Carefully, they picked up the pace, moving forward toward what they hoped was the exit.

Water crashed down inside the small dome-shaped interior directly behind the waterfalls as Eva breached the water. Bobbing in the water lifelessly, water running off her face, her nose instantly picked up the scent of life nearby.

Struggling out of the water, she crawled onto the rocks, her limited eyesight even worse inside this dimly lit area. Bringing her hands to her wet face, she wiped the water away before feeling down to the large open hole on her throat.

Vague memories populated her mind about a large man biting into her flesh and taking her life. Shallow memories then surfaced of the men who had their way with her, sometimes more than one at a time, ripping her clothes off, biting her, forcing their tongues and other things inside her roughly. Used and then tossed aside and forgotten, another conquest by men that took advantage of her naivety. Those painful, demeaning times had been her life, before the new Eva. With newfound determination, she followed the scent leading to an opening behind the water she had floated through.

Behind her, several other and far more rotten corpses floated forward. Blindly following their new leader across the pond, they now lost limbs from the immense pressure of traversing under a waterfall. The first and largest of the group attempted to climb out of the water but its wrist snapped. Still attempting to crawl onto the ledge, it struggled but was unable to climb. Four more zombified corpses used him to pull themselves up, over his back and onto solid ground.

Four made it up, then moved toward the woman whose

human scent they could pick up slightly, following after her into the cave, their mouths snapping hungrily.

16
THE CRATER HIDEOUT

The Cessna Citation flew low, its passengers peering out from their respective windows. In the distance, storm clouds were approaching while the vastness of the ocean lay below. Vaz considered recommending a refuel but thought better of it. The longer they were in the air, the further agitated Paim seemed to get. The meager food and drink on board was dwindling and that was likely adding to his shortness.

After several more minutes passed, Vaz could wait no longer. They had to turn back or risk ditching the plane in the ocean if they continued on with this fiasco. He cleared his throat, dreading the rage from Paim when he announced his intentions.

"Mr. Paim," Vaz began, then stopped, staring out the

windshield. He blinked. "It looks as though a storm is approaching from the west. There are islands up ahead, I'm going to make a pass and check them out. If nothing turns up..." He paused, then decided to keep his mouth shut after no response from his boss came back.

Pushing forward on the steering yoke, the plane dipped down. As they got closer to the remote island, something else caught Vaz's eye. Something shiny. The closer the plane got, the more it became apparent that whatever was down there was not a part of the island.

"Gentlemen, I can't believe I'm saying this, but we may have something here. I'm going to fly over it here in a few seconds."

"That's my plane," Paim said, though they were still too far away to identify it.

Vaz held his tongue and continued on. The Cessna zipped by the shiny object in the water near the beach. "This island is undocumented; it doesn't show up on any maps that I'm aware of. Something must have smashed into it a long time ago judging by that crater down there."

"Can you land on the beach?" Paim shot back quickly, uninterested in craters and documented islands.

Surprised they had actually found the missing plane, Vaz stuttered, "Um, yeah, yes, sir. I suppose we could, judging by the length of that beach. If your briefcases are still on that plane down there, someone is going to have to do some swimming. But that storm..."

"You're the pilot, land and we'll take care of everything else! Don't concern yourself with the storm," Paim replied coldly, still peering out his window at the downed Seneca 8088N.

How was this guy so damn sure he was going to find something and not care about a storm creeping their way? *I guess that's why he's top dog. He's just that damn confident,* Vaz thought. He was just glad they found something that could put this mission to rest. He checked his fuel. They were cutting it close. With perfect conditions, they would make it back to the nearest airport on fumes.

"Damnit, damnit all to hell," Vaz muttered as he circled around and lowered the landing gear.

Sam and Laura reached the end of the tunnel and came out of the hole they had traversed, both guns drawn as sunlight hit their eyes. Laura squinted around at her new surroundings.

"What is this place? It's beautiful!" Sam said, turning around and taking it all in.

Surrounding them was lush vegetation and numerous Violet Laceflower plants. Water trickled above the hollowed-out crater they found themselves inside.

"That water must lead to the waterfalls we swam under!" Laura exclaimed, pointing up at the top rim of the wide crater that encircled it and likely held water. She continued to stare at the natural beauty around them.

"Well, we definitely climbed in elevation going through that tunnel. I'm guessing this place must be around seventy-five feet up to the rim, possibly more? Just look at this lush plant life!" Sam said as he walked through the vegetation.

Numerous fruit trees in various colors and sizes filled the area, most of which looked oddly foreign.

"Seeing this fruit is reminding me that we need to get some food in us," Laura said, picking a pineapple off of a nearby plant.

Sam pulled out his knife and she held the pineapple out for him as he sliced into it, causing pineapple juice to instantly ooze out. The sweet smell of the ripened fruit hit their noses at the same time.

"Oh wow, I've never smelled any fruit that good!" Laura exclaimed as Sam cut a chunk out, handing it to her. She quickly took and biting into it, closed her eyes. "That is without a doubt the best pineapple I've ever tasted!"

"I'd like to take your word for it, but I'll have to see for myself." He held the pineapple in one hand and the knife in the other. Seeing his hands full, Laura took the remaining piece she had and held it to his mouth. He took it and she smiled softly.

"Yeah, hot damn, that's delicious," Sam replied.

"I know it is. I've been tending them for a year now," came a voice behind them.

They both quickly turned, Sam dropping the pineapple to the ground and quickly drawing his revolver.

A figure walked out from behind the thick vegetation.

"Dad," Laura whispered.

"Laura? My dear Laura, is that you?" The frail bearded man with long stringy, greying hair cautiously approached the new arrivals.

William Joyner stopped in front of Sam and Laura.

"You…" he stammered, "You're here!"

Newly formed tears dripped from Laura's eyes, seeing her dad for the first time in over two years.

"Laura, it really is you!" William said, extending his arms.

Laura rushed forward, wrapping her arms tightly around her dear father.

William put his arms around his daughter, squeezing hard, then he pulled her back, looking into her wet eyes. "I am sure you have questions, my dear, Laura, as do I."

"Papa, I have literally spent the past two years trying to track you down! Why, Dad? Why all of…this?" Laura replied, tears continuing to run down her face. She wiped them off sadly, not breaking eye contact.

"I will answer all questions, but first, who are you?" The thin, bearded man looked from his daughter over to the man standing beside her.

Sam slowly extended his hand. "Name is Sam Berry. From Burbank, California."

"Both of you were in the plane that went down, I assume. I saw it fall from the sky yesterday shortly after that major storm passed by," William replied, taking Sam's hand and shaking it.

Sam could tell quickly that the man didn't have much meat on his bones. Yet, for someone with brain cancer, he looked rather healthy.

Glancing at Laura, who was still reeling at seeing her father again after so long, William continued, "Come, follow me. I will show you my home and get you something to eat and drink. I would very much like to hear about the plane that crashed."

He turned to walk away but Laura spoke up. "What happened to the father that played with me in the back yard? Making bobby traps, going on adventures with his only daughter? Did that man die when he got his news from the doctor back in Texas?"

William stopped but didn't turn around. Sighing, he replied softly, "I understand your anger and frustration but please, come to my home and I will explain."

"Dad, I've been watching my mother die a little more each day not knowing what happened to her husband! You left us and I vowed that no matter what, I was going to find you and ask you straight to your face why you couldn't have included us in this. We spoke several times after you left, then no more contact! I made countless phone calls, wrote countless letters to the locals, all to try to find you! All I knew about was this supposed doctor you found, about a potential cure. That doctor, by the way, is back in that church we slept in last night. A rotten corpse!"

William sighed heavily. "That would explain the revolver. I have not been back to that church in a long time. I have not ventured past the waterfalls in nearly a year. It is why I did not check for survivors of the plane crash."

He turned back to face Sam and Laura once more. "I have indeed found the cure for brain cancer. It works! But the price for this is my enslavement to this island. There is no way off and no way to communicate with the outside world. The things out there, I...I cannot believe you both made it this far. Anyway, please, come with me?" His eyes pleaded with his daughter.

Laura fell silent, feeling Sam's eyes on her. She glanced over at him.

Sam gently put his hand on her shoulder. This small act of kindness calmed her as together, they followed Laura's estranged father deeper into the vegetation-filled crater.

As they walked, several species of tropical birds took flight from the thick tree cover. Laura looked up, watching the multi-colored animals flapping their wings. It was a beautiful sight and one that was much welcome in a place like this filled with the living dead.

Sam and Laura followed William through the clearing. Inside it, against the back of the crater, was a hut made from bamboo shoots and supplies that likely had come from the church. Sam surmised that the structure itself was slightly over four hundred square feet and, while makeshift, was likely sturdy enough to withstand tropical storms that passed through the island due to its secure proximity to the far crater wall.

Laura eyed the structure as they walked to its front entrance made of bamboo tied snugly together. The roof had several peculiar squares on it, reflecting the sun's light. William opened the door and motioned for them to enter.

Laura walked through first, not looking at her father, while Sam glanced at the old man and gave a friendly nod of thanks.

Inside the house was a bed against the corner connected to a small kitchen with shelving, a chair made of animal fur and bamboo, and what appeared to be a workstation complete with desk and another homemade chair.

Closing the door behind him, William headed to the kitchen area and took out several colorful fruits and a plate of what appeared to be cured meat. "Not sure exactly what this species of fruit is, but it's sweet and delicious. Also, I've become quite good at curing meats here. This particular meat is what is known as Golden Ringtail Possum."

Not hesitating, Sam hungrily took some and began eating. "Thank you, Mr. Joyner. This is quite good."

"William, just William."

Sam nodded his understanding politely.

William offered a bit to his daughter who declined with a quick shake of the head. "So, you must be wondering how I've lived here this long…" he began.

"I'm wondering why you left us. That's what I'm wondering and that's the reason I traveled around the world to find my answer. And here it is, sitting in a little shack inside a crater on an island populated by zombies. Was it worth it?" Laura said fighting back her frustration and resentment for a man she deeply loved and had missed for years now.

William sighed again. "I have a lot of explaining to do, I know. Laura, how do I say this? I was dying, and I saw an opportunity to possibly be cured and deliver that cure to the whole world! I knew your mother wouldn't let me part ways. So, I left and spared you both the indignity of watching me wither away to nothing. Little did I know that there is a cure for this debilitating disease, and it only grows on this island."

Finishing up the meat, Sam looked around the small

room this man had called home for the past year. Reaching into his backpack, Sam pulled out the few notebooks he had taken from the church. "There is a lot of damning stuff in here, sir. Lots of experimenting on these people without their knowing what was really going on. Using them as guinea pigs."

"And that is where Dr. Pedroso and I parted ways on our ideology. Eventually, it drove me out of the church. When I met the man, he had promised me a cure for my disease was to be found on this island. Well, he was right about that, there is a cure for brain cancer, and it is here and found within the plant named Violet Laceflower—mixed with the right amount of NR 485, Dr. Pedroso's serum."

William took a gulp of water before continuing, shaking his head as he came to grips with actual humans standing in front of him, one of which was his dear, sweet daughter. "Forgive me, I haven't spoken to anyone in so long, I am trying to compose myself here."

"Take your time," Sam said compassionately, seeing the man struggling.

"Thank you, Sam. So, our disagreements over how to handle the people here stricken with leprosy lasted night and day. I didn't want them used as guinea pigs and he felt that they would die off anyway, even though it was an incredibly slow process. Actually, stunningly slow, they should have all died off from their leprosy many years ago, before the infection took over. And they would have, until a full syringe of NR 485 was inadvertently injected into one of them. It accentuated the disease and made what they have even more contagious by way of saliva."

"How are they still alive? This zombie virus happened a year ago?" Sam asked, glancing at Laura who kept her eyes on her father, studying him.

"It spread, quickly. These people were dying, banished to the sea roughly ten years earlier by their peers on the Solomon Islands to die of an incurable, very rare form of leprosy. They luckily found this island and claimed it as their new home. Then, we showed up and it went to hell. Once infected with Dr. Pedroso's high-dosed serum, they died and came back. Or hell, maybe they didn't even die at all. But they changed from docile to deadly. Still rotting from the leprosy but also death rot. Their brain activity remains and feeds their senses, keeps them going. Speeds up their metabolism, as well. Once you're bit, forget about it…" He shook his head sadly.

"Yeah, but, with nothing to eat, won't they eventually shrivel up to nothing? The ones we've seen are disgusting," Sam continued.

"The wildlife here on the island, that's one theory as to how they're still shambling on," William said. "But I think it's something else, something about this island and these flowers. This crater you're standing in and the tunnel you came through to get here. Something from up there slammed into this island, likely hundreds of thousands of years ago. I think some of this strange vegetation resulted from it, these flowers included. Also, the storms. You obviously noticed that storm? Well, they are frequent and range in intensity. It's as if this island doesn't want to be found out here. Or, maybe, whatever smashed into it caused something in the atmosphere too, I don't know, severe weather patterns, perhaps…"

Laura chimed in, "Up there? You mean, outer space?"

Looking at his daughter, he nodded. "It is why I still live and those things out there haven't rotted to nothing. It extends life. Dr. Pedroso didn't buy it but I've done the research. The plant life, especially inside this crater, doesn't exist in this exact form anywhere else. Sure, it spreads out into the rest of the island, but it is primarily concentrated here."

"And the Violet Laceflower and NR 485 serum, how did you find the right consistency? Why not use it on those things out there?" Sam asked.

William answered, "You want to go out and get close to one of them? Once you're bit, that's it. You're infected. I've had a lot of time. I found this place a long time ago when visiting the village I'm guessing you passed. Back before they were infected with Pedroso's mistaken dose. I perfected the right consistency of flowers that I grind up into powder and a single drop of the NR 485 serum. Injecting into me and living inside this crater has quite literally saved my life. I'll die of old age before the NR 485 runs out. I took it from the church. This crater and the flowers that are ground up and mixed with the serum are my life, I'm afraid to say. Mother Nature combined with man-made medicine has created a true cure for brain tumors. Too bad it won't be shared with the rest of the world."

"Why stay here? If that's the case, Dad, why not leave!" Laura exclaimed, trying to keep her cool.

"Get back how?" William asked.

"By boat! There's a boat here, right? The recording said that…" Laura started.

William shook his head. "Not anymore there isn't. As soon as the new, manmade virus spread, those not infected on the initial wave made their way to the boat we traveled in on. They were pursued by family, friends, loved ones. When they got to the boat I can only surmise that the infected got to them, turned them, and then made sure to destroy the boat, ensuring that those who had made their miserable lives even worse would never leave the island. That's how I pieced it together, anyway, once I surveyed the damage later. Now, here I am, the lone survivor. Laura, you have to believe me, I think about you and your mother every single day. I have missed you both more than I can express."

Laura pulled out the letter from her father from her front pocket and held it tightly. William glanced at it, saw what it was, and had to choke back tears.

"No boat? So, we're stuck here?" Sam said incredulously.

William answered, "It would seem that way. This island isn't on the main flight path and is still undiscovered. Needle in a haystack, especially with those storms that constantly swirl by. There are a lot of islands like this one scattered throughout the Solomon Sea. It's small enough that no one would think to chart it. I've heard planes on occasion fly far overhead when the weather is cooperating, but what can I do? With those things out there I've decided to stick close to this crater. Only going out to hunt for wild game on occasion. And I've booby trapped the area leading into it."

Laura, arms crossed, looked at the floor, saddened at the

entire situation. Angry at a God that allowed her dear father to be diagnosed with incurable brain cancer and the poor people of this island that had been manipulated in the name of science. She felt conflicted, her emotions running high.

Seeing her ruminating, Sam responded, "Yes, the bamboo spiked holes and the trip wires. I got hung up in one, actually. Laura helped me out. You did all that by yourself?"

William looked from his daughter over to Sam. "Yes, I did. I'm stuck here and my main goal is to keep those things away. They've actually learned over time that the lake spells doom. I've killed enough of them that they seem to stay away. Occasionally, one will get too close and fall into one of my traps. You see, when they all turned, they were already heavily diseased. I don't know how this disease works on healthy humans. My only experience is with the lepers, although I know I have seen my old assistant, Luiz Velho near the village. He was bitten and is one of them."

Sam looked around at the small space once again. "I see you have some equipment over there. A microscope and, is that a lamp?"

William glanced at the items in question. "Ah, yes, I have found a way to power several items taken when I abandoned Dr. Pedroso. It wasn't easy getting them up here but there is a way to get back and forth without going through the waterfalls as you both have. Solar power is the way of the future and with small pieces of silicon and glass casing, I was able to create my own power source to continue my research here. It's not much, but it's made life here slightly more bearable."

Sam and Laura looked at one another, trying to take in the magnitude of what they had stumbled upon here in this place. Her father. A cure for brain cancer. Meteors. Zombies. It was all too much to process, so they remained quiet for a few moments.

"I assumed whoever was onboard your plane perished?" William asked, trying to move the subject to more familiar ground.

"Remember Eva? Eva Barnes?" Laura said sadly.

"Yes, I do. I never much liked her, but you were old enough to make your own friends. Why? She wasn't on that plane, was she?" William said with concern.

"The pilot, copilot, Sam's friend and Eva. All dead," Laura said, getting angry. She squeezed the letter from her father in her hand.

Sighing heavily, William shook his head in sadness. "I'm sorry, I'm sorry that you came all this way trying to find me, costing the lives of your friends and pilots."

"The pilots were drug runners, so no loss there," Sam added.

"And your friend?" William pressed.

"Ed, his name was Edward Brandt. He was mortally wounded in the crash and died on the beach. Then one of those things bit him—we killed it, I think, or I should say, I hope. Then buried his body."

William's demeanor changed. His expression suddenly turned deadly serious. "Laura, what of Eva? What happened to her?"

Laura saw the sudden change to intense concern. "She

was bit by one of them. It killed her, she's back close to the village. In fact, the one that killed her didn't look quite as rotted as the others we've encountered. From my limited knowledge of leprosy in medical school, that is."

"Oh, Lord. You left her there? And the man? On the beach, you buried him?" William asked hurriedly.

"Yes," Laura and Sam said at nearly the same time.

"And the pilot, he was killed on the beach, we think," Sam added.

"They will all come back because they are not truly dead."

Sam and Laura looked at each other worriedly before Sam spoke. "Gunshot to the head, that's the death blow to those things, isn't it? I got one on the beach. Shot it in the shoulder and it wasn't fazed. I mean, this woman was barely even a rotted corpse, but she kept going. Until I shot her in the head, then she dropped instantly," Sam said grimly, thinking back to their beach encounter.

"You would be correct. Blunt force to the brain, which is essentially what is keeping them going," William nodded.

Laura walked over to William's workstation and picked up a vial of clear liquid marked NR 485. She inspected it then opened the letter in her hand, turned to face her father, cleared her throat and read it out loud.

After a few moments of silence, while Laura folded the letter back up and put it in her pocket, William spoke. "I can't believe you traveled this far to find me, Laura." Tears dripped freely from his eyes.

"I love you, Dad. You've always been my best friend,

and you up and left. And I needed to find you. I would have found a way to travel to the moon if I knew that's where you had run off to," Laura replied sadly.

"My dear Laura. My dear sweet…"

He fell silent. Standing up, he gently walked over to Laura and wrapped his arms around her. She instantly leaned into him as hot tears streamed down her cheeks. She couldn't stay angry at him, no matter how hard she tried. They stood in silence, letting their full emotions run their course.

Sam remained silent. Through the hell they had thus far endured, it was nice to see such a shared love and bond between these two kindhearted people. In this instant, he was glad they hadn't barreled onward to the beach, instead focusing on finding her father who might be their only hope of surviving.

Suddenly, a hum could be heard from outside. Laura and her father broke their embrace instantly, wiping their eyes. They looked at one another, then, one by one, quickly ran out of William's house.

Outside, they peered up into the sky as a small plane circled the island.

17
HOME INVASION

William, Laura, and Sam watched the plane circle overhead. "They've likely spotted the downed plane. We're going to be rescued!" Laura exclaimed.

Sam's mind went to the large quantities of cocaine left on the beach. *That plane, what if it isn't here to rescue, what if it's here to collect?* He gripped his revolver tightly. In the pit of his stomach, he felt as though this was going to make things worse, much worse.

"I have one flare left in my flare gun, here goes nothing," Sam said, looking over at William and Laura.

Raising it in the air, he pulled the trigger. Nothing happened.

"Oh no, no! The water, that swim, it's not working, damnit!" Sam exclaimed as he continued pulling the trigger while holding the flare gun in the air. He looked around desperately. "That boat you came in on, there's no way of repairing it?"

"No way, trust me, I tried. Unless a burnt-out husk of a boat can be salvaged, no boat," William replied, still staring up at the plane.

Sam put the flare gun back into the backpack, hoping it was just temporarily waterlogged and they could use it another time. "How did the people originally get here? I doubt they were flown in. Where is their means of transportation?" he asked William.

William shook his head. "When we arrived, the most I could get out of these people was their own ship was lost to the sea after they had disembarked. None of them thought they would live more than a few months. Most died off before we got here. Ten years later, any remaining have all turned into what you now see. Even then, they've been slowly whittled down through my traps, as well as finally succumbing to the mutated disease."

"Well, there's one less on the beach, the one I shot through the head, and one stuck in one of your traps down there," Sam said.

"And the one that got to Eva, the big one. He looked more...fresh than the rest," Laura added.

"Must have been Velho," William replied, glancing up at the thick line of black storm clouds far out at sea.

"William, the plane we were on, we found out after it was too late that the pilot and copilot were drug runners that had stolen quite a bit of cocaine from their boss. So, that plane overhead, it may not be rescue. It's just a hunch,"

Sam said gravely.

Turning to face him, Williams eyes widened. "Drug dealers? Laura, what the hell were you doing traveling with drug dealers?"

"Trust me, we didn't know what they were up to. We got a private flight from Kokoda airport to the Solomon Islands. Supposedly, from what our illustrious pilot told us, it's quite a common thing in Papua New Guinea. Small charter flights to the islands out in the Solomon Sea. We had no clue!" Laura answered.

Sighing, William replied, "Yes, you are right. However, as Sam said, this may complicate getting out of here, depending on who is on that airplane. Do you know if the drugs survived the crash?"

"Yes, the pilot dragged the briefcases from the wreckage to the beach. I buried them but not well. They'll be found, unless one of those zombies up and carries them off," Laura said shaking her head.

"Not them. But you buried your friend Ed on the beach too? He was bit?" William asked.

"Yes. But he was dead. I'm sure of it," Sam replied.

The plane dipped below their vantage point, its engines roaring as it slowed down in its attempt to land.

William looked them both in the eyes, getting their attention. "I'm afraid your friends are not dead. At least not anymore. Burning the bodies, decapitation, or brain death by bullet or any other sharp object is the only way to put them down for good. Do you understand what I am saying?"

Sam and Laura stared at him in utter horror, not wanting

to believe some zombie versions of their friends were out there now, un-dead.

William continued. "And that's not all. They will likely be much more aware of their surrounds. Their brains are still slowly changing and being taken over by the alien host virus. From the research I have been able to conduct here, it can take years before all traces of what was once a human life with memories is wiped out along with the physical body. So, these friends of yours, if they have indeed been bitten and infected, they're—how shall I say this—*fresh*, for now both in mind and body. But they will get worse and worse as time goes on. That is a certainty."

"How do you know they'll turn out like the lepers on this island?" Sam questioned.

William shot back, "Because, once you're bit, it's over. I may have found the cure for brain cancer, but there is no cure from this virus. Just prolonged agony. Whatever happens from this point on, this virus cannot leave this island, do you understand?"

Laura shuddered at the thought of them being stuck on the island as her father had been now for two years and counting.

They heard in the far distance the plane's loud engine powering down. "For better or worse, that is our ticket out of here, whatever happens, we need to get to that plane," she said, determined to keep hoping.

"You're right. I'm ready when you are," Sam said, glancing over at William.

Laura looked at her father. Sadness replaced the anger

she felt for the man. He had indeed abandoned them, but in the process, had discovered the cure for the disease which had been a death sentence for him and many others across the world. *My dad did that,* she thought proudly.

"Dad, would you like to get off this island along with that cure you've discovered?" Laura asked respectfully.

Staring at his daughter, he pondered this for a bit. "I would be welcomed back into the Joyner home?"

"I may be upset that you left us, but we're family. And I do love you, or I wouldn't have traveled halfway across the globe to find you. I suppose if there is such a thing as divine providence, you ending up here and me finding you after a plane crash, well, that's a one-in-a-million chance. So, either someone or something up there is looking out for us, or after much bad luck, the gods have decided to throw us a bone."

"I'll pack my things as quickly as I can," William replied with a small smile. He headed back inside his house.

Sam and Laura hung back. They turned to face each other. "What are you thinking?" Laura asked.

"That it's good to see this reunion of sorts. I don't know this man, hell, I barely know you. But you both seem like very good people, and one thing in this life that is important, in my honest opinion, is family. My parents are overprotective, have always been. And have they ever pissed me off from time to time, but right now, I can't think of anyone I would rather see than them. To hug and kiss them and thank them for loving me unconditionally. Even when I decided to become best friends with that fuck up, Ed." Sam paused, contemplating these things.

Laura found herself even more attracted to this man and smiled warmly at him as she felt a lump in her throat.

William looked out his window at his lovely daughter. His pride and joy that he had abandoned years ago, even if his reasoning was sound. He didn't want her to see him rot away, especially when dangling in front of him had been the possibility of a cure. Only the cure had come at great cost, a new and deadly strain, devastating to all infected. He felt ashamed for what he had helped create, even if in the process, a true cure for brain cancer had been discovered.

He watched Laura and Sam talk, cooperating with each other, enjoying each other's company. He smiled. "Good girl, Dad is proud of you and loves you so much."

Tears filled his eyes as he looked away, packing a few things into a small cloth sack. Among them, a vial of the NR 485 serum, ground up Violet Laceflower in the correct quantities for injecting into terminal patients, and detailed notes on how he had come to finding the cure and how it was administered. Then he grabbed a rock, the size of his fist. Part of the meteor that had crashed on the island so long ago, bringing with it the Violet Laceflower DNA of what he could only surmise came from a distant world.

He grabbed a few more odds and ends, including a picture of Laura, Alicia, and himself at the beach when Laura was a little girl, put it in the sack cloth and tied it with twine. Then, pulling out his own small revolver and a few remaining shells, he stuck the gun onto his side and walked out to his waiting daughter and Sam.

"You both know we'll need to pass close to the village

on our way to the other side of the island, likely encountering more of the infected. I'm not the spryest man anymore, due to my time on this island, but I will go as fast as I can and try not to slow us down," William said.

Laura nodded in agreement, sad to see the frail state her dad was indeed in.

William then pointed in the direction they would be heading, a different one than the way Sam and Laura had entered.

"We're ready," Laura said, gripping her gun tightly, glancing over at a determined Sam who gave a nod in agreement.

William turned around, gazing one last time at his home for the past year. Sam stood beside him. "William, let's consolidate here and make it easier. I can put that small sack you're holding in my backpack. It's nearly empty anyway, and that's one less thing to carry. Sound good?"

William was surprised at the kind gesture and handed Sam the small cloth sack with his few belongings that easily slid into the much larger and nearly empty backpack. "Thank you, Sam, we can take turns lugging that thing back to the plane, okay?"

"Sure thing," Sam replied with a smile.

William continued on through the thick vegetation, followed by Laura and Sam.

"So, this meteor crashes here, bringing along, what? Alien DNA or space dust? Over hundreds of thousands of years new species of plant life pop up, including this flower that can literally heal brain cancer? I wonder what else here has healing properties?" Sam asked William, ever curious of his surroundings.

William replied, "I've done much research on the plant life here and numerous plants have shown to contain foreign DNA. I'm at a loss as to what they are, but I have my doubts they are from this planet. I'm a medical doctor and not necessarily a scientist, but these truly seem alien to me."

Taking in the beauty around them, they continued through the lush plant life with William leading the way. "As I said, there is a back way through this crater. One the infected have never discovered and likely never will. It is well concealed, but I must warn you, there are animals on this island that are as dangerous or even more than the lepers out there. At least the infected are slow moving. Come on, through here," he pointed to a crack in the side of the crater up ahead.

On either side of their path, several low moans could suddenly be heard. William froze in place, quickly raising his revolver. Laura's eyes widened as she raised her gun along with Sam. "Did I just hear what I thought I heard?" she asked in a whisper.

"Shit, those things must have followed us in through the waterfalls!" Sam whispered back.

"But that's impossible. Their brains are too far gone to forcibly travel through that torrential downpour. Plus, they've been programmed to avoid this area with all the booby traps I set up around the perimeter!" William replied quietly.

They scanned the thick foliage and saw movement. All three had their respective guns raised, trying to get a clean shot.

Two of the leper zombies drudged forward, one on either side of them. William was the first to get a shot off, blasting what appeared to have once been a teenage boy. The slug blasted the top of his head off, dropping him instantly.

The other zombie reached out, grabbing hold of Laura's shoulder. She screamed out in terror as Sam smashed the back of its head with the butt of his gun. The zombie released its grip on Laura's shoulder and turned to face Sam. Laura raised her revolver, put it against the zombie's skull and pulled the trigger. Most of its head exploded, sending particles of rotted brain matter cascading across the vegetation nearby.

Laura quickly scanned the rest of their immediate area. While no moans could be heard, there was a shuffling behind them on the narrow, overgrown path. All three pointed their weapons toward the noise. "Come on, I know my way around here," William muttered, motioning them to follow forward, away from the advancing zombies.

William led the way faster now, with Laura and Sam on either side of him, one step behind and keeping watch of their respective sides. "They didn't come here on their own. Someone led them here," William whispered.

"Eva," Laura replied.

Stepping out slowly from behind them stood Eva. Still wet from her trip under the waterfalls, a large chunk on the side of her neck was missing but no longer bleeding. She looked ghastly: her hair, no longer in pigtails, was tangled and wet and hung loosely atop her head, her eyes a milky-white consistency which locked in on Laura.

All that was good at one time inside of Eva had ceased

to exist, while her worst attributes seemed to bubble up to the forefront of her still active mind. She had always struggled with doing the right thing but now those shackles had been removed. Jealousy, pride, envy, lust, gluttony, and most importantly, murder had all taken over. The disease that now pumped through her slowly rotting arteries had altered her DNA, bringing out the dark side of Eva.

Laura raised her gun, aiming it at her friend who appeared to be biting at the air. Then Eva did something unexpected; she spoke one word in a guttural growl, "You…"

Seeing the gun, she leapt back into the thick brush, out of sight.

No one said a word. Laura was stunned at the sight of her recently resurrected friend, now a zombie, having just spoken directly to her.

"I have never seen this before, even from Velho, our assistant, a really big man, compared to the lepers in the village. When he turned, he was animalistic. He was fast but he never spoke."

Laura remained silent. Still staring out ahead for any more movement. Trees rustled, and thick plant life seemed to be taunting them with swaying leaves, but there were no moans.

"Come on, we need to keep moving. We don't know how many she brought with her," William said, cautiously taking small steps forward, his revolver at the ready.

They were near the tight walkway in the side of the crater and no one had spotted any more zombies, but movement deep in the brush could still be heard along with low moans on either side of the small path.

"Don't fire unless you have a clean shot, we need to save our ammo," Sam said.

Nodding, Laura continued looking for her old friend, no longer a friend at all. She couldn't shake the feeling that this woman was after her in particular.

"I sure as hell am not looking forward to squeezing through there," Sam said, pointing at the narrow walkway on the side of the crater wall with its sharp, jagged rock on either side of path forward.

"You can say that again," Laura replied.

From behind them, another leper zombie stepped out directly behind Sam, grabbing hold of him. Sam stumbled forward and fell on his face, his gun dropping out of his hand at the sudden jolt of his body slamming onto the ground.

Laura hollered out, "Sam! No!"

William turned to see a naked zombie-woman covered with the same grotesque lesions that covered the rest of the unfortunate souls of the infected island. Skinny and rotten, its flesh was leathery and barely hanging on to the bones underneath.

William aimed his gun but was unable to get a clear shot, as the leper zombie frantically tried to bite into the back of Sam's neck while he struggled and squirmed, then was whipped over onto his back just as the zombie's jaws were about to sink into flesh.

"Someone get this damn thing off me!" He grunted as he pushed up on the creature's shoulders, forcing its snapping teeth away from him.

Another zombie grabbed hold of William, who had his back turned away from where Eva had stood. Impulsively, he spun around, gun in hand, placed it under its chin and pulled the trigger. The dead man's rotted brains exploded out the top of its head, dropping it instantly.

Sam had managed to roll over on top of the woman corpse who continued biting at him. Laura aimed her gun at the rotted corpse but couldn't get a shot without risking hitting Sam.

With one hand around her throat, keeping her secure, Sam pulled out his knife with his free hand, raised it and then slammed it into the front of the zombie's skull before twisting the blade.

The biting ceased as the pathetic creature dropped its struggling arms and lay still.

William and Laura took hold of each of Sam's arms, helping him to his feet. "You okay?" William asked.

"I wasn't bit so, yeah, I'm good," he replied shakily, brushing himself off.

Laura squeezed his arm in relief before letting go and looking around for more zombies.

All was quiet in the thick tropical forest. What would normally be a beautiful view of trees, flowers and lush vegetation had taken on a sinister and ominous feel. Anything could be hiding in the camouflaged dense green landscape.

A slight rustle of leaves was the only warning as Eva jumped out from the midst of several tall plants, grabbed hold of William's arm and, snapping her jaws, lunged in to bite it, his gun flying into the brush at the sudden movement.

Laura, who was closest to her father, screamed out, "Eva, no! Look at me!"

William's eyes widened in horror as the girl he once knew many years ago, now a walking corpse, tried to bite him. He wrenched his arm back, her teeth and strong jaws biting the air and missing his own flesh by mere inches.

Eva glanced over at the sound of Laura's voice.

"Laura, look out!" Sam shouted.

Eva lunged forward onto Laura, slamming her against the side of a large tree. William scooped up his dropped firearm, aimed it at Eva and squeezed the trigger. The blast missed her head as she was moving too quickly in her attempts to sink her teeth into Laura's exposed throat, instead hitting her just under the left shoulder blade.

Sam, meanwhile, had scooped up his dropped revolver from the ground and raised it up to his chest.

Eva felt no pain but knew *something* had happened to her. The force of the bullet knocked her off of Laura, but she hopped up, her milky-white eyes moving from William, still holding the gun, to Sam, also holding a gun, to her one-time friend. She quickly slid back into the thick vegetation before any of them were able to squeeze off another shot.

As she moved backward, Laura caught a fleeting glimpse of her once more, Eva's white eyes boring holes in her. *She's glaring at me,* Laura thought as Eva disappeared.

William squeezed the trigger in an attempt to thwart the fleeing zombie from doing any more damage, but the bullet sailed past her head as she ducked down and crept away.

Laura turned quickly to her father. "Dad, did she bite

you?"

William brushed himself off, looking at his arm. There were marks where she had gripped tightly, but no skin had broken. "I'm good, that one there is smart and cunning, we need to move, now."

Smart was never something Laura associated with the usually ditzy Eva. Cunning though, that checked out. That was how she had lived her life, for better or worse, getting what she wanted, when she wanted it. Like insisting this trip was for her—vacationing, getting drunk, and getting laid.

Putting his hands on her shoulders, Sam looked at Laura. "Are you okay? You hit that tree pretty hard." She was favoring her right side. "Here, let me see," he gently raised her tank top slightly to take a look at the injury while William kept his revolver trained on the forest where Eva had disappeared. Sam grimaced at the deep cut oozing blood on her back.

"It's cut and bleeding, must have hit a sharp branch, but it could be worse," Sam said, trying to mask his concern.

"We'll worry about that later, right now we need to get the hell out of here. I feel like a trapped animal in this crater and time's wasting," Laura said, grimacing at the sharp pain. She could tell from the tone of Sam's voice he wasn't being entirely forthcoming about the injury she sustained. The cut on her back was fairly deep and would likely need stitches at some point. Likely sooner than later. Her back was wet and warm. *Blood.*

Sam gently pulled her tank top back down and gave her an encouraging smile, which she forced in return. They both glanced over to see William, roughly twenty feet away, standing by the crack in the crater's side, waiting anxiously.

Sam walked over to the corpse on the ground and pulled the knife out of the zombie's now lifeless body on the ground. He looked at William then cautiously into the crater opening, "Lead the way," he said, pointing to the jagged exit against the crater wall.

Before entering the narrow opening, Laura turned back to the thick tropical foliage and scanned the area once more in the hopes of seeing Eva. "I fear you and I aren't done yet," she whispered. She turned and quickly made her way into the tight wall.

William moved forward, squeezing in between the cracked crater walls. Laura, shaking her head at what they had just encountered and her now aching back, followed with Sam close behind, making sure she was protected in the center.

"Hold up," Sam said.

They stopped and glanced back as Sam raised his revolver. He had three shells left and Laura's gun had four. William had five remaining shells in his own revolver.

"Hope this works," Sam said, and pulled the trigger near the entrance, hitting an outstretched piece of loose crater rock above them.

The shot reverberated loudly as dust and debris fell along with the large chunk of stone, smashing against and blocking the entrance of the narrow crack in the crater wall.

Hidden in the thick cover of the crater's lush vegetation, Eva continued hungrily peering in the direction of her one-time friend, now blocked by a large rock across the opening of a narrow entrance.

18
"PISS-POOR LANDING"

Near the village, Ed sleepily looked up toward the sky as the plane flew overhead, his milky-white eyes taking in the sight. The village offered his mind little explanation as to its existence. Small, dilapidated huts lined the dirt street that was now overgrown. Beings that had many years ago resembled humans now shuffled slowly back and forth the length of the village. As if they remembered this place as being someplace *special*.

Ed, however, had no such memories. But he did have memories of airplanes. Airplanes carried passengers, of which he had recently been one. Passengers meant *food*. His white eyes followed the plane, the now scuffed-up black briefcase still clenched in his hand. He looked down at it, unsure why he continued carrying it. Somewhere in the dark recesses of his damaged, disease-riddled mind, he knew it was of some importance.

"This is going to be a bumpy landing, hang on," Vaz said as he lined up the plane to the long stretch of clear sandy beach. His comment was met with silence from the rear, which didn't surprise him.

He was still stunned that his abrupt and rather random change in their original flight path earlier had led to the discovery of the plane they had been searching for over the past day. This was a bad idea, landing on a stretch of beach with just enough fuel to make it back to the nearest airport. So many things could go wrong. *Please, God, let me see my wife and daughter again. Please, God...*

The Cessna Citation made a sudden drop in altitude as Vaz slowed the plane down. He spoke quietly, walking himself through the steps to get them safely on the ground as he kept his eyes on the Altitude Indicator while keeping the correct pitch. "Full rudder up. Slowing speed to one-hundred knots. Extending flaps and increasing pitch...now."

He wiped sweat off his increasingly perspiring brow then double checked the landing gear as the plane dipped lower and lower. Clearing his throat, he continued with the procedures. "Centerline looks good, all things considered. And the wind seems to be giving me some pushback. Increasing speed to one-hundred twenty knots. Syncing round out rate...now. Watch out for those rocks, Vaz, here goes nothing."

The sandy beach was heading toward them fast as Vaz continued to keep the plane from stalling out while still dropping speed to land. The Cessna's wheels cleared a patch of large rocks by mere feet before reaching the beach. Vaz dropped the plane immediately, pulling back on the yoke as soon as the rear wheels hit the sand. He kept the nose wheel off the ground for a few brief seconds as he continued applying the brakes to the plane as hard as he could.

The plane ran over small rocks in the sand, jostling all aboard around violently. No one said a word as they looked on. The engine roared loudly as Vaz slammed on the brakes. The plane felt as though it was about to completely fall apart. The flaps pulled back as wind hit the wings hard. The plane was slowing down enough that Vaz dropped the nose wheel to the sand. Once it hit, the plane rocked hard, hitting a larger round rock buried under the sand causing everyone to fly out of their seats slightly, even with their seat belts secured.

Applying more pressure to the brakes, the plane jutted forward. In front of it, the short makeshift sandy runway was quickly coming to an end. That end was a series of large rocks that would crush the front of the plane, making any attempt to leave impossible.

"Stop this damn plane!" came the angry response from Paim behind him.

"I'm trying!" Vaz shot back. *Oh shit, I don't know if I can get us stopped in time!*

Amanda and Angelina were back home waiting for him, he had made a promise. Gritting his teeth, Vaz continued with the brakes and the flaps, trying to keep the plane from tilting in the sand either way. The looming sandy colored rocks piled high were growing larger and larger in the front windshield. They were mere seconds away from smashing into them as the plane continued sliding forward.

The plane shuttered as its wheels ground over small rocks in the sand. Twenty feet to the rocks ahead. Fifteen feet. Ten feet. Eight, seven, six. At five feet the small Cessna Citation came to a complete full stop. The shuddering ceased as the engine slowed.

Vaz sat back in his seat, sweat dripping off his face and soaking his shirt. He blew out a big, heavy sigh.

"Piss-poor landing, but we're in one piece, I suppose," Paim said coldly.

Instant rage engulfed Vaz who turned to look at what were now essentially his captors. "You hired me to do a job. A damn near impossible one at that, and I got us here in one piece. You should hope and pray I can get this plane backed up and have enough runway to clear a takeoff. So, cut me some slack, okay?"

Paim's eyebrows raised. He wasn't used to this kind of talk from anyone. His henchmen Ruiz and Vidal leaned forward, glaring at Vaz. Seeing this, Paim raised his hands. "Easy, boys. It's okay, he's right. Mr. Vaz, you are correct. And for what it's worth, you did get us here in relative safety. You will be compensated accordingly once we are back at the Kokoda airport."

Vaz acknowledged this small gesture, nodded his thanks and said, "Before powering down and letting you out, I need to get this plane turned around and ready for takeoff."

"I don't have time for this!" Paim responded angrily.

Gritting his teeth, Vaz said, "It could cost us valuable fuel if we attempt this upon leaving. Please, let me take care of this."

"Do it quick," Paim replied, sitting back.

"You'd think I've never flown a plane before, you piece of shit," Vaz whispered to himself as began to back the plane up and turn the yoke sharply. While the engines of the plane were still powered up and Paim and his men would likely not hear him, he tried the radio.

"This is Cessna Citation 649, come in. Does anyone copy?" Vaz muttered.

Nothing but static came back.

Damnit, damnit all to hell. He clicked the radio off.

"Hey! What are you doing up there! Are you communicating with someone?" Paim shouted from his seat.

"Nope, just walking myself through backing this thing up."

Paim sat back, buying the lie.

Vaz bit his bottom lip once more, glaring out the front of the plane as he maneuvered it correctly through the sand. Once in position, the plane was finally powered down, sounding as weary as its pilot.

"Gentlemen, this goes without saying, if Barroso and Pinto are still alive, they are to remain alive until my drugs are back in our possession," Paim muttered with both men beside him nodding. "Before we go out to the downed plane, we first search the beach in case it's here. I would rather none of you have to swim out there if they don't have to, however,

I will want to find the bodies, is that understood?"

"Yes, sir," came the stoic replies.

Vaz took that as his cue to open the hatch and let his captors out.

Upon exiting the plane, Paim, Ruiz and Vidal drew their guns and surveyed the beach while Vaz climbed out wearily, stretched his arms and looked toward the crashed plane still hung up on the islet.

"How could anyone survive that?" he muttered quietly shaking his head at the destruction.

"Boss, you need to see this," Ruiz said from a distance up ahead on the beach.

Paim and Vidal began moving up to where Ruiz stood, stopping at a dead woman's corpse, her head nearly destroyed by a gunshot.

"What the hell," Vidal said with eyes wide, peering down at the rotted corpse.

Vaz quickly made his way to where they stood and instantly turned his head in revulsion. "My God, what happened to her? I think it's a her."

"Whatever happened, guns were involved. This woman was shot," Paim said, continuing to scan the beach.

His eyes fell on more victims. Without a word, Paim headed toward them, Ruiz and Vidal following suit with Vaz in the rear. They soon saw that one in particular appeared different from the rest. While the others, a child included, had severe head trauma, one had literally been ripped to shreds. The area looked as though someone had exploded from the inside. Tiny pieces of body parts and bones were all that remained.

No one spoke, all surveying the carnage strewn about.

"This one of yours?" Vaz asked, pointing at the head of a man half-buried in the sand. Part of the man's spinal cord was still connected to the head but the skull had been bashed in and it appeared as though the brains had been removed.

Paim walked over to where Vaz stood and looked down. Instantly, he saw the face of Pinto, his mouth half-opened and missing his tongue. Paim nudged the head with his black shoe, turning it over and inspecting it.

"Whatever did this tore the head from his body, this head wasn't cut with a knife or sharp object," Vaz said.

Not bothering to respond, Paim surveyed the rest of the area but there was no sign of the stolen black briefcases full of dope. "We need to check the plane," Paim muttered, unfazed by the bodies strewn about.

"What the hell? Something awful is going on here! These bodies look infected with some type of disease, leprosy or worse. Looks like they've been dead for a while, but that body is a fresh kill," Vaz said pointing to the head of Pinto in the sand.

"Why don't you let us worry about these things? I have seen and have inflicted much worse. This doesn't bother me. In fact, it's one less problem I have to deal with. Once we find Barroso and my drugs, we can leave, and this will all be behind us," Paim paused then looked Vaz in the eye. "I need you Mr. Pilot, to go check my downed plane out there. Check for survivors and check for my drugs."

"Why would I do something like that?" Vaz replied,

standing up to the brutish, large man.

"Because, Augusto, while we need you to fly us back to civilization. Once there, you are disposable. As is your wife and child. Do not make me threaten you. Do as I say. I'll even be nice about it: *Please* go check the plane. Ruiz, you go along. If my drugs are still onboard, I'll need you to transport them back here."

"Yes, sir," Ruiz replied emotionlessly.

Vaz stared at Paim in disbelief for several seconds before turning and walking toward the beach, while Paim and Vidal continued scouring the beach for more clues as to what happened and, more importantly, the drugs.

Come on, Vaz, swim out there, check out the plane then get back. We're almost there, just find his damn drugs and we're out of here, back home. "Looks like we're gonna get wet," Vaz muttered to the large man chosen as his chaperone.

"It appears so. Come on, time's wasting," he replied, staring out into the sea at the plane hung up on the islet.

Vaz agreed with the big oaf on that. Time was wasting and he wanted to be home.

They made their way out into the water, going deeper into the ocean and closer to the downed Seneca.

Vaz got to the plane first and surveyed the extensive damage. The plane was destroyed. He wondered how anyone could have made it off the plane alive. Ruiz joined him and stood with him on the small islet.

"You check the cockpit and I'll check the cargo hold," Ruiz commanded.

"Yes, sir," Vaz shot back, not meaning to sound as

sarcastic as it did. He wasn't liking the order taking and his mood took a further nosedive being stuck with this job.

Ignoring him, Ruiz waded through the water toward the back of the plane while Vaz found footing on the nose and pulled himself up onto it, careful not to slip on the wet metal. He peered inside the busted-out cockpit window.

"Dead body here in the copilot seat, I'm guessing it's Barroso!" Vaz called out.

Ruiz glanced back and replied, "Climb inside. Look for more bodies."

"Of course," Vaz replied to himself. He glanced back at the beach and was no longer able to see Paim and Vidal, who had likely started investigating the jungle area past the beach.

The slight smell of Barroso's already baking body in the sun hit his nose. "Oh shit, this is in a whole other realm of fucked-up right here."

He contemplated lying to Ruiz and telling him he had sifted through the plane but reasoned that might not be a wise choice. These guys were cold-blooded, hardened killers. Sure, they needed him, for now. *Just do what you're told, Vaz.*

"Sonofabitch," Vaz mumbled as he climbed through the broken windshield into the cockpit. Once inside he felt his stomach gurgle and started to heave at to the sight of Barroso's mutilated neck and the stench permeating from it. He gagged but was thankful very little came up, due to his nearly empty stomach.

He made his way slowly to the passenger area. It was corpse-free. "Well, I'll be damned, we might actually have some survivors on this island that aren't the bad guys. The plot thickens," Vaz muttered. His eyes fell on the seat once inhabited by Edward. What wasn't submerged in ocean water was stained with blood. *At least one injured, or dead, somewhere on the island.*

His mind went to the bodies on the beach. None resembled anything close to human. More like diseased mutations that had been long dead. Yet they were dead, all with head trauma. "So, who killed Mr. headless Pinto if they're all truly dead?" Vaz shuddered at the thought of more of those things out there. *What the hell kind of island is this?*

Moving back to the cockpit, Vaz was about to climb out then looked over at the nearly decapitated Barroso and figured he was already waist-deep in the guy's bloody, rotting body, so why not? He reached over and felt around the dead man's body. Under the man's shirt, he felt a hard bump. Vaz held his breath, then as quickly as he could, raised Barroso's shirt. His stomach was becoming bloated and showing signs of rigor mortis setting in. Gritting his teeth at the revulsion he felt, he fought through it until he found what he was after, the dead man's gun.

He quickly pulled the Smith & Wesson 9MM revolver from the man's holster, turning it over in his hand. Vaz let out the air he'd been holding in, and for the moment, forgot about the rancid smell in the cockpit. The gun had an off-color silver stock and black handle and from the looks of it, it had been used before, showing scratches and a distinct lack of sheen to the barrel. He was no fan of guns, but in this bad situation he had been thrust into, this was a Godsend.

After a bit of fidgeting, Vaz figured out how to release the magazine by pressing a small knob near the trigger and saw it appeared fully loaded with seven bullets total. He slammed the magazine back and pulled back on the chamber, securing a bullet into the barrel.

Play it cool. If everything went as planned and the drugs were found they could leave here, no problem, but if things went sideways, like they had every step of the way, *I've got this*, Vaz thought, looking over the gun once more before sticking it in the front of his pants and covering it with his shirt. *Just don't shoot your pecker off.*

He slowly climbed up and out of the opening in the cockpit and was once more on top of the nose of the plane. Looking toward the beach, he still saw no Paim and Vidal. "Good, you do your thing, and I'll do mine."

"What was that?" a voice behind him yelled up.

Glancing back, Vaz saw Ruiz wading through the water near the nose of the plane, looking at him suspiciously. "What did you say up there, flyboy?"

"Nothing, just talking to myself. Did you find what you were looking for back there?" Vaz asked, wanting to change the subject.

"Yeah, well, don't talk to yourself. It makes me edgy, and if I'm edgy, my boss gets edgy. Just do what we fucking tell you and keep your damn mouth shut, got it?" Ruiz spat out.

"I got it," Vaz said, glaring down at the large, imposing man. *I'm no killer, but it would give me great pleasure to blow your brains out right now, you bully scumbag. You and that big ox sidekick with you.*

"Then get your ass down here and let's head back to

the beach. Unless you found something inside the cockpit?" Ruiz shot back.

Vaz's heart suddenly raced, wondering if the man could tell he was hiding something. "I'm coming, hold on," he called out, trying to sound nonchalant.

"Don't tell me to hold on, you cocksucker," Ruiz mumbled loud enough for Vaz to hear as he waded past the plane, moving toward the beach.

Vaz ignored the insult and slid down into the water, making sure to avoid any unnecessary contact with his newfound friend jammed in the front of his pants. If he dropped it in the water, it was a lost cause.

Once he was in water past his waist, he began following Ruiz who had obviously found nothing as he was leaving the crash site empty-handed. Which meant either the drugs flew out during the crash or they were on the island.

Ruiz looked back to see where Vaz was, shouting, "Hurry up, you're falling too far behind!"

Vaz mumbled to himself, "That was you on the trip out to the downed plane, you overgrown thick-necked fucker."

He looked up at the sky warily as the black clouds, while still a good distance away, seemed to be slowly creeping toward the island. He looked back to the beach once more and saw Paim and Vidal walking near the edge of the sand by the tree line near the carnage. Neither one had any briefcases, they haven't found anything yet, which meant he wasn't going anywhere for the...

Vaz saw something else, near Ruiz. "Is that what I think it is?" Vaz muttered, his eyes widening in terror.

Ruiz turned around once more. "If I have to tell you again to swim your skinny ass closer to where I can see you, I'm going to take the butt of my gun and smash it over your—"

The fin was less than twenty feet from Ruiz, the very tip protruding out of the water, then it was gone.

"Shark!" Vaz yelled.

Ruiz, caught completely off-guard, turned to look in the direction Vaz was pointing. One second later, his body violently shifted to the right. Instant pain and shock sailed through his body as the fourteen-foot tiger shark latched its sharp jaws around his legs, biting down ferociously into the meat.

Panicked, Vaz looked toward the shore where a puzzled Paim and Vidal watched as the horror unfolded. *Do something! Get to the shore, go now!* As fast as his arms and legs could kick and paddle, Vaz began swimming to the shore.

A mere thirty feet to the right of Vaz, Ruiz suddenly slipped under the water. As he gulped for air, he shouted out, "Help me, you sonofabitch!" Blood was pooling up around him while the shark continued to thrash violently, ripping his legs to pieces. It released him and circled back. Ruiz grew weaker from the sheer amount of blood pouring out of his deep wounds. Water filled his lungs as he could no longer stay afloat, his mind fading. The last thing Ruiz saw under the water was the tiger shark making its second attack, this time sinking its jaws into his exposed upper chest. Seconds later, his life ceased while the shark pulled his body out to sea.

Vaz, meanwhile, frantically swimming for his life, was

unsure if any more sharks remained in the immediate area. *They smell the blood and rotting carcass of the copilot, get your ass to shore now!* The shore seemed farther than he remembered it. More than Paim and his lunkhead goons, this shark was at the top of the food chain he was fleeing from now.

He was cognizant of the Smith and Wesson 9MM still jammed in the front of his pants and just hoped it wouldn't spill out from him thrashing around frantically in the water. The closer he got to the shore, the more he could hear shouting from Vidal. He didn't once glance back to see if any more fins were sticking up, following after him for a second course.

Finally, after what seemed like an eternity, Vaz washed up on shore and lay in the sand while Vidal and Paim stood over him, not offering any assistance.

"You motherfucker! That was my brother and you let him be eaten alive by a shark! I ought to kill you right here and now!" Vidal shouted.

"Easy, easy, there, Vidal. This man needs to fly us back to the mainland. And besides, there was nothing he could do. Get up, pilot," Paim exclaimed coldly.

Sitting up on the sand, Vaz peered up at his captors. Vidal looked as though he had murder on his mind, glaring at the man who had just escaped a shark attack. He hated these two more with each passing second.

Vaz stood slowly to his feet, glad his soaking wet shirt hung loosely on his body. Unless he was frisked, they would have no clue he was packing heat.

"I am to assume nothing was found?" Paim asked,

standing in front of an out-of-breath Vaz.

Catching his breath, Vaz replied, "Copilot is dead. The crash nearly severed his head from his neck. No other bodies were found, Ruiz hadn't taken anything either. So, your precious drugs either got sucked out of the plane when it went down, or they're somewhere here. Where the hell did you two go?"

Paim responded, "We went to investigate several gunshots. They're likely on the other side of the island. So, it looks like it's time to go hunting. That includes *you*, Mr. Vaz. Now, be a good boy and go fetch me the key to the plane. I wouldn't want you getting any funny ideas before we're damn good and ready to leave here."

Gritting his teeth, Vaz remained silent and did as he was told. Once he got to the Seneca, he pulled the ignition key and looked at it. "I could just jump into the plane right now and try to make a run for it," he paused, thinking to himself. "They'd shoot me dead before the plane leaves the ground. Plus, there is likely survivors here somewhere. This just keeps getting better and better."

He returned to where Ruiz and Paim stood and placed the key in Paim's outstretched hand.

"Good doggie," Paim said with an snide grin, placing the key into the pocket on this shirt.

I'll be getting that key back one way or another you bastard, Vaz thought.

19
PAIM'S
MISSING DOPE

Paim, Luiz, and Vaz once more walked past the carnage on the beach. None of them looked down but simply walked past it toward the island jungle. Vaz took one last look at the plane he had spent far too much time in over the last twenty-four hours, hoping beyond hope that he would soon be back in the pilot's seat on his way home. He continually pushed away the thought of never seeing his wife and child again.

Once they reached the thick, green growth, Paim looked at Vaz. "You go first."

"Wait, why me? You're the ones with guns. You're the ones that…" Vaz began.

"Shut the fuck up, I'm paying you and after what we

saw on the beach, you're going first," Paim replied calmly.

"But I'm the pilot!" Vaz retorted. "You need me to get out of here! There is likely more of whatever those things were on the beach in there!"

"It's like this, Mr. Vaz. This is why I took the key to the airplane for safe keeping. I trust myself and Ruiz. You? I don't trust. Now *move your ass.*" Paim patted the shirt pocket on his right side.

Shaking his head, Vaz moved forward past Paim and Ruiz, careful that the bump under his shirt remained concealed.

Pushing through the tall overgrowth, they walked cautiously into the jungle. "Which direction am I taking you two?" Vaz asked smugly.

"Just move forward. I saw what looked like the top of a chapel from the beach. That's where we're heading. My drugs are here, I know it," Paim muttered.

"Sure thing, boss," Vaz replied sarcastically.

"Wait a minute. Look, boss!" Ruiz exclaimed pointing to something on the ground.

Crouching down, Paim saw instantly what it was. One of twenty well-wrapped packages of white powdery cocaine. "So, it is here. Just as I suspected." Paim scooped up the dropped package, inspecting it. It was still sealed and untampered with.

"Boss, take a look at this," Ruiz said as he bent down. In his hand was another package of cocaine.

Paim looked from it to the forest ahead. "Either someone is fucking with us or one of those rotting ghouls has my briefcases and is unknowingly spilling them out. Either way, it's here. We find it and we leave."

Ruiz nodded, glaring at Vaz. He had been relatively quiet, which was no surprise, but Vaz could tell the man was shaken by the killing of his brother. *Good, maybe one of those things on this island will rip your ass to shreds as well. One less scumbag I may have to contend with.*

"Footprints, relatively fresh, going to that church," Ruiz stated observing the print of a shoe in a bit of soft ground.

The lunkhead is good for something other than muscle, Vaz thought smugly. They followed the trail of dropped packages until eight of the ten total from the first briefcase were collected.

They pushed on through the thick forest. Insects made noises but little else could be heard. The ocean crashing against the shore had long since faded and all that remained was the totally foreign and dangerous jungle now surrounding them. Thick palm trees that anywhere else would look beautiful here were ominous and shrouded the sun from view.

To Vaz, it felt as though the jungle itself wanted to rip them to pieces, much like the ill-fated Pinto on the beach. Every now and then, when the ground became softer, a shoe-print could be made out.

There was a light rustling in the tall, jungle foliage near their path.

"Hold up. I hear something," Vaz said, holding his hand up.

Paim and Ruiz came to a stop, close behind him, both raising their guns.

"I hear nothing," Paim said after listening intently.

"Shh, there's something out there," Vaz replied.

"It's an animal, we're in a jungle. Now get moving!" Paim shot back.

Vaz looked at his surroundings before cautiously starting to move forward. He desperately wanted to pull his gun out for his own protection, but he knew that wasn't an option. *Keep that Ace in your pocket until you really need it, Vaz! It might be your only ticket out of this hell.*

The last remaining cocaine packages were found along their path and, once collected, Vaz was given the unenviable task of carrying his share until they found something to properly carry them in.

He chose not to grumble about the job and instead focused on getting to the small church in the hopes that the person or persons responsible would be there with the rest of the dope so they could get the hell off the island. This, of course, meant those who took it would be executed immediately. *What a sonofabitch no-good rotten bit of luck I've gotten myself into here.*

The church appeared up ahead in a clearing. Pushing though the tall brush, Vaz could swear he head more rustling as he continued to suspect something, or someone, was following them. Without drawing unneeded attention, he glanced quickly from side to side, Paim and Ruiz following closely behind him. Vaz was on high alert, almost expecting something to leap out of them at any second. *Survive this, get the hell out of Dodge, get back to your wife and your little girl, Vaz! Keep your shit together.*

They stepped into the clearing in front of the church

to see the front door open and, laying just outside of it, the empty dope briefcase.

"What the hell is going on?" Ruiz mumbled to himself, glancing over at Paim who remained stern-faced.

Sweat dripped from Paim's brow. The man was strong and worked out frequently to keep up his good looks, but hiking through the jungle wasn't something he was accustomed to. His clothes were sweaty and dirty, something that normally would have disgusted him but right now, all Paim cared about was winning. And winning meant securing his drugs while knowing both his ex-employees were dead.

Paim had already made a mental note of tracking down both men's relatives. They would all suffer for the misdeeds of these two thieves. And when their murders would be eventually discovered, word would travel far and wide about what happens to those that cross the powerful Sérgio Melo Paim.

Cautiously, Paim raised his gun to the church entrance and along with Ruiz, pushed past Vaz who was happy to fall back. Once at the door, Ruiz bent down and retrieved the briefcase carefully without setting foot in the church, that would come later. He placed his cocaine packages back inside first.

"Here," Ruiz said, displaying the opened briefcase for Vaz and Paim, who dropped their packages into it. "Should we make flyboy here carry this around until we leave?" he asked, glaring at Vaz.

"No, keep it on you at all times. We find the other one, then we leave. Come on, let's check out the church here," Paim replied. Looking at Vaz, he muttered, pointing at the church's open door. "Well? Get moving! God's waiting."

Shuddering at the disrespectful comment, Vaz, a lifelong Catholic that had in recent years lapsed, was really wishing he would have been absolved before the ordeal he found himself in. *Too late for that, just survive and make things right after this mess.*

Glancing to one side of the building, he saw old grave markers, on the other, near the rear, sat an old generator. Taking a deep breath, Vaz moved forward into the church, scanning the room for dead bodies and instantly smelling the stench.

"There are bodies in here, looks like they've been dead for a long time though," he called out as he glanced around and grimaced at the smell of old, rotted bodies.

Paim and Ruiz walked in and surveyed the small church. "Someone's been here recently," Ruiz said, bending down and picking up an empty granola bar wrapper.

"Floor is dusty, judging by the tracks left, there's three of them. Which, by my calculations, means someone isn't accounted for. Pilot, copilot, and four other passengers were on board that plane." Paim pointed to the area of floor where Sam, Laura, and Eva had slept the previous night.

"What the hell was going on in here? This isn't a church, at least not anymore. It looks like an operating room," Vaz said, scanning his surroundings.

Ruiz sifted through several scattered papers laying on the floor near the desk, reading over some of the notes. "Says here this place is some kind of leper colony. Or was. Their village is somewhere past this church. A Dr. Pedroso was working on a cure. This here is his lab, of sorts." He paused and looked at the pile of bodies in the corner. Paim had pulled an old bloody sheet off of them, one of which was wearing a doctor's lab coat and had a bullet in the head of his rotten corpse.

"Those things on the beach must have been some of the villagers," Ruiz mumbled, glancing at Paim who appeared to be preoccupied with the uncovered corpses.

"I am not interested in lepers or whatever went on here. I am only interested in securing my second briefcase and leaving this island. Pinto and Barroso are already dead. Their passengers can rot here for all I care," Paim said, standing to his feet after viewing the three corpses in the corner. He wiped his sweaty black hair back over his head.

"Speaking of which, you've got one briefcase, which is better than nothing," Vaz said, hinting for a departure.

"And there's another one left. That we will find, I'm sure of it. It's likely in that village, let's go," Paim replied curtly.

"Suit yourself," Vaz mumbled, exiting the church.

Outside, the eerie silence Vaz had felt in the thick tropical forest had followed them here as well. He listened without moving.

"Come on, get going!" Ruiz exclaimed, giving Vaz a small shove and, for a brief second, pausing and scanning the area.

"Let's go, what's with both of you?" Paim said, carrying the briefcase out with him.

"Boss, listen," Ruiz said.

They all listened intently to the utter silence around

them. Then a low moan emanated from somewhere past the thick vegetation.

"What is that?" Paim said quietly, his eyes darting around their perimeter.

"A moan, I think it was a moan," Vaz said, glancing down at his shirt, hoping he wouldn't have to give up his ace.

Ruiz walked forward to the edge of the tree line, looking out into darkened jungle, then turned back to face Paim, pointing behind him toward the foliage. "I think Vaz is right, I think something is out—"

Something reached out, grabbing hold of Ruiz's outstretched arm and pulling the surprised man into the tree cover. Ruiz had no time to react upon seeing the tall, skeletal being whose face was a mutation of blisters and scabs, the skin peeling from its scalp hanging down over the right side of its face and covering its ear. Its eyes were milky-white and what clothes it had once worn were little more than thin rags hanging off its lesion-covered, corpse-like shell.

Its dead eyes peered at Ruiz who was about to let out a scream but was cut short when the corpse, still holding his arm, bit down onto his thumb, index, and middle finger, biting them off completely. It frantically chewed its fresh food as Ruiz stumbled backward into the clearing screaming. He aimed his gun into the forest and began firing.

Paim ran to the injured Ruiz, staring in horror at the hand missing three of its fingers. Ruiz had emptied his handgun into the forest but was still pulling the trigger on the emptied gun.

"Ruiz, stop!" Paim shouted.

Ruiz dropped his gun to the ground and cupped his injured hand. "Sonofabitch fucker bit my *fucking* fingers off!" He roared in pain.

Vaz cautiously stepped forward, staring at the wound dripping a steady flow of blood onto the now blood-covered ground in front of him.

"My hand! My fucking hand!" Ruiz groaned loudly.

"Listen," Vaz said as Paim continued to look at Ruiz's hand then out into the forest with his gun raised.

"You continue shouting commands at me, pilot, and you'll soon find that you will need to fly the plane with only one functioning eye!" Paim threatened.

"I said listen, damnit!" Vaz shouted, ignoring the threat.

Paim turned around with a scowl on his face, ready to tell the pilot to shut the hell up but Vaz pointed to the forest and put his finger to his lips for silence.

Ruiz, meanwhile, kept groaning loudly at the severe pain on his bloody hand.

Turning to his remaining goon, Paim muttered, "Shut the fuck up, Ruiz."

Ruiz fell silent at the look on his boss's face. Fighting back more cries of pain and shock, he continued cradling his hand.

Silence fell over the area surrounding the church once more. Then the sound of numerous moans rose from beyond the cover of trees and foliage, coming from all directions at once.

"Fuck this! Boss, we need to get back to the plane and get out of here!" Ruiz whispered.

Paim didn't reply but continued staring out into the dark jungle past the church. "I see someone, through the trees, over there," he pointed slightly east of their current location by the old church.

Vaz walked forward, squinting to see. "Yes, I see them, but," he paused, continuing to peer through the trees. He saw a man that certainly didn't look to be a native of the island. If it was a corpse, it was a fresh one—its clothes relatively new, albeit covered in blood. He was carrying something in his left hand. It was a briefcase.

"Sérgio, please, this man needs to get to a hospital immediately," Vaz said urgently, wanting nothing more to do with this island and its cursed inhabitants.

"Oh, you care about him now? I think not," Paim shot back.

Ed, who had been peering at them from afar on a lush, vegetation-covered hill, could make out weapons in their hands. He remembered the shiny things outstretched, pointing into the jungle forest. His hunger was overwhelming, but his mind told him to keep moving and avoid them. If he was to feast, he would need to be more calculated.

Vaz was about to continue when the grotesque corpse that bit off Ruiz's fingers minutes earlier stepped out of the forest. Three fresh bullet holes were lodged in its chest, yet it still walked. It let out a low, guttural moan as it moved toward Ruiz, whose back was turned as he contended with the throbbing pain in his hand along with the disorienting shock.

"Ruiz! Look out!" Vaz cried out, as he instinctively

began reaching for his concealed pistol under his shirt.

A gun blast reverberated from behind him, zipping by his ear and connecting with the approaching zombie's open eye and blowing out the back of its head, dropping it immediately to a lifeless heap on the ground just of out of reach from Ruiz.

Vaz whipped around, glaring at Paim. "You damn near shot my head off!" he shouted with ears ringing.

Paim ignored him and pointed to the jungle past the church. "That's where we're heading. I saw that thing moving that way and it was carrying my second briefcase."

"I'm bleeding bad here," Ruiz said.

"Then the sooner we nab the sonofabitch in the jungle, the sooner we can get out of here and get you all fixed up," Paim replied.

Vaz looked from Paim to Ruiz in disbelief.

"Yes, boss," Ruiz mumbled and walked toward Paim.

"Come on, let's go," Paim ordered Vaz.

Shaking his head, Vaz moved forward, back into the jungle to follow the drugs, moans emanating all around them. Paim made sure Vaz was in the lead, himself and his briefcase safely in the center, and bringing up the rear, the injured Ruiz, leaving a trail of blood behind.

Climbing over old fallen trees, pushing through thick foliage, they continued in the direction where Paim had seen the man with the briefcase. The moans continued, almost as if beckoning them forward.

"Up there, I see a village, at least I think it's a village," Vaz said as he pushed through lush, green vegetation.

Paim caught up, peering over his shoulder. "I see people

in that village, though not many of them." He paused, squinting. "There! There he is! The one with my briefcase! I knew this persistence would pay off!" Paim said proudly.

Vaz peered in the direction Paim had pointed. He was right, there was a man carrying a briefcase. He could immediately tell something was wrong by the way the man staggered, but he didn't look like the rotting cadavers they had seen. He was wearing clothes and didn't resemble a mummy covered in sores.

"Soon we will be on our way home, my friend, and you will get the medical help you…" Paim began then fell silent, hearing grunting behind him. And…*was something snarling?*

Both Paim and Vaz turned around at the mysterious sound and saw that Ruiz had stopped walking roughly twenty feet back. He was looking down at his hand and shaking his head back and forth rapidly.

"What the hell is he doing? Ruiz, come on! Almost there!" Paim said with more than a hint of concern.

Still shaking his head, Ruiz began stomping his feet on the ground as he continued to growl, snarl, and make guttural, animal-like noises.

Vaz began backing up and noticed Paim doing the same. Even in the sinister and violent world of the drug trade, this unnatural behavior instantly put up one's defenses.

Now flailing his arms wildly and stomping his feet, Ruiz began spitting up blood. Small streams of it trickled out of his mouth at first, then turned to projectile vomiting onto the grassy trail leading to the village.

Suddenly, Ruiz was no longer concerned with his bit

hand. Both arms hung loosely at his sides while his vomiting ceased and he let his head hang down, as if staring at something intently on the ground. His breathing appeared shallow and slow. The ground around him was sprayed with digestive juices and thick blood.

Vaz watched in horror, his mind suddenly recalling a popular American horror movie he had watched the previous year at the cinema. *Dawn of the Dead.* Humans were bit, then turned into the walking dead. Just like what appeared to be happening here.

"The bite, he's turning into one of those…things," Vaz whispered.

"No! This cannot be!" Paim shouted, drawing the attention of meandering villager zombies.

"Shh! We're going to draw more of those things to us!" Vaz said, glaring at Paim.

"Don't you tell me to—" Paim began.

Ruiz slowly looked up, straight at his boss. He recognized the men in front of him. One had ordered his brother into the water, causing his death. The other had watched his brother die in the water and survived. His eyes turned milky-white, his mouth and clothes covered in vomited blood. He stared at the living beings in front of him angrily, and then, hungrily. *Food.* He began biting at the air, gnashing his teeth together as if rabid, streams of red-tinted saliva dripping from his hungry mouth.

20
CAT ENCOUNTER

va peered into the crack on the side of the crater past the large fallen rock. Her mind tried to process what she was to do. She had watched as a man she had vague and short memories of fire a weapon. *Guns, they are called guns, and they can hurt me.* The blast had caused a large rock to fall, blocking her from them. *Sneaky, very sneaky.*

Seeing it was pointless to continue any attempts at entry, Eva turned around determinedly, surveying the fallen leper zombies that had followed her up to this area. She remembered death, she had always been terrified of dying, but now she realized, it wasn't so bad. In fact, it was quite freeing.

Other than the pain in her stomach that would be relieved once she devoured Laura, she no longer had concerns for anything other than her immediate needs. Even her looks no longer mattered. *Food* was all that mattered. Food and revenge.

She made her way back to the crater entrance where she and her cohorts had traveled up earlier. *Be persistent, you will find them again, try to run. Like you used to, before...* Still having much of her strength and no longer feeling the pain on her ankle, Eva ran forward, entering the tunnel, back to the waterfalls.

William led the way through the crater's small, slip opening. Behind him, Laura struggled with the pain of her open wound administered by Eva. Sam continued moving through the incredibly tight fit. Not helping things was the backpack he had to carry instead of wear. He had considered dropping it but the notebooks, flare gun, William's thin briefcase, and possibly the most important thing, Violet Laceflower plants he had picked earlier. If they made it off this island, those plants might be of interest to a great number of people.

His knife was at his side and his revolver remained in his right hand. Sam could tell Laura was struggling and called out to William in front. "William, when will we be out of this tight squeeze?"

"Soon," William called back, his frail body tired from the quick trek through the dangerous wall of the crater.

The further into the side of the crater they moved, the darker it got.

"I hope you know the way through here," Laura said, grimacing as her back bumped a jutted-out rock.

They continued on, Sam continually glancing back and was relieved to not see any more signs of Eva pursuing them.

He doubted she would. The large rock that had fallen had pretty much ensured that. He feared they hadn't seen the last of her, though.

Shaking the zombified corpse of Eva out of his mind, he once more focused on Laura. She was struggling but quite well at covering up how uncomfortable she must be in this tight space. After her injury, Sam was more confident than ever they had made the right choice to move through the small side passage in the crater instead of risking a trip through the darkened tunnel, not knowing whether Eva would be stalking them or what lay in wait below.

Get her mind off of this, talk to her.

"Laura, when we get back to America, what's the first thing you're going to eat?" Sam asked.

"I know what she'd eat if it were available," William called out from the front.

At the same time, she and her dad replied, "Cheeseburger, fries, strawberry milkshake."

"What? Am I missing something?" Sam said, forcing a chuckle out, glad he was lightening the mood slightly.

"Cheeseburger, fries, strawberry milkshake. My dad and I would often go on dates. We went to this local diner, Sal's Burger Digs. Damn were those some good burgers," Laura said, smiling at the fond memory.

Smiling, William added, "We would go there, pig out, then I would take her to the cinema, and whatever was playing on that two-screen theater we would watch. And I mean anything. Remember that time we went to see that Christopher Lee movie? *Dracula: Prince of Darkness* I believe it was called? You were nine years old. Oh, how you squeezed my hand tightly through most of that one!"

"He would always get one large milkshake and make us split it. I always, always begged for my own but you would say it's more special to share something sweet together out of the same glass, and I would say I didn't want your cooties," Laura replied, now chuckling at the warm memories.

"It was a tradition, Sal's and a movie…" William trailed off.

"The last time we went on our father-daughter date you told me you had an important doctor's appointment the next day due to your increasingly severe headaches. After you got the news, everything changed. For all of us."

They all fell silent before Sam chimed in. "Well, I suppose wherever we end up, there's got to be a place that can grill up a hamburger and make some french fries. I'm more of a chocolate milkshake kind of guy, but damn if a strawberry milkshake doesn't sound positively delicious right about now."

Laura glanced back at him and smiled. "Come to Port Aransas, Texas and you'll sink your teeth into the best burger your mouth has ever tasted."

"I'll take you up on that, Laura," Sam replied softly.

William, keeping quiet in the lead, smiled broadly. His daughter, his crowning achievement in this life, was with him once more, and with her was a decent man.

The dim amount of light from the crater's entrance behind them had faded. Now, new light could be seen up ahead. Pointing, William exclaimed, "There, up there is our exit!"

With newfound determination, all three of them pushed on through the tight fit. Laura, ignoring the pain on her back, focused on the light growing brighter and brighter. "How did you find this?" she asked her father.

"I realized that even with some of my bobby-trap concoctions around the waterfalls, it may not keep them out for good," William said. "And that would mean I would be trapped, backed up into a corner. So, I did some exploring around the exterior of the crater, found the crack on its outside, forced myself to be brave and trekked through it, coming out at where we entered."

"What if those things had found your little walkway?" Laura asked, genuinely curious and impressed by her dad's ingenuity as they continued their descent forward.

"Good question. You'll see in a minute," William replied as the light grew brighter the closer they got.

Laura glanced backed at Sam, puzzled by what they were about to discover at the other end of the narrow, jagged walkway. He returned the look with a shrug and grin.

Sam liked the Joyners. He could tell they loved each other and had gone through so much. He reflected briefly on his initial reluctance to helping track down Laura's father, and now saw that he had indeed made the correct choice. Seeing just how resilient Laura was, and her deep love for her father, was endearing her to Sam even more. She was gentle but determined, even when continually fighting through obviously intense pain on her back. She wasn't giving up on their survival and neither was he.

The bond Laura and William obviously shared made

him miss his own mom and dad. Overprotective as they were, it was out of sheer love for him, their only child. He had taken them for granted numerous times, including going on this very trip with a guy like Ed. Now, all he cared about was seeing to it that Laura and her estranged father made it off this hellish island, and wrapping his arms around his mom and dad tightly, back in the relative safety of Burbank, California. Soon, he hoped.

They arrived at their exit. William pushed back a grouping of sticks lined with bamboo leaves strung together to form a sort of makeshift camouflage doorway propped up against the opening. Stepping out into the sunlight, Laura and Sam followed close behind. Sam was truly impressed with William's handiwork. It blended in perfectly with the rest of the greenery that surrounded it. No one would be able to see that a hidden walkway led directly behind the man-made construction.

Sam glanced at his compass and quickly realized that they had made their way to the far north side of the crater. They had made it to the opposite end of the island. Directly behind them, about a hundred feet back, water crashed on a beach with heavy seaweed cover. Resting on the beach, turned on its side, was a boat, or what was left of it. It appeared to have been set on fire exactly as William had told them.

"Well, that's not an option," Sam said, peering at their surroundings.

"Exactly, the natives made short work of it. Which is why I gave up on any and all attempts of escape, until now," William answered sadly.

"We need to make our way to that airplane that just landed," Laura chimed in.

"Yes, we do indeed, but first," Sam began as he pulled another shirt from his backpack, took out his knife and cut it into long pieces.

"Sam, we don't have time," Laura began.

"Yes, we do, take off your shirt," he responded, seeing the back of her tank top caked with blood.

She looked at him trustingly as William turned around, facing the ocean, letting this man take care of his ailing daughter.

Nodding, she carefully peeled off her shirt. "Ouch, damn this hurts," Laura shuddered.

Sam took the two remaining pain tablets from the church and a small container of water out of the backpack and gently poured it over the exposed wound. Seeing her grimace at the cold water hitting the cut, he softly said, "Hang in there, trust me, I'm an Eagle Scout." He handed her the pain meds which she popped into her mouth and swallowed.

She chuckled then felt his strong, firm hands against her back, gently dabbing at her bloodied wound with a spare cloth out of the backpack. Pouring a bit of water on the soiled wash towel, he wrung it out then pressed it against the cut, holding it in place. He tossed his bloodied tank top off to the side and gently wrapped his ripped shirt around her back against the cool, wet towel, bringing it to the front just below her bra. He then tied it into a knot securely without being too snug.

"Here you go, my last shirt. Nothing fancy and don't

laugh." He motioned for her to raise her arms as he slid the t-shirt carefully over her raised arms and head, gently pulling it down over her exposed chest, making sure he kept his eyes on hers.

She looked into his eyes as he finished pulling the shirt down carefully then stood up. They were standing close to each other; he could feel her warm breath on him. Her beautiful brown eyes locked onto his. Neither smiled, both for a brief second enjoying the closeness.

William glanced back and once more smiled to himself then cleared his throat.

Snapping back to the matter at hand, Sam looked over at William. "Okay, good to go, lead the way. Back to the other side, I suppose."

Laura smiled to herself, glancing down at the shirt she now wore. It was white and in the middle of it in red and black letters were the words in a science fiction font, *May the Force Be With You*. Directly under the words were the two small cartoon characters, R2D2 and C3PO. C3PO was waving at anyone who looked at the shirt.

Seeing her smile, Sam muttered, "Birthday present from my mom. You and your dad had your traditions, well, my mom, God bless her, still thinks of me as her little boy."

"I love it, thank you, Sam. Thanks for, well, a second shirt. Looks like I'm cleaning you out of shirts," Laura replied, still smiling and immediately feeling significantly more comfortable with the makeshift bandage.

"Think nothing of it," Sam replied softly.

Laura smiled and glanced away, suddenly very aware

of her attraction to him and sensing the feeling was mutual.

William had found a long bamboo with a jagged broken tip. Using it as a walking stick, he moved forward past Sam and Laura, pointing in the direction they would be heading. "Now, we're pretty far from the other side of the island. Large, jagged rocks, likely from the meteor that crashed here, are spread out around the perimeter, making it impossible to walk around the rim. During my years here, I've learned the best, quickest way to reach the other side is straight on through. Past the village. The good news is, I know all the little shortcuts. The bad news is, they still lead us close to the village. When I was alone, I got really good at sneaking around, but there are three of us, so silence is the key once we get close, got it?"

They nodded in agreement as they took off into the jungle.

"I'm surprised they can see with those glazed-over eyes," Laura observed as they hiked through the dense jungle forest.

William nodded. "Oh, they can see, alright. I'm not sure how well. Their sense of smell, however, is heightened even in their advanced state of decomposition. Likely better than when they were alive. Laura, that cut you've got, it's a good thing Sam had some extra supplies, they can really sense blood. I found that out when I was setting up those traps around the lake, sliced my hand good. It didn't take long before I heard the moans drudging over in my direction from the village. Two of them actually, they didn't make it far."

Sam glanced over. "Why? What happened?"

William raised his revolver and shook it slightly.

"Ah, got it," Sam nodded.

"I'm a doctor, one that hates guns, as Laura well knows. Even if I'm from the great state of Texas. But I had to get cozy with them relatively fast once Dr. Pedroso's man-made infection spread. It actually started when I was setting up camp in that crater. We were barely on speaking terms at that point." William fell silent, thinking back to things going from bad to worse to deadly.

"How's the bandage holding up?" Sam asked Laura who appeared to be keeping up quite well.

"Good, Sam, thanks again. You're pretty good with this survival stuff. Well, other than stepping into one of my dad's traps over by the lake." She chuckled.

"That's right, you did tell me you got hung up in one of my traps. Well, better that than run through with the bamboo spikes," William joked lightly.

Grinning, Sam replied, "My parents, well, mainly my dad, wanted me in Boy Scouts. So, I was enrolled at ten years old. A little over six years later I made it to Eagle Scout. By that time, I had a lot more on my mind than scouting. Driving a car being top of the list. But I must say, looking back, those were good years of my life and well worth it. Made my dad quite proud. I still remember his face when I reached Eagle Scout." He fell silent, reminiscing of better times.

"Well, Sam, my apologies for you being stuck here and for the loss of your friend. But not all hope has been lost, it seems," William said.

"Oh, I intend to get off this island with the both of you on that plane, and I'm not giving up," Laura said firmly.

"Damn right," Sam quickly fired back.

"Well, by the looks of those clouds out there, the clock is ticking. That's a nasty one, similar to what you apparently flew through yesterday. However, this one's trajectory appears to be heading over the island."

"How long until it makes landfall?" Laura asked.

"Likely a few hours, maybe more but, maybe less," William replied.

The three of them, almost in unison, picked up their pace while still being wary of their surroundings.

"Hold up," William said, raising his hand. "I hear something."

They stopped and fell silent. Insects could be heard buzzing by, the flapping of birds wings high in the air.

Out of the brush in front of them, something large charged forward, heading straight toward them.

"Look out!" William shouted as what appeared to be a medium-sized jungle cat with red stripes and white fur charged them. Sam grabbed Laura instinctively, both jumping to the side of their trail, while William, with his outstretched bamboo stick held his ground.

The creature came to a stop in front of him, snarling and growling while swiping its claws at the outstretched, sharp bamboo.

Sam held out his revolver, pointing it at the animal's head. It glanced at him, piercing yellow eyes, looking hungry. He pulled back on the hammer, but William said steadily, "No, Sam, don't fire that gun. Just take it easy."

Sam kept the gun pointed and found that Laura had

joined him, standing right beside him, her own gun drawn.

"What are we doing here, William?" Sam asked urgently.

Jabbing at the cat, who swatted at the bamboo, William replied quietly, "Shh, we've likely stepped into her den, or are near it. I've encountered these animals before, never seen them anywhere else on earth so my guess is they are a product of the island's evolution after the meteor hit, much like everything else here. Just, stay calm."

"Easy for you to say," Sam replied, "That thing looks like it wants to have us for breakfast, lunch, and dinner."

The cat's long tail swished back and forth as if trying to decide what to do with her intruders. It continually snarled, showing them her large, sharp fangs.

"How many of these things are on this island? It's not that big!" Laura said, staring at it, wide-eyed.

"Not many in my experience, they keep to themselves due to the infected. It's like they know something is off-kilter here. Come on, girl, easy does it. We'll go our way, you go yours," William said calmly, keeping his eyes on the cat.

They all remained silent as the cat seemed to be contemplating what her next move was. It smelled the air while keeping its eyes on them. Then slowly, it started backing up.

Sam's eyes widened, watching the animal standing down.

Laura grabbed onto Sam's arm. "I can't believe this, she's leaving!"

"That's a good girl, easy does it. You go your way, we go ours," William repeated as he kept his eyes locked on the cat until it was far enough away that it quickly turned and jumped back into the thick foliage, completely out of sight.

"Whew," Laura exclaimed, releasing Sam's arm. "That was intense. And on an island that continues to throw more intense shit at us every hour we're here."

"Try living here for two years. Those aren't the only strange animals that, if I were to wager a guess, are only found on this particular island," William came back, lowering his bamboo staff.

"She was smelling us. I thought for sure she smelled my wound," Laura said quietly.

William began leading the way once more, giving them a wide berth from where the cat had jumped away. "You're right, she smelled your blood. It smelled untainted. The few animal species on this island are picked off by the infected. It's the only food source the natives have. The animals are used to their smell, the smell of death itself, and they've grown accustomed to fearing the zombies. We, on the other hand, well, you get the picture."

"That cat was beautiful, I've never seen a species that remotely looked like it," Sam said in amazement.

"Oh, there are more out there," William replied. "Monkeys, birds, smaller rodents. I kill only to survive, and only the very minimum. Like the meat you ate back at my humble abode. This island has been through much since us humans invaded its natural habitat. This island is special, and we humans have most certainly corrupted it by our presence."

"Well, I'll be happy to leave it be as soon as possible," Sam added.

They walked in silence, only stopping for short rests, to check on Laura's injured back, and to rehydrate. They crossed several hills filled with beautiful plant life. Flowers not seen before anywhere else on earth. Small flowing streams of water lining the trail periodically.

"Come on, the village is getting close," William said in a near whisper.

"Yeah, and so is that storm cloud," Laura said, glancing up into the still sunny sky while behind it rolled the black beast.

Eva had quickly made her way down the tunnel, past the still-floating zombie under the waterfalls that was doomed to stay there, struggling in vain to escape. She dropped into the water and quickly found herself out the other side, back in the lake. She feebly swam to the shore then pulled herself out of the water.

Still in the bloodied shirt Sam had provided for her in what felt like a lifetime ago, it snagged on a rock as she walked forward and quickly ripped off her body. She walked on past the lake, past the booby traps, only her small cut-off shorts covering her lower half. Her milky-white eyes looked down at her still-firm breasts. She had vague memories of using them to her advantage. This was no longer needed. Only *food*.

She snapped at the air with her mouth and took deep breaths in, trying to locate warm- blooded humans in the vicinity. Her keen sense of smell picked up the scent as she started toward the village in the distance.

21
RUIZ'S FATE

Ruiz looked hazily toward the ground, the whites of his eyes eating away at his pupils until his brown eyes were completely replaced by a milky-white substance. With a glazed-over expression he looked at his hand, missing three digits and dripping blood.

Slowly raising his head, his foggy eyes looked out at a new world. *Where am I? What am I doing here? I'm so hungry!* Raising his severely wounded hand, he stuck the two remaining fingers into his mouth and bit down hard. They easily came off, leaving behind a stump. His ears heard yelling but it was muffled. Staring ahead, he could make out two figures standing in front of him as he chewed up his fingers hungrily.

"Ruiz! What the hell are you doing?" Paim exclaimed, watching in horror as his employee of over seven years chewed off the remaining digits on his left hand.

Staring on in equal revulsion, Vaz whispered, "He's infected with whatever has taken over the people on this island. We must leave at once or we're stuck here until that storm passes." As if on cue, in the distance, a boom echoed from over the ocean. Thunder from the now quickly approaching storm.

"What the hell type of island is this?" Paim shouted, for the first time beginning to show a bit of concern for his own well-being. A rare occurrence. The man was untouchable and nearly invincible in his homeland, but here, this was another story completely.

Clenching the briefcase of cocaine tightly, he raised his gun at Ruiz, then hesitated. His loyal employee, along with Vidal, being picked off in rapid succession. Paim glanced back to see if the man in possession of his second briefcase remained in eyesight back at the village but was dismayed to see he had vanished. *Shit! This is going downhill fast,* he thought.

Ruiz continued his transformation from human to something else entirely. The saliva of the leper zombie infecting him rapidly, entering his bloodstream and killing off the part that made him human. His mind was scrambled but still coherent enough to know this was not normal, but he had no way of stopping it. He felt rage, hateful, angry and most importantly, *ravenous.*

His nose twitched, he smelled something wonderful, something warm and delicious. His hollow eyes peered out at the two figures. One, he barely recognized, while the other, he knew well. In another time, maybe he had been friends with this one. The man was large, and dangerous. *But I am more dangerous now.*

He swallowed the chewed-up the flesh, bone, and gristle of his two remaining fingers, but this did little to curb his appetite. In fact, it was somewhat revolting. It tasted of death. But the delectable smell of the two in front of him was tantalizing.

"He needs to be put down, Paim," Vaz said quietly.

Raising his gun at Ruiz, Paim put his finger on the trigger, then hesitated.

"Do it! He's changed! Shoot him and cut your losses!" Vaz said louder.

Paim glared over at Vaz then looked once more at his rapidly changing employee. His hand began to shake. He had murdered before—often, actually. But never a loyal employee such as Ruiz who was essentially his right-hand man. Now, literally, with only his right hand remaining.

Thick, infected saliva dripped from Ruiz's hungry, waiting lips. His eyes fell on the shiny silver object held out in front of the large person in front of him. He remembered this thing. He had used one like it numerous times to end others' lives. Now it was pointed at him. *This person intends to do me harm.*

Vaz kept his eyes on Paim as his hand slowly inched its way to the copilot's revolver under his sweat-covered shirt. "Do it, come on, Paim!"

"You shut the fuck up, pilot man! What do you know of murder? You don't tell me what to—"

Above, a loud crack of thunder reverberated through the sky, setting everything that followed in rapid motion.

Ruiz took off in a dead sprint toward his potential victims just as Paim pulled the trigger on his large, silver Browning 9MM pistol. The bullet erupted out of its barrel toward its intended target. But Ruiz's instincts had kicked in; he knew the man in front of him would do this and shifted ever so slightly to his left as the bullet zinged by his head, missing it by mere centimeters as he continued rushing forward.

Vaz pulled his revolver out from under his shirt. Without hesitating, he raised it and fired, hitting Ruiz in the throat as he leapt in the air toward Paim. Ruiz instantly dropped to the ground at his boss's feet.

Paim instantly looked over to Vaz, who now had the revolver trained on him. "How *dare* you! Where did you get that sidearm?"

Behind both men, a gathering of zombie lepers from the village, hearing, seeing, and most importantly, smelling the commotion unfolding nearby, shambled over to where the standoff was occurring. Groans wafted up from the nameless and, in some cases, faceless corpses, filling the increasingly windy air.

"You're going to give me that key to the airplane and that gun. Or, I swear to God, I will blow your brains out right here and now, you sonofabitch," Vaz uttered coldly.

Paim stared at his new adversary, unblinking, the silver Browning 9MM revolver at his side in his right hand and the briefcase full of cocaine in the other. He recognized the revolver Vaz held in his hand. "You got that Smith & Wesson hand cannon off of Barroso when you were out searching the downed plane, didn't you?"

Vaz, also unblinking, with his gun raised and aimed directly at Paim's head, nodded.

"You sneaky little fucker, you, I knew I shouldn't have trusted you from the get-go. I only use my own people, but you? You're quite the anomaly, and what you're doing will not only cost you your life but the life of your wife and your ch—"

Vaz pulled the trigger just as Paim flinched, blasting his right ear completely off.

Paim screamed out, dropping the briefcase onto the ground and lifting his hand to the bloody hole where his ear had just been. Blood began pumping steadily out, seeping through his cupped hand and spreading onto his shirt. "You shot me!" Paim shouted.

Vaz pulled back on the hammer of Barroso's 9MM revolver. "Next one goes through your eye. I'm not a murderer, yet. Now, drop your gun and give me that key, you two-bit drug peddling *piece of shit*."

Staring at Vaz with eyes full of pain and rage, Paim took his hand from the side of his bleeding face and hesitated.

"I mean it," Vaz said slowly, still unblinking.

With his blood-drenched hand, Paim dug into the front pocket of his loose-fitting designer shirt and produced the key to the Cessna. He closed his fist, making sure the key was covered in his blood, then opened his hand and dropped it onto the ground.

The moans behind them grew louder, as did the wind.

Paim glanced back, seeing the approaching horde as his eyes widened in horror.

Vaz, however, kept his eyes trained on his opponent. "Now the gun. Drop it, then step way back," he said steadily.

"What are you going to do? Leave me here?" Paim shouted, continually glancing back.

Something grabbed his foot while a sharp pain ripped through his ankle. He looked down to see Ruiz, with half his neck completely blown off, had grabbed hold of him and sunk his teeth directly into the side of his ankle. He shouted out in pain while Ruiz bit down and through flesh, muscle, and bone.

Vaz, caught off-guard by the sudden and strange turn of events, blinked. His eyes fell to the dropped bloody key on the ground near Paim's unbitten foot.

This time, Paim didn't hesitate, aiming his Browning 9MM directly at the top of Ruiz's head and pulling the trigger. Black hair, skull fragments and brain matter exploded outward, dropping Ruiz's head to the ground. His mouth, however, was still locked tightly around Paim's blood-soaked ankle.

At the immense agony of both his shot-off ear and throbbing ankle, Paim dropped to the ground.

Vaz charged forward, scooping up the dropped key while Paim pushed at the lifeless Ruiz's obliterated head, trying to free the teeth from his blood-covered foot.

Vaz stood back beside the dropped briefcase full of cocaine and looked at it. He picked it up, shouting, "I'm leaving this damned island without you! Then, I'm going to take this garbage back to the Kokoda airport and hand it in to the authorities."

"No, no! You sonofabitch! You can't do this to me!" Paim shouted, then aimed his Browning at Vaz, who was much quicker than his severely injured captor. The bullet easily missed him, instead zinging by and smashing into a nearby tree.

Vaz suddenly heard moaning behind him. He whipped around to see three leper zombies within an arm's length of him. With no time to raise his gun and pull its trigger, Vaz did the only thing that came to his frantic mind, he swung the briefcase as hard as he could at the approaching zombies. The briefcase connected with the nearest walking corpse, what had likely in its miserable life been a man but now resembled a skeleton with sickly green skin wrapped around its bones. It was biting at the air when the briefcase made contact, snapping its head backwards with such ferocity that it broke its neck. With nothing to hold it up, the head fell backwards, resting lazily against the pathetic creature's back. Unable to see forward, the zombie shuffled several steps then fell to the ground.

Another gunshot rang out, missing Vaz's head by barely an inch.

"If I'm not getting out of here alive, neither are you!" Paim shouted. But it was in vain, as four more zombies had arrived, one a man in a bloody, torn-up Black Sabbath shirt. In his hand was the second briefcase. They all stood over Paim, looking down hungrily at him.

Paim unloaded the rest of his Browning's bullets into his

assailants until the only thing emanating from the gun was empty clicks. Only two of his shots had connected with the heads of the zombies, dropping them instantly. The other two remained unharmed, and hungry.

Meanwhile, Vaz had two more zombies to contend with. The first was a woman, likely in her mid-twenties before the disease that plagued this island took her over. One sagging breast was all that remained, a hideous monstrosity of rotting skin with thick, puss-filled lesions oozing out of open sores and a mouth that only had half its teeth remaining. The woman was biting down frantically, trying to get a taste of what she was smelling in this close proximity to a living human being.

This time, Vaz was able to get his gun in time. Remembering the zombie movie he'd once seen, he carefully but quickly aimed at her forehead as she grabbed for him. He pulled the trigger and her forehead, along with all the contents inside of it, exploded backwards, covering the thick green grass in red. She instantly fell lifelessly to the ground.

Paim swung wildly with his gun and made contact with an older looking zombie. The gun smashed against his chest hard. Paim could hear brittle bones inside cracking from the impact. However, this did little to stop him. His hungry jaws chomped at the air the closer he got to Paim.

The last of the four, the man with the Black Sabbath shirt still carrying Paim's drug-filled briefcase, hovered over him but didn't attack. It just stared at him, almost as if it were thinking what its next move would be. Paim looked warily up at the man carrying what belonged to him. "Why aren't you attacking me! Come on, you fucker!"

Ed tilted his head, contemplating. He smelled the air but already, the scent of fresh human blood was beginning to fade. This man was becoming what he now was. With his white eyes, he stared down at the bloody foot with a chunk of flesh ripped out of it.

Paim leapt forward, grabbing hold of the sides of the briefcase and yanking it from Ed's hands.

Ed contemplated this, slowly opening and closing his mouth, grinding his teeth together. He looked back to the rage-filled man who was now quickly attempting to stand to his feet. Ed's foggy mind kicked into gear, but the still-human Paim was quicker.

Hobbling, Paim swung the briefcase, connecting with Ed's head, and knocked him backwards onto the green foliage below.

Ed's eyes narrowed as his dark side bubbled up deep within his psyche.

"Stay down, you fucking disgusting zombie shit! I saw what you and your kind did to my employee, Pinto, back on the beach!" the man shouted at him before turning away, staring at the village beyond.

Ed began standing back to his feet, but Paim had already fled, hobbling as fast as he could, considering the injury to his ankle. As he moved, a line of blood was left in his wake on the ground below. The side of his face was throbbing from the missing ear and a loud ringing continually reverberated inside his fog-filled head. He made his way toward the village fighting through the agony.

Ed glanced back at Vaz who was struggling with the other zombies, then watched as Paim hobbled slowly away. *Pinto*, the giant man had said. This man was the cause of all of this. *The cause of me! Follow this man. See to it that his life ends. Permanently.*

Vaz was dealing with the last of his immediate threats and for him, the saddest. A child. Possibly no older than ten, judging from its height and body structure. However, what had been a child at one point was now something straight out of a ghastly horror movie. Its eyes were wide and white. Large open scabs covered its body, and it no longer had a scalp. Instead, the dull and grotesque sight of its exposed skull was visible. Vaz wasn't even sure the sex of the child, due to its heavy state of decomposition.

Aiming his Smith & Wesson at the pathetic being, he hesitated, thinking of his own daughter, likely the same age. He shook his head sadly. "Nope."

He stepped backward, away from the approaching child, nearly tripping over the remaining zombie with its neck broken backwards. It lay helplessly on the ground, slowly moving its mouth open then closed. Vaz raised his foot and brought it down onto the zombie's head, easily busting it open. It immediately stopped squirming.

Repulsed by the carnage, Vaz turned his attention to where Paim had fallen but discovered he was no longer there. The huge, broad-shouldered man was instead hobbling away toward the village carrying the second briefcase. Following him was the dead man with the Black Sabbath t-shirt.

"Where in the hell are you going, Paim?" Vaz turned to

look further into the jungle, past the village, near the crater, talking to himself. "This young guy in the Black Sabbath shirt must have been a passenger on that doomed plane. His wounds look fresh, and he looks to be an American. Now he's one of these…things. Are the rest of them turned as well? Damnit!"

He sighed, trying to decide what to do next. What if there were more survivors out there? *And you're going to leave them here on zombie island.* How could he even find them, if he did decide to stay? *It's a fool's errand. You promised your daughter, Vaz!*

Sighing, he turned back toward the beach, still avoiding the small child that slowly and aimlessly shuffled toward him. The bloody key now rested in his front pocket, the briefcase of cocaine in his one hand, and the Smith & Wesson in the other with several bullets remaining.

Vaz glanced up at the sky, the black cloud was nearing, and the sun was setting. He glanced at his watch. 7:56 PM. If he made a run for it, he might be airborne before the storm hit. He looked back toward the village and beyond.

Fuck.

22
NOSE CANDY

Paim wasn't the only one heading to the village where the aimless dead shuffled as their rotten brains had dim memories of the streets and huts lining them. A topless blond woman had made her way from the lake back to the village. Her mind was getting quite good at knowing the lay of the land, recalling the beach, church, village, then crater. All within walking distance on this small island that was now her home.

She had a bullet hole in her back and a large bite taken from her neck, but neither gave her any discomfort. The only discomfort she felt was inside her stomach. The insatiable lust for flesh. *Living human flesh.* She peered on from her well-hidden vantage point in a cluster of palm trees and thick bushes near the village, seeing the man in the Black Sabbath shirt carrying something. She had seen that item; it was a black briefcase.

She heard gunshots ring out in what looked to be a stand-off near a long row of huts, between several men with guns and several islanders. Many of *her kind* had been destroyed. A bulky, muscular man with big biceps had been injured in the scuffle and was now heading toward the village. Behind him was…*Ed. Yes, that was his name. He is one of us now.*

Another man nearby carried the other briefcase. The air smelled *human.*

Keeping a close eye on the approaching storm cloud, William, Sam, and Laura traversed through the jungle back toward the village. It had been a slow trek due to Laura's aching back and the frail state William was in. "Hold up, I need to rest just a second!" he sighed as the huts came into view in the distance.

They stopped and all drank some water.

"Those storm clouds, I've seen plenty, and this storm looks to be a real sonofabitch. We should keep moving. Sam, I can carry the backpack for a bit," William stated.

Sam shook his head. "I'm good. Thanks for the offer."

William nodded his appreciation. He could tell Sam knew he was struggling in his current shape.

"We still have the flare gun, want to give it another go?" Laura asked Sam.

He looked up at the rolling clouds and the setting sun and sighed. "I'm not holding out much hope for this thing to work but I can give it a try." Sam reached into the backpack and drew the flare gun out with one remaining flare.

William and Laura watched as he raised it into the air.

Sam pulled the trigger, but again, the flare didn't ignite. Shaking his head, he tried it again and still, nothing. "This thing is spent," he muttered, lowering the flare gun.

Laura came up beside him. "It must have gotten damaged in the water. At least you got that one shot out. It saved our lives."

Disappointed, Sam nodded and popped open the chamber, removing the flare. He tossed the useless flare gun to the side then reconsidering it, hung onto the flare, sticking it into his pocket. He glanced over at William and Laura. "You never know," he said, hopeful.

Laura patted him on the back. "One way or another, Sam, we're getting out of here."

"We're gonna damn well try," he replied.

Lightning cracked above them as darkness swept over the island.

Paim felt woozy from the heavy loss of blood but there was something else too. Something alien inside of him coursing through his system, and it hurt. *This feels like what I would imagine acid feels like burning the skin!* He pushed away the thought of a particularly gruesome fate several of his inner circle had inflicted on a rival drug lord's family several years ago. *Is this my fate after a life of inflicting terror on others?*

He arrived at the row of huts as night fell. *Or was it*

dark from the storm clouds? It didn't matter, all that mattered was the incredible pain he felt on the side of his face and his ankle but more importantly, in his blood.

He peered into the village. It was dilapidated and utterly depressing. Shambling through the streets were more of the things that had infected Ruiz. Seeing this beastly man and smelling his blood, they began making their way toward him.

"Come on, you fuckers! I'll take on every last one of you rotting pieces of shit!" Paim hollered before suddenly bending over and groaning at the sudden sharp pain in his abdomen. *Hungry, I'm so...hungry!* He was without a weapon and felt his strength draining. Coming to the first small hut he saw, he stumbled inside and closed the door, latching it shut with a meager piece of wood that had once been used to hold the door in place, glad to find it empty of any of the zombies roaming the streets.

He fell onto a dirty mattress covered in what looked to be old, dried feces and urine. He couldn't be sure, and he didn't care. He could barely stand any longer. Looking around the tiny one-room "house" he saw what must have been a child's doll covered in dust and spider webs. Several other odds and ends were scattered about the floor, eating utensils, plates and several articles of abandoned clothing.

"Hungry, so damn hungry," Paim muttered, putting his hand to the hole on the side of his face where his ear had once been. As his hand touched it, he noticed that the pain he had felt mere minutes ago was beginning to subside while the hunger was increasing.

He looked at the bite on his ankle. It was severely

mangled. Leaning forward, he touched that as well; it still stung, but far less than before. Paim doubled over as the hunger ripped through his body. "Fuck me, this hurts! Ahh!" he shouted out as he grabbed hold of his hair, ripping clumps of it out.

There was a pounding on the hut's door. After several attempts, the nearly rotted-through wood holding it closed busted apart and the door flew open. Several rotten lepers stood in the doorway, peering inside. Paim looked at them. *This is it. I'm done for.* He scooted himself back against the far wall, looking around for something to protect himself with.

The lepers biting at the air appeared to be trying to smell. Slowly, with blank stares across their rotted, lesion-infested faces, they turned and left the doorway, shuffling back out onto the dirt-covered street.

Why didn't they attack me? Oh no, oh shit! I'm becoming...

His mind spun as he had a difficult time recalling why he was here and what he was after. Looking down, sitting beside him on the rotted mattress, lay the black briefcase. For a moment he felt intense relief, and something like joy. Then confusion.

How do I open this? What's inside? It's important, I remember that.

As his mind continued to regress, he frantically tried to open it, fumbling with the latches. He was able to unhook the first latch, but his fingers began shaking with pain, his head spun, and his stomach was on fire. Saliva dripped from his hungry open mouth onto the briefcase, causing his fingers to slip. Frustrated, he began smashing his fists against it and finally, standing to his feet, he threw it against the side of the hut. The final latch came undone, spilling its contents out onto the dirt floor.

He peered down at the packages that lay spread out haphazardly, tightly wrapped and taped shut in clear bags. A white substance inside. *Think, you know what this is, this belongs to you! What is my name, though? I can't remember my name! Do I have a name?* He shook his head violently, trying to grasp what was happening to him.

Paim dropped to his knees, crawling over to the nearest package of cocaine and picking it up. Inspecting it, he had vague recollections of this substance from another life. It gave pleasure to those that ingested it. *Through the nose.*

He tore open the package, spilling its contents onto the floor. He stared at the white powder as his mind continued to slip. Unlike Eva's, his was devoid of nearly anything decent or humane. His worst tendencies were chaos in every form. His hands shook almost uncontrollably, his head twitching as the virus coursed through his veins.

Then, everything went black.

Drops of rain began falling on William, Sam, and Laura. "Well, the storm has arrived. I guess we try and make it to the church?" Sam asked.

"Great, another night in that place," Laura muttered.

Moving forward, staring back at the village they were

passing, William nodded his approval at their plan. "Just remember, keep quiet. The rain is a good thing right now, it will mask our scent. At least for the leper zombies. I can't be sure about Eva, she's much keener than the rest of them."

"Is there no chance of avoiding the village completely?" Sam asked.

"With this weather and the thick, dense foliage, it's more dangerous than going this route. Lord knows, I've tried. There are sudden drops in the land's elevation that'll break your leg. Plus, that cat we bumped into earlier—there's more of them and other nocturnal animals out there and they can see at night. We can't. At this distance, we are still on relatively flat land and they can't pick up our scent."

"Duly noted," Sam replied quietly as a streak of lightning flashed through the sky, lighting up their surroundings. The village appeared roughly four hundred yards away and in it, shapes could be seen shambling aimlessly.

Laura shuddered at the ghastly sight of the undead moving about in the rain. They were truly lost souls, damned to spend the rest of their lives here until their bodies rotted away completely.

A loud boom overhead followed by another lightning strike, this time closer to where they stood. "This is what I imagine hell would be like," Laura said grimly.

Nodding, Sam whispered, "Come on, let's get moving."

With William in the lead, they quietly crept past the village in the distance, making sure to keep an eye out for wayward, roaming lepers that may have picked up their scent.

Laura, tight beside Sam, whispered, "Your shirt's gonna

get wet, sorry. But that bandage job was a real lifesaver. Thanks."

"The shirt is yours now. A souvenir from your time on Hell Island, in what truly feels like a galaxy far, far away," Sam quietly joked back.

Laura smiled, a nice reprieve from the terror she felt, made all the more ominous by the lighting and thunder crashing overhead. Each time a crack flashed through the sky, the outlined figures lit up. Like demons in the hell they came from.

All three clenched their guns tightly. Sam had Ed's knife in his left hand and Pinto's gun in his right. William was also wielding the bamboo spear.

The rain was steady but thankfully wasn't a downpour, yet. It was getting harder for the three of them to see.

"William, I hope you know where you're going, I can barely see ahead of me anymore!" Sam said through the rain.

"Stay alert, we're heading in the right direction!" he replied.

Another crack of lightning. They were right beside the village. Closer than they had ever been thus far. Through the rain, moans of agonizing hunger echoed through the streets.

They crept silently, Sam and Laura stepping where William stepped. Another crack of thunder and lightning.

"Ed! I saw Ed!" Sam said in a loud whisper, pointing at the village.

"Come on, we need to keep moving!" William replied.

The moans grew louder.

Nearby, inside a small hut in the village, Paim's eyes

opened, now fully glazed-over and white. Drool and blood leaked from his open mouth onto the pile of cocaine in front of him. *Hungry. I'm so, hungry!* He looked at his surroundings. They were foreign to him. In the darkness, his hand ran across the floor immediately in front of him, he felt something soft running between his fingers. Grabbing a handful, he lifted it to his face. *This isn't food.* He was about to drop the handful of white powder, but his mind remembered. He moaned loudly.

This is mine, it is why I am here. This may help me get food quicker, must have food!

Raising it to his face, he buried his nose in the powder. *Breathe in. This is how it works. Remember?*

Paim, while unable to breathe any longer, could still suck in air through his nose. He sniffed as hard as he was able. The pure, uncut cocaine entered Paim's body. The euphoric feeling hit almost immediately, reviving his senses, giving him profound clarity and unmitigated strength.

He stood to his feet, no longer hampered by the pain previously felt in his ankle and the side of his face. Now, he felt...*invincible.*

Looking down at his hand, still covered in white powder, he raised it again, sniffing hard. This made him clench his fists tightly together. Even his hearing from his one ear seemed to improve. He could now easily hear the moans of the dead scattered throughout the village of the damned he had died and been reborn in.

This village in now mine.

Paim smashed open the thin door of the hut, bursting

out into the rain-filled street. He took in his surroundings. Numerous rotten shells of what once had been human beings shuffled past him. A small child stood lifelessly in front of him, its brain trying to comprehend the new beastly presence in their village. Paim looked down at it, then noticed, behind the child, stood a man. *I know this man. This is the one that had my briefcase. He followed me here.*

While not taking his eyes off of Ed, Paim grabbed hold of the child's head and effortlessly twisted it, snapping its neck. He yanked up, ripping the head off of its torso. The body slumped over onto the rain drenched ground. Paim, still looking at Ed, dropped the head in front of him and stepped on it as he made his way forward.

Another crack of thunder and lightning.

"What the hell is *that?*" Laura uttered, catching a glimpse of Paim.

"Whatever it is, it looks like it's about to square off against Ed!" Sam exclaimed.

William, noticing Laura and Sam had slowed, called out to them, "Both of you, we must hurry!"

Boom. Lightning crossed the sky. Ed no longer faced the giant of a man but stared now at William, Laura, and Sam. The large man also saw them in the blinding white streak of lightning.

Darkness fell once more across the island as it waited for the next lightning strike. The rain poured, drenching everything. In the darkness, a man bellowed out. The sound was no longer human but that of a rabid beast.

A leper corpse came up behind the three travelers, grabbing at Laura who screamed.

"Laura!" Sam shouted, kicking the shadowed figured off of her before it could attempt a bite.

William turned and, with his bamboo staff, slammed the sharpened tip into the dark shape's head, dropping it instantly.

"Run!" William shouted.

William, Sam, and Laura took off running past the village while more moans rose up in unison, as if the giant had ushered a call to arms.

Paim stepped forward, now focusing on the fresh meat his nose had picked up, no longer interested in the skinny dead man standing in front of him.

However, Ed was still interested in him. He moved to block Paim's way forward, staring blankly at him. His mind worked hard at understanding what he had just seen—his best friend from another life and the woman he had traveled with. And a man. *Father of woman. Searching for father. Found.* The man in front of him meant to harm them, and everything in this place Ed now recognized as his own afterlife.

Bumping against Ed, Paim glared down at him.

Ed grabbed the man by his throat, digging his nails into the man's dead flesh. Thick blood began to ooze out from between his fingers. This had no effect on Paim, however. Instead, the large man shoved Ed to the ground, quickly grabbing hold of Ed's still outstretched left arm and twisting. Bones and tendons snapped and tore, much like the leper zombie child, as Paim pulled until Ed's arm ripped free from his torso.

Ed's mind tried to comprehend the new injuries his body was sustaining. This man was clearly more powerful than he was. But this man was going to go after Sam. *His Sam.* He looked up at Paim then to the stump where his left arm had been, the tiny part of his remaining human brain trying to comprehend what was happening.

Looking down with crazed, unblinking white eyes, Paim raised the severed arm above his head, and brought it down, over and over on Ed's head until the arm itself had disintegrated into useless pieces of limp meat.

Looking down at Ed's bashed head, satisfied he had put an end to the man's miserable existence, he tossed the remaining arm on top of an unmoving Ed then looked up at the jungle where he had seen the fresh human meat. Stepping on top of Ed's body, he moved forward quickly, determined to catch up with his food. His cocaine-fueled mind processed where they might be heading, and one word floated to the surface. *Church.*

Behind him, a host of the living dead had also caught the scent and, seeing this new member of the island on the hunt, they began shuffling after him.

23
NOWHERE
TO HIDE

Fatigued and sore, William tried to mask his weariness from Sam and Laura as he led the way through the wet jungle. Rain continued pelting them as they tried navigating their way forward. Coming upon a fallen tree, William attempted to jump over it and instantly realized he was going down. His foot slipped out from under him on the muddy ground as he landed in the damp grass, the slick mud causing him to stumble forward in the dark. Trying to catch his fall, he dropped the bamboo staff in front of him as he went down.

Sam reached out, trying to stop his fall, but it was too late. The wet ground moved forward, almost in slow motion, toward William's face as he crashed down, his foot pinned between two rocks. Something snapped inside his leg as he landed with a hard thud. He cried out at the instant pain shooting up his leg.

"Dad! No!" Laura shouted out, immediately rushing to his side with Sam.

"William!" Sam said, putting his hand on the older man's sprawled-out body.

Shaking his head at the pain, William said, "I'm pretty sure my fibula is broken, right above my foot. Damnit!"

"We've got to get you to the church!" Laura exclaimed.

Biting through the pain, William pushed his frail body up with the help of Sam and his daughter. "My gun, I dropped my gun!"

Moans echoed through the jungle behind them, getting closer. Sam and Laura looked at each other worriedly. Sam scanned the immediate area but it was out of sight, lost in the darkness and the rain cloud dumping on them.

"I'm sorry, William, we don't have time to look for it. Laura and I still have ours," Sam said.

"Hand me my bamboo again, I'll be needing it," William said shakily.

"We can help you," Laura said gently.

Lightning cracked through the sky, illuminating the tropical jungle. Now on his feet and looking nervously behind him, William shouted, "They're coming!"

In the flash of light, they saw silhouettes moving through the forest in their direction, moans wafting toward their intended victims. Along with that sound was another more sinister one: a man, growling and attempting to speak. The three of them could barely make out his slurred gibberish, but the message was loud and clear. *We are coming for you.*

Using the bamboo stick as a crutch, William moved forward slowly with the help of Sam toward the church in the distance, guided only by the continuous lightning and Sam's occasional glances at his compass. The broken leg had slowed them down exponentially.

Laura glanced behind them, hearing the moans growing louder.

Another lightning bolt cracked through the sky, lighting up the zombie horde and their new leader, the monstrous, cocaine-fueled Sérgio Paim in the not-too-far distance. Slowly shuffling onward.

They smell us and are following the scent, she thought with a shudder.

Sam glanced back at her and immediately saw the fear. "Come on, Laura, we're almost there!" He pointed forward through the thick tropical forest to the church.

"There it is! Up ahead, I see it!" Laura yelled out over the pounding rain. Sam's *Star Wars* shirt clung to her wet, cold body and had effectively undone the makeshift bandage Sam had applied earlier. She felt the pain and desperately wanted to stop and catch her breath but knew this would lead to instant death. Between her and Sam, they simply didn't have enough bullets or strength to fend off the infected lepers advancing.

They had been hiking through the dangerous, wet, dark terrain between the village and the church for over an hour, but it felt like several hours, due to the slow drudgery in the rain and their weary and injured bodies. The moans behind them continued growing closer.

Sam glanced back worriedly at the approaching undead. "We have to keep moving!" he exclaimed, seeing that the lepers had gained ground on them with William's increasingly slowed pace from his injured leg.

Pushing through tall, wet foliage along with numerous other lepers of the island, Paim, meanwhile, still high on the cocaine, wanted to move quicker but the severe foot trauma he had sustained earlier at the hands of Ruiz made this impossible. Although he felt no pain, his constant movement had torn more tendons and his foot at this point was nearly useless. He was forced to hobble along with the rest of the leper zombies at a greatly reduced speed. *Church, they are going there. And that will be their end.*

As lightning flashed across the sky, he could make out the three fleeing living humans. They were still further ahead but their movements indicated that they had slowed down significantly. Seeing this, Paim forced himself to move faster on his broken, bleeding ankle.

So intense were his hunger and rage that Paim continually tried to speak, but all that he was able to produce were gurgles, grunts, and shrieks. His mind raced as it tried to connect dots that were no longer there. He couldn't accept the fact that he was dead and this was his new existence, yet he knew something was terribly off.

Laura continued glancing back behind her, hearing the strange guttural roars. Whoever the beastly figure was that they had seen back in the village must certainly be more dangerous than the rotted zombies they had encountered thus far.

The rain continued pelting them and to Laura it felt like every drop was another lashing from a whip across her back. She felt her strength waning from the lack of food and ever increasing pain. "Sam! I don't know how much farther I can go! I've lost a lot of blood, I'm feeling a bit dizzy."

Without missing a beat, Sam, letting go of William momentarily, spun around and grabbed her just as she was collapsing. He held her tightly and carefully slung her arm around his neck.

The weary, pain-wracked William looked out past them as another lightning crack flashed, followed by more moans and the slow movement of impending doom. "Hang onto my daughter tightly, Sam! We're nearly to the church!" he shouted.

William, with a broken fibula, hobbled with his makeshift crutch toward the small building now clearly in view.

Sam met Laura's eyes. "I'm not letting you go; I got you. Just hang on to that gun and move your feet," he said through the rain.

She nodded slowly, glancing back as another flash of lightning cracked followed by booming thunder. An outline of one of the leper zombies was far too close. Shaking, Laura raised her gun, pointed and pulled the trigger, connecting with its head and dropping it instantly.

"Good shot!" Sam said as they neared the church, Laura resting much of her weight on Sam. She bit her lip, fighting through her pain, as well as the agony and misery of their situation, thankful for Sam's strong shoulder as blood ran down her back onto the wet ground below.

The church was less than fifty yards away now. Sam and Laura caught up with William, who shouted through the rain, "I don't know how we're going to keep those things out once we get there!"

"We'll find a way! Come on, we're almost there!" Sam shouted back.

At the sound of a roar behind them, the three turned around in terror, coming face to face with the beast of a man that had been pursuing them since the village. He looked crazed and deranged, his head shaking, his face covered in white paste, his arms trembling. He opened his jaws, biting into the rain as blood tricked from his mouth, nose, and hole where his ear had been.

He reached forward, about to grab both Sam and Laura before they had a chance to aim and fire their guns, when another gunshot echoed through the pouring rain and smashed into Paim's face. In an instant, his nose was gone, leaving a large cavity in its place. Paim fell backward into the sopping-wet, muddy ground, twitching.

The three survivors turned back toward the church to see a man running toward them from the old cemetery. Lightning flashed, revealing a black-haired man holding a gun. Instinctively, Sam quickly raised his gun at the approaching man while still clinging tightly to Laura who attempted to raise her own gun with difficulty.

"Wait! Hold your fire!" the man shouted. "My name is Augusto Vaz! I am the pilot of the airplane back on the beach!"

Staring in wide-eyed amazement, the three survivors

stood speechless.

"Here, we must get to the church now!" Vaz continued, offering his help to William, seeing him use the bamboo as a crutch.

William warily accepted the help, putting his arm around the man who quickly led him to the church, Sam and Laura following close behind as moans from the living-dead continued wafting up from the jungle behind.

On the ground lay a motionless, hideously deformed and mangled Paim, thunder and lightning crashing over him.

At the entrance to the church, Vaz pushed the door open with his foot and they all entered.

Vaz quicky took William to the nearest chair and sat him down while Sam carefully attended to Laura.

Quickly closing the door and latching it shut tightly with the lock, Vaz turned to look at the three people he had just rescued from certain death at the hands of the violent walking corpse, Paim.

Several candles were lit inside the church, bringing much needed light to the proceedings. Sam fished through his own backpack, pulling out the candle taken from the church earlier. "Here, the more the merrier," he said, handing the candle to Vaz who took it and nodded, touching its wick to one of the lit candles sitting atop the operating table.

"I would ask if you guys are okay, but..." Vaz began.

"We're pretty damn far from okay, but we're alive," Sam replied, wiping the moisture from his face. "I think I speak for all of us when I say thank you for what you did out there. Your shot was perfectly timed."

Looking at the three, Vaz nodded and said, "I cannot offer you much of anything. I landed here not long after you, and only decided to stay because I knew there were survivors left here. At least, I assumed there were. My intuition paid off. Not that we have much of a chance of making it out of here alive at this point. With that storm and those damn rotting corpses out there soon surrounding us."

William examined his swollen ankle and leg while Sam knelt down beside Laura, wiping the rain from her face. "Name's William Joyner by the way, over there is my daughter Laura and her, um, traveling companion, Sam."

"That looks broken," Vaz muttered, pointing to his leg.

"Tell me something I don't know. I need to get it set or I'm not going anywhere but this seat," William said shaking his head in dismay.

"I saw your name in some of these here notes earlier. How long have you been here, Dr. Joyner?" Vaz asked.

"Just William. Too damn long. Help me set this leg if you don't mind," William said sighing.

"I don't know the first thing about setting," Vaz began.

"I'm a doctor, I'll guide you. First, you will need to apply traction."

"And that is?" Vaz answered shakily.

"Set the bone. You have to get the bone into its proper place. In my case, you'll have to pull on my leg by grabbing hold of my ankle," William said.

"Okay, I'll do my best. Any pain meds in here?" Vaz asked.

"Nope, Laura took the few remaining pills earlier, for

her deep cut on her back," Sam answered.

"Hot damn, I said it before, but it bears repeating, you guys are in bad shape," Vaz replied shaking his head at the sorry lot in front of him.

"You could say that," Sam answered.

"But we aren't dead, so thank you, Mr. Vaz, for not leaving us here. We saw you land and made our way through hell to get here," Laura said with eyes closed as blood trickled from her lower back to the floor.

"There should be some twine in one of those desk drawers. We used it to tie down the…" William began then fell silent.

Nodding, Vaz located the twine, grabbed the bamboo, and with his leg, brought the bamboo staff down hard, snapping the end off. "This is gonna hurt like a sonofabitch, here bite down on this," he said, handing William a cloth laying on the desk.

William nodded and bit down. Vaz looked gravely at Sam who nodded his approval.

Vaz wiped the sweat from his own face and took hold of William's foot. "Ready?"

William nodded.

There was a *crunch* as Vaz pulled on William's foot.

The rag fell from William's mouth as he let out a deafening scream of pain. "More! Pull again!" he cried out.

Vaz obliged, pulling at the broken leg once more until they all heard an audible *pop*.

William cried out once more, then sighed. "Thank God, bone is in place. Quick, wrap the bamboo around and tie it tightly with the twine."

Sam quicky handed Vaz his knife to cut pieces of twine for the quick and dirty stint.

Vaz cut the twine and tied knots around the broken fibula held in place by the bamboo as William winced in pain, then he stood to his feet while William closed his eyes, resting and catching his breath.

Sam pulled out the water and tiny bit of food they brought from William's hut earlier and dispersed it. Laura took a small bit and nodded, noticing that he didn't take any himself.

"Sam, you've got to eat something too," she whispered.

He quickly shook his head. "You and your father need it more than me. I'll eat when we're back on the mainland. And we *are* getting back to the mainland, right Vaz?" He turned to face the man who nodded his thanks for the small bit of cured meat.

"Let me see the cut again, Laura," Sam said calmly.

Hesitating a bit, Laura nodded and leaned forward in her seat. Sam gently lifted up the back of her shirt. It had begun bleeding again. Assessing it closer, Sam said, "You need stitches. You've been losing a lot of blood and we have to get that cut closed up."

Vaz came over and inspected the deep wound. "Your friend is right."

"Top drawer in the desk," William said as he pointed.

Quickly, Sam hopped up, went to the desk and pulled the drawer open. Near the back was stitching string. He yanked it out, inspecting it.

"We tended to the villagers' many ailments here, including stitching them up when they would inevitably lose a limb. There should be needles somewhere in there too, along with a bottle of rubbing alcohol to disinfect the wound," William continued.

"Got it," Sam said, heading back to Laura.

Vaz crouched down along with Sam. "So, I am assuming you've never done this before, right?"

"Nope," Sam replied.

Vaz held out his hand. "Here, allow me. I actually stitched up my little girl. She took a fall over a year ago, cut her arm pretty bad. We don't have much money and I could not afford a large medical bill. So, I stitched Angelina up. It was only three stitches, and she was a trooper. This, however, will take more."

"You have a brave daughter. Maybe we can share battle scars once we get out of this. Do it," Laura said, biting through the pain.

"How did this happen?" Vaz asked, inspecting the cut that was roughly two inches long and slightly off to the right of her spinal cord.

"One of those things, actually, my friend that has been turned, attacked us up in the crater. Slammed me against a tree with a protruding branch. As bad as this is, it could have been much worse, she could have bit me," Laura answered through the pain.

Nodding, Vaz replied, "Sorry to hear about your friend. This island, for all its initial outward beauty, is a true sonofabitch. You're going to feel some pain, here goes." He quickly poured a bit of the rubbing alcohol onto her wound, causing Laura to scream in pain. Setting it down, Vaz inspected the cleaned wound. "It's deep, but no vital organs seem to have been hit. Just muscle tissue. You just need stitching up."

Carefully, he began threading the needle. Sam, on his knees, stayed close to Laura and held out his hand as Vaz eyed the wound. Laura took his hand into hers.

"Squeeze as hard as you need to, okay?" Sam said softly.

Tears fell from her eyes at the immense pain. She nodded and looked to her dad who had tears in his own eyes. He gave his little girl a nod of encouragement and mouthed, "You're so brave."

The needle went into her flesh as she once more screamed in pain and squeezed Sam's hand tightly. After several stitches, she grew quiet. She had passed out.

Vaz quickly finished up the stitches, zigzagging them haphazardly to take the least amount of time It took ten stitches to roughly cover the area.

Once he was done, he sat back on the floor and nodded to Sam. "All done, let's hope they hold."

"Thank you, Vaz. Thanks for saving our asses," Sam said wearily.

Vaz nodded then got to his feet. "People, here is the situation. The plane has maybe, and I do mean maybe, enough fuel to get us back to the Kokoda airport. It's going to be close but regardless, we cannot take off in this storm. It's a suicide mission if we attempt it."

"Okay," Sam began, "so the only option is, stay here and hold out until the storm breaks, then make our way to the beach, get into the plane, and get the hell out of Dodge while evading those things out there. All this with two of us having injuries, am I correct?"

"Correct, that's the plan," Vaz replied.

"How much ammunition do you have in that gun, Vaz?" Sam asked.

Vaz inspected the gun. "Looks like five bullets."

"I've got three and," Sam paused picking up Laura's gun. "This one also has three. Eleven, total. Versus what looked like a horde of those things making their way toward us. Definitely more of them than there are bullets."

They all fell silent.

"Also, I have this," Sam pulled out the remaining flare from the flare gun, holding it up for Vaz to see.

"Well, we've got nowhere to hide. This church is our last stand. It's the only thing that'll keep us alive from here to the airplane." Vaz inspected the flare, "What happened to the gun?"

"Didn't fire. This thing might be fucked as well. But I didn't want to discard it just yet."

"Good. Good man, Mr. Sam," Vaz shot back. "This church is going to have to hold them off for the time being," he added, looking around at the old walls.

"Well, you took out the big one—that's a win, I suppose—but with their sheer numbers, they could break through," Sam said.

"And if they do, we'll kill as many as we can, deal?" William said, his eyes remaining closed.

They all fell silent once more.

"That big one, he wasn't like the others. He with you?" Sam asked.

Nodding, Vaz replied, "Oh, you could say that. He was the man that hired me to fly him here. To find this." He pointed to the briefcase sitting in the corner.

"And it all comes full circle. The damn drugs," Sam said angrily.

"Yep. The second briefcase that bastard took off the zombie with a Black Sabbath shirt. He one of yours?" Vaz asked.

Sighing, Sam nodded. "My friend, Edward. Died on the beach. Well, died as in, he's dead but clearly up and walking around."

"He's not the only one," Laura said, waking up and grimacing at the pain in her back.

"There's one more out there not from this island. The one I mentioned before and the cause of the gash on my back. She's still out there. I'm surprised we haven't seen her since the crater."

"Well, let's hope we don't have to deal with her. The fresh ones, those seem to have more strength than the old rotten ones," William said grimly.

"I'm guessing that's a fairly accurate assumption," Vaz answered.

"That big one, you sure he's dead? Like, completely dead?" Sam asked.

"I shot him in the face, so yes. But I'm not ruling anything out. Not here."

"Okay, then, we should shore up the door and windows. Vaz, can you give me a hand?" Sam asked.

"Should be some nails in one of those drawers. We had to continually be securing this old building…" William trailed off, pointing to the drawer in question.

Vaz quickly opened it and saw a small box of nails and a hammer in the back. Pulling them out, he gave a handful to Sam who had quickly found a paper weight on the desk that appeared heavy enough to withstand being smashed against nails and wood.

While William and Laura rested with their wounds, Vaz and Sam both began driving nails into weakened areas most vulnerable to the lepers outside.

"They're outside the church now," Sam said, moving to the window he had closed earlier to ensure it remained closed tight, driving several nails into its sides. Satisfied it would hold, he moved back to Laura, "How you holding up?"

She nodded and gave him a slight smile.

"Good, just get your rest for now. We still have to huff it to the airplane once the storm breaks, and you've got ten stitches in your back now," Sam said.

"And I feel every single one of them," Laura said wincing.

Silence fell once more until a dull thud on the door sounded, followed by low moans.

"Well, the dead have come a' knockin'," William said wearily.

"It seems they have. It's gonna be a long night," Sam answered.

They looked gravely at one other as more moans and thuds surrounded the church.

24
BURN THE SONOFABITCH DOWN

Eva silently slipped past the village, seeing it was nearly empty. She came upon the thick body of a man with his head almost completely destroyed. Rolling him over, she ripped open his shirt and with long fingernails, dug into his stomach, pulling out his intestines. Her appetite for meat was almost insatiable. She hungrily began feasting on the tainted organs and choked. They were rotten from the cursed virus that plagued the island.

She forced down several more bites before regurgitating it all back up on top of Ruiz's desecrated body, standing to her feet. Her nearly naked, drenched body was neither cold nor in any pain, except for the insatiable craving deep in her belly. She sniffed the air, but the rain and wind had deadened any trail there may have been toward the delectable flesh she so craved.

What now? In the distance, even through the pouring rain, she heard the faint moans of the living dead lepers. *Church building. They are there.*

With jaws biting, she continued on. *They will pay with their lives, and I will be satisfied.*

Inside the church, the candles continued lighting the room dimly while rain pounded the roof and soaked the undead that staggered around the church grounds, aimless and unsure of what to do next with the church sealed tightly shut.

While the survivors waited for the storm to pass, William shared what he could with Vaz about the island's inhabitants and why he had been there for the past two years. Vaz listened with rapt attention, forgetting about the groans and knocking outside.

"You mean to tell me you found a cure for brain cancer?" Vaz asked astounded.

William nodded. "I did. But at a great cost, as you have seen in the short time you have been here."

"What do you plan on doing with the cocaine, Vaz?" Sam asked warily.

Vaz slapped the top of the briefcase. "Well, I was planning on throwing it into the ocean when and if I make it back to the plane. Then, on second thought, I figured the police back in town would be quite interested in this large haul. But since that damn briefcase is the reason we're all in this shit, it stays here. I'd like to burn it up, actually, as a final middle finger to its owner."

Sam nodded, then turning to William he asked, "How long do these storms usually last?"

Thinking for a second, he replied, "At least once a week one of these big bastards comes through. The last one brought the plane you were in down but missed the island. More often than not, however, they go right over top of us, as you're seeing now. The good news is, they rarely last more than half a day, or in this case, night."

"So, the plan is, we hole up here and at first light, we bust out of here and make a run for it, all in agreement?" Vaz stated.

"If I can't keep up, you leave me behind, got it?" William stated, glancing at his daughter.

"No! We all go!" Laura shot back quickly.

William was about to protest but Sam chimed in. "We're all getting off this damn island, one way or another."

"I'm so sorry for all of this. For you risking your life to find me, Laura, and you, Sam…" William fell silent.

"We can all make apologies and slap high fives and dance for joy after we land at Kokoda airport," Vaz said shifting his eyes to his new traveling companions.

They all fell silent, listening to the rain come down along with the rapping on the walls of the church and the moans of the dead.

Laura shook her head and rubbed her eyes. The church was empty and only the two candles brought any light to the dusty old room. "Sam? Dad? Where are you?" She slowly stood to her feet, instantly frightened.

Thunder and lightning raged on outside but there was no longer pounding on the walls of the church. She moved forward toward the door. "Hello? Anyone there? Vaz, where are you? Where the hell is everyone?"

They're gone, but I am here, a voice came from the farthest shadowed corner of the room.

Laura whipped around, pain shooting up her back at the sudden movement. A nearly naked Eva stepped out. At least, what had been Eva at one point. Now, she was little more than a rotted-through corpse. The side of her head was caved in and what little remained of her hair was stringy and hanging limply over her face in a tangled mess. Most of her flesh had been stripped away, revealing muscle tissue and bones.

"Eva!" Laura shouted out.

Oh, I used to be Eva. But I am so much more. And I have you to thank for it. I will live forever, slowly rotting away until merely bones are all that remains. All because you had to find Daddy. Eva stepped toward Laura as she backed away from the hideous monstrosity before her.

"Stay away from me!" Laura shouted.

You made me this way, and now you will join me. But not before I feast on you until I have reached my fill. Oh, you will never escape me! I will be with you always! Eva leapt at Laura, her boney hands outstretched, reaching for her throat.

Laura's back hit the door to the church causing her to shriek out in pain, her stitches bursting open at the hard blow.

"Oh God! No, Eva!" Laura shouted out, shaking herself awake.

"Laura!" Sam said, running to where she had awakened on the floor toward the back of the church building.

She blinked and looked up at Sam standing over her. "What—?" she muttered as she tried to get her bearings.

"You were asleep, but you're okay now," Sam answered.

She slowly stood to her feet, grimacing at the pain in her back. "What time is it?"

Sam glanced at his watch, "It's five-thirty in the morning."

"How long have I been asleep?" she responded, yawning.

"Not long," Sam lied, placing his hand on her shoulder gently, glad she was able to get sleep after their hellish previous day and even worse night of running.

William, sitting in the same chair where the makeshift bone setting had occurred earlier, rested his mended leg and smiled at his daughter. He loved her so much and was happy to see what he sensed was a true budding romance in its very early stages. "How are the stitches holding up?"

Laura looked at her dad. "About as good as that stint you've got." They both smiled wearily at each other. Noticing the utter silence around them, Laura asked, "Wait a minute, the rain, did it stop? I don't hear any moaning out there, either, or do my ears deceive me?"

"It did indeed, not long ago. We aren't sure what happened to the lepers out there but we're about to find out. We've been planning our route as best we can and it's time to go, Laura," Vaz said, then held up a broken-off wooden leg of a chair. Its end was wrapped in white cloth and was wet.

"What's that?" Laura asked.

"We were able to get a bit of rubbing alcohol out of that bottle we used on you last night onto a torn sheet. It's a torch."

"I like it. Okay, let's do it." She sighed with the gun in hand. "Dad, how's the leg?"

"It's been better, but the splint should hopefully hold out until we get to the plane," William replied.

They all stood by the front door. Sam had on his backpack, with William's small sack still inside, and his own gun at the ready with the three bullets remaining.

"I'm going to try something. It may buy us some time and take a few of those things out as well," Sam said nervously as he pulled out the final flare, glancing down at the briefcase of cocaine still sitting in the corner where Vaz placed it earlier.

"Whatever you've got cooking, make it quick," Vaz said as he lit the torch with the remaining burning candle before unlatching the door lock and standing back. "Time to get the hell off this island."

"What are you going to do, Sam?" Laura asked him anxiously.

"I'm going to try and light things up a bit." He leaned forward and gave her a quick but soft kiss on the lips.

Laura, eyes wide, was pleasantly surprised. She glanced over at her father instinctively who was grinning.

Sam threw the door open and they stepped out into a rain-free dawn on the island of death. The leper zombies were still in the area but had given up on breaking the door down. The deathly shapes turned to face the humans, their white eyes staring blankly at the church. Moans of hunger slowly emanated from their lifeless mouths once again.

"Let's go!" Vaz exclaimed, waving the torch in front of him.

Without hesitating, Sam moved past them, taking off in a sprint around the small building while Vaz, Laura, and William stepped forward.

The nearest leper zombie made its move, shuffling toward them. Vaz raised his gun, aimed, and pulled the trigger, instantly vaporizing much of the zombie's head, dropping it to the ground instantly. He then aimed at a staggering female zombie moving in and fired, connecting with the side of her head, causing enough damage to drop her.

The three hurried as fast as they could from the church, their injuries barely keeping them ahead of the slow-moving leper zombies. The flame from the torch was having the intended effect, keeping the living-dead at bay.

"Get back, you fuckers!" Vaz shouted, pointing his gun and waving the torch which caught a nearby female leper zombie's dress, sending it up in flames.

Sam, meanwhile, headed to the generator at the rear of the church and, as fast as he could with shaking hands, unscrewed the gas tank cap. He took a quick whiff, smelling the likely tiny bit of remaining gasoline he had poured in earlier. "Please work, *please* work."

He jammed the flare's tip into the opening, shoving it into the tank as far as it could go. When he was satisfied it was secure, he stood to his feet to see a nearly faceless giant of a man approaching from around the church building. It was the one Vaz had called *Paim*. What was left of his face didn't resemble anything human any longer. Most of it was caved in. One eye was completely missing while the other rested lazily in its socket. Most of its mouth, however, remained. It was biting at the air, its top and bottom rows of teeth clearly not aligning due to the close-range blast he had taken the previous night. His brain remained intact, and therefore, this monstrosity hadn't been finished off.

Sam tried to shout out, but zombie Paim grabbed him around his throat, squeezing tightly. Laura glanced back from the clearing in front of the building, seeing what was happening by the generator. "Sam! No!"

"Damnit!" Vaz exclaimed, when he saw Paim at the rear of the church.

There was no clean shot for either Vaz or Laura who looked on in horror as Sam was lifted up off the ground by his throat.

Sam gagged as the huge man's large hand wrapped around his throat, choking the life out of him. He hadn't dropped the revolver in the surprise encounter and he raised it now under Paim's mangled chin.

Paim, however, saw this with his one remaining eye and quickly slammed Sam against the side of the church, almost causing him to drop the gun.

A crooked, grotesque smile seemed to form on Paim's nearly destroyed face. He pulled Sam in, opening his jaws wide.

Sam could smell the stench of already rotting flesh on the man along with the exposed insides of his head. Still clasping his gun, Sam tilted it toward his face and pulled the trigger. The bullet entered the front of his neck and shot out the back, having little effect on the already dead man.

William, meanwhile, had taken Sam's knife as protection and was swinging it at an approaching zombie, ramming it into the side of the feeble being's head. The creature stopped moving, its long since degenerated brain unable to comprehend what was happening to it. William yanked back on the handle and the knife was pulled out, causing the zombie to drop into an unmoving heap on the dirt.

Laura was doing her best to protect her crippled father from the zombie horde that had newfound interest in the fleeing human flesh. Knowing she only had three remaining bullets in her own revolver, she was hesitant to pull the trigger until one man with his ribcage fully exposed grabbed hold of her back. Instant pain shook her, causing her to scream out. She turned to her aggressor, placed the revolver under its chin and blew the top of its head off.

Directly behind the fallen zombie was another, nearly identical one with its arms outstretched, attempting to grab Laura by her throat. It was met with a bullet to the forehead.

Vaz tried to figure out a way to help Sam with the man three times his size who was clearly getting the upper hand.

But he couldn't risk Sam being killed or gravely injured in the process. He aimed as best he could at Paim's mangled foot and pulled the trigger of his Smith & Wesson. The slug connected with Paim's ankle, disintegrating his entire foot and a portion of his lower leg. Vaz pulled the trigger again and Paim's other foot blasted off completely.

Paim was instantly unable to keep his footing and fell sideways, releasing Sam from his grasp and falling to the muddy ground.

Sam raised his gun at Paim then stopped. Standing above the fallen Paim was his mangled friend, Ed, missing his left arm, and his head so bashed in it barely resembled his old friend at all. However, the Black Sabbath shirt, while now in shreds, was still draped over his body. Sam pushed himself back through the mud, away from Paim and his deceased friend.

With his remaining eye, Paim looked up to see Ed standing over top of him. In his hand was a sharp rock. Paim opened his jaws, trying to speak, but no words came out. He was about to swipe out with his hand at the man standing over him but was instead met with the sharp end of the rock smashing into his forehead.

Looking on in horror, Sam crawled to his feet, aiming his revolver at the dueling zombies, but hesitated as Ed smashed the rock over and over onto Paim's forehead until the beast of a man ceased to move, his brains spilling out entirely onto the mud.

Ed slowly stood to his feet, staring at Sam.

"Sam, come on, damnit! We've got to move!" Vaz

exclaimed, flailing his torch at nearby zombies and blasting one that had gotten too close in the face. Behind him William and Laura relentlessly continued to keep the slow-moving leper zombies at bay.

Sam began moving backward, away from Ed.

With his remaining arm, Ed pointed to Sam's gun, opened his mouth and tried to speak. Only grunts came out. He raised his finger, pointing at his forehead.

He wants me to kill him, for good.

Behind him, Vaz was yelling but it was drowned out by his thoughts. Ed, his best friend. Ed, the crazy sonofabitch that always got into trouble, but always had his back. Ed, the man who had spent countless hours talking to him about what he wanted to do after he had sowed his "wild oats"—have a wife and kids, eventually. All of that now lost. A distant memory.

Sam nodded his understanding and raised his gun and aimed.

Ed was able to get one single, if nearly incoherent, word out of his mangled mouth. "Friend."

Instant tears dropped from Sam's eyes as he pulled the trigger. One second Ed was standing in front of him, the next, he lay motionless on the ground beside the once human, now beast, Paim.

"I'm sorry, Ed," Sam said as he quickly wiped his eyes and ran back to a waiting Vaz, Laura, and William who were now at the edge of the clearing where the church stood.

"We have got to go, now!" Vaz shouted, pointing at the zombie lepers encompassing them.

"One last thing! Time to burn this sonofabitch down. Stand back!" Sam shouted, thinking of the black cocaine briefcase inside the old, decrepit and desecrated church.

He turned around, aimed his revolver at the flare jammed in the generator's gas tank and fired. The bullet connected with the tank, which in turn ignited the last remaining flare. The generator immediately exploded, causing a chain reaction as the church next to it also exploded. Pieces of burning wood and debris flew outward and into the sky in a violent display of smoke and fire. Ten lepers near the building that had turned to begin their pursuit of Vaz and the crew instantly caught fire and were incinerated.

Sam, closest to the explosion, was knocked down, dropping his empty gun, but Vaz instantly scooped him back up and pulled him into the jungle.

Quickly catching up to William and Laura who were both in intense pain by now, Vaz shouted, "What's the ammo count?"

"I've got one bullet left, if I'm counting correctly!" Laura exclaimed.

"I'm down to one myself, so let's make these count," Vaz replied.

Sam came alongside William, putting his arm around the struggling man and helping him along.

Laura glanced at Sam. "You okay?"

Sam simply nodded, not wanting to think more on what he had just done. *I shot my best friend in the head.*

"You did the only thing you could do, okay?" Laura said, walking hurriedly beside him.

"I guess so," Sam replied.

"You just gave the living a fighting chance. Thank you, Sam Berry," Laura came back.

This brought a smile to his face.

They continued on their perilous trek through the jungle toward the waiting airplane on the beach, Sam glancing at his compass to make sure they were still heading in the right direction. Behind them, plumes of smoke lifted up into the sky as the remnants of what was once a church, then a place of experiments and death, was burnt entirely to its foundation. Scattered about the area were numerous leper zombies, finally, at long last, resting in peace.

The remaining dwindling zombie horde shambled toward the beach in pursuit of the warm-blooded humans attempting to flee the confines of the hellish island.

All were shambling but one. One watched from a distance, knowing where they were heading. It had taken off through the jungle forest ahead of them and was waiting for revenge.

25
BLOODY BEACH

The four survivors trudged for almost two hours through the damp, thick green foliage, now undeterred, toward the waiting beach. The closer they got to their destination, the more fatigued William became, hobbling on his throbbing leg. He had found another bamboo makeshift crutch but it was cumbersome and, at times, made him even more unstable in the uneven and muddy jungle terrain.

Laura, meanwhile, was dealing with her own pain and was in desperate need of meds, but there were none to be had. The only thing keeping them going was the possibility that an actual escape sat waiting, parked on the beach.

Sam continued trying to push away the thought of his friend whose final order was for Sam to put an end to his miserable existence. It was something he knew he would have to live with, and deal with, the rest of his life.

The ground was still wet and slick from the torrential downpour the previous night, making travel significantly more slippery and, therefore, much more arduous with William's broken fibula. He tried to mask the pain but it was growing increasingly more difficult to take any steps at all, even with Sam at his side, holding him up along with his crutch.

The torch Vaz had constructed back at the church still burned and remained a potential weapon if they needed it.

Laura was the most nervous of all of them, fearing her one-time friend, now seemingly arch enemy, lay in wait somewhere in the jungle. Or could she be waiting inside the airplane? She pushed the nightmare from earlier out of her head and focused on the task at hand. *Make your way to the beach, then go from there. One step at a time, Laura.*

Vaz glanced at Sam. "That was a beautiful thing you did back there. Up in smoke went the drugs, I guess you could say, so there's some justice in that."

"I hope God can forgive us for the hell that has happened on this island," Sam replied grimly.

"God wants no part of this rock in the middle of the Solomon Sea, I'm afraid. It belongs to that meteor and the dead that it keeps from fully resting in peace," William said, wincing at the pain.

They all fell silent, focusing ahead several hundred feet where the palm trees and dense foliage came to an end and the beach lay immediately beyond.

"Come on, we're almost there," Vaz said.

At long last, they stepped out of the jungle into powdery,

white sand. The bright sun shone down, growing hotter as the morning hours passed. Scanning their surroundings, they saw several bodies strewn about. All leper zombies except one. Pieces of Pinto lay rotting in the sun, devoured by the living dead. All four turned their heads in revulsion at the ghastly sight.

Near the crashing water at the edge of the beach sat the Cessna Citation.

Laura looked out to the ocean. "The plane we were on. It's gone!" she exclaimed, pointing to where it had once rested on the islet.

"The storm likely took it out to sea, along with the rising and falling tide," William said, out of breath from the walk through the jungle with his broken leg.

All four survivors looked up at the beautiful, tropical morning sky. The storm had indeed passed.

"Well, this is what I call as perfect flying weather as we could ask for, all things considered," Vaz observed, shielding his eyes from the bright, rising sun.

"I can't believe I'm actually looking at this right now," Sam said almost reverently, staring at their escape in red and white with the numbers 649 on its side.

Vaz led the way with Sam and Laura close behind.

"Come on, Dad, almost there," Laura said over her shoulder as he came to a stop on the beach.

Sighing, William replied, "Give me just a few seconds. My leg is killing me."

Laura scanned the surroundings, which appeared to be secluded, and took several steps toward Vaz and Sam. *No, stay with your father.* "Hey, hold up!" she shouted up ahead, about to turn around to fetch her slightly trailing father.

"Come on, the sooner we can get boarded the—" Vaz began, glancing back, seeing movement that stopped him in his tracks.

Behind William, near several large rocks jutting out of the sand, a grotesque woman rose out of the water, only the whites of her eyes showing through clumps of matted and muddy blond hair hanging down her face. Large lesions had sprung up around her exposed torso and chest.

Creeping up past the rocks, she made her way onto the sandy beach. Stealthily, she moved on them, arms outstretched, ready to attack.

Vaz shouted as she came into view, raising his gun, "William, look out!"

Laura and Sam turned around at the same time, both realizing what was happening. Laura took off toward her father, but Eva had made too much headway in the powdery soft sand.

Leaping forward, Eva landed on top of William's back, easily knocking the man down in the surprise attack as well as the instability of his broken leg in the soft sand. Wasting no time, Eva sunk her teeth into the back of William's exposed neck. Biting through flesh and muscle until she had a mouthful, she ripped upwards, pulling a large chunk of William along with her.

William yelled in surprise and pain at the violation just as Laura, too, cried out as loud as her lungs could manage. With one bullet left in the chamber of her revolver, she lifted it up and pointed at her adversary.

Behind her, Sam ran through the sand, trying to get to her while Vaz shouted out, "The head, she must be shot in the head!"

Eva lunged forward, off of William who lay twitching in the hot beach with his lifeblood spilling from the back of his neck onto the sand.

As if in slow motion, while Eva was airborne, Laura pulled the trigger but missed her head, instead sending her final bullet into Eva's heart, a shot that would instantly kill any human. But Eva was no longer human at all, nor did she have any need for a working heart.

She landed on top of Laura who dropped to the sand. Instant pain shot through her body as the coarse sand rubbed against her fresh stitches. Eva, now on top of her, spit a mouthful of her father's blood onto her face. Laura closed her eyes and mouth tight in revulsion and a primal instinct to survive.

Thick blood from Eva's fresh bullet hole seeped out onto Laura's shirt as she fought with her assailant. *Must not get her bodily fluids mixed with mine!*

Sam reached the women first as Vaz ran toward the ensuing chaos. Sam's top priority was to save Laura, and he plunged the knife Ed had gifted him into the back of Eva's head, driving it through the skull and cranium. Leaving the knife in, he grabbed hold of her arm and yanked as hard as he could, pulling her off of Laura who quickly rolled away.

Eva instantly jumped to her feet, blood oozing out of her mouth, the bullet hole and the knife sticking out the back of her head. Her face was a mess of caked blood, sand, and grotesque lesions beginning to form as she chewed on the remaining meat from Laura's father still in her mouth. Swallowing it, she grinned, raised her hand and slowly pulled the knife out of her head, not taking her eyes off of Sam.

Her head bobbed back and forth and her body was shaking. The knife would soon be her end. She felt her foggy mind begin to slip, this time permanently. Her brain functions were shutting down and the control she once had over her rotting body was ceasing.

Holding the knife in her hand, she licked the blood from it, her lips in a permanent grotesque smile that she could no longer control.

"Crazy—" Sam began.

"Bitch!" Laura finished from behind Eva, smashing the back of her head with a jagged, black rock, sending bits of skull and hair to the sand below.

Now it was Eva that was knocked to the ground, and Laura wasted no time rolling her over and smashing the rock on her head. After the first few hits, Eva's evil sneer was destroyed and her face broken open. Several more and the skull cracked and caved in. A few more and all that was left was a nearly flattened head. What remained of Eva lay twitching in the sand.

Laura stood to her feet with the help of Sam, tears falling at what had just happened to her father and what she was forced to do to her once friend.

Vaz stood beside the still moving Eva. He lowered the lit torch and dropped it on top of her body. "I doubt this will burn you completely, but it's a start."

Turning her attention away from what remained of Eva, Laura hurried over to her father, still laying in the sand, bleeding out.

Dropping to her knees along with Sam, she looked at his wound. It was bad. Not only was it an infectious bite, but a life-ending one. He had already lost far too much blood.

"Oh, Dad, no!" Laura wailed.

William slowly rolled over to look at his daughter. He was near death, or at least, his first death.

"We're gonna get you out of here! The plane, we're so close!" Laura exclaimed.

"Laura, my sweet daughter. It's over, you have to go. Please," he mumbled as blood began trickling from his mouth.

Behind them, in the jungle forest, moans began rising up, growing closer. The remaining leper-dead were making their way to the beach.

Vaz looked up nervously then glanced at Sam and shook his head. Sam knew it was time to go. He gently put his hand on her shoulder, "Laura,"

"No, no! I traveled halfway around the world to find you, damnit, and it's not going to end like this! You cured brain cancer!" Laura cried.

"And the cure is inside this fine young man's backpack. Take it, use it. Save lives. I would say it is going to be my legacy, but I would be wrong. You, Laura, are my legacy. And I cannot begin to tell you how proud I am of you," he whispered.

Laura dropped her head and rested it on her father's

chest, sobbing. His breathing was shallow and heavy. He was in the throes of death.

William gently stroked her hair as his mind raced through vivid memories of his little girl with the same long brown hair. Dropping her off at kindergarten for the first time, her first car, graduating high school. His mind was fading yet still coherent.

He looked up at Sam standing over them. "You take care of my baby. I couldn't, but you…" his voice trailed off.

Sam felt a lump forming in his throat. He barely knew this man and his daughter but already felt a deep intimate connection with them after all of the horrors they had endured together. He nodded his understanding to the dying man.

Behind them, the moans echoed louder through the tall palm trees on the edge of the beach.

Looking toward the ominous moans in the distance then back at Laura, William whispered, "Go, tell your mama you found me and that I'm sorry, sorry for everything." He fell silent as he tried to lightly push her away.

Sam gently took Laura's arm, lifting her up. She struggled at first then buried her face in Sam's chest. He put his arm around her, careful not to touch the stitching on her lower back.

William looked at Vaz and slowly lifted his hand, pointing at the gun.

Nodding his understanding, Vaz bent down pulled the hammer back and placed it in William's outstretched hand.

"Get them home, promise me…" the older man whispered.

Vaz quietly replied, "I give you my word, William."

Turning from the dying man, Vaz glanced at the tree line. Shapes of what appeared to be six leper zombies were arriving, making their way slowly through the dense, dark green lush foliage. Pointing to the plane, he said firmly, "We must leave, now."

"Come on, Laura, time to go," Sam said, picking his knife up from the sand and guiding her to the plane.

She never looked back. If she had, she would have seen William Joyner mouth the words, "I love you, my Laura," as he placed the Smith & Wesson under his chin.

Vaz pulled the key out of his front pocket near the plane and quickly motioned for them to climb in as he hopped into the pilot's seat.

Sam guided Laura in first, then took the backpack off of his already sweaty back and placed it on the floor then hopped in. He glanced back to see the approaching leper-zombies had reached the beach and were moving toward the dying William. He closed the door to the plane as a shot from the revolver rang out. Laura, sobbing softly, buried her hands in her face.

On the beach, the slow, plodding footsteps of the dead made their way toward the recently deceased William, smelling fresh blood. Inside the Cessna, Vaz quickly placed the key into the ignition and began firing up the plane.

"If you're religious, time to pray. We're going to need some divine intervention if we haven't already received it. Not only is there hardly any runway, our biggest problem is the fuel, or lack thereof," Vaz said grimly.

Sam nodded, Laura still reeling over having to leave her father on the beach.

"If those things out there get in front of us, we won't be able to build enough speed on this damn beach to lift off!" Vaz shouted, glancing back before hurriedly going over all his piloting instruments.

Sam looked at Laura who had stopped crying and now wiped her eyes as he reached over and gave her hand a quick squeeze. She took hold and held it tightly in hers.

"Throttle is good, rudder is good, engine is running good. Okay, time to get the hell out of Dodge," Vaz muttered to himself, glancing out his side window to the beach, seeing the living dead shuffling toward them. One in particular caught his eye. It was the ten-year-old child he had spared earlier.

He pushed forward on the throttle and the propellers inside the engines on either side of the plane spun faster. Ready for takeoff.

Several leper zombies walked blindly toward the moving airplane, gazing at it in wonder.

Shaking his head in disgust, Vaz moved the yoke and the wheels began to move just as the small zombie child stepped in front of the plane twenty feet away, then stopped. Staring blankly at the Cessna, peering up at Vaz himself sitting in the pilot's seat, she didn't move or bite at the air.

"What the hell," Vaz mumbled to himself in amazement.

The rest of the zombies were now attempting to move in front of and around the plane.

Sighing, Vaz closed his eyes and moved the steer yoke forward.

"What is that small one doing?" Sam said from the seat behind Vaz.

"I can't believe I'm saying this, but I think it wants us to end its existence! We can't wait, the others are nearly in front of us as well," Vaz replied sadly.

They all fell silent inside the plane while Vaz pushed forward. After a few seconds of movement, a brief thud came from outside as the wheels pulled the child under them, then all was quiet except for the rapidly increasing propeller and engine noise of the Cessna reaching full power for their attempted takeoff.

"Okay, gang, this is going to be quick and dirty. I've got to get this thing up to sixty knots in order for it to take off. The room for error is literally, zero. We have one shot! If we miss it, we either smash into the rocks up ahead a way or—" Vaz paused.

Laura, who had regained her composure somewhat, answered for him, "Or we crash into the ocean upon takeoff."

"That would be correct. So, ladies and gentlemen, fasten your seatbelts, make sure your tray tables are in an upright position, and hang on to your asses. Here we go."

26
RUNNING
ON FUMES

Vaz gave the Cessna all he could for the short beach runway they were on. Trying to figure out the length he would need to achieve liftoff along with the small pebbles their wheels were bumping over was a nearly impossible task, so he decided to err on the side of full throttle even if doing so could potentially result in over torquing.

"Please don't stall on me, baby," Vaz muttered, already feeling beads of sweat forming on his brow. The plane shuddered and bumped on the rocks at the force with which Vaz was attempting takeoff. Normally, he would need nearly five-thousand feet to get airborne and he was short by several hundred. He also had to figure in the wind, which the plane would be fighting against.

The Cessna moved faster, the rocks on the opposite end of their bumpy, sandy runway approaching quickly. Sam looked on, trying not to wince while Laura simply closed her eyes, prepared to meet death if that was their ultimate destiny.

Vaz gritted his teeth, glaring out the windshield. "Come on, come on, more power!" he shouted, continuing to go full throttle.

The wheels of the Cessna bumped over the stones on the beach, shaking the survivors in their seats. It felt as though the plane was going to fly apart from the immense shaking. Sam continued holding Laura's hand tightly and said a quick and quiet, *Our Father* prayer.

Pulling back as hard as he could on the steering yoke, Vaz lifted the Cessna up, off the beach mere feet from the large, jagged rocks at the end of the runway. On the way up, the front wheel clipped the nearest rock and instantly a warning light went off in the cockpit.

Ignoring it, Vaz continued pulling back on the steering yoke, thankful that the rear landing gear remained untouched by the rocks.

The plane lifted up quickly and continued to vibrate from the rapid acceleration. Behind it, la Isla de Sebria grew smaller and smaller until it vanished, as if it had never existed at all. None of the passengers aboard the Cessna once glanced back at it.

Vaz turned the warning light off and raised the landing gear. "Wow, that was a close one. All things considered, we should thank our lucky stars we've made it this far."

"Good flying, Vaz," Sam said graciously.

"Yes, Vaz, you literally saved our lives," Laura said.

Nodding his appreciation for their kind words, he replied, "Don't thank me just yet. We aren't out of the shit by a long shot." He continued looking over his readouts in front of him. Everything seemed good, except the fuel. *Hot damn, this is gonna be a close one.*

"How are the stitches holding up, Laura?" Sam asked.

"It hurts but I'll be okay," she answered.

He smiled at her and looked down; they were still holding hands and they remained so as they all fell silent, each in their own worlds, replaying the events of the past several days. The harrowing escapes and near-death experiences.

"We're gonna make it," Laura said calmly.

I hope you're right, Laura, I truly do, Vaz thought, looking warily at the fuel gauge then glancing out his side window at the island quickly disappearing from view, like a mirage in the middle of the ocean.

He called back, getting Sam and Laura's attention. "Listen, I've been thinking. That island, pretty sure it wants to be left alone. I can't explain the severe storms that constantly circulate this part of the Solomon Sea. I can't explain the insanity we experienced there, either. Yeah, there's notes and whatnot, but I don't believe in zombies. And we just fended off zombies. We barely made it out of there with our lives, and some of us didn't. So, if we get back to land and by some miracle we land this thing, we need to have a story that lines up. One that doesn't involve anyone attempting to find this island, ever. We can't risk whatever those leper zombies are infected with spreading."

Sam and Laura nodded in agreement.

Laura added, "That virus could spread exponentially at a rapid pace that likely couldn't be contained. I agree, Vaz. The island's location stays hidden."

"I don't want what happened to Ed and Eva or even those gangsters to happen to anyone else. My lips are sealed," Sam added.

They all fell quiet, thinking through how they would present information to the authorities and loved ones when and if they survived this final leg of the harrowing journey.

Sam pulled out his backpack, unzipped it, and pulled out William's small, cloth sack. Opening it, he looked over the doctor's notes and samples of ground Violet Laceflower and the NR 485 serum he included. Inside his own backpack, he had a handful of what should have been wilting or even dead Violet Laceflowers along with some of Dr. Pedroso's notebooks. Flipping through each, he looked puzzled.

Laura looked over. "What? What is it?"

"Much of this makes no sense to me, it's beyond my scope of knowledge, but what do you make of it?" he replied, handing the notes over to Laura.

After briefly flipping through them, she said, "Well, this seems to line up with what my dad was telling us earlier. It could be a possible cure for terminal brain cancer. These details in my father's notes, plus the samples along with Dr. Pedroso's own research would need to be tested, but if it works, this could literally save millions of lives moving forward. All thanks to my dad's discovery on that island!"

She fell silent, already missing her dear father. Sam

held something out to her. She looked down, and in his outstretched hand was the picture her father had with him during his years on the island. A picture of Laura, Alicia, and himself at Siesta Key beach in Sarasota, Florida when Laura was just a little girl. She took it and looked it over, a flood of memories crashing down on her.

"I remember this trip. I remember this day. It was so beautiful outside, and we had rented a condo down by the ocean. We had just eaten ice cream before this picture was taken. Mama will be happy to see the picture came back with me." She quieted then, reminiscing over her memories of their family.

"Laura, I wish there was something I could do to change..." Sam trailed off.

Laura shook her head and Sam, taking the hint, fell silent.

He put the doctor's contents back in the briefcase and stored them again in the backpack. He then looked over the knife Ed had given him, seeing it still had Eva's blood on it. He quickly shoved it into the backpack, out of Laura's sight, then glanced over. She still wore his *Star Wars* shirt, now covered in both her father's and Eva's blood on the front and her own on the back. He thought of what her father had said to her as he neared his end: "You take care of my baby. I couldn't, but you..."

He leaned his head back, physically, mentally, and emotionally drained. He hadn't really slept since his final night in the hostel back in Kokoda before leaving with Ed for what he had assumed were the Solomon Islands.

Just going to rest my eyes for a little, he thought as he instantly fell asleep.

Vaz glanced back and saw both his passengers were sound asleep. He was lost in his own thoughts. Of traveling to the Honiara Solomon Islands airport and their interaction with the shady Logan Pabon and whatever grizzly fate befell the man named Fabian Amill. Of what he had been forced to do all at the threat of death to him and likely his family. Of watching a man eaten alive by a shark.

"Sonofabitch, what a hell of a last few days. I'm coming home baby girl," Vaz mumbled to himself and yawned. He wasn't sure when he had slept last and was beyond tired himself.

"Tell me about your wife and little girl, Vaz," a voice behind him asked.

He glanced back to see Laura wearily looking at him.

"I thought you were asleep," he responded.

Laura yawned. "I could. Or, I could keep you awake and alert. I got some sleep last night and honestly, I could use some conversation right now, to help get my mind off of..." she fell silent.

Vaz glanced back at her, happy to change the painful subject. "My wife's name is Amanda and my daughter's name is Angelina Sophia Vaz, she's my little angel."

"How old is she?" Laura asked.

"She's ten and growing up far too fast already," Vaz said, instantly missing her.

"Well, you'll see her soon," Laura replied.

"I certainly hope so. I promised I would take her shopping for a dress she really wanted. Then this nightmare happened." Vaz wiped his weary face of sweat.

"Vaz, we would literally have been doomed there had it not been for you. Thank you for all you've done for us. And, I should add, are still doing," Laura said kindly.

"Not out of this yet. Speaking of which," Vaz started, then clicked on his headset. "Kokoda airport, this is Cessna Citation I number six four nine. Requesting emergency assistance, please respond, over."

After a brief silence, a man on the other end answered, "Cessna Citation I, reading you loud and clear, Augusto Vaz, is that you?"

"Santana! Good to hear your voice!" Vaz responded happily.

"Vaz, my friend! Tell me where you are! I am assuming you are traveling with passengers?" Santana answered warily.

"Two passengers. And neither are ones I initially left with. Long story, trust me. I have with me two survivors of flight number 8088N, Pinto's plane," Vaz answered.

"What the hell have you gotten into, Vaz?" Santana responded.

Vaz sighed heavily. "I'll tell you all about it over a beer but first, here's the situation. Our front landing gear got a bit banged up but that's not the worst of it, at least not yet. We are running on fumes, buddy."

"Oh, shit. Well, first things first. I've got your location on my radar. You're about one-hundred and fifty miles out. Think you can make it?" Santana replied.

Vaz glanced at his fuel gauge and shook his head. *Fuck!*

We're not going to make it.

"I'm not sure," Vaz replied, wracking his brain for a solution. Something came to mind, but it was a long shot. "I'll keep you appraised of our progress, just be ready for us. One way or another, this plane is coming down, Vaz out," he said grimly.

As soon as Santana got off the com with Vaz, he speedily dialed Vaz's wife, Amanda. After several rings, she answered.

"Hello," a weary, tired voice said.

"Amanda, this is Santana over at the Kokoda airport. Your husband, he's on his way in."

Gasping, Amanda answered, "Santana! We will be there in minutes! Angelina! Papa is coming home!"

Santana could her a little girl yell out, "Papa! Papa is coming home! Finally!"

"Listen to me, Amanda. Please listen, there's something else…"

"What?! What is it?"

"His plane, it's…" He paused. "It's out of fuel."

He heard the phone drop.

Vaz turned to face Laura and a now awakened Sam. "I'm going to shoot straight with you both. We don't have the fuel to get us safely to the Kokoda airport. Close, but no cigar. So, I'm flying this bitch in until she runs out of fuel completely then we coast it down, hopefully on the runway and not into a nearby field."

Sam shook the sleep off and blinked, coming to terms with what Vaz had just told them. "So, let me get this right. We don't have enough fuel and a bum front landing gear. We're gonna coast it down and land on the rear wheels then come to a full stop and hop on off this here plane?"

Nodding, Vaz replied, "Yeah. Yep, that's about right."

Looking over at Laura, Sam said, "Alright, we're in."

Vaz grinned nervously and pushed the Cessna onward, toward the coast of Papua New Guinea where the waiting Kokoda airport was located.

The rest of the trip was tense as land drew closer and the reality of another ditched plane was looking likely. Sam offered Laura the small bit of remaining food in the backpack, but she declined. Vaz, however, thankfully took it and gulped it down hungrily, realizing just how famished he was.

He thanked Sam and got back to the task at hand.

"Ladies and gentlemen, we are now over Papua New Guinea. Kokoda airport should be approaching soon. Then we shall see..." Vaz began.

"You're gonna land this plane, I know you are. *We* know you are, Vaz! Your little girl needs that new dress," Laura said confidently.

Vaz gripped the yoke tightly and began his initial descent toward the Kokoda airport. He decided to keep the plane higher in the sky than normal as he guessed he would need all of the coasting room he could get. Out his front windshield, the plane cut through beautiful, white puffy clouds.

Engine one began sputtering and a red fuel light blinked once more.

"I know, I know," Vaz said annoyed, hastily flipping the warning off.

Looking out her window, Laura said almost casually, "Takes you back to the good old days of our first plane crash, doesn't it?"

The sudden and unexpected joke caught Sam off-guard as he let out a small laugh, trying not to disturb Vaz.

The sputtering ceased and the engine grew silent.

"Engine one is finished. Shouldn't be long now until…"

Engine two began sputtering.

"There it is," Vaz said grimly.

No one spoke as engine two continued sputtering. Vaz kept the plane going as fast as he dared. They were getting closer to the airport but would still easily fall shy of the runway.

Engine two fell silent.

"And that, ladies and gentlemen, is the fat lady singing, so to speak," Vaz said, glancing back.

"What now?" Sam asked, attempting to mask the sudden dread that fell over him.

Sighing heavily, Vaz leaned back in his seat. "Good news is the wind is on our tail. Pushing us forward. Bad news is, well, we all know the bad news. I'll keep her up in the air for as long as I can. But it's going to drop, just a matter of when and how rapidly."

No sooner had Vaz uttered the words than the plane began to descend slowly.

"Santana, come in," Vaz said.

Seconds later, the com clicked on. "Santana here. Give me some good news, Vaz."

"Well, one way or another, this plane is going to be on the ground in very short order. Either in pieces or whole."

"We'll have firetrucks here at the ready," Santana said, then added, "I've got you on my radar. You're almost there, good buddy."

Amanda hastily got her daughter situated in the passenger seat of her 1975 VW Beetle. Most couples didn't have two vehicles in the small, poor town of Kokoda but the VW had been purchased way under its value, thanks to Vaz's smooth negotiating skills. She hadn't found it necessary to use until today as his Cutlass Supreme had remained at the airport.

"Mama? Is Papa going to be okay?" Angelina said, noticing the urgency as her mother got them ready to head to the airport.

"Angelina, here is what we are going to do on our way to the airport. We are going to pray our Rosary. You know how to pray your Rosary, so that is what we are going to do for your father. He needs our prayers, okay?" Amanda answered her daughter who now looked scared.

Amanda ground the gears of the VW as she reversed the car out of their driveway, slammed it into first gear and taking off down the road, kicking up dirt as she went.

"Our Father, who art in heaven," Angelina began in her tiny, innocent voice.

Vaz clicked off the com after speaking with Santana and pushed on the steering yoke. An eerie silence had fallen over them all. Wind whistled against the plane's outer hull. Thankfully, there had been very little turbulence up to that point.

"There, up ahead, I see it, Kokoda airport," Vaz said pointing out his front windshield.

Laura and Sam peered out. It seemed far away on the horizon.

The Cessna continued its slow, downward path, shaking and bumping against the wind.

Sam and Laura gripped their arm rests while Vaz continued wrestling with the yoke, trying to keep the Cessna's nose up as long as possible.

The airport was now clearly visible from the plane. Its single runway lay in front of them along with the control tower where Santana sat by awaiting their arrival. Several trucks were now pulling in. *Firetrucks.*

The plane dipped lower yet with the turbulence becoming stronger and more pronounced.

"Deploying landing gear," Vaz said, hitting the switch.

Under the plane, all three wheels popped out, the front one only releasing part of the way then stopping. Another blinking red warning light flashed in front of Vaz.

"Okay, front wheel is partially released. Not ideal, but at least there's something there," Vaz called back.

The turbulence continued to shake the plane violently up and down while the wind howled outside. Sam leaned his head back against his seat while Laura put her hands over the back of her neck and looked at the floor.

"Cabin pressure is still good, speed looks good," Vaz said to himself.

On the ground, police cars spread out alongside the firetrucks. They were now less than one mile out from the runway.

The wings swayed up and down as Vaz wrestled with the yoke, trying to keep the plane straight and steady.

"Come on, baby, hold yourself together, we're almost there," Vaz spoke to the plane. The yoke was shaking so badly at this point it was vibrating his whole body. He forced the yoke up, keeping the nose from dipping too far down.

The runway was approaching fast but it was almost impossible to keep the plane straight. As Vaz fought with the yoke, he yanked up on the flaps. "Closer, closer, come on, damnit! You can do this, Vaz!"

Asphalt rushed forward as the back wheels slammed onto the runway far too hard, causing the plane to bounce up into the air slightly and tilt to the left. The tip of the Cessna's wing nipped the edge of the runway, pushing it back to a somewhat level position.

While Sam and Laura hung on for dear life behind him, Vaz pulled back once more on the yoke, but the nose came down. The damaged front landing gear hit the ground and instantly sparks flew out.

Inside the cabin, an awful grinding sound emanated while the landing gear buckled under the immense speed and pressure and snapped off. The nose slammed onto the asphalt, sending everyone forward as seat belts pushed against them, stopping them from flying up, against the windshield in the cockpit.

The rear wheels were on the ground and the plane was slowing rapidly but causing serious damage to the nose. Inside the cockpit, numerous alarms were sounding and smoke was beginning to waft through the entire cabin.

Another loud crunch.

The rear left wheel had broken off and the rest of the landing gear was crushed. The left wing once more hit the runway but now with full force, causing the rest of the plane to veer sharply to the left and into the grass beside the tarmac.

The rear right side landing gear could no longer withstand bearing the majority of the weight of the Cessna, along with bouncing off of the runway, and it broke off. Now, with no landing gear at all, the plane continued to slide in the grass, leaving in its path a stretch of dust, smoke, and debris.

Inside the cockpit, Vaz strung together obscenities mixed with prayers as he continued doing all he could to keep the plane from erupting into flames with the ever-increasing smoke inside the cabin. Behind him, Sam and Laura coughed and fanned their faces.

The Cessna kept sliding off to the side of the runway, inching closer and closer to the control tower over on its left side. *If I hit that building, this plane is gonna catch fire and we'll be burnt alive.* With newfound determination, Vaz ground his teeth, pulling up on the flaps, now that breaks meant nothing due to the complete loss of the landing gear.

Finally, the plane came to a grinding halt. Warning lights

blinking throughout the cockpit in front of a dazed Vaz who put his hands on his face, making sure he was indeed, alive. He quickly unbuckled his seatbelt and jumped up.

"Both of you, we aren't out of this yet! Quick, out of the plane!" he shouted back to Sam and Laura who were both dazed, but alive.

He pushed the door open, thankful that it hadn't been damaged in the crash landing. It swung open, creaking on its hinges. He peered out in the distance to see an ambulance, police cars, and firetrucks racing over. He felt disoriented, as though they were still in another country.

Sam picked up his backpack, making sure Laura was out of the plane first. Because the landing gear was gone, getting outside the plane was as easy as stepping outside onto the grass.

Laura looked back to Sam and Vaz. "The engine is on fire!" she exclaimed.

In seconds, Sam and Vaz joined Laura on the grass outside the plane and without turning around, began running away from the burning engine. Once far enough away, they slowed as firetrucks raced past.

Covered in dirt, smoke, sweat, and blood they stumbled onto the tarmac as the ambulance pulled up. Behind them, the Cessna Citation I was now covered in flames. Its right engine exploded, sending debris flying through the air. Ducking slightly, the three survivors shielded their faces from the immediate heat of the blast.

Several paramedics jumped out of the ambulance and ran over as Vaz muttered to his traveling companions, "Thanks for flying Zombie Crime Lord Airlines. Have a nice day."

Sam smiled and draped his arm around the exhausted man who had just saved their lives, yet again. "I'd fly with you anywhere. Thanks for getting us back as safely as you could, all things considered."

Vaz nodded while Laura simply sat down on the tarmac, unable to grasp the full effect of all that had happened. Sam quickly sat down beside her as the paramedics began examining them and asking questions.

In the parking lot near the airport, Angelina wrapped up her prayer with an "Amen," as her mom came to a sliding stop.

Wrenching the parking brake up, Amanda unbuckled her daughter's seatbelt and motioned for her to get out. Looking on in terror at a plane on fire off the tarmac, she felt the tears streaming down her face. *Oh God, no.*

"Is Papa still going to get me that dress?" the sweet voice of her innocent daughter asked.

Have faith, Amanda. Have faith. Taking a breath and wiping her eyes, she looked at her daughter and confidently said, "Yes, Angelina, my dear. Let's go get your dad."

A police officer noticed the woman in a white dress with the little girl who had jumped out of a light blue VW Beetle and were running up to the tarmac. He quickly put his hand up, stopping them and asking them questions.

Vaz looked up from the paramedic checking his vitals who was insisting he get onto a stretcher and be taken to the local hospital. "Amanda? Angelina?" He quickly pushed the paramedic away and started to run toward his family who, in seconds, were with him, all three wrapping their arms around each other and kissing each other.

Sitting on the edge of the tarmac, Sam and Laura looked at the man who had saved their lives. "Hell of a first date, Laura," Sam said with the slightest of grins, running his hands through his dirty blond hair.

Laura glanced at him and slid closer until their bodies touched, then she leaned over and gently kissed him on his dirt-covered cheek, resting her head on his shoulder.

Santana walked over from the control tower quickly to find Vaz, Amanda, and Angelina shedding tears of joy. He overheard the girl ask, "Dad, does this mean we can't get that new dress?"

"Honey, the first thing I plan on doing once I'm cleared here is getting you that dress!" Vaz replied warmly.

Amanda wiped tears from her eyes then grew stone-faced when Santana walked up. She glared at him silently as police cars, ambulance sirens, and firetrucks blared in the background.

"Um, excuse me for interrupting. But, Augusto, my friend, you saved the life of my family and I just want to tell your wife how sorry I am for having dragged you into this," Santana stuttered.

Amanda was about to reply but Vaz beat her to it. "Pay times three, maybe four? And the bill for the airplanes, send them to the Paim estates. They can square up with the town of Kokoda and the Kokoda police department. May he rest in peace."

Santana's eyes widened.

"Come on, honey, let's get Daddy cleared and out of here." Vaz took his daughter's hand and walked away. Amanda said nothing to Santana, but turned and joined her husband who was now talking to the police.

"Sonofabitch. Paim is dead. Paim…is…*dead!*" Santana muttered to himself.

A new day had come to the people and town of Kokoda.

27
THREE
YEARS LATER

William Joyner's discovery of the cure for terminal brain cancer had indeed been a success and the flowers Sam had picked and stored inside his backpack on la Isla de Sebria survived and were able to be harvested. Along with both doctors' notes and the NR 485 serum, the cure was tested then replicated and mass produced in the years that followed the mysterious incident somewhere in the middle of the Solomon Sea.

The William Joyner Cancer Research Association, commonly referred to as WJCR, set up in honor of the late doctor to continue his work in finding cures for terminal cancer patients, was already showing great success in other areas apart from brain cancer. All thanks to the Violet Laceflower that not one doctor could find a reason for existing on earth.

Sam, Laura, and Vaz shared their experience on la Isla de Sebria with the authorities both in Papua New Guinea as well as back in the states. None could recall the exact location of the island, due to the storms happening when they'd arrived, something the three of them had discussed among themselves before being questioned. The constant storms caused numerous searches to falter until locating the mysterious island was considered a lost cause.

They did speak of the leper colony doomed to die a slow death on the island, along with the mysterious plant life and new species of animals found within its jungles. Much of this was met with puzzled and confused looks and, at times, outright disbelief, as it sounded too far-fetched. Except that the Violent Laceflower was proof of something totally alien out somewhere in the middle of the Solomon Sea.

The local law enforcement back on Kokoda had pieced the story together from both Vaz and Santana, but also several other police forces around the Solomon Islands, that Sérgio Melo Paim had either vanished without a trace or was killed. Either way, his operation was quickly infiltrated and much of his workforce arrested, including Officer Logan Pabon of the Royal Islands Solomon Police Force on suspicion of aiding and abetting a known drug lord. That, and the murder of one Fabian Amill, employee of the Honiara airport, whose body was discovered upon thorough investigation of the officer's whereabouts shortly after the man's disappearance. Pabon, however, had quickly surrounded himself with Sérgio Paim's lawyers who agreed to work on the ongoing trial.

The dirty cops, and there were plenty, found guilty of taking payouts from Paim were quickly arrested and replaced. Still, the Paim empire, while severely crippled, existed in a significantly truncated version after the head of the snake had been cut off.

Vaz, Laura, and Sam were cleared of any wrongdoing, although Edward and Eva's disappearances were tough for their families to take. Both Sam and Laura showed great sensitivity in explaining to them how they had perished in the Piper Turbo plane crash near the mysterious island. They agreed it was best to leave out the part about zombies and flesh eating.

Laura's mother, however, heard the story in its entirety and accepted her husband's fate.

Sam and Laura sat inside Sal's Burger Digs, each finishing off their respective cheeseburgers. Sam took a sip of Laura's strawberry milkshake and set it back down on the table, wiping a thin line of whipped cream from his top lip. "Hot damn, that is one good milkshake!"

"I know right? *Much* better than the chocolate ones!" she teased.

Sam picked up his own chocolate shake and took a big swallow of the thick cold goodness. "No matter how many times we eat here, I have to hand it to your father, this was a great tradition he started."

Alicia, now sixty-one years old and a proud grandmother,

came back to the booth carrying a small boy. "Want to go to Mama?" she asked little brown-haired William Edward Berry.

The small child reached his hands toward his smiling mother who happily took him into her arms.

Alicia sat down with them at the table. Her once brown hair was now gray, but Sam noted again that Laura had obviously gotten her naturally good looks from her mother.

"I really wish you weren't heading back to California tomorrow," Alicia said sadly.

"I know, Mom, but Papa here has to get back to work. We'll be back to visit this summer. Sam's got a lot of time off coming up," Laura said, giving her husband of two years a wink.

"Indeed, I do. Your late husband's research is never finished and the advancements we've made—" Sam began.

"No talk of work at Sal's. Only cheeseburgers, fries, and milkshakes!" Alicia joked.

"Duly noted," Sam replied with a smile, raising his chocolate shake and clinking it against his mother-in-law's glass.

After finishing their meal, the four of them went back to Alicia's to say their goodbyes and get their luggage. While Laura, young Willy Jr. as he was called, and her mother were in the living room, Sam made a quick call to his friend all the way down in Papua New Guinea.

"Hello?" answered the groggy voice on the other end after numerous rings.

"Well, hello there, Mr. Sleepy!" Sam said with a chuckle.

"Sam! How are you? Wait, why the hell are you calling

me at nine o'clock in the morning? I have a late flight today, and you're interrupting my beauty sleep," Vaz said sleepily.

Sam replied with a grin, "It's five o'clock here in sunny Texas so consider this your wake-up call."

"Alright, alright. How are things? How's little Willy Jr.?" Vaz asked yawning. Behind him, Angelina could be heard asking who was on the other end. "It's Sam. Yes, I'll tell him. Angelina says hi."

"Hi, Angelina," Sam replied laughing.

"That girl is thirteen going on sixteen. Can you believe my baby has a boy that's been passing her little love notes at sch—" Vaz began before Angelina shushed him. "Okay, okay! Go find your mom!"

"Vaz, I promise, this summer Laura, Will, and I are coming to visit. Angelina can babysit and we'll hit the town, sound good?" Sam said.

"Deal," Vaz replied warmly. He was thankful they had stayed in close contact since their ordeal back on the island three years prior. He now considered them dear friends. Each took turns visiting the other at least once a year and stayed in touch via phone calls.

"So, Vaz, the reason for my call," Sam began then sighed. "It looks like the higher-ups at The William Joyner Cancer Research Association are bound, set, and determined to find that damn island. Against your government's wishes, and ours for that matter, they're planning on setting sail with a small group of locals in the hopes of finding it, doing research, and collecting data on the plant and animal life. They're convinced there are more foreign plants that could be used for further research and development in the field of cancer. But beyond that, they're convinced a cure could be found there for this new AIDS virus. I can't stop them. Lord knows, I've tried."

He was met with silence on the other end. Finally, Vaz spoke. "Sam, numerous organizations have tried, but those storms and it's geometric location…"

"I know, right?" Sam replied. Then added, "They've got some heavy-duty boat, supposedly can weather most any storm. My concern isn't that they can actually make it there. My concern is what they find. That disease cannot leave that island."

"What do you want me to do, Sam?" Vaz asked, now fully awake.

"Let the right people know. That boat cannot leave Papua New Guinea."

After another pause, Vaz asked quietly, "You still have the knife?"

"I do. With Eva's blood still on it," Sam answered.

"Damnit, Sam! I told you to—" Vaz began.

"I know, I know. But listen, I did my own analysis on the blood. It's still alive! And just as infectious as it was when she was stuck with it!"

"You know what would happen if that virus-tainted knife fell into the wrong hands?" Vaz asked grimly.

"I do. Trust me, I do. It's safe. Once I figure out a true and definitive cure for whatever that virus is, I'll dispose of the blood. But until then, if anyone ever does find the island, and if they are infected, and if they make it back to the mainland, well, you catch my drift. We need an antidote before that happens and I've been working diligently on it, but thus far, no luck. And I know as well as you do, someone, sometime, is going to find that island. The way it's looking, sooner than later."

"I get it, Sam. Thanks for the heads up," Vaz replied.

"Look, I gotta go, we need to get to the airport. Keep your ear to the ground for anything suspicious with regards to ships making their way through the Solomon Sea that have no business being there," Sam said.

"And if I find something?" Vaz questioned.

"No matter where I'm at or what I'm doing, get in touch me with, then we'll cross that bridge when we get there," Sam said gravely.

"Stay safe, my friend," Vaz said.

"You as well," Sam answered as he hung up then made his way out to a waiting wife and fussy little Willy Jr.

They said their goodbyes to Laura's mom, promising they would see her again soon, and left for the San Antonio airport with a layover in Chicago before their final destination, Burbank, California.

Sam and Laura spoke briefly about his call to Vaz once they arrived back in Burbank, but this topic was usually avoided, due to Laura's vivid memories of her father's death and the two plane crashes they had been involved in. Even resulting in the occasional argument when Sam pressed the issue of what may or may not still be residing on the island.

She was, however, a wonderful wife and quite literally, the best thing to ever happen to Sam. His parents not only welcomed her into the Berry family, but hoped for many more grandkids and quickly referred to her as "the daughter they never had that the good Lord in his infinite wisdom had blessed them with."

Laura had her own demons, dealing with nightmares of a naked corpse-Eva mutation biting the air, eyes white and full of rage. In the dreams, she would continually stop at nothing to get to Laura as she attempted to flee in vain from a blood-covered beach with thunder and lightning crashing overhead. Laura always woke up in a cold sweat, sometimes letting out a scream of terror. Instinctively, she would reach to her back, feeling the healed-over scar given to her by her one-time friend on the other side of the planet. It was on those nights that Sam knew the final chapter of la Isla de Sebria had yet to be written.

Willy Jr. slept soundly in the other room of Sam and Laura's house. The married couple lay together in each other's arms after a much-needed night of lovemaking after their time in Texas at Laura's mother's house. Laura drifted off to sleep, happy and satisfied, while Sam stared at the ceiling. Alone with his thoughts. Alone with his waking nightmares.

"This isn't over yet. It may only get worse," Sam mumbled before drifting off to sleep.

EPILOGUE "WE'VE FOUND SOMETHING, SIR!"

The 1980 Viking 43 double-cabin motor yacht sped through the Solomon Sea. Three of its five occupants had arrived in the East New Britain Province of Malmal in Papua New Guinea at the Jacquinot Bay Airport a day earlier before making their way to the rendezvous point in the small town of Malaua in the Jacquinot Bay.

The 1980-built yacht had been retrofitted with modern stealth, radar-blocking technology, along with new, black paint covering its exterior, and black tinted windows. The large fuel capacity made this particular yacht the correct choice for the mission at hand, and the one in which the three Papua New Guinea pirates had been commissioned to take their clients out in to the middle of the Solomon Sea.

The three-hundred-fifty-gallon diesel fuel tank, along with added fuel tanks, was more than enough to get the travelers to where they needed to go and back again. It's twin six-hundred-twenty horsepower dual engines roared as the boat sliced through the rocky waves. All forty-three feet of the retrofitted yacht was utilized for speed, agility, and stealth. All of which were precisely needed for the mission they were on.

The torrential rain had been pummeling the Viking for what seemed like hours as it continued on, almost in vain, searching for the mysterious island known as la Isla de Sebria. The yacht tossed and turned violently but stayed afloat while it rode the high waves.

Inside, seated in the captain's chair, Pedro Wari gripped the helm tightly, doing his best to navigate the storm that even a weathered sea-farer such as himself wasn't prepared for.

"This boat is built for storms, but this is a whole other level of danger here!" Wari shouted to his passengers behind him, all of which were gripping their seats tightly.

Wiping cold sweat from his brow, thirty-year-old Sullivan Reeves called out, "How much longer can a storm like this last?"

The attractive Helena Banks answered, "I hope this was worth it." She glanced at the man on her other side. "We've traveled halfway around the world to find your damn island, Ethan! If anyone at the WJCR connects the dots, it's our asses!"

"No one is going to find out until we're back, and by then, with what we've collected, we'll have to fend off all but the highest bidders!" Ethan Davis, another upstart employee of WJCR, exclaimed as the usually arrogant man nervously ran his hand through his wavy brown hair.

"You talk of highest bidders, but I am going to say this once more. We get paid *first*. Is that understood?" the man behind them said grimly, showing no fear at the turbulent weather smashing all sides of the Viking.

Only Ethan glanced back and nodded. Helena and Sullivan were almost instantly afraid of the man that had been hired on by captain Pedro Wari.

"You've already been paid for the first half of this expedition, and you will be compensated the rest once we make it back to the mainland and have secured proper transportation back to the United States. Like we agreed," Ethan retorted, trying to mask his apprehension at standing up to the one clearly in charge.

Another wave smashed into the front of the Viking, sending it upward, then crashing back down into the ocean. The rain was coming down so hard it looked at times as though it was raining sideways. Yet, the boat continued its path forward.

As though the storm finally gave up on its quest to push the unwanted travelers back where they came from, it began easing up. The rain went from sideways to a downpour on top of them and, while still windy, the waves started to calm. The black sky remained dark but out of the front windshield it appeared as though sunlight was attempting to peek through.

The man behind Ethan, Sullivan, and Helena leaned forward, looking out the window, then shifted his gaze to

Ethan and, in a calm, almost soft voice said, "Out here, I am the shark. You are the seal. If you raise your voice to me again, I will bleed you dry, American."

The three employees fell silent. None looked back but all got the message, loud and clear.

Logan Pabon sat back quietly in his seat behind them.

"It looks like we've found something, sir! Look!" exclaimed the rattled and sweat- covered Pedro Wari, taking his hand off the helm and pointing out the windshield.

In the distance, roughly one nautical mile out, sat an island.

About the Author

Eugene Weaver was born on August 8, 1974 in Millersburg, Ohio. He and his wife Joani have been married for 20 years and have two boys. They currently live in Canton area in Ohio.

Eugene has been an avid lover of movies, music, and the arts nearly all his life. At 12 years old, he wrote his first novel, Pivoron *Mountain*, in longhand cursive. At the persuasion of his boys thirty-six years later, he decided to take up writing once more. His first novel, *Thunder Stone Realm*, and its two sequels were published in 2023 and 2024. He has published two subsequent novels since completing his Thunder Stone Realm trilogy: *Battle for Quadrant 8304* and *The Amulet of Visimar*, the first in a three-part series. *Crimson Paradise* is his sixth novel.